THE HOUSE IN THE WATER

VICTORIA DARKE

Boldwood

First published in Great Britain in 2024 by Boldwood Books Ltd.

Cover Design by Becky Glibbery

Cover Images: Shutterstock, Alamy and [Richard Nixon] / Arcangel

A CIP catalogue record for this book is available from the British Library.

Paperback ISBN 978-1-83561-691-8

Large Print ISBN 978-1-83561-692-5

Hardback ISBN 978-1-83561-690-1

Ebook ISBN 978-1-83561-693-2

Kindle ISBN 978-1-83561-694-9

Audio CD ISBN 978-1-83561-685-7

MP3 CD ISBN 978-1-83561-686-4

Digital audio download ISBN 978-1-83561-687-1

Boldwood Books Ltd
23 Bowerdean Street
London SW6 3TN
www.boldwoodbooks.com

For my fellow Thames island-dwellers – because river people do stick together.

PROLOGUE

SUMMER 2013

Edward Pepperidge scratches the back of his neck, moves his hand to the throttle and pushes it forwards. The gentle hum of the boat's engine becomes a roar. He feels the wind in his face and what remains of his hair lift, and he breaks into a broad smile. Yes, this is what he needs today. *Escape. Freedom. Speed.*

He's left the densely packed banks of Walton-on-Thames behind. Up here, there are only a few properties dotted about beside the bank. That makes it an ideal stretch to let the boat have a run, safe in the knowledge that he'll be long gone before gardens are doused by its wake.

Within minutes, he's closing in on May Day Island. About a hundred metres long by about thirty metres wide, it sits in the centre of the Thames, dividing it into two channels. Edward takes the channel to the right, and although he'd usually bomb past here towards the weir and the lock beyond, something makes him slow down to take a closer look.

Once you glance its way, May Day House is impossible to ignore. The mouldering Victorian mansion commands attention and respect, despite the screen of dense trees threatening to encase it, like a spellbound castle. Glimpses reveal windows which have been either smashed by local teenagers or smothered in ivy; gutters which are hosting saplings and bushes; and an orangery whose glass ceiling has been shattered by ornamental trees growing within when the house was finally abandoned.

Edward's attention is drawn away from the building by a bright red *For Sale* sign, which is affixed to a wooden stake on the bank. That is new. And news, too, for everyone who lives in the area. Most have never known May Day House occupied, although there are many stories exchanged about its mysterious past. He reduces his engine to a trickle and draws closer in.

His eyes catch movement amongst the trees. The island's uninhabited still, he's sure, but he supposes it might be an estate agent, or maybe a local kid up to no good. They wouldn't be the first teenager to do that around here; some have even come a cropper trying to swim across for a dare. But he knows better. This river's an untamed beast. It commands respect.

Edward brings his boat even closer to the bank. At first, he can see nothing but tangled weeds; rubbish chucked onto the island by passing hobby-boaters; decaying walls and overgrown roses. He's about to give up, in fact, when he sees something in his peripheral vision.

It isn't in the garden, though.

He's horrified to see a man in the river, directly in front of his boat.

No, actually, it isn't a man, *it's a boy*. A teenager, maybe. He's swimming in slow motion, his arms waving above his head, his face partially submerged. Edward rams his boat's engine into reverse.

'Swim, damn you. *Swim away*!' he yells.

But it is too late. He closes his eyes as the boat collides with the boy. He knows what is going to happen. He doesn't need to see it.

A few seconds pass, and Edward opens his eyes.

The first thing he does is turn off the engine. It has undoubtedly masked the sound of the impact, for which he is grateful. He's now a good few metres away from the point of impact, and he has to see, urgently, what state the boy is in.

The second thing he does is pull out his phone, ready to call the emergency services. But as he does so, he pauses. *Will I be accused of manslaughter?* he wonders. What if someone saw him speeding earlier? But he hadn't been speeding when he'd hit him, had he, and the boy had been in the river without a float, without anything to mark him out. He'd have to explain that the boy had come out of nowhere. *Yes,* yes, he thinks. *It'll be OK. They'll understand it was an accident.*

Edward moves to the back of the boat with his phone in his hand and looks down into the murky waters beneath. He's expecting to see a – he struggles to even think about the word – a *body.* Yes, he's expecting to see a body floating on the surface, or some blood, some torn clothing, even him swimming, still alive. But there's nothing. Not a trace.

Can he really have sunk just like that? That quickly? Surely not, he thinks. Not satisfied, he climbs onto the prow of his boat, just to check the boy hasn't become snagged on something. He peers over. There's nothing there.

Edward assesses his options. He could call the police and tell them what happened, but without a body they'll either think it's a wind up or a cover up. Or, he could leave it. Just push off and see what happens. And if a body does turn up, he could always turn himself in and explain he'd done everything he could, couldn't he? The boy had probably swum away and hidden himself on the island. And he *had* looked for him, hadn't he, and he'd have called an ambulance if it had been required. He's a good person, a good citizen. Edward shakes out his arms as if physically shedding his anxiety and turns the key in the ignition. Yes, he'll leave it for now, and keep an eye on the news.

As the boat begins to pull away, he turns to look at May Day House for one final time.

It's then he notices the face at the window.

It's the boy! The same one he'd seen in the water, but now he's in one of May Day's upstairs rooms, staring out towards the river. He's looking straight ahead, not in Edward's direction, but it's definitely him.

Relief floods through him. He's alive after all! Happy days.

Edward inhales the misty morning air. *Thank God for that*, he thinks.

It takes him a minute or two to realise what was wrong with what he just saw.

Bloody hell, he thinks, a shiver running down his spine. *That boy at the window wasn't wet.*

And would he have even had time to get up there? And actually, when he'd been in the water, waving frantically as if his life had depended on it, he hadn't made a sound. Not one. He'd been... *unnaturally* silent.

Edward pushes the throttle to maximum. Every sinew of his body wants to take him as far away from that house as he can physically go.

Because the boy he hit, the boy he saw at that window – there's absolutely no way he could have been a living, breathing human.

1

MEREDITH

October 2013

'Left a bit... Yes, that's it... Just lower it a bit more...'

Meredith winces as the removal firm wrestle with the box that contains their crystal glasses – a wedding present. The well-spoken, immaculately dressed man who'd quoted for the job had promised a seamless, stress-free move from their second-floor flat in Putney to the island, but even she can see his staff are now doubting they can deliver on his promises.

It isn't really their fault. It's incredibly unlikely they've ever had to use a boat to move someone's stuff before. Meredith now wishes they'd gone with the specialist river removal firm the estate agent had suggested, but Philip had insisted they use this one, because they had a royal crest on their van. That's because Philip is impressed by royalty, something Meredith outwardly respects, while keeping her own views on the subject to herself.

She takes a step back and tries to focus on the island opposite, instead of the possibility of losing their belongings in the river's rapid autumnal flow. She takes in the thick screen of trees marking the water's edge, the wildly overgrown garden beyond, and behind all of that, now visible after high winds stripped away a fortress of leaves, May Day House itself.

Can we really be here? she thinks. *Can we really be doing this?*

It had begun as a dream, a bit of window shopping on a property app. After she'd run some provisional figures, though, and worked out they could just about manage it, May Day Island had rapidly become her obsession. It had felt – in fact, it still feels – as if the house has been waiting for them. It's a perfect project, a new beginning, a new adventure. And serendipitous, too, that she's been able to bring Philip back to the area he grew up in.

She'd arranged the viewing of the island as a surprise. She hadn't told him anything about her plans for the day, and when they'd driven down Weybridge high street, he'd thought she'd brought him to see his parents, who live in a retirement flat in the town. But instead, they'd taken an abrupt right turn down a bumpy track between two high hedgerows and parked up in a small gravel car park. From there, she'd taken his hand with a conspiratorial smile and led him through a small apple orchard to the riverbank, where a man wearing a tweed jacket, salmon pink trousers and pointy, shiny brown shoes had been waiting for them beside a small wooden rowing boat.

'We're going to have a look around May Day House,' she'd said, beaming at him.

'May Day?' he'd replied, his face reflecting his shock at this turn of events.

'Yes. We can afford it. Just. And it's just... Oh Phil, it's just the most amazing place. The photos... we could make something incredible here. I just know it.'

She had been pleading with him, like a child begging for sweets. He'd seen the look of wonder and hope in her eyes and responded as he always had, ever since they'd met, and particularly in the last couple of years.

'OK,' he said. 'But... it's just a look, all right? We can't get carried away. It must be almost a ruin now.'

She had grinned and turned immediately to the man who was waiting for them.

'This man is Charles O'Connor, Phil. He's from O'Connors, the estate agents.'

'Oh.' That was all he'd said as they'd followed him and climbed on board the boat. Philip had instinctively taken the oars and begun to row the three of them across to the island, with strong, confident strokes, his years spent in his university's first rowing eight still evident more than two decades later.

'Yes, nice to meet you, Mr Holland. As Mrs Holland says, I'm Charles,' the estate agent said, shuddering for a moment when a splash of water flew off the right oar and landed on his blazer, but recovering his composure swiftly; probably, Meredith thought, because he'd remembered his cut. 'I'm delighted you've come to see the island. It's a very special place.'

Although there has been a building on the island for centuries, the present May Day House was conjured up by a Victorian artist who had married into money and indulged his whimsy with wild abandon. Built in the Gothic Revival style from a mixture of red and white stone and brick, it has round turrets, arched windows and flying buttresses.

'Mr and Mrs Chevalier, who designed and built the house, unfortunately had no children, so the property was put on the open market when Mrs Chevalier died in 1920, and then it was sold to the Wilkinson family, who owned several West End theatres,' the estate agent had said after they'd tied up the boat and disembarked, the gentle breeze off the water wicking away the moisture on their skin. 'They used it as a venue for weekend entertaining for many years, but then came World War Two. It was requisitioned by the government then, I believe, and then afterwards, unfortunately, the family firm experienced money troubles and their children and grandchildren were unable to maintain it adequately,' he continued, now forging his way through waist-high grasses and brambles, which were snagging his jacket. 'Nevertheless, the last Mrs Wilkinson lived here until her death. Then the family argued over it for years, before finally agreeing to sell it once they'd finished wrangling over her will. It took two decades, would you believe. Families. Anyway, as you can see, it is now in a state of disrepair…'

This had been an understatement of epic proportions. During that visit, Meredith had seen, even from a distance, that nature had reclaimed much of the ground floor. Ivy was growing through rotten window frames; weeds were sprouting out of crumbling brickwork and there was a tree thrusting out of the orangery roof. It was also clear that the main roof was missing many tiles and that one of the chimneys was listing at an alarming angle. And yet, despite the state of it, the house had pulled Meredith into its spell. It had been instinctive. After the immense weight of the previous few years, the endless questioning, she'd been seeking an answer, and May Day House had provided it. And Philip, who'd been so worried about her for so long, had acquiesced.

So now the deal making, surveying and conveyancing is finally done, and they are here with their entire life, such as it is, in neatly labelled boxes, waiting for a new chapter to begin.

And it is going far from smoothly. The removal firm has struggled to load a barge borrowed from a local property developer, because the island is miles away from a suitable slipway. The transfer across the bank is slippery and uneven, the old steps and landing stages long gone. It is all taking a great deal of time.

'The sun's going to start setting in a few hours,' Philip says, visibly tense. It has been an exhausting, stressful day, the confirmation of completion only coming through at lunchtime, and no doubt he is now regretting his choice of removal firm. He is always so definite in his decisions and easily wounded if they prove to be less than stellar.

'It's OK. They said they can come back tomorrow if they don't get everything in today,' Meredith replies, putting her arm around her husband's slim, toned waist, a testament to his obsession with running and all other manners of exercise, a trait Meredith feels comes perilously close to self-flagellation. 'We'll manage. They've loaded the mattress and the microwave, so we've got somewhere to sleep, and we can heat up dinner.'

'Yeah. You're right. Sorry. I just wanted today to be perfect, you know? You deserve it.'

Meredith squeezes him tightly.

'It *is* perfect,' she says. 'I'm with *you*, and we're starting again, in the most magical place. It's brilliant. It can't not be.'

'But are we absolutely mad?' he asks, as the removal men manage to slide an armchair onto the barge. Meredith smiles and maintains her grasp, determined not to let this injection of doubt be infectious. They had discussed their decision at length before making an offer on the island, drawing up lists of pluses and negatives, trying to be as realistic as they possibly could be while keeping the dream alive. They had *more* than thought it through. In fact, they had practically written a dissertation on it. And anyway, there could be no turning back now.

'Yes,' she replies, still smiling. 'Absolutely bonkers.'

'Well *they* definitely think we're insane,' says Philip, gesturing towards the red-faced removals men, who've returned to the van for another load. 'I mean, who on earth would move to a crumbling house with no central heating on an island with no bridge and no mains water, which will probably flood tomorrow?'

'It's a good point,' says Meredith, looking over at the island, feeling her well of optimism refill as soon as she sees the outline of the house, despite her husband's proclamations. *It's going to be OK*, she thinks. *That house will look after us. I'm sure of it.* 'Well, shall we? No time like the present to get started, as they say.'

Philip leads her down to the water's edge and takes her hand as they both clamber into the same wooden rowing boat they'd used for their first visit that summer. As he unties the ropes and pushes them away from the bank, Meredith spots movement on the towpath, where they were just standing.

'Oh, hello,' says a woman Meredith can't see. Her words are clearly a question rather than a greeting, her voice deep and confident, her accent firmly home counties. 'I saw the vans arrive when I was out walking the dog earlier and I just wanted to pop along and say hello.' The woman emerges from behind a tree trunk. She is short, slim as a whippet and has blonde highlighted hair cut into an angular bob. Her skin is an unseasonal caramel, the kind that can only be achieved via a sunbed or expensive tanning products. 'I'm Elinor. Elinor Pepperidge. I'm the chair of the local residents committee. We're so excited that the island has new owners, I can't tell you.'

She certainly appears excited. Her grin is broad and her teeth, gleaming and neatly aligned, are all on show.

'Oh, hi,' says Philip, grabbing hold of the branch hanging off the bank to stop the current from carrying their boat downstream. 'Hi, Elinor. I'm sorry we can't shake hands, we're about to head over, as you see...'

'Yes, typical me, turning up at the wrong moment. Not to worry. I just wanted to say hello, to welcome you to the area. It's a lovely spot, as you know.'

'Yes,' replies Philip, his voice loud, confident and jaunty, a tone Meredith knows he usually reserves for addressing his passengers. 'We know.'

'Yes. I hear you're local?'

Philip blinks, so quickly that someone who didn't know him well would not even have noticed. But Meredith notices. Of course she does. She loves him. He's thinking about Stuart, she thinks, the small seed of doubt she's been trying to suppress since they'd decided to buy the house, resurfacing. *Has he been humouring me?* she wonders. *After all, this area must evoke such conflicting emotions for him. Will he cope, being so close to where it happened? Have I been selfish and foolish?*

'Yes, yes, I was here as a boy,' Philip says to Elinor. 'But I haven't lived around here since I left for university. So, it feels quite new, in a way. A new start.'

I do hope that's the truth, thinks Meredith.

'Absolutely. Yes. How wonderful,' says Elinor, her smile unmoved, even though Meredith suspects she was hoping for much more detail. 'Well, I'll let you get on. Perhaps you'd like to come for tea sometime at my place? We're up the lane just here, second on the left. Old Stone Cottage. It's old and made of stone. Does what it says on the tin.'

'Great, yes. We'll pop round soon,' says Philip, releasing the branch and taking hold of the oars – a move, Meredith suspects, designed to ensure Elinor has no chance to try to firm up arrangements.

Meredith waves and smiles politely as the boat glides across the water towards the island. As they cross the invisible and yet tangible border that marks the beginning of their side of the river, she hears her husband exhale.

'Thank heavens for that. I thought we were going to be stuck with her for ages,' he says, grabbing hold of a tuft of grass on the overgrown landing stage and pulling their boat alongside.

'She's harmless, I'm sure,' replies Meredith as he steps onto the island and begins to tie the craft up to a large metal ring which is covered in weeds. 'People must be desperate to know who we are, and what we plan to do with the place. It's human nature, isn't it? They've all been walking past here for years, staring at the house, and now here we are, new folk turning up full of new ideas. I don't blame them.'

'You are so much more forgiving than me,' says Philip, smiling.

'I know,' replies Meredith, taking the hand he's proffered and stepping onto the landing stage. She's taking a deep breath, overwhelmed suddenly by her new surroundings and all they mean, when Philip grabs her by the waist without warning and lifts her into the air. For a second, she thinks he might be about to throw her into the water as a prank, but she's wrong. Instead, he slings her over his shoulder and walks, slowly and with a disturbing wobble, down the weedy path that leads to the house.

'*Put. Me. Down,*' she shouts, in mock outrage.

'No! I can't do that. It's tradition. I need to carry you over the threshold,' he says, stumbling slightly when his foot catches under the root of a fallen tree.

'Damn it, Phil, you'll kill us both.' Meredith can feel the blood running to her head, which feels uncomfortably close to the ground.

'Arse. You're right, as usual.' He halts and lowers her, feet first. He's panting, his face red.

'You idiot,' she says, leaning in to kiss him. 'I like the gesture, but I don't fancy a broken neck.'

'Yeah, fair enough,' he says, wiping his forehead with the back of his right hand. They stand there for a moment while he gets his breath back. They're about twenty metres or so from the house's main entrance, standing on a pathway made of crazy paving, crowned with a rotten wooden pergola more than ten feet long, through which untold varieties of roses have knitted a summer blanket. When they'd visited the first time, their scent had been intoxicating. Meredith can't wait for them to flower again. To their right is a wilderness of weeds, felled trees and saplings planted by the winds and the birds, and to their left there are remnants of a circular formal garden, designed around a weather-beaten statue of a young woman wearing a crown of flowers in her hair.

There's more land on the other side of the house, too, including some raised beds previously used as a kitchen garden, a well which had at one stage been the only source of drinking water on the island, and a patio and seating area which have become a nesting spot for ducks and geese. *A great deal to be getting on with*, Meredith thinks. *And that's just the garden. The house, meanwhile...*

'Shall we go in, Lady May Day?' says Philip, interrupting her thoughts.

'Yes, let's, my lord.'

Meredith laughs as he takes her hand. They'd started calling each other that almost as soon as the deal had been agreed, making light of the enormity of the task ahead of them, the realisation of a dream which sometimes felt impossible.

But it has to be possible, she thinks. *It has to be. We need this, after all we've been through.*

2

ELLEN

October 1943

'Are you sure this is the right place?'

It is pitch black. Ellen can hear there's water nearby; fast-moving, angry sounding water, but she can't see it.

'Yeh. Hang on a minute.' The man who'd picked her up from the station, who'd said his name was Bob, is standing close enough to her for her to both smell the tobacco on his breath and make out his faint outline, even on this cloudy night. She sees him reach into his pocket, pull out an object and shake it hard. It's a bell, and it rings out clearly and deeply, like the one that called her to Mass every Sunday at home. 'That will bring 'em over,' he says. 'You just wait by the edge, over there' – she sees him pointing to the left, but not what he's actually pointing at – 'and they should be here in a few minutes.'

He puts the bell back in his pocket and begins to walk back in the direction of the car.

'Are you going?'

'Yeh. I've got a few more jobs to do, miss. But you'll be fine. They know you're coming, and they'll have heard me.'

He continues walking, and she can no longer see him. She wants to run after him and beg him to stay with her, for two reasons. They are both, she realises, somewhat ridiculous, given why she is here. The first thing is that she is terrified of the dark. And secondly, she is also terrified of water. Her reasons for both of these fears are real and incontrovertible but cannot be openly acknowledged if she wishes to come here and be useful. And she does, so she bites her lip and digs her fingernails into her palms to stop herself calling out for him to return. She has to work her way through her fear. That's something Dr Lovell would say, and she likes Dr Lovell. He is right about many things. So right now, she needs to do as he says. She has to. She can't fail this placement, or they'll send her back.

'*Hello, there*!' Thank goodness for that! Someone's coming for her. She can see the dim light of a torch bouncing around in the darkness, like a gigantic firefly.

'Hello,' she replies, loudly, so whoever this man is can hear she's waiting for him.

'*I'll be with yer in a minute*.' She can hear the rhythmic sloshing as a boat's oars fight against the water flow, and the deep breathing of the man propelling them.

Ellen's eyes are growing accustomed to the darkness now, and even in the cloud-covered, crescent moonlight she can just about make out the riverbank to the left and beyond it, across the water, the outline of a very large building. There are no lights in its windows, as is to be expected given the blackout, but it is undoubtedly there.

'There we go,' says the man, who Ellen can see is now on her side of the bank. He's drawing up to a wooden landing stage which is down a small flight of steps. She walks over, lugging her leather suitcase behind her.

'I've tied her up now. Yer can hop in.'

Ellen knows she will not be hopping anywhere with her ludicrously heavy bag, but she does her best, making sure to hold on tight to the railing next to the steps to avoid falling into the river weighed down by her uniform, her nylons, a smart dress she is unlikely to ever need, three novels, a notebook, several pairs of shoes and her favourite hairbrush. 'Give me yer bag,' he says, heaving it up with both hands and lifting it towards him with a grunt before placing it in the boat. 'Take my hand, love.'

Ellen can't make out his face yet, but she can see he's holding out his hand, and she takes it. She wobbles a little as she gets in, largely due to her state of mind rather than her physical condition, which is surprisingly decent, given the circumstances.

'There you go, love. All in? Lovely. Let's head back over.' The man starts rowing and Ellen tries to take a few deep breaths to calm her racing heart. 'Yer been here before? May Day, I mean?' he adds, filling a silence Ellen had actually been enjoying.

'No.'

'Ah. Yeah, well, it's an unusual place. But special, too. Being on an island and all.'

When she'd been told that her next assignment was to be at a hospital for recovering soldiers situated in a large house in the middle of the Thames, Ellen had been intrigued. The only islands she'd visited had been the Arans, and then only once, to go camping, when her father had been feeling a bit flush. She supposes being cut off from everyone by water might make for a strange environment in a medical institution, but then, what hospital isn't oddly cut off from the world? They all are, she thinks, even if their rivers, fences and ditches are invisible.

'I can imagine,' she replies.

'Yer Irish?'

'Yes.'

'Yer a nurse, then?'

'Yes.'

'Army nursing service?'

'Yes.'

'Yer don't say much, do yer?'

'No.'

'Seen much action?'

Suddenly, Ellen is thrown into a memory she has no desire to remember. It's dark, the stench is extraordinary, and the noise… The noise is all-consuming.

'A bit.' *Please stop asking me questions,* she thinks. *I've come here to work, not tell my life story.*

'I really admire your lot. I was in the Great War, yer know? Out in France. I was injured. Gammy leg. Your girls sorted me out. But that's why I'm not, yer know, giving Hitler what for in this one.'

Ellen softens. Although she still can't see his face, his voice tells her he's also haunted by things he'd rather not discuss.

'Taking people like me across to the hospital is vital work too,' she says, smiling, hoping he will be able to detect this in her voice.

'Yeah. And the river is pretty fierce at the moment, let me tell yer,' he adds. 'Not easy work. I'm Brian, by the way. I'm on ferry duty most of the time, but I also do work on the grounds sometimes, me and my boy Neil.'

'Nice to meet you, Brian.'

'Nice to meet yer too. Now, we're almost there. Could yer do me a favour? If I climb out, can yer hold on to the landing stage while I tie us up?'

'Of course.'

Ellen can see they've pulled up beside a long wooden pontoon. She clings on to a metal ring just by her shoulder, and she watches Brian launch himself out and pull himself up to standing, his breathing laboured. Then he leans down and ties a rope around a tall metal post.

'Do you need a hand getting out?'

'I might,' she replies, leaning over to pick up her bag.

'Don't worry about yer bag, love, I'll bring that. Here, give me yer hand again.' For the second time that night, Ellen places her life in this man's hands, and allows him to pull her safely onto the island. She is incredibly relieved to feel the grass beneath her feet.

'Yer head up to the house. I need to finish tying up the boat. I'll bring yer bag in a bit, all right?'

'Yes, thank you,' she replies, as she takes in what she can make out of May Day House. It looks huge from here, looming. She can see it's three storeys high, and either side of her are gardens, but whether they're ornamental or practical, very necessary kitchen gardens, she can't really tell. She can see a path leading from the landing stage up to the front door, and she follows it, walking through what feels like a long green tunnel. When she reaches the door, she takes hold of the knocker and raps hard, twice.

3

MEREDITH

October 2013

Meredith's eyes are focused on May Day House's oak front door and its tarnished brass knocker. She watches as her husband fishes into his pocket and pulls out the oversized metal key the estate agent had given them earlier, when the money had officially landed in the right accounts. He passes it between his hands, as if he's weighing up its importance.

'Shall we?' he asks as he inserts it into the lock. She realises his hands are shaking.

'Yep.'

She holds her breath as he turns it. They're both aware of the symbolism of the moment. They are quite literally opening a door to a new life, a new start. Preferably, she hopes, free of the pain that's been part of their lives for far too long.

There's a clunk, a click and a screech as Philip opens the lock and leans against the door, its hinges whining in complaint.

Meredith steps over the threshold and there's a crunch as her feet meet a carpet of dried leaves which must have been lying on the tiled floor of the hallway since last autumn. Cleaning the floors is just one of the many jobs on their lengthy, urgent to-do list. Many of the windows are broken, meaning nature is entering the house with alacrity. She stands still and breathes in the scent of the historic house, of the walnut and birch used in the panelling on the hallway walls, the must of damp, the sweetness of decay.

'What was that?' says Meredith, reacting to a loud thump. It's impossible to tell where it came from.

'Might just be the wind knocking something over upstairs, maybe?' says Philip.

It's possible. The house is stuffed full of dark furniture of mysterious origins and knick-knacks bought on foreign adventures or given as gifts by grateful house guests. In some places, they're piled up high like miniature barricades.

'Yes, maybe,' she says, hoping that whatever's broken isn't valuable. They intend to get the house contents valued and assessed soon, to see what is worth keeping, and if they can, sell anything that's particularly valuable to help with the cost of refurbishment.

'I'll go up and look,' Philip says, and Meredith watches him climb the threadbare red carpet on the broad wooden staircase straight ahead of them. Halfway up, before the stairs twist to the left, there's a spectacular, arched stained-glass window, which is, miraculously, still intact. It depicts, appropriately enough, May Day celebrations in what appears to be a woodland on a perfect early summer's day. Trees bearing leaves in the first flush of youth line up in the background, and in the foreground, young girls wearing long white dresses and crowns of fresh flowers are dancing around a Maypole. Just to their right, an oversized wicker hobby horse stands and waits.

Philip has just walked past the window when there's a heavy knock on the front door.

Meredith pivots and goes to answer it. She pulls it open and is greeted by the leader of the removals team. His short brown hair is plastered to his forehead and his cheeks are bright red. He appears far from happy in his work.

'Where are you wanting all of your boxes put?' he asks, panting.

'Oh, you can just put them in any of the downstairs rooms,' she replies, and she sees his face lift when he realises he and his team won't have to tackle the stairs.

Meredith and Philip are planning to live downstairs for now. The house's last resident, who'd lived here until her death, had converted an old study on the ground floor into her bedroom and an adjacent downstairs toilet into a bathroom when the stairs had got too much. The rooms are dirty and ageing but watertight, so they will do. 'The bed goes into the third room to the left.'

'Rightio,' he says, turning and nodding at his colleagues, who are standing a few metres away bracing a box each. 'Let's crack on.'

Meredith moves to the side of the hallway and they troop in, nodding at her as they pass. She's quite embarrassed by the physical effort they're having to make on her behalf, despite having paid them handsomely for it, so she's relieved to see Philip coming back down the stairs.

'Trying to figure out what's only just fallen over and what's been lying on its side up there for decades is like trying to count grains of sand,' Philip says, walking towards her. 'But it was probably the wind. It's blowing so hard through the broken panes on both upper floors and the leaky frames that it sounds a bit like someone's shrieking.'

'Shall we go outside?' says Meredith, suddenly desperate for some fresh air.

'Yes, why not. I need to check the water pump, anyway. I turned a tap on upstairs and nothing came out.'

Meredith's heart sinks. She is prepared for what amounts to camping in a junk shop, but managing without running water is something she simply is not willing to do. *What are we doing?* she thinks. The thought is unwelcome and dismissed almost as soon as it appears. It's almost as if she's imagined it.

She follows Philip to the house's rear entrance. It's a glass panel door off the kitchen, which Meredith adores. If it were not for the microwave, kettle and toaster the removals men have just deposited in here, you could easily be back in the 1920s, and dealing with the fallout following Cook's decision to walk off the job after a very large and laborious dinner party.

It's far larger than the traditional scullery of most average Victorian houses, because it was designed and built for entertaining. There's a rectangular oak table and matching chairs in the centre, the floor is covered in black and white tiles, the walls in a light blue. There's also a large oblong porcelain sink and a wooden drying rack, and its walls are lined with a hodgepodge of dark wood, glass-fronted cupboards, painted wooden shelves and enamel-fronted units. It hasn't ever been properly modernised; the existing electric free-standing hob probably needs to be condemned and the surfaces are covered in an unholy mix of grease, dust and pigeon droppings, but Meredith doesn't care. She dreams of setting the table with fresh flowers and home-grown produce for wedding couples and writers and artists on retreat, the room filled with laughter and hope. She knows it will take a lot of effort just to make it safe to prepare food in, but she's actually quite looking forward to the challenge.

Philip removes the keys from his pocket, searches for something that looks like it might fit, and inserts it in the lock. He's lucky on his first try, and he grins in triumph as he turns the lock and the back door swings open.

'Ta-da,' he says, stepping onto the crazy paving beyond. Meredith follows, and then the door slams shut behind her with no warning. She feels her heart beating faster, because the impact of wood meeting wood at speed had sounded like a gunshot. 'Must be the wind again,' he says, and she knows he's right. Of course it's the wind. The removal guys are going in and out of the front door, and physics explains this perfectly. She needs to calm down. She's on edge today, a combination of tiredness, anxiety and stress. An ugly cocktail, as her old counsellor would put it.

She passes the old well and follows Philip over to the brick outhouse, where they know the water pump is located. He flicks on the light as they enter the windowless one-room building, and they are both relieved that at least the electrics work.

'Can you go and turn on the outside tap, darling, and we'll see what this does?'

'Sure.'

Meredith walks over to the back wall of the house, beneath the kitchen window, and turns on the tap that's poking out of the brickwork. Nothing happens.

'Is it on?'

'Yes, I think so!' she shouts. 'I tried turning it both ways.'

'Shit,' he yells back.

Meredith is about to re-join Philip when she spots a splash of blue through the trees, and hears the roar of an engine, which dims quickly and then a man's voice calls out.

'Are you guys OK?'

She abandons the useless tap and walks over towards the bank, where she can now see a small blue wooden boat is waiting. In it is a man who looks to be in his late thirties or early forties. He's got medium-length brown hair peppered with grey, which is sticking out at interesting angles. He's sporting stubble a couple of days old, and he's wearing a red hooded top with an indistinguishable, washed-out white logo and dirty blue jeans. He's smiling at her, and it's a warm smile, welcoming.

'Sorry, I didn't mean to be nosy. I just heard swearing...'

'Yep. Sorry. My husband is having trouble with our water pump.'

'You're the new owners of the island, are you? Great. Welcome.'

It's the second time today a new neighbour has welcomed them to the area, and it feels good. Meredith smiles back.

'Yes, we are,' she replies. 'For our sins. I'm not sure we'll manage to survive without water, though.'

'Yeah, that's the problem with these places, isn't it. Look, sorry, I should have introduced myself,' he says, bringing the boat in closer and throwing a rope around a nearby tree trunk. 'I'm Damon. I live just along the river in a houseboat. We've all been wondering when the new owners were going to arrive. This island is a popular topic of conversation around here, see.'

'Nice to meet you, Damon.'

'Likewise. Now, should I see if I can help? I'm used to water pumps. I use one on the boat. I could take a look?'

Meredith is discombobulated. She'd once struggled up the stairs to their flat in London with the contents of three boxes of tiles a delivery guy had refused to bring to their door, and she'd passed three different neighbours in the four trips up the stairs it had taken, and not a single one of them had offered to help. This was unexpected. Astonishing. Like a different world.

'Are you sure? I don't want to bother you...'

'Course. We river dwellers look after our own, you know.'

Damon grins and for the first time that day, the lurking fear about the risk they've taken moving here vanishes. This neighbourliness is incredibly reassuring. He is still smiling at her, in fact, when Philip comes out of the pump house to try to find where she's gone.

'I think we'll need to call a plumb... Oh,' Philip says, spotting Damon, who's now grabbing hold of a bunch of weeds to steady himself as he climbs out of his boat and onto the island.

'Hi, I'm Damon,' says their new neighbour, holding out his arm as he walks towards Philip with a smile. Her husband seems startled. No doubt, she thinks, feeling just as confused as she does by the different attitudes of people here.

'Hi...' he says, not taking his hand. Meredith is taken aback by Philip's rudeness. There's an awkward silence, and then Damon fills it.

'I was just saying to...'

'Meredith,' she says.

'Yes, Meredith, that I came over when I heard you shout.'

'Yes, we've got some issues with the water pump. But I'm sure we can find someone to come and fix it. And in the meantime, we can probably just use the well.' Philip sounds formal now, intensely in control, as if he's at work.

'Yeah, Meredith said. And I was telling her actually I'm quite handy with those sorts of things. Shall I come and take a look and see what I can do? Might save you some bother.'

'No, we're fine, thank you.'

'Come on, Phil...' says Meredith, both embarrassed by her husband's rudeness and keen to have some water for tonight. She knows they won't get a plumber until tomorrow morning at the earliest.

'It really is no bother,' says Damon, smiling at Meredith. 'Not at all.'

'Why don't we see if Damon can work some magic?' says Meredith, and she sees Philip soften slightly. 'Otherwise we've got an expensive problem on our hands.'

'Yes. OK.' Philip blinks furiously. She can see this turn of events might be denting his pride. He's a very capable man, Philip, in professional terms, but he's not great at DIY. Neither of them are, in fact. Which is something they both need to work on urgently if they're ever going to make a go of this place.

'Right, let's see what we've got,' Damon says, walking into the pump house. Philip follows him and stands in the doorway and Meredith loiters behind.

There's some tapping and a squeak.

'It doesn't seem to be responding when you…' says Philip, just as there's a hum and water starts to spurt out of the outside tap. Meredith walks over to turn it off.

'It just needed tightening up,' says Damon, ambling out of the door and past Philip, who looks, Meredith thinks, quite abashed. 'Hadn't been used for a while.'

'Yes, clearly,' says Philip. He sounds a lot less grateful than Meredith thinks he *should* sound.

'Wow, thanks, Damon.' She's eager to cover for her husband's behaviour, which she assumes is due to the stress of the day. 'That's amazingly helpful, thank you.'

'Like I said, it's what river people do.' Damon runs his hand through his hair and smiles.

'Yes, thank you, you've been very helpful,' says Philip, clearly remembering his manners.

Meredith considers asking Damon in for tea, and then remembers they haven't unpacked anything yet. 'I'm so sorry, I would offer you something to drink, but I don't even know where the teabags are…'

'No worries,' Damon says, holding his hands up to show he's at ease. 'It's chaos when you've just moved in somewhere. But maybe some other time?'

'Yes, of course,' says Meredith.

'You'll find me in the little red narrowboat about 300 metres that way,' he says, pointing upstream. 'If there's smoke coming out of the chimney, I'll be in. See you whenever.'

As Damon makes his way back to his boat, Philip walks over to Meredith and slides his arm around her waist.

'Why were you so rude to him?' she whispers, pulling away.

'He's clearly one of the river people, Merry. They live illegally in hideous boats beside the towpath, discharge their sewage into the water and probably steal to get by. I don't like them. No one round here does.'

'He seemed nice to me.'

'Yes, well, you're too kind-hearted. Don't trust him. Don't trust any of them.'

'Come on, Phil. Lighten up. He did us a favour. It was a stroke of luck he was passing by, wasn't it,' she says as they hear him start his engine and head off downstream.

'Yes, very helpful of him.'

'Come on, darling. Let it go. We have a working pump now.'

'Of course. Yes,' he says, returning his arm to her waist. Meredith leans into him.

'I think we're going to like it here,' she says, noting the distant look in his eyes. She can guess what he's thinking, and she knows he needs comfort. 'It's going to be all right, you know. We're going to be fine.'

'Of course it'll be OK, my lovely,' he says as a cold breeze bounces off the boat's wake and flies into their eyes and nostrils. 'Of course it will.'

4

ELLEN

October 1943

The front door of May Day House swings open and warm light floods onto the stone steps.

'Well come in, come in. It's a cold night,' says a senior nurse, her scarlet-edged cape swirling as she turns around and beckons Ellen inside.

When the door closes behind her, Ellen allows herself a moment to take in where she is, and how far she's come to get here. She has survived the water and the darkness, and now she is back on familiar territory, in a world of science, of order, of cleanliness.

'So, you're Lieutenant Quinn, I presume? It's good to have you with us. Was your journey satisfactory?'

The nurse is mid-thirties, Ellen thinks, although the war has been hard on everyone, so she could be younger than that, perhaps. A badge just above her left breast announces her to be Captain Huntingford. Her hair – what Ellen can see of it beneath her white starched veil – is dark brown, almost black. She speaks 'well', as Mammy would say, and she seems friendly, if brusque, but that is pretty standard in Queen Alexandra's Imperial Military Nursing Service. It goes with the job. She is working hard at trying to meet that standard, although it really doesn't come naturally to her.

Ellen looks around her. She's in a long wood-panelled corridor. Faint rectangular outlines show it has been stripped of its previous finery. There are two wooden desks lined up against the walls on the left-hand side, and a woman and a man in army uniform are sitting at them, answering phones, scribbling notes and occasionally sliding files into a bank of large metal filing cabinets on the opposite wall.

'Shall I show you where you'll be sleeping?'

Ellen nods and follows the captain down the corridor and up the stairs at the end, passing a large stained-glass window, which has been boarded up on the other side to protect it from the bombs.

They arrive at the first-floor landing, where thick red carpet has been covered with sticky, dusty plastic sheeting. 'The vast majority of the patient rooms are on this floor,' the matron says, 'and a few more are downstairs, where you'll also find the dining hall and treatment rooms. Staff sleep on the top floor.'

Ellen follows her without comment, aware as a junior rank that her role is to listen, act and not question. The sister leads her down a long corridor with white, glossy walls, and turns into a room on the left. 'This will be yours,' she says. 'You'll be sharing with another young nurse, Lieutenant Rebecca Hanson. She's on duty at the moment, but you'll meet her tomorrow morning.'

Ellen enters the sparsely furnished room. The window is covered with stiff, thick green curtains, and under her feet are bare floorboards. There are two neatly made metal-framed single beds, one on each side wall, with a small metal bedside table each, atop of which sits a grey Anglepoise lamp. An alarm clock and a novel on a table are the only signs someone has already laid claim to the bed on the right. In the left-hand corner is a rectangular porcelain sink with a mirror above it, and in the other corner stands a walnut-effect wardrobe with several drawers beneath. There is nothing on the walls.

'The bathroom is down the hall at the end. We all share, I'm afraid, so pick your time wisely and don't dawdle.'

Ellen nods, and she's about to ask where her suitcase might be when she hears heavy breathing and matching footsteps. Seconds later Brian arrives at the doorway brandishing it, his face the colour of a ripe Cox apple.

'Thank you, Brian,' says Captain Huntingford. 'Much appreciated.' He tips his cap and retreats, his uneven, heavy gait echoing down the empty corridor. 'Right, well, I'll leave you to settle in. If you're hungry, you might find Chef can rustle you up a sandwich. If not, I suggest you get an early night. You're on the roster for tomorrow morning: 7 a.m. sharp.'

Ellen nods once more and smiles, hoping to elicit the same from her superior, but without success. Instead, Captain Huntingford simply turns around and marches back down the hallway.

Ellen pulls the door closed and sits on the bed that hasn't been reserved, the one on the left. She is dog-tired. The one night's leave they'd allocated her after her long journey, which she'd spent in a tired boarding house in South London, had not been enough. Travelling in wartime is not for the faint-hearted, and frankly, Ellen thinks her heart is pretty faint these days. She briefly considers going downstairs in search of food but decides on balance that her need for rest is greater than her need for nourishment. So, she unlaces her shoes, places them neatly at the end of the bed, brushes her teeth and face at the sink, removes her coat, dress, underwear and stockings and stores them in the wardrobe, and dons her cotton pyjamas.

Before she pulls back the blankets on the bed, Ellen decides to turn off the lights and open the curtains. When her eyes adjust to the darkness once more, the dim but persistent light of the moon shows her the bedroom has a view over the gardens to the front of the house. The willows and birch trees which stand sentry over the water's edge are swaying in the wind, which is also tearing leaves from their branches, sending them flying towards the swollen river and the mainland beyond. It will not be long before they are stripped clean. Ellen wonders what lies beyond them. Daylight will help answer that question, at least.

Ellen realises how peaceful this view, this place, is making her feel. Although it's a scene flooded by darkness, it's also a scene full of natural things, things that have an order and can be predicted, observed, and relied upon. This place, this strange, isolated place, feels like it has the answers she's seeking.

It's going to be all right, she thinks, for the first time in a long while. *Yes. It is going to be all right.*

5

MEREDITH

October 2013

Meredith's muscles and joints ache so much she feels every one of her thirty-five years. In fact, she thinks, possibly even an additional twenty this morning. She pulls herself up from the mattress on the floor, puts on her dressing gown, stretches gently and slides her feet into her slippers. The floor is both freezing and filthy.

Their first week of owning May Day has passed in a blur of punishing, constant movement. Her every waking moment has been spent pulling up, clearing out, vacuuming over or sorting through. She is grateful she bought several pairs of heavy-duty rubber gloves before they moved, because she has certainly needed them. She's lost count of the dead mice she has found, the rat droppings, the fox poo. She even spent one horrific afternoon disposing of the rotting carcass of a swan.

It is not, she reminds herself, Phil's fault he only managed to get two days' leave for their move. The airline disposed of the automatic entitlement to such leave for pilots during the last round of cost-cutting measures, and he only has a few days of annual leave left, given the time he had to take off to support her in the spring. No, this is not his fault, and he would rather be here. Of that she is certain.

They've been inseparable ever since they met online five years previously. Philip, a decade older than Meredith, had been just out of a long-term relationship which had gone sour. Meredith, meanwhile, had been in a relationship with someone from university which had lasted a few years but had put her career first after their breakup and had only decided to look for a partner again just before her thirtieth birthday.

She clearly remembers opening the dating app for the first time and seeing Philip's face. She'd found him attractive immediately. It had felt immediately right between them, as if they'd always known each other. That they'd get married was never in question, and they hadn't waited long. Six months to the day of their first date, they'd tied the knot in a little church in Putney. Her parents had loved him and had never questioned whether their rush to get married was questionable. Well, not to her, anyway.

Philip often texts or calls her from exotic places which sound idyllic to her, telling her how lonely he feels without her, how nothing, even something amazingly beautiful, feels right without her there with him, and she believes him. Some of her friends think she's being played, but then, *some* friends are, she suspects, jealous.

She understands why. From the outside, her life appears extraordinary. She has had a successful career in banking, has met and married a handsome airline pilot, and now she can afford to take an indefinite career break from her high-powered job and buy her own Thames Island. I mean, who wouldn't be jealous of that?

It isn't their fault they have a false impression of our lives, she thinks. After all, we have deliberately given them one.

They have done a great job of hiding their pain from pretty much everyone. It was her idea to do so, because she simply can't bear people asking her about it all the time. Every time someone does that, it sends her right back, back into the room with the sonographer and the screen and the silent speakers. She has been there twice now. The first time she'd gone in with the optimism and enthusiasm of a child certain of presents on Christmas morning. The second time, she'd felt more like a convict begging for parole. Those visits and the months that followed etched scars on her heart she knows will never heal, and so she prefers not to think about them, to try to preserve what strength she has left. Her friends have struggled to accept this. They have urged her to talk about it, to continue seeing the counsellor, to just take a sabbatical, not to throw her career away. They don't understand the depth of her pain. She no longer replies to their messages, which are becoming increasingly rare.

And then there is the reason for the money, the money that helped them buy May Day Island. She supposes people assume it's from her bonuses and Philip's wages, but in fact their savings are fairly modest. Philip's salary is reasonable but not amazing, a product of the modern era of aviation where every airline is busy taking part in an incredible race to the bottom. And her bonuses, such as they have been over the years – always less than her male colleagues', she's pretty certain about that – went mostly on the mortgage for their lovely old flat, the running of a car and on their four cycles of IVF, which resulted in two pregnancies and two gut-wrenching, world-imploding miscarriages.

No, the money that enabled them to take the leap of faith they needed to buy this place is her parents'. Or rather, from their estate.

Mum and Dad. Emma and James. Mr and Mrs Sale. Whichever way she refers to them, they are never going to come back. So, like her history of miscarriages, she keeps quiet about their deaths, too. She does not want pity. It only makes their absence seem more real.

In fact, she thinks as she reaches the kitchen, their very different relationships with their parents have probably been the only major difference between them. Philip had never understood why she wanted to speak to her mum and dad several times a week, or why she'd always favoured Christmas at their place to a romantic day a deux in their flat.

Philip is not close to his parents, and that's the reality. Despite the fact they had lived less than an hour's drive away from Putney, they had only visited for occasional stilted lunches which had felt like a duty rather than a joy, with Meredith doing most of the talking – she returned exhausted after every occasion. And despite moving within a few miles of them now, there has not been any sign of Philip wanting to see them more. Meredith had hoped, privately, that things might improve between them after the move. She knows that the family were never the same after Stuart drowned – she now has significant experience, of course, of grief and all its grasping fingers, which linger for far longer than society would like – but it bothers her that he has living parents who he doesn't really see or enjoy. Can it really only be grief that's made them all so distant? Philip shuts her down when she tries to get him to talk about it. It seems to be a family trait. She notices that they never seem to say anything to each other of any importance, and she wonders about the damage being done by what is left unsaid.

Meredith walks over to the small area she's managed to organise, which includes a small under-counter fridge which is old but still working, the sink, a microwave, a toaster, a kettle, an air fryer and a coffee machine. The latter two are remnants of their days in a well-appointed, upmarket kitchen in Putney.

She leans down and opens the fridge door and peers inside. She is hoping for milk at the very least, because she desperately needs coffee. She's going to start tackling the top floor today, and for this she needs as much energy as she can muster.

There is no milk. On closer examination, actually, there is very little of anything. She remembers she finished the last of the milk in her tea yesterday. At the time, she'd made a mental note to go out and get some more, but that was a mental note that harked back to the days when she could just walk outside their front door, turn left and walk two hundred paces to a corner shop with every staple in stock, and much more besides. Now, things are different. Now, she will have to row herself to the mainland to go to the shops, and she hasn't done that yet, not by herself.

Philip has done a deal with the family who own the local boatyard, the Stirlings, to ferry him across the river for work, so she always has their boat for her own use. He gave her a basic rundown before he left: how to untie the boat, unlock the oars, what to do with her hands, arms and back, and of course how to tie the boat up safely on the other side. However, she hadn't really paid much attention, mainly because she'd hoped she wouldn't need to do it while he was away on this trip. He suggested she should leave all of the rubbish from the house in strong black sacks in a pile on the patio, and that's what she's been doing, avoiding having to ferry them to their wheelie bin on the mainland. Phil will do that when he gets back. But the milk and the food in general, well, it would seem she has little choice but to take to the water by herself today. If she waits until he gets back, she might find she only has rice and stale cornflakes left to eat, and more to the point, she detests black coffee.

Meredith lets out a loud performative sigh, for no one's benefit but her own, and walks into their makeshift bedroom and grabs some underwear, a pair of jeans, a T-shirt, a hoodie and some socks from the pile on a chair in the corner. They all need a wash, but the washing machine they ordered hasn't been delivered yet. Then she goes into the bathroom next door to brush her teeth, noting how greasy her hair is in the partially de-silvered mirror above the sink. That's because they currently only have cold water, and she's been doing flannel washes from a bucket. She needs to find a plumber to come and look at their immersion heater, urgently. She will search online for one later, when she gets back from her mission to the supermarket.

When she's ready, she pulls on her padded green coat and trainers, grabs her keys, locks the front door behind her and walks to the riverbank. Their rowing boat is tied up in two places, to a tree and to a large, rusty metal ring covered in weeds. It takes her ages to figure out how to undo the knots Philip's tied; clearly there is knowledge river dwellers have that she has yet to learn. She remembers him telling her their dad had bought them a little dinghy when they'd been small, and he and Stuart had been allowed to row themselves around in the summer, when the Thames had resembled more of a lake than a river. They'd been in the sea cadets, too, hence the rope tying tricks.

She wonders if she'll ever learn about any of it. It all seems so overwhelming. There are too many things to learn and too many jobs to do. Every time she thinks she's achieved a small task, something else breaks, chipping away at the tiny bit of progress she's made. It's like trying to rock climb on a sand dune.

Finally, she manages to untie both ropes, and launches herself, inelegantly, into the boat. Then she grabs the handles of the oars and nudges the right one against the bank to push the boat off. She succeeds. She pushes one oar back in the water a few times so she is facing the far bank, takes a deep breath and then yanks both back. She tries to do as Philip has taught her, but the river feels different today. It's like stirring treacle on an enormous scale. And to make things worse, the boat doesn't respond in the way she hopes. Instead of going directly across in something approximating a straight line, she's going around in a circle.

As she's battling with the oars, Meredith spots a white dot in the distance and realises a motorised boat is heading directly for her. She can't tell how fast it's going, but what she does know is her own boat is moving painfully slowly. She panics and pulls the oars as hard as she can, but she just spins around faster. She checks on the white dot. It's more of a golf ball now. Closer.

Come on Meredith, she thinks. *You're a grown, competent, professional woman. You can do this.*

She checks the white golf ball once more, and it's now football sized. *Right*, she thinks. *If pulling them at the same time doesn't work, I'll pull them alternately*.

This works, although it's incredibly slow going. She's now about four metres from the bank. The boat is bearing down on her. Have they spotted her? She bloody hopes so, although their engine is still whining insistently, and showing no signs of quieting.

Just a few more strokes, she thinks, her heart pulverising her rib cage. It is a huge relief when she is finally within touching distance of the trees that hang over the water's edge, and she almost cries when the boat bumps into the bank. She leans forward to try to throw a rope around the nearest tree trunk.

Then the boat races past her.

She is so relieved to still be alive she doesn't even think about the wave – the wake – that is heading straight for her, the result of that boat's reckless speed.

It is a large one, large enough both to delight children at the seaside, and to cause her boat to rock violently.

It all happens so fast.

She loses her balance. The rope slips out of her hand. Her head tips forward. Her body follows. And then she finds herself hurtling downwards, her arms spread wide as if she feels she might fly. Her upper body hits the bank so hard all of the air is forced out of her lungs. The bottom half of her body, meanwhile, sinks into the water. It's incredibly cold, and she gasps in shock.

'Jesus, are you OK?' says a woman's voice. Meredith had been so busy focusing on trying to row she hadn't seen there was anyone there, and the fact there is, is both embarrassing and a huge relief. She looks up briefly and is even more relieved that it isn't the busybody woman they'd met on moving day. If it had been, she'd never live this down. They'd all be dining out on this in the local pubs by dinnertime. 'I mean, of course you're not OK, what a stupid thing to say. You must be cold and very wet. And are you hurt?'

Meredith shakes her head. She doesn't feel in pain at the moment, although it does occur to her it might be the shock.

'OK, well, that's something. Look, give me your hand, and I'll pull you out.'

'My legs... might be... stuck...'

'In the mud? Oh yeah, it's soft and deep that stuff, isn't it? But don't worry, it's not quicksand. You'll have dirty legs, but you'll be fine.'

Meredith is doubtful, but she doesn't argue. She is five foot ten, a size fourteen and she's wearing a heavy coat. But on the other hand, she wants to get out of here, right now. So she puts her hand out and the other woman pulls hard.

To her astonishment, her feet begin to shift and she does her best to help by using her spare arm to pull herself up out of the water.

It works. She imagines she looks rather like a walrus basking in the sun, but she's out of the water, and that's what matters. And then she remembers.

'Oh God... the boat. I haven't tied it up.'

'Don't worry lovely, I've got it,' says her saviour, who switches her focus to the boat, which Meredith can see from a sideways glance has fortunately been caught by a nearby tree. It's several feet away from the bank, however, and Meredith can't see how this woman thinks she can get it back. But then she throws off her long, camouflage-style padded coat and reveals a bright pink swimming costume beneath, and before Meredith can stop her, she is in the water and splashing her way over to the boat. She takes hold of it within seconds, grabs a rope, and pulls it back to the bank before pushing herself out of the river with a grace Meredith can only dream of.

'Bloody hell,' says Meredith, her teeth chattering involuntarily from the cold. 'That was mad. Amazing.'

The woman grins as she ties the boat up to the tree.

'I'd only just got out from my morning swim, to be honest, so it wasn't too much of a shock to get back in,' she says, pulling her long coat back on. It's then Meredith notices the bright pink float at her feet.

'You swim in there, at this time of year?' says Meredith with disbelief, as she pulls herself up to a sitting position.

'Oh yes, all year round.'

'Blimey.'

'Yes, lots of people say that. Well, look, let's get you warm and dry. You'll be needing a change of clothes, too. My place is only a short walk away. Come with me.'

Meredith is too shocked and too cold to argue. She follows her rescuer along the towpath. She's shorter than Meredith, maybe five foot four, very slim with short brown hair cut into an angular bob. Meredith thinks she's probably in her early thirties. After about a hundred metres, they turn sharply left via a small gap in the hedge and arrive at a log cabin with a pretty picket fence on the boundary. The woman swings a gate open and leads Meredith through the garden, which is a magical mix of meandering stone pathways and colourful, textured planting, with many still flowering, despite the arrival of autumn. There's also a wishing well, an old cartwheel and a statue of Buddha.

'Here we are.'

Meredith enters her home, which smells of jasmine and pine. The wooden walls of the cabin are exposed inside and beautifully varnished. The effect is warm and inviting. 'Now, let me get you a towel, and you can have a shower. And then I'll lend you some of my clothes.'

'Thank you. By the way... I'm Meredith. Merry.'

'And I'm Holly.'

'Thank you, Holly,' she says, taking off her shoes.

'Honestly, it's fine. Saving people from a watery death before breakfast really gets your heart pumping. You did me a favour.'

The two women smile at each other, and Holly goes off in search of a towel and a change of clothes. Her home has one large living and kitchen room. There are fairy lights strung over a fireplace which houses a wood burner, there's a fluffy cream rug on the floor, a rustic oak kitchen to the right, a round oak dining table and two large yellow sofas.

Meredith walks over to the burner, taking care to avoid the rug so she doesn't deposit river mud on it. The burner is alight, and she puts her feet nearest the heat, trying to thaw them out.

'Here you go,' says Holly, returning with a pile of clothes and a large fluffy grey towel. 'Why don't you go and take those soaking clothes off and warm up properly in the shower. Take your time.'

Meredith nods gratefully and follows her host down a small corridor, which leads to a bedroom to the left, and a bathroom to the right. Its walls are covered in blue and white tiles, a large, trailing house plant is hanging from the ceiling, and there's a naked statue of a woman in the corner, next to the sink.

When Meredith shuts the door behind her and finally peels her wet clothes off, she realises she is shaking. When she turns the shower on and surrenders to the warm water, she starts to cry. They are tears of relief, certainly, but they are also tears she's been keeping back for months: tears of grief and of fear and of frustration.

* * *

'Better?'

'Much.'

'Good. Are the clothes OK?'

Meredith smiles. She's wearing ripped jeans and a large, red jumper. They are absolutely not what she'd normally wear, but she feels great in them.

'Yes, thank you. They're great. I'm amazed they fit.'

'I've got a whole range of sizes from years of yo-yo dieting,' replies Holly. 'So I estimated what you might be. I'm glad I got it right.'

'You did.'

'Awesome. You can keep them, by the way.'

'I couldn't.'

'Yes, you could. Don't be silly. Now, will you join me in some breakfast?'

Meredith wonders whether she might be overstaying her welcome, but her hunger and her lack of food back on the island persuades her to accept.

'That would be lovely, thank you.' Holly busies herself in the kitchen, putting on the kettle and getting out bread, crumpets, jam, butter, cereal and milk. 'You have a gorgeous place.'

'Oh, thank you. It's a bit rustic, I know, but I love it. So, are you... new around here?' she asks, as she puts plates, bowls and cutlery on the dining table.

'Yes. I've just moved onto May Day Island with my husband.'

Holly's eyes light up.

'Oh, have you? How amazing. I love that place.'

'Have you been on it, then?' Meredith asks, walking over to the table and standing beside it.

'Oh, we've all been on it at one time or another.' Meredith blinks, and Holly sees her shock. 'Oh, you didn't know? Yeah, all the local river dwellers have picnicked on there, or spent the night wild camping on it, at some point. It's been empty for years. It's too tempting, having it there and not being allowed to go on it, you know? Human nature. Don't worry, though, we'll stop now! We aren't going to trespass on your property. I promise.'

Meredith tries to hide her discomfort. She had not considered that other people might feel they have a claim to the island. Since she'd found it online and they'd decided to buy it, it has always felt entirely theirs.

'Of course, I'm not worried about that,' she says, not really convincing even herself.

'Coffee?' asks Holly, and Meredith accepts eagerly. No doubt, Holly will actually have milk. 'It's such a funny place, isn't it?' Holly continues, turning round to flick the kettle on and spoon coffee into a cafetiere. 'It looks older than it is. It feels older, I think. And do you know why it's called that?'

'May Day?'

'Yes. I might be wrong, I'm only going on local gossip, but I heard that it was because Mr Chevalier, the man who had it built, was desperate to have an heir. He'd been married for a few years before he bought the island, and he and his wife were having no joy. And May Day, well, it's linked to all of those ancient fertility rituals, isn't it? Spring, new life, all that jazz. So he reckoned if he called it that, and built that fertility goddess statue in the garden, and put those figures in the stained glass, they might be able to have a baby.' Meredith is struck dumb for a moment. She can't believe she hadn't noticed this before. Now she's been told, of course, she will not be able to unhear it, to unsee it. It will taint everything. She feels the panic rising in her stomach, but she doesn't want to tell Holly why. Not talking about her pain seems to help; it means she doesn't have to relive it constantly. 'But anyway, enough of that,' says Holly, clearly unaware how this news has affected her. 'How are you finding it? It must need a lot of work.'

'It's... hard going,' says Meredith, breathing slowly and deeply to try to calm herself down. She doesn't want to talk about anything painful today. She will process how she feels about this news later, she decides. Much later.

'I bet. It's a bit of a ruin, isn't it?'

'Yes. You could say that.'

'But worth it?'

'Yes. I think so. We both think so. Me and Phil.'

'Good you have each other there,' Holly says, pouring hot water into the cafetiere and giving it a stir. 'It's quite a place to be on your own in.'

'Yes, it's helpful to have someone to work through the enormous DIY to-do list with,' replies Meredith as Holly places a mug in front of her and a jug of milk.

'Oh no, I didn't mean it like that. I meant that it's a bit... creepy, you know? Some of the locals say they've seen...' She stops, just as she carries the cafetiere over to the table. 'Actually, don't mind me. It's just silly gossip.'

'Seen what?' says Meredith, her stomach tightening.

'Oh, nothing. Honestly. How do you like your coffee? Black? White? Just a splash of milk? Or loads?'

'Tell me. Please. Seen what?'

Holly looks chastened.

'Look, this is just silly local gossip, all right? But I did hear some people say they've seen a… figure over there.'

'Like a human? Someone visiting the island?'

'No. Like a ghost.'

Meredith's mouth runs dry. An instinct she's had, a feeling she's suppressed, begins to seep out of the mental safe she's put it in.

'Oh.'

'Like I said, it's just silly gossip,' says Holly, pouring coffee into her mug. 'Milk?'

'Yes please,' she answers, her voice catching.

'Seriously, don't give it a second thought. I shouldn't have said anything. It's just people being silly. Old buildings give people ideas.'

'Yes, they do.' Meredith is thinking of the sounds she's heard upstairs, of the doors that have slammed, of the prickle she's felt in the hairs on her neck sometimes when she's been alone.

'And ghosts don't exist, anyway.'

'No.'

'Anyway, tell me. What big plans do you have for the place?'

Before they'd moved, this had been one of Meredith's favourite topics. The restoration of the formal gardens, of the wedding services in the orangery, of the beautiful honeymoon suite she planned on the first floor. But now, the exhaustion she feels, that niggling unease, coupled with this morning's tumble into the river – they have all curbed her enthusiasm. She doesn't feel the love at all.

'Oh, lots of plans. But lots of work first. We have to clear the house and the garden and fix the roof and windows…' She puts her head in her hands. 'Oh bloody hell, I'm knackered. Sorry.'

'Don't be. Anyone would feel like that after your shock this morning,' says Holly, squeezing her arm. 'I take it you're not an experienced oarswoman?'

This makes Meredith laugh.

'How on earth did you work that out?'

'Just a hunch,' says Holly, mirroring Meredith's sarcasm. She sits down opposite her, cradling her own coffee.

'Seriously, though, I *am* going to have to get better at it. I've got to get some stuff from the supermarket today, and we've got bags and bags of rubbish to bring over after that.'

'You've got time. And what you need is a boat with a motor, anyway. No messing.'

'I've got no idea how to use one of those either.'

'I thought your husband grew up by the river?'

Meredith blinks. She's momentarily taken aback that this woman she has only just met knows about her husband's childhood. But then she checks herself, reasoning that Holly is also a local. And locals seem to talk to other locals.

'Did you know Phil when he lived near here, then?'

Until Stuart died, that is, Meredith thinks.

'Oh, nah. I was too young. Your husband's about ten years older than me, I think?'

'Oh, are you thirty-five too?'

'Just turned thirty-five! Samesies.' The two women smile at each other. 'But yeah, my parents knew his family, I think. And I saw Elinor walking the dog the other day, and she mentioned that a local had bought the place, so I asked who it was.' Holly takes a large gulp of coffee and swallows hard. 'I was sort of surprised to hear he was so keen on buying the island, to be honest. Given what happened to his brother so close by.' This reference to Philip's childhood agony shocks Meredith. They rarely discuss it and his parents never want to, so the fact that someone she barely knows is aware of what happened to Stuart is distinctly unsettling. Her eyes dart towards Holly, who is staring fixedly into her mug. 'I'm sorry... I probably shouldn't have said that. My stupid mouth. It's just when we all heard you guys had bought the house, well, everyone's first thought was about what happened to his brother. It was a long time ago, but... people haven't forgotten around here. You don't, when someone local dies in the river...'

'It's OK,' replies Meredith, quietly relieved to be able to talk about Stuart, someone she'd never met but whose ghost she feels she lives with daily. He had been eighteen months younger than Philip, and apparently very much in awe of him. They had looked alike, could even have been mistaken for twins in the right light. Their personalities, however, had been very different. Unlike Philip, Stuart had apparently been quiet, unassuming; shy, even. 'I worried a lot about whether moving here would stir things up. I mean, he never wanted to come and walk along here when we visited his parents, and we hardly ever talk about what happened.'

'Yeah. At least you can't see the bridge from the island. It's a bit further along, at least.'

The bridge. Meredith shivers thinking about it. Stuart had jumped from there into the river, egged on by his mates.

'Yes.'

'Kids still jump from there in the summer, you know.'

'Really?'

'Yeah. Kids are kids, aren't they? They think they'll live forever. And most of them are fine, of course. But someone seems to die in this stretch of the river every couple of years. The occasional suicide, you know, but mostly not by choice.'

'God. It's so awful. Phil still feels guilty, you know. About not being there.'

Holly looks thoughtful.

'I can imagine.' There's an awkward silence. 'But obviously he must feel OK enough about it to live here now? He must see returning as a positive thing?'

'Yes,' replies Meredith, glad of the change of topic. 'He says he sees buying the island as an opportunity to make peace with the area and with himself. He wants to put down happy memories here now, instead.'

'Makes sense, I suppose.'

'Well, I think my love for the island is infectious.'

'I bet.'

'I just wish Phil's affinity with boats was also infectious. I am rubbish at it. But his job takes him away so much, I have to be able to cope by myself.'

'What's his job?'

'Oh, I thought you'd have heard about that, too. He's a pilot. An airline pilot.'

'Nice.'

'Sort of. It's less glamorous than it looks. Not so well paid these days as it used to be, and he's constantly tired and he's away loads. It makes... things hard.'

'I can imagine. Although the holidays must be nice?'

Meredith smiles. It's much easier to talk about this rather than the important days he's missed, the difficulty trying to conceive, his absence on key days during their IVF journey.

'Yes, we're very lucky. But no holidays for a while yet, though. We need to spend all our money on this place. And sort out the boat situation.'

'Ah, the rewards will be worth it. And you'll learn! You can ask at the boat shop by the lock. The owner there, Rob, the older guy, he services outboard engines. He might have one you could buy?'

'Good idea.'

Meredith makes a mental note to talk to Philip about it when he's back.

'Right. Food. Toast? Crumpets? I have either.'

'A crumpet would be great.'

'Coming up.' Holly walks over to the counter and pops two crumpets in a toaster.

'So how about you? You obviously liked this area so much, you decided to stay?' Meredith asks, keen to learn more about her new friend.

'Oh, yeah. My parents bought an old chalet on this spot and brought me up here. It was a bit rustic, you know, but it was lovely. I played in the river all summer, made loads of local friends. I did leave for a bit, went travelling, lived overseas for a while, but I came back here to look after them before they died. And after that, well, I put all the money I had into rebuilding it. I love it here. I never want to leave.'

'I can imagine. I feel like that now, even after the week I've had.'

'Yeah, there's something about the water. I can't explain it really, but it's addictive, calming, you know? Restorative. I know I sound like a hippy. Although I am a bit of a hippy, to be fair.'

'What do you do for a living?'

'Oh, I run meditation classes and yoga retreats. I picked up the habit when I was living in Thailand, and it's never left me.'

'Sounds amazing.'

'It is. You should come to one of my classes.'

Meredith nods with enthusiasm as the crumpets pop up, and Holly brings them to the table along with butter and jam.

'So what do you do?'

'Well, at the moment, the renovation of May Day Island. But not very well, obviously,' says Meredith, laughing. 'I've taken a career break from my job in banking to give it a go. It felt like the right time to try to follow a dream, you know?'

'Yeah. You've always got to do that. If you don't, you'll always wonder.'

'Yes,' says Meredith, digging into the jam jar. 'Exactly. Yes.'

* * *

It's nearly lunchtime when Meredith rows herself back over to the island, with Holly coaching her from the bank. Her first foray to the shops has been successful, and she reckons she has enough food in the bags stowed by her feet to last until Philip gets back, at least. She's feeling more positive than she did this morning, less defeated. Meeting Holly has cheered her up. It's good to know she has a friend nearby.

She waves in triumph at Holly as she successfully navigates the tying up and disembarking of the boat, bags and all, and watches as she turns and walks back to her home. As she's walking back through the pergola to the house, her phone buzzes. It's a message from Philip.

> Flight fine, just heading to hotel. You OK, darling? How's the big clear out going? So sorry I can't be there. Bloody work.

Yes, *bloody work*, mumbles Meredith. She respects his choice of career and knows it's much harder than it looks, but on days like these, when he's about to spend twenty-four hours in the Abu Dhabi sunshine, she can't help but feel resentful. She will reply later. She has a lot of tidying to do first. She promised herself she'd clear out at least one of the upstairs rooms before bed, and her sojourn at Holly's has delayed her.

After she has deposited her groceries in the kitchen, she finds a couple of strong black bin bags and one of her new pairs of rubber gloves and walks up the two flights of stairs to the attic rooms.

She coughs as she reaches the top floor, the dust up here catching in her throat. *It might be worth buying a mask,* she thinks. Her lungs are probably full of the stuff by now, and that can't be healthy.

She decides to start in the room that's furthest away, at the end of the corridor. As she walks there, the floorboards creak and groan beneath her feet, and she wonders whether they might be rotten. She checks her phone is still in her back pocket, in case she has to ring for help. Although how long they'd take to get to her, she has no idea. Do the fire service have boats? She doubts it.

She reaches the final room on the left and pushes the door open. She is relieved to find it's not stuffed to the rafters with crap, as quite a few of the rooms are. This one should be a relatively easy one at least. There are two rusting metal bed frames resting on their sides beneath the window, there's a wardrobe on the right that's missing a door, and on the left there are several wooden packing boxes and a couple of disintegrating suitcases.

Meredith rolls up her sleeves, opens up her phone and selects one of the cleaning playlists she's created to help keep her entertained. As the music fills the room, she decides to tackle the boxes first. There is not much worth keeping in here, she thinks. It's mostly old magazines and newspapers, receipts from the sixties, and Christmas cards from and to people she will never meet, and who are most likely dead. Whoever packed this box was determined to keep every single piece of evidence of their existence, and while it's frustrating for Meredith, she has some sympathy with them. Who doesn't want to have something survive of them? She certainly does. That was at least part of the reason why she put herself through fertility treatment. And then, a large part of the reason why she and Philip bought May Day House, trying to restore it to its former glory. They want to make it their legacy.

The boxes done, Meredith decides to move onto the wardrobe. There's nothing hanging in it, so she pulls out the drawers. It's full of folded white linen, and when she pulls the sheets out, a cloud of dust and several moths fills the air. She coughs, dumps the sheets in a pile to her right and looks in the drawer to check she hasn't missed anything.

Then she notices the lump in the drawer liner. There must be something under there, she realises. She reaches over and peels the liner back. Beneath it is a small blue book, its cloth cover disintegrating at the corners. It's a notebook. She scans its early pages, but there's no sign of a name to show who it belonged to. What there is, however, are pages and pages of handwritten notes. And there are dates, starting from October 1943.

But they're not just notes, she realises.

Some of them are letters.

And the first one begins: 'Dear Mammy...'

6

ELLEN

October 1943

Dear Mammy,

I've now been at May Day House a week. It's been exhausting and overwhelming, not helped at all by the journey here, which was also really difficult. I knew of course that leaving Egypt would mean yet another long journey by boat, and of course you know how I feel about that, but I didn't have a choice. This was a particularly long one too.

We met the ship on the Red Sea coast. They would not let us travel via the Suez Canal, because the area was not safe, and so we had to traverse the whole of Africa instead. They send me where they send me, as you know! I had to make the best of it.

I managed to hold myself together on the long voyage by keeping busy. We were bringing back a large number of severely injured men, so I set about my duties; cleaning, feeding, listening, jollying, doing whatever they needed to help them get better.

We stopped off for ten days at a place called Durban in South Africa, so they could restock the boat and everyone could rest. It's so beautiful there Mammy, you'd love it. The sea is the most astonishing sort of blue and it's so warm, like a bath. And one of the matrons took a group of us off for the day in an open-back truck to see some wild animals, and it was a dream, a complete dream. I saw elephants, lions and rhino, and I was only a little bit scared. You would have been proud! I wish you could have been there. I really do.

The second part of our journey was the worst. The weather was bad in the Atlantic and there was so much sickness, including from me, I'm afraid to say. Our ship was tossed around like a little toy, and I don't mind admitting that I felt very fearful, and I think that made me feel all the more nauseous. I do not want to see another basin for the rest of my days, I tell you.

We were all very relieved to arrive in Portsmouth, even though it was raining. After all that time in the sunshine, it made me think of home. Then I had to take the train up to London. That was difficult, as the timetables nowadays are very unreliable, and at one point we stopped in a siding for a good two hours, and no one knew when we might set off again. Anyway, I had one day off in London, and I used my wages to pay for a guest house, which was cheap but cheerful. I didn't go out, even though I know I should have. I was just so tired, so I slept and slept and only came out for meals. I departed early for Weybridge after lunch the following day. After another eventful journey, I was picked up from the station in a van and driven to a funny little parking area beside the river, which I now know belongs to May Day Island. There, in the pitch black (due to the blackout) I met a friendly man who helped me into a little rowing boat and took me to my new posting, which as you might have guessed from the name, is on an island.

Yes, an island! In the Thames! I didn't even know there were any. Anyway, I'm now at May Day House, which is a Victorian mansion being used as a hospital for war-damaged soldiers. I've only done a few shifts so far, so I'm still getting my head around it all, but it's an unusual sort of place. It's not full of people with physical wounds, although there are a few who do have some minor physical injuries. Instead, it is hosting soldiers with a sickness of the mind.

Did I tell you that I'm here because of a psychiatrist I met in Cairo, Dr Lovell? He recommended me to the management here. Dr Lovell has been very kind to me, and he was also, I felt, very kind to the men he looked after, some of whom had been written off as constitutional neurotics. He has theories about mental breakdown and experimented with all sorts of new therapies in Cairo, some of which I am told they may introduce here.

Not everyone is as forward thinking as him, however, I am afraid to say. There are at least two doctors whose behaviour seems to me to border on cruelty.

So far, I have witnessed one or two very unpleasant public dressing-downs, which I feel cannot possibly help a man feel stronger in his brain or his body. But it is not my place to question a doctor's work, so I do not do so. Instead, I'm concentrating on making a difference where I can, by feeding them nutritional food, making them comfortable, and helping them look their best. It is all I can do.

I will write more soon.

Your ever-loving daughter x

* * *

'Are you coming, then? The boat leaves in a few minutes.'

Ellen snaps the notebook shut and places it in the drawer of her bedside table.

'Oh, yes, sorry. I lost track of time.'

She snatches her handbag from the end of the bed, takes her coat out of the wardrobe and follows her new roommate down the stairs to the entrance hall.

Ellen has the afternoon off. Luckily, so does Rebecca, and she has persuaded Ellen to come with her on the ferry over to the mainland so that they can walk into Weybridge and visit the Lyon's Corner House. It will be good to get to know her properly, thinks Ellen. Despite sharing a room, their shifts have meant they've rarely had time to talk to each other.

She follows Rebecca down the path to the boat dock. It's a bright autumnal day, and everything looks and feels very different to the night she arrived. The tunnel of roses possesses faded beauty; the river is meandering, not torrential; the house is elegant, not imposing. Nevertheless, she is pleased to board the boat and leave May Day for a short while. Her first couple of shifts have been exhausting, and the atmosphere on the island is both claustrophobic and intense.

As Brian rows them across, Ellen examines Rebecca. She's elegantly turned out in a tweed skirt and matching jacket, low-heeled shoes and a white shirt. A red scarf adds a dash of colour, and a ruby and gold brooch is pinned close to her heart.

'That's beautiful,' says Ellen. 'Your brooch.'

'Oh, thank you,' says Rebecca in an accent so perfect, Ellen reckons she wouldn't be out of place reading the news on the BBC. 'It's from my mother.'

Ellen looks down at her own clothes – an ageing blue skirt, tatty white shirt and a jumper a colleague had knitted for her as a gift on the ship back to England – and feels embarrassed.

'I like your sweater. It's so jolly,' says Rebecca with a broad smile, and Ellen immediately feels better. 'Mother always buys me muted colours. I bought this red scarf myself.'

'Do you see your parents often?' Ellen asks after they've disembarked and begun the walk into the town.

'Goodness no. They sent me away to boarding school as soon I turned eleven, and I have only really been back for short visits ever since. I trained as a nurse as soon as I could.'

'You don't like each other, then?' Ellen finds it hard to imagine anyone not liking their mother. But then, perhaps she's lucky. Which is a strange thought, given how unlucky she feels in general.

'Not dislike, exactly. I would say it's all rather neutral. They aren't great at expressing any kind of affection, and I suppose I've got used to it. Are you close to your parents?'

Flashes of the past come to Ellen: her mother's warm embrace; the bitter bite of her father's belt; her hot tears falling on the flagstones of their kitchen.

'My mother, yes. But I haven't been back to Ireland in a long while.'

'Are you Catholic?' she asks as they pass the Three Horseshoes pub on their right. They are nearing the high street now.

'I am, yes.'

'From the south?'

Ellen glances at Rebecca's expression, trying to ascertain whether she's being judged. She's not political, but she knows the partition of Ireland two decades earlier is still a subject of discussion and disagreement.

'Yes.'

'How lovely. I've always wanted to visit.'

'If you do go, I can tell you where to avoid,' says Ellen with relief, and they both laugh.

'Do you have brothers and sisters?'

Ellen feels a lump form in her throat. She misses her siblings dreadfully.

'Yes. I have two brothers and two sisters.'

'Younger or older?'

'All younger. Do you have siblings?' Ellen is keen to move the conversation on.

'I did have an older brother, yes. But he was shot down and killed during the Battle of Britain.'

'Oh goodness. I'm so sorry.'

'So many people have lost people, haven't they? I don't have a monopoly on that. But thank you. I miss Sebastian a great deal. He was the best of us.'

Ellen doesn't know what to say, so she lets silence fall as they cross the road and walk along the high street, stopping outside the tearoom, whose fogged-up windows mark it out as one of the most popular destinations in the area. 'After you,' says Rebecca, opening the door and beckoning Ellen inside.

They are shown to a table in the corner, next to the counter.

'I'm sorry if talking about your brother upset you. I didn't mean to bring up painful memories,' says Ellen, taking a seat opposite her roommate.

'Oh, I'm glad to talk about him. It's a relief, if I'm honest. When I last had leave, I visited my parents. It was as if Sebastian had never existed. All we talked about was the weather and the performance of this year's crops.'

'Did you grow up on a farm, then?' asks Ellen, who had several friends from Irish farming families.

'Yes.'

'Small or big?' asks Ellen, accepting a menu.

'About five hundred hectares,' replies Rebecca, receiving the same.

'Oh.'

Ellen's friends had lived on farms a fifth of this size.

'Seriously, Ellen, please don't be impressed,' says Rebecca, noting her shock. 'My father inherited it and has tenants doing all the hard work. I'm embarrassed, if anything, by how much he has for so little effort. He thinks being a nurse is a mug's game, by the way. I'm pretty much doing this to annoy him.'

'My motives are similar,' says Ellen. They grin at each other. Ellen finds herself warming to her new friend.

'How are you finding it so far? May Day House?' Rebecca asks.

'Tiring. Different.'

'You were in Egypt before, weren't you?'

'Yes. We were dealing with battle fatigue there too, but this is... different. More medical, you know? I find some of the methods a bit... upsetting.'

'You'll get used to it. It does work, for some of the men, at least.'

'That's good to hear.'

The two women order two Eccles cakes and a pot of tea.

'I do find some of the other staff a bit abrasive, though,' says Ellen, who is thinking of the matron, who has been incredibly curt with her during her first two shifts.

'Oh, don't be too put off by old Huntingford. Her bark is definitely worse than her bite.'

Ellen raises an eyebrow.

'Hmm. I'll take your word for it.'

'And the men are generally a good lot. I've found the work to be quite rewarding,' says Rebecca as the waitress brings a pot of tea to the table and places two cups down in front of them. 'And it definitely beats working on the front line.'

Ellen swallows hard, determined not to let painful memories surface. She watches the other woman pour two cups of tea, the brown liquid eddying on the surface.

'Yes,' is all Ellen can manage to say. She's using all of her energy to keep herself on an even keel. Rebecca doesn't seem to notice. She pours milk into the cups, stirs them and hands one to Ellen.

'Here's to no May Days at May Day House,' says Rebecca, holding up a teacup.

'Cheers to that,' says Ellen, raising her own cup, and hoping that her friend can't see that her hands are shaking. 'Please God, cheers to that.'

7
MEREDITH

October 2013

'Come on, Merry, put that down. Let's go and eat.'

Meredith puts the notebook down with reluctance. She'd read the first letter just after she'd found it, but then she'd chastised herself for wasting time. So she'd put it to one side, only finding it again and opening it last night when she'd been upstairs searching for an electric heater.

It's not named, but it clearly belonged to a nurse who worked at the house during the war, and Meredith is fascinated by it. The estate agent had mentioned that May Day had been requisitioned during the Second World War, but this little book promises to tell her so much more.

'Yes, I know. Sorry. It's just so interesting, you know?' she says, returning it to her bedside table.

'I know.' Philip reaches across the bed and encircles Meredith in his arms. 'And I completely understand. But we also need to focus on telling May Day's next story.'

Meredith sinks into the warm space between his chin and his shoulder and looks up at the ceiling, from which hangs a dusty but beautiful chandelier.

'Do you think they'll let us? Make the changes we need to, I mean?' she says, noting a spider has knitted an intricate web about the light fitting as elegant as a bridal veil.

'They'd better,' says Philip, rubbing his eyes. He's still recovering from a night flight. His sleep is often disrupted for the entirety of the time he's at home between trips. 'Otherwise, this place is going to fall apart, isn't it? They'll have to.'

Their architect had submitted their plans for May Day the previous day, after extensive consultation with the council planning officer. In them, they have detailed plans for new windows throughout; a larger replacement for the decrepit orangery, designed to accommodate weddings; the rebuilding of an old gazebo in the gardens, perfect for photographs and outdoor classes of all kinds; and finally, a small outbuilding near the existing pump house, from which they want to run a small dayboat hire business, with access provided via private ferry. Meredith knows she'll have to get better at steering boats if they're going to make a success of this particular venture.

'But it's listed. You know what they're like about listed buildings.'

'Yes. But we're not extending it, not really, except the orangery, and that won't make a huge difference anyway, will it, to the footprint?'

'I suppose not.'

Meredith is more frightened by the prospect of a refusal from the council than she wants to admit. Despite her inheritance, their existing funds will only stretch so far. She reckons they have enough to fix the roof, to do some basic gardening and perhaps refurb one or two rooms on their existing budget. They are relying on planning permission being granted to enable them to secure a business loan, which will allow them to get the house ready for visitors. They know it needs to be special to command the sort of money they are hoping to charge. Without the changes they are planning, they may struggle to even pay their existing mortgage.

Perhaps I should go back to work, she thinks. *Yes, I could always go back to work.*

The thought calms and reassures her. The fact she has the capability to go out and earn a decent living is an important safety net she suspects they both value greatly.

'Shall I make us some coffee?'

Meredith smiles and nods. Philip kisses her on the cheek and launches himself out of the bed, wrapping himself in a dressing gown immediately. She didn't manage to find a heater, and the house is freezing. As soon as he leaves the room, Meredith also gets out of bed and reaches for her dressing gown and slippers. She will lay the fire in one of the ground floor rooms later, where they've made a sort of den with two comfortable chairs and a coffee table. There's also a piano in there, which, while ageing and slightly out of tune, has provided a welcome respite from clearing, cleaning and sorting. She hasn't played the piano since school, and she's enjoying rediscovering it.

Meredith follows Philip into the kitchen, where he's standing at the counter scooping coffee into the expensive machine they'd bought when they had been two well-paid professionals with no kids and, she thinks, no worries, not really. Now they still have no kids, but they only have one salary and a whole load of worries which neither of them is talking about. She makes a resolution to talk to Philip honestly about how she feels later. *This can't be healthy,* she thinks.

'Would you like a bacon sandwich? I think we have some bacon,' he says, hitting the button on the machine and grabbing two cappuccino mugs from a cupboard. 'And I got some of that kefir stuff you seem to like, you mad fool. Shall I pour you some?'

'Oh yes please,' says Meredith with a grin, desperate to appear happier than she feels. She doesn't want to ruin the moment. He's only just got back from his last trip and she wants to make the most of his spell at home.

'Coming up.'

'What time do we have to be at Elinor's?'

'Half past ten. We've got an hour.'

They had hoped to avoid meeting with their enthusiastic new neighbour for a while yet, but Elinor has been insistent, even going so far as sending them a welcome card with a suggested date and time. So they've agreed, reluctantly, to give up some of their precious time together to sit in her living room, no doubt eating expensive Waitrose biscuits and being mined for potential local gossip.

Philip is getting milk out of the fridge when there is an incredibly loud bang.

'What the hell was that?' he says.

Meredith's heart is racing. She hasn't really acknowledged to herself how she's felt since that conversation with Holly, the one about the ghosts. She hasn't seen anything out of the ordinary, but she definitely feels uncomfortable here when she's alone, and there've been all sorts of strange noises at all times of the day and night. Of course, there are lots of reasonable, straightforward explanations for those noises – animals, gusts of wind, dodgy roof tiles, a creaking old house – but that doesn't change her instinctive fear. She's slightly embarrassed by it, however, so she wants to hide how she feels from Philip.

'Sounded like it was outside?'

'Maybe. Wait here,' says Philip, opening the back door and marching outside. Meredith follows him. She instinctively does not want to be left alone.

It's even colder outside, though, and she's not wearing a coat. She shoves her hands in her dressing gown pockets and runs to catch up with Philip as he walks round to the front of the house, to the patio which borders the old formal gardens. He comes to an abrupt halt a few feet from the rose garden.

'What the...?'

There's a man in their garden.

He's wearing jeans, a wax jacket and a bucket hat. He's in the overgrown wilderness near the boat dock, and his back is turned, so they can't see his face.

'Excuse me?' says Philip, loudly and firmly, but the man does not turn round. 'Hello? *Excuse me*?' he shouts, but there is no response. The man doesn't move an inch.

'We'll have to go over there,' says Meredith.

'Yes. Stay here.'

'Don't be silly. I'll come with you.'

They approach him very slowly, keen not to startle him and provoke a violent response. When they're close enough, Philip taps the man on the shoulder.

The man turns around. He's not at all what she expected. He's a pensioner, she reckons, an old one at that. He has a wispy moustache and deep, dark wells beneath bloodshot eyes. He looks tired. And not at all dangerous. In fact, it's him who looks scared.

'Who are you?' he says. His accent is local, she thinks. A hint of London.

'We live here. We own this place,' replies Philip, his chest puffing up, and his earlier understandable fear subsiding.

'Sorry?'

It is clear the old man is rather deaf.

'*We own this place*,' says Philip, louder this time.

'Do you? I didn't think anyone owned this place any more,' says the man, pulling out a handkerchief from his trouser pocket and wiping his eyes.

'We heard a noise,' says Philip.

'Did you? Oh yes. I was getting a rake out of the shed and I knocked over a plant pot.'

'Why are you here?' Philip says, his exasperation clear.

'I look after the place,' says the man. 'I always have.'

Philip clearly does not know how to respond to this, so Meredith steps in.

'Hello. I'm Merry. Phil and I have bought May Day.' She holds out her hand and he takes it and shakes it.

'Hello. I'm Graham. Sorry, I'm just a bit shocked to find anyone here. And usually, anyone here is up to no good. I apologise for my rudeness.'

'That's OK. I'm sure it's a bit of a surprise. But didn't you see it was for sale?'

'Oh yes. But it's been on the market for so long, I assumed no one would ever buy it. It's such a mess, isn't it?'

Meredith feels her thin veneer of confidence and optimism slip once more. Up until very recently she was convinced they had made the right decision, but each time someone implies they haven't, a little bit of her resilience is chipped away.

'Well, it certainly needs work,' says Philip.

'Yes,' says Graham, sniffing.

'When you say you look after May Day, what do you mean?' asks Meredith.

'Oh, I keep an eye on the place. And I try to contain the garden. But I'm afraid it has got the better of me.' His eyes dart around him, his eyelids hooded, and his upper back and neck bent forwards, as if he's waiting for a blessing. 'I'm not young any more.'

This is a definite understatement. He looks at least ninety.

'Well, don't worry. You don't need to worry any more. We're here,' says Meredith, reaching out to rub the old man's shoulder, a gesture of reassurance and thanks.

'Oh, no, I'll stay anyway.' Graham's eyes aren't looking at either Meredith or Philip, but staring into the distance, towards the house and the weir beyond.

'We can't afford to pay you,' says Philip.

'Oh, I don't want paying. No one's paid me for years. I'm fine with my pension, anyway.'

It seems impossible to refuse him, even though neither of them wants an elderly man randomly arriving on the island whenever he feels like it, at best gardening ineffectually, at worst, actually getting in the way or falling and injuring himself. But they are polite people, painfully polite, and neither of them can bring themselves to say so.

'Well if you're coming, do you think you could call me first? So I know to expect you?' It's the best compromise Meredith can think of. 'Do you have a phone? I could text you my number?'

The old man shakes his head.

'I'll run and find a piece of paper, and write it down,' she says. Graham nods.

By the time Meredith has gone inside the house, found something to write on and a pen and run back outside, Philip is helping Graham into a small, rigid, plastic boat with an outboard motor.

'Here you go,' she says, handing Graham the piece of paper, which he receives without comment, and puts in his coat pocket. 'Let us know when you're coming next,' she shouts as the engine fires up and his boat begins to pull away, but Graham does not turn back to acknowledge what she's said. *It might be he hadn't heard her*, she thinks. *Or perhaps he's actually ignoring her?*

'Well, that was weird,' says Philip, taking hold of her hand.

'Yes.'

'Do you think he's... all there?'

'It's impossible to say.'

'He's so bloody old, he must feel exhausted just getting here.'

'Poor old guy. Maybe this is his routine? Maybe he doesn't have anything else to do?'

'Maybe. So you think he'll come back?' asks Philip.

'I'd say so. But I doubt he'll call.'

Philip nods. There was something about the old man that suggested he was a man outside of time, or perhaps, just in his own time, with a complete disregard for the rules of others.

'Oh well. I doubt he'll do us any harm.'

* * *

Old Stone Cottage is grander than Elinor had made it sound. Meredith suspects it is probably well over two centuries old, and it's looking good on it. It has a very smart, bright red front door, elegant sash windows and the remnants of wisteria draped over its frontage. It also has a well-groomed front garden, protected from the road by a finely tuned box hedge.

Philip pushes open the wooden gate and Meredith follows behind, clasping the flowers they've bought from Waitrose as a gift. He presses the video doorbell, and they both wait with ludicrous smiles on their faces, aware they are probably being observed.

The door is answered by a man in his sixties. He's wearing salmon-coloured chinos and a pink-and-blue checked, button-down shirt.

'You must be Philip and Meredith,' he says, his face a rigid scowl. Meredith feels like she's about to be told off by the headmaster. She senses immediately that the atmosphere is absolutely not what they'd expected.

'Yes,' says Philip, stepping over the threshold into the open doorway. She can't see his face, but she assumes he's also sensing something amiss.

'Come through,' he says, 'into the drawing room.'

He gestures to the left, and they follow him into a room with a low, beamed ceiling, an inglenook fireplace, which is lit, walls covered in rural prints, and two light blue sofas positioned either side of a rectangular glass coffee table.

'Elinor will be with you shortly,' he says and withdraws.

'That was a bit... cold,' says Philip, who's still holding onto the flowers.

'I hope Elinor is feeling more friendly,' Meredith says, trying her best to sound chipper.

But Elinor is not feeling more friendly. She enters almost as soon as her husband leaves, her face stony, her megawatt smile conspicuously empty.

'Would you like tea or coffee?' she says, with the enthusiasm of a parent taking kids to the park on a wet weekend.

'Coffee, please,' says Philip.

'Same.'

Elinor does not ask whether they take milk, Meredith notes.

She nods and leaves at speed.

'Oh dear,' whispers Philip, sitting down on the sofa facing the window and placing the flowers down on the table. 'I'm guessing we're no longer very welcome in the neighbourhood.'

Meredith joins him on the sofa and grasps his hand.

'It can only be the planning application,' she says, feeling anxiety begin to sweep over her.

'But it only went online yesterday.'

'Don't they send letters, though? To neighbours?'

'They're not close enough.'

'Then what, then?'

'I don't know. But I suspect we're about to find out.'

Elinor sweeps back into the room with a tray bearing three cups of white coffee, and no biscuits. She places it down on the coffee table, takes one for herself, and sits down on the sofa opposite.

'I'm glad we arranged this meeting,' says Elinor, taking a sip of her steaming hot coffee. *A meeting,* Meredith thinks. *Uh-oh.* 'Because it is perfect timing. As you know from our brief chat when you moved in, I'm the chair of the local residents' association. And it is in that regard we need to have a chat.'

Meredith picks up her coffee and blows on it, as Philip squeezes her left hand.

'How so?' he says.

'We were made aware late yesterday that you've already submitted a planning application for May Day House, without consulting with us.'

Blimey, Meredith thinks. *That was speedy*. Do they have a mole in the planning department?

'We weren't aware we were legally required to?'

Elinor shuffles in her seat.

'Not legally, no, but when anyone moves into an area like this, with so much history and with such strong community bonds, we would expect to be consulted. Especially when it will affect all of us.'

Philip's grip is tightening, and Meredith can tell his temper, which is usually firmly under control, is threatening to flare. She decides to step in.

'We aren't making any significant changes to the house,' she says, holding her mug near her chin, like a shield. 'Not really. But it needs to be made watertight if we are going to...'

'You're going to make it an entertainment venue,' says Elinor, the word 'entertainment' clearly causing her considerable pain.

'It's not going to be a theme park,' says Philip. 'We are hoping eventually to host weddings and retreats. That's all.'

'With all the associated noise, parking issues and potential pollution,' says Elinor, without missing a beat.

'There will be council restrictions on noise, Elinor, as there always are, and we'll adhere to them. We have our own car park on the mainland, as you know, and will arrange if necessary for parking on private land elsewhere. But pollution? What on earth do you mean?'

Philip's angry response has caused Elinor to move forward on the sofa, her tiny, bony bottom just resting on the edge of the cushion. She is leaning forward, her head only a few feet away from Meredith and Philip.

'May Day House is not on mains drainage. We have legitimate concerns about whether your septic tank is big enough and whether the watercourse will be affected. Then there are potential issues with the expansion of the footprint of the house, given the flood risk. All new houses are required to have flood voids and water holding tanks...'

'But this is not a new house, and we are only extending the orangery, which is essentially a very large conservatory.'

Elinor puts her mug back down on the tray with a thump.

'Mr and Mrs Holland, I think there are a lot of things you don't quite understand. Obviously, you have only just arrived and you aren't aware of the very real concerns local people have about the future of May Day Island. That island has been part of the lives of local people long before you or I were born. There are many with very strong connections to it, all around here. And the thing is, we had assumed anyone who moved in would take the time to get to know their neighbours, to test the waters, so to speak, before putting in plans for the house. And we are shocked you haven't done so.'

'Look, Elinor,' says Philip, attempting a smile. 'I understand you might have hoped for that, but the truth is, we don't have the luxury of time. We need to start making money from the house soon, or our funds will run out. Our savings will barely scratch the surface of the work that needs to be done. But we do want to work with the community here, of course we do. We're very happy to meet to show you the plans in more detail, and to explain what we hope to do with the place. We don't want to cause ill feeling.'

Meredith examines Elinor's face for any signs that Philip's attempt to show willing is having the desired effect, but finds none.

'That is good to hear, but too little, too late,' says Elinor, 'unless you're prepared to withdraw the plans?'

'We can't do that,' says Philip. 'We've paid the council to register them, and our architect spoke at length to the planning officer before she submitted them, to make sure they were acceptable. There are no grounds to withdraw them.'

'Well then,' says Elinor. 'I'm afraid to say we are at an impasse. I will meet with my colleagues on the residents' committee to pass on what you've said.'

'We would be very happy to host you all on the island, if you'd like to come?' says Meredith.

'I think it's too late for that, given the plans are apparently set in stone,' says Elinor. And then Philip, who has drunk no more than a few gulps of his coffee, stands up and makes to leave.

Meredith almost tries to pull him back down, to try to somehow pull the situation back from the brink, but then thinks better of it. She can tell it would be useless.

'I'm afraid that's right, Elinor,' he says, pulling on his coat, which he'd folded on the floor next to the sofa. 'We aren't going to change them. But we also don't want to fall out. If you want to come and see us, as Merry says, for reassurance and an explanation of what we're going to do, you are more than welcome to do so.'

Elinor stands up too, and Meredith realises she has no choice but to follow. She reaches down for her coat, puts it on and zips it up.

'I must warn you both that a recommendation for refusal from the local residents' committee carries a great deal of weight with the council,' says Elinor.

'Well, let's see,' he says, walking towards the door, with Meredith following him.

'Thank you for inviting us over,' she says, trying to salvage some sort of warmth from the meeting, but Elinor's mouth doesn't even twitch.

'Mr Holland, if you think you are going to win on this, you are absolutely mistaken,' she says, opening the front door for them. They both step outside, to find it has started to rain. 'And trust me, you need friends around here. River residents stick together, you know.'

'Well, let's remain friends then, Elinor,' replies Philip. 'Goodbye. Do come and visit us.'

Elinor does not reply, and Meredith doesn't make any further attempt to be polite. Instead, she follows her husband back down the path and through the gate, which shuts with a clatter behind them.

They are back on their own land, in the small gravel car park, before either of them speaks.

'Shit,' says Philip. 'Shit, shit, *shit*.'

All of the confidence and bravado he displayed in Elinor's drawing room has disappeared. Now he's undone, unravelling, unguarded. She knows his reaction is not just about the planning permission, and not just about the money. At least Elinor didn't mention Stuart, and for that Meredith is grateful. But she knows it weighs heavily on him.

She rarely sees the man she loves like this, and she does the only thing she knows will help – she pulls him into her embrace while he weeps. He has done this for her so many times, when she has felt the earth giving way beneath her feet and the future turning to dust. *This is all my fault,* she thinks. *If I hadn't seen the house and persuaded him that we should buy it, he wouldn't be feeling like this.*

'It will be OK, my love,' she says as he sobs, wishing desperately for him to believe it. 'We'll find a way through this. I know we will.'

8

ELLEN

October 1943

Ellen is struggling to keep her eyes open, but she can't let them close, not even for a second. The young man beside her is depending on her.

He's undergoing something called modified insulin therapy, something she'd never heard of until she'd got here, and something she's still trying to get used to. In fact, all of the patients in this room are getting the same treatment. It involves the nurses injecting these otherwise physically healthy, non-diabetic young men with insulin, which lowers their blood sugar. This makes them sweat, salivate and become restless, before inducing something akin to a coma. Then the nurses are charged with keeping them in this half-asleep, half-awake state, all the while making sure they are clean, as comfortable as possible and have sufficient water and nutrients to keep them alive.

One of Ellen's colleagues has told her that earlier in the war, they'd given them enough insulin to knock them out completely for at least ten days, a practice which she knows is incredibly dangerous. That sort of dose can easily lead to death. Now, however, there's an insulin shortage, so the doctors at May Day have switched to this 'modified' version, which involves keeping them at least slightly awake by feeding them sugary tea through a nasal tube at regular intervals. Ellen has to keep very detailed notes for all of the men in the room, making sure their insulin and tea doses are administered on schedule and in exactly the right doses.

It's warm and airless in the room, and she has been stuck in here for more than eight hours. She has two more hours to go. She wipes her forehead with the back of her hand and looks around her at the linen-covered, thin bodies laid out neatly in lines, like corpses recovered from the battlefield. It's getting dark outside, and the angled metal lamps beside each bed are casting golden circles on the polished parquet floor. *It looks so peaceful here now,* she thinks, *you couldn't even imagine the horrors this house has seen.*

And they do seem like horrors to Ellen, even though Captain Huntingford has explained each procedure to her in some detail, keen to educate her in the psychiatry practised at May Day. Modified insulin therapy, she says, is designed to disrupt a chronically disordered mind, inducing a feeling of peace and a fresh slate. Quality sleep, undisturbed by terrors, she has been told, is vital, hence the use of medication to induce it. And as for the convulsion therapies – the use of Cardiazol, which causes terrible seizures – Ellen just cannot get her head around this at all. That's not to say the treatments she has seen and helped administer to men fresh off the battlefield in the past have been gentle. Some have been brutal. She has seen gaping wounds, partially amputated limbs and faces half-blown off, and she has helped emergency surgeons sew, saw and save as much as they can. But it is easier to understand taking drastic action in those circumstances, she thinks, than it is when a man appears to be physically healthy.

None of the treatments she's seen so far at May Day seem to be influenced by the work of her former colleague Dr Lovell, although Captain Huntingford has told her some elements of his work are due to be introduced here soon. When they'd worked together in Egypt, Dr Lovell had told her he believed that when given the opportunity to work as a collective, to see they are needed for the common good, men will find their own path to healing, and therefore, back to battle. He advocates team exercises and entertainment, and of talking therapy as a treatment. He told her of how he organised wards so men moved closer and closer towards the door as they went through their treatment, giving them physical evidence of their progress.

But then, it seems to her to be far harder to treat someone whose disease is in the mind. The doctors can't see what they're dealing with, so in many ways, they're treating in the dark. And there is a great deal of darkness. She knows some of what brought these men here. She has seen it with her own eyes. All of them have been through hell. In fact, some of them still seem to be living in it.

She knows the names of these men who are neither asleep nor awake, neither soldier nor civilian, but nothing about their personalities or their past. Despite caring for them so intimately in the fortnight since she arrived, she has yet to talk to any of them. But she does know about their nightmares, for when their bodies fight their way out of the induced coma, they shout, they scream and they whimper. They also call out for comfort, from their wives, from their girlfriends, from their mothers.

There are other patients here, however, in other wards, who are awake and lucid. They are either graduates of this treatment or those whose mental illness is considered less severe. If she didn't know why they were here, she might not have guessed they were ill. She has passed the time of day with them in the corridors and the day room, discussed the headlines in the papers or assisted with the cryptic crossword, and their conversation has been entirely normal, average, unnoteworthy. And yet when they are in crisis, either induced or naturally occurring, it is clear why they are here and not on the battlefield. Their scars might be invisible, but they are no less real.

'Ellen?'

Her head snaps up and she sees her roommate, Rebecca Hanson, at the door.

'I've come to relieve you. We've got a new arrival for ward four, and I thought you might appreciate the opportunity for some fresh air?'

'Are you sure?'

Ellen is aching to get outside, but she knows Rebecca has also done her fair share of shifts in the twilight zone.

'I'm sure. Go on. I won't tell the captain if you don't.'

Ellen doesn't ask twice.

'When are they due?' she asks Rebecca when she reaches the door.

'I think imminently. I just heard the bell.'

Ellen smiles at her friend as they switch places. Then she picks up her grey cape from a row of hooks in the hallway, pulls it on and walks out of the front door.

It's 6.30 p.m. and dark, so Ellen picks her footing carefully on the paved path that leads down to the boat landing. When her eyes begin to adjust, she can make out the shadow of a boat crossing the river. She's glad she's not late. May Day House protocol dictates that all new patients must be met off the boat by a member of the medical staff when they arrive.

'Here yer go, sir,' says Brian, whose large, lumbering shape she can just make out in the boat beside the jetty.

'Thank you, Brian,' says a man, his voice clipped, polished, educated.

She sees the shadow of her new patient lean over to try to carry his own bag.

'No, don't worry about that sir,' Brian says. 'I'll bring it.'

'If you insist,' says the man, stepping off the boat with far more grace than Ellen. It's then he spots her. She decides this is the moment to introduce herself.

'Hello, sir. I'm Lieutenant Quinn. I'm one of the nurses here. I've come to meet you and show you where you'll be staying.'

'Thank you. Nice to meet you. I'm Flying Officer Hennessey.'

They have a few RAF pilots in their care now, alongside a small group of sailors, to add to the majority, who belong to the army. Ellen smiles in greeting, even though it's unlikely he'll be able to see it in the dark. He holds out a hand, and she takes it.

'Nice to meet you, too. Follow me.'

She leads him to the front door through the pergola of roses, which are now preparing for their long winter sleep.

'How long have you worked here, Lieutenant Quinn?' he says as they walk.

'Oh, only a couple of weeks.'

'Nice to know I'm not the only one who's new.'

As she holds the door open for him, the hallway lights allow her to see him properly for the first time. He's at least five inches taller than her, with dark brown hair parted at the side, prominent cheekbones and a strong jaw, and a well-trimmed moustache. He has a small scar on his right cheek which Ellen thinks might have been obtained in action, but apart from that, his skin is clear and well shaven.

Later in life, much later, Ellen will replay this moment in her head, remembering the way she felt: the surge of blood through her veins, the widening of her eyes, the fading out of all vision on the periphery. For a split second it had felt like there were only the two of them in the world, and she had known without doubt that meeting him would change her life.

'Lieutenant Quinn?' says Captain Huntingford, walking down the staircase and into the hallway.

'Yes ma'am.'

'Are you going to show this man to his ward? Or are you going to clutter up the hallway all evening?'

'Sorry Captain, of course. Come this way, Flying Officer Hennessey.' Ellen walks down the corridor and up to the first floor, looking straight ahead in an attempt to hide how blindsided she is feeling. *It is completely unprofessional to even have thoughts like this,* she thinks, *and if the captain knew about them she'd be out on her ear immediately.* 'Ward four is just up here on the left,' she says, as she reaches the top of the stairs. She turns around and is surprised to see Flying Officer Hennessey is lagging behind.

'Sorry, don't mind me,' he says as he climbs the last few steps. 'I've done myself an injury. A physical one,' he says, raising an eyebrow.

'I'm sorry to hear that. Do you want one of the doctors to take a look? I can put it in the notes if you like.'

'No,' he sniffs, holding onto the bannister at the top while he recovers himself. 'I think they've got more than enough to be getting on with.'

Ellen wonders what his diagnosis is, or even if he has one. The men here have been variously diagnosed with Conversion Hysteria – where symptoms like blindness or partial paralysis are thought to have a psychological rather than physical trigger – battle exhaustion or mental breakdown. The latter two of which, Ellen thinks, seem to be catch-all terms for anyone suffering mental disturbance as a result of the war.

'Did you travel a long way today?' she asks, taking advantage of his need to catch his breath to try to learn more about him.

'Not too far. I'm stationed on the south coast.'

'It looks nice there. Well, the bits I saw from the train on my way up from Portsmouth, anyway.'

'You're not from these parts, obviously.'

'No,' Ellen smiles. 'As you can tell, I'm Irish. But I've been in England, France, Egypt and South Africa since the war began, so I've travelled a lot.'

'More than me, Lieutenant. Much more than me. I see France occasionally from the cockpit, but that's it for travel, I'm afraid. I do know Ireland, though.'

'Oh?'

'Yes, my mother's family are from there. She took me to visit relatives there quite a few times when I was young. The family seat is in Wicklow. I remember it being very green, very hilly and there were lots of cows.'

Ellen laughs. 'Yes, there are plenty of those, Flying Officer Hennessey. And it is very pretty in Wicklow. Less so where my family are from, though. I'm from a town.'

'Which one?'

'Dundalk, in County Louth. Do you know it?'

'Yes. It has a pub. And a greengrocer. And a man who sits on a bench called Paddy.'

'I think you're pulling my leg, Flying Officer Hennessey.'

'I am, Lieutenant Quinn, and I'm sorry for it. And please call me Harry.'

'We're not allowed to use first names in here,' Ellen whispers.

'Shame.'

'Yes,' says Ellen formally, as one of the senior nurses emerges from one of the wards and walks towards them. 'Anyway, shall we get you to your new quarters?'

'Why not.'

Ellen leads him to the left and turns into a large room which is furnished with five hospital beds. There are four men in here already. Three of them are playing cards at a small table in the middle, and the fourth is reading in bed. They look up briefly when she enters the room but then return to their pastimes, a reflection of how used they are to nurses visiting them at all times of the day and night.

'Here you are. This is ward four. This is where you'll be.'

Harry is about to ask her something when she hears Brian climbing up the stairs with his bag. She gets out of the way so he can bring it inside the room.

'Well, I'll leave you now,' she says, as Brian passes her and deposits Harry's bag beside his bed. 'I have a shift to finish in another ward. If you'd like supper, ask the sister on duty in the office – that's the room at the end of the hall – and she'll ask Chef to make you something.'

'Fine. Thank you.'

She turns to leave.

'Will I see you tomorrow?' he asks, his voice low, so the noise of his card-playing ward-mates eclipses it. She wonders if he's joking again, but he seems serious. Nervous, even.

'I don't think so, Flying Officer Hennessey. I'm not assigned to this ward for a week or so.'

'That's a shame.' He looks for a moment like a lost child.

'I'll pop in if I'm passing by,' she says, taking pity on him.

'Super. Well, thank you very much, Lieutenant Quinn. I shall see you anon.'

She watches him walk over to his bed, his poise and confidence apparently restored. She turns and walks swiftly down the stairs and returns to her original ward to relieve Rebecca.

'How was it?' she whispers when Ellen walks over to her seat, which is beside one of the beds.

'Oh, fine. He was quite chatty, really.'

'Ah. One of those.'

'What do you mean?'

'The ones who use their charm and their wit to mask their pain.'

'Do they do that a lot?'

'Yes, many of them. They've had to do it, you know, in their squadrons and their units, so they carry on doing it here, at least for a bit. But the doctors will soon peel back the layers. They always do. I've seen it done. It's hard to watch, to be honest.'

Ellen has seen several of their patients in acute distress in the time since she's arrived, but somehow, she can't imagine jolly, friendly, handsome Hennessey behaving like that at all. She wonders how he's feeling now. Whether he's scared of what might be coming. Because she knows this is no holiday camp; he has good reason to be fearful.

'Well, I'll leave you to it,' says Rebecca, gladly giving up her post.

'Yes. See you later,' says Ellen as her friend disappears through the door and out of sight.

As she settles back into the room, her routine and her responsibilities, Ellen takes a moment to acknowledge what has just happened. She's met hundreds of men during her time in the QAIMNS, maybe even thousands. And she knew almost all the local boys in Dundalk, although she never cared for any of them. Yet she had known Harry for less than a few minutes before something significant had shifted inside of her. It hadn't been a choice; it had been an imperative. An instinct. And unlike the fears that threaten to overcome her daily, this is not something she wants to fight.

9

MEREDITH

November 2013

'Are you sure you're happy with it?'

'Yes, yes, I'll manage. It'll be fine.'

'Shall I stay until you're safely back?'

'No, no, you go.'

Meredith does not want an audience for what she's about to do.

They've bought a new boat. It's a fibreglass four-seater with a 40 hp outboard engine, which should be enough to do battle with the river over the winter. Philip has just brought it over and moored it by the towpath, but Meredith is now going to attempt to take it back to the island. She's not actually sure it'll be fine, as she's a complete beginner when it comes to boats, but she doesn't want to tell her husband that. He's in a strange mood this morning; restless. She knows a run will help him. She'd rather he was working off his stresses than staring at her, his teeth clenched, and his fists furled, from the bank.

'OK. But call me if you need to. See you in a bit.'

Meredith watches his back, his strides long and smooth, until the river bends nearer Walton and he disappears from view. Then she sits back in the boat and closes her eyes, letting the weak winter sun warm her face.

She listens to the sounds of the river which are now becoming so familiar: the clatter of the geese, the whispers of the trees as the wind whips through them, panting dogs enjoying long walks, the rhythmic beating of swans' wings as they soar over the water. When she opens her eyes, she feels a little calmer, but no more ready to tackle the river crossing by herself.

This is ridiculous, she thinks, coming to a sudden decision with relief. *I'll go for a walk instead and wait until Philip finishes his run.*

She checks she has the engine keys with her and that the boat is securely tied to a tree before climbing out onto the towpath. She decides not to go in the same direction as Philip and turns instead towards Weybridge. There's something down here she wants to see.

Meredith keeps looking over her shoulder as she walks down the path, unable to shift a feeling of unease and, yes, guilt. *Which is ridiculous,* she thinks. *Why on earth should I feel guilty about visiting somewhere hundreds of members of the public walk past every day?* And yet they have never been here together, and she feels as if she's trespassing.

It takes her about twenty minutes to reach it.

The bridge is concrete, about thirty metres wide, and is covered in both ivy and graffiti, the latter only ugly tags rather than artistic drawings. There is thick woodland on either side and it looms above her, making her feel as if she's walking through a deep railway cutting. There are steep concrete steps immediately to the left which lead upwards, and Meredith takes them, her heart beating fast. When she reaches the top, she turns back on herself and walks slowly onto the bridge, in the direction of Desborough Island. It's quiet up here. This road is only used by people driving to the rugby club, so it's rarely used; another reason why teenagers are drawn to it like bees to a honeypot. They are usually not disturbed.

She approaches the iron railings with trepidation. This is where Stuart jumped. Although Philip rarely talks about it, she has been told enough to know this is the place where his brother died.

It had been a summer's afternoon, a Saturday. Stuart and Philip had been hanging out with friends, swimming in the river and drinking in the woods. A few hours in, Philip had decided he wanted to go home. He'd really been itching to get back to his studies. He'd just finished the first year of sixth form and had been determined to become a pilot. Stuart, meanwhile, eighteen months his junior, had wanted to stay.

Several hours later, the police had interrupted a balmy evening meal in the garden to tell their parents that their youngest son had been found unresponsive in the water.

They had all been changed irrevocably that afternoon.

Philip had been devastated, wracked with guilt that he hadn't been there to dissuade Stuart, or to jump into the water to try to save him. His parents, meanwhile, had been consumed with grief. Whatever their family life was like before that afternoon, it is long gone, thinks Meredith. Even now, decades later.

She peers over the side of the bridge. The river is fast and furious, and it's a long way down. The dark water, an emulsion of earth, mesmerises her.

Then, just for a moment, she sees herself from above. In fact, is she inching towards the edge? Are her feet lifting, and does she feel a hand on her back?

Meredith springs back and gulps for air. She feels nauseous. She needs to leave.

She turns and heads for the steps, but as she does so, she spots something on the other side of the bridge. She walks over and picks it up. It's a small bouquet of flowers wrapped in cellophane, so old that the flowers – freesias and dahlias, by the looks of things – are crumbling into dust. She can see there's a card nestled amongst the stems. She pulls it out. Rain has long since obscured the writing, except for the first word, which seems to be Stuart.

Someone must have put these here over the summer, she thinks. But who would do that? It's not Philip's writing, and anyway, he never comes here. His parents, perhaps? But it doesn't look like their writing, either. She replaces the bouquet and makes her way down the steps onto the towpath.

As she walks slowly back in the direction of the island, Meredith continues to ponder who it might be. A friend of Stuart, maybe. Someone who was with him at the time? Ideally, she'd ask Philip about it, but she knows better than that now. It will only make him more on edge, and she doesn't want that before he leaves for a flight. He needs to be calm and put together, not emotionally compromised. And anyway, Meredith has accepted that she will never know or understand the depth of damage done to Philip and his parents that day, just as he will never understand the extent of her own pain. Some feelings simply cannot be put into words.

* * *

'You can just call Tom or Euan at the boatyard if you can't get it to start, or whatever.'

It's three hours later, and they are back in the boat by the towpath. This time, Philip is dressed in his uniform. He's about to head off for four days, and she has just brought the boat back over under his supervision. She's glad she didn't try the return journey alone earlier, and she thinks he was, too. He doesn't know she went for a walk to the bridge, however. She'd lied and told him she'd walked into town for a coffee. He hadn't questioned it.

'Have you got everything? Your flight bag? Your hat?'

They have already learned it is a sensible precaution to run through anything they might have forgotten at this stage, before it's too late.

'Yes. I have. Look after yourself, darling,' he says, leaning over for a final kiss.

'I will. Now be off with you. I don't want you to be late.'

Philip walks away, waving as he does so. When he's out of sight, Meredith considers her options. She could simply untie the boat and head back, but she's far from confident about that. What she needs, she thinks, are lessons in operating her boat. If she can become proficient by herself, that'll be a weight off her husband's mind. Then, she has an idea.

Meredith walks for about five minutes down the towpath, away from town, where the land behind the towpath gives way to fields; vital green lungs amongst urban sprawl. She passes an eclectic collection of lived-in boats, from barges with makeshift wooden structures perched on top to repurposed lifeboats from North Sea oil platforms. She knows these are all illegally moored, and their presence is resented by many in the area – Philip included, clearly. She can certainly appreciate some of the more ramshackle ones would be an eyesore to live opposite, and there must be issues about safety and pollution, but she also assumes that without these boats, these people would be homeless. Like so many issues Britain is currently wrangling with, she thinks, there is no clear-cut solution, and far too many angry voices on both sides.

She stops when she arrives at a red narrowboat. Just as Damon had told her when they'd met on their first day at May Day House, there is smoke coming out of its shiny metal chimney. He's home. Meredith makes her way down the bank and steps onto the back of the boat carefully, grabbing hold of a rail to steady herself before knocking on the wooden double doors.

'Just a second.'

She hears a rustling, a few clicks and the sliding back of a bolt.

'Well hi! What a nice surprise,' says Damon, smiling broadly.

'Hello. I'm so sorry to turn up without warning. But I wanted to say thank you for fixing our water pump. It was very kind of you,' she says, cringing at the thought of how rude Philip had been. 'And I also wanted to ask you for another favour. It's just I'm after a few lessons about boat stuff, and I thought you might be the guy to ask.'

'Ah, yeah, I reckon I'm your man,' he says, and she feels instantly more at ease. 'Come in, I'm just making a brew. Watch your head.'

Meredith ducks as she enters the boat. It's a lot tidier inside than she'd expected, despite its small proportions. There's a futon, currently folded back, along one wall, a small galley kitchen with a gas hob and a wood burning stove at the end with a couple of wooden chairs either side.

'Welcome to my world,' says Damon. 'It's about the size of a one-man tent, but it'll do.'

'It's lovely.'

'Well, it's not really. It's always damp and at this time of year, bloody cold. But it's OK.'

'It's very tidy.'

'You can't not be on a boat this size. If you leave your dinner plates out on the surface you're risking a landslide.'

'I can imagine.'

'Do you want a cuppa?'

'Yes, that'd be lovely.'

'Take a seat.'

Damon gestures towards the wooden chairs by the fire, and Meredith walks over and sits down.

'Milk? Sugar?'

'Milk and one, please. Strong.'

Meredith examines the pictures on the wall at this end of the boat. There are photos of Damon with an older man and two younger men, who she assumes might be his brothers; there's a map showing the route of the Thames; and a picture of Damon at the wheel of a classic car.

'Is that your car?' she asks.

'That thing? Nah. It was my dad's. He sold it, though. Sadly. He ended up selling a lot of things. He was shit with money. And at controlling himself when it came to booze.'

'I'm sorry to hear that.'

'Yeah. It is what it is. Anyway, here you go,' he says, handing her a mug of steaming tea and sitting down in the chair next to her. 'So, what is it you need help with?'

'Well, the thing is… It seems I'm absolutely diabolical at anything to do with boats,' she says, tugging her left sleeve down. 'And I can't be. Not now. Not given where I live.'

'Right. I see.'

'We've bought a new boat with an outboard motor. I've told Phil I know how to use and maintain it, but I don't really, and I don't want to tell him I didn't understand when he tried to explain it, because he's so busy and so tired. And I don't know any of those nautical knots you all use, either.'

'Ah.'

'I was wondering whether you have time to show me? I could pay you?'

'Nah, don't be silly. I don't want paying. But yes, I'll help you. Shall we finish this tea and go?'

Meredith laughs with relief.

'What's funny?' asks Damon.

'Oh, if I'd asked my neighbour in Putney for a cup of sugar, he'd have had to think about it.'

'Well, you're not in Putney now, my dear.'

* * *

'So you push the primer button a couple of times to start the flow of fuel. Not too many times, or else you'll flood it. Yeah, that's it. Then you pull on the starter cord a few times. That's it! It's firing. But if it doesn't start, open the choke and pull it a few more times. If it sounds rough, adjust the choke.'

The motor behind Meredith is now humming contentedly, mirroring her mood. It feels good to be out on the water, and it feels good to be in control.

'Now twist the tiller handle clockwise to accelerate. If you twist it the other way, you'll slow down.'

Meredith twists the handle and the prow of the boat lifts out of the water. The resulting cold wind blows her long hair off her face and energises her skin, reminding her of the feeling you get when you're facing the sea in a storm.

'There you go, you've got it. Piece of piss, right?'

She grins. They seem to be flying down the river towards Walton-on-Thames; pubs, waterfront homes, houseboats and gaggles of geese pass by in a brilliant blur.

'Now turn it down a bit. We're getting to a busier area, so you don't want to speed too much.' Meredith turns the handle back a little in the other direction. 'Yeah, that's it.'

They sit in companionable silence for a while, as she takes in the people walking their dogs on the towpath, the young couples holding hands, the teenage boys vaping by the bushes.

'So how are your plans for the house coming along?' Damon asks, and Meredith sighs inwardly. Their planning application and the numerous angry representations from members of the local residents' committee have become the talk of the town.

'Not great,' she says.

'Really?'

She's surprised he hasn't heard about it, but then, he's not on the committee and he's not likely to be plugged into local politics. 'Yeah. It turns out local people aren't interested in the house being restored.'

'Who's making a fuss?'

'This woman called Elinor, who heads up the residents' committee, and she's got loads of her mates to write in and complain too.'

'What reasons are they giving?'

'Oh, all sorts of stuff. Concerns about overdevelopment, pollution, noise, destruction of natural habitat, sewage – you name it, they're pissed off about it.'

'The classic "not in my back yard", right?'

'Yes. Exactly.'

'Figures. They're trying to get rid of us, you know. Us boat people.'

'Are they?'

'Yeah. Apparently, we're ruining their morning jogging routes. Scaring their children. Lowering their house values. Anyway – shall we turn? Just slow down a bit, and then turn the tiller to the left, and we'll do a U-turn and go back.'

Meredith nods and does as he suggests, and begins steering the craft back up the river, against the stream.

'Anyway, they're selfish arses. The council will see through it, won't they? They'll see that the house needs some TLC and that you guys are the people to make a go of it.'

'I hope so.'

'I mean, surely there's money to be made there?'

'Oh, I think so, but we need a cash injection to do it. So much needs fixing.'

'Turn the power up a bit. You'll need a bit more, now you're fighting the current.'

'OK,' she says, and does so.

'That's it,' he says as they speed up.

'The consultant we used says we've pushed the boundaries a bit with what we've asked for anyway, so... I don't know. I'm nervous.'

They stop talking for a bit, and Meredith is glad. She is enjoying this experience of being out on the water under her own steam, and she doesn't want to think about money, or their business, or the lack of it if they don't get the plans through. She is enjoying just being.

'Right, we're nearly there. Shall I bring it into the dock, or do you want to?'

'I'll do it. I need to get better at this.'

She follows Damon's advice, coming in slowly and hitting reverse gently just before contact with the bank, to avoid hitting it. She is absolutely delighted when she brings the boat alongside the towpath without drama or damage.

'There you go! Nothing to it.'

She is beaming. He shows her how to twist the rope and drop it over a post, ensuring it won't slip. It's all so much easier than she'd thought.

'Thanks so much. That was amazing,' she says, high on her own success.

'Ah, it was no bother. Any time,' he replies, running his hand through his wayward hair, his smile genuine.

Meredith is then hit with a burst of dopamine and reaches out to hug him. Damon looks momentarily surprised before hugging her back.

'Honestly, thank you,' she says into his shoulder as they embrace.

'No, thank you,' he says afterwards, waving as he walks away in the direction of his boat. Then she holds her hand up to her right cheek, and realises she is blushing.

* * *

Meredith spends the rest of the day on her latest project, which is scrubbing the kitchen to within an inch of its life, removing decades of grease, dust and spiders' webs. When that's done, she flips open her laptop and checks the council planning application portal. There are two new objections on there and no letters of support. Her heart sinks.

To distract herself, she decides to take a bath to wash away the kitchen grime. They recently celebrated a small victory when they'd found a plumber to fix their immersion heater. So, while they still have no heating, they do have hot water, and after a long time washing in a bucket, it is glorious. She walks into the bathroom, turns on the hot tap and lights a couple of candles. She undresses quickly and sits in the bath even before it's filled, swirling the water around her, her limbs occasionally making contact with the freezing cold enamel, the shock sending shivers down her spine. Then she selects a bottle of bubble bath, takes the lid off and tips a liberal amount into the water.

It's 5 p.m. now and almost dark. She hasn't turned the overhead light on, so the only light in the room is from the two candles on the bath. Meredith shuts the hot off, adjusts the temperature with some cold, lies back into the bubbles and closes her eyes. She drifts away for a moment, feeling that week's pressures – the increasing bad feeling amongst their neighbours, the mountain of clearing they still have to do, Philip's increasingly stressed state of mind – begin to lift. She wonders whether she can do anything to help Philip. This is a new thing for him, really. Aside from his six-monthly simulator checks, she has rarely seen him even slightly anxious. He is so much more contained than she is, so much more in control of his emotions. But their financial position is concerning him even more than it is her, it seems. She knows they may never manage to finish refurbishing the house without planning permission and another loan, but she also knows she could probably go back to work to make some money. It would slow their business plans down considerably, but they'd survive. She's tried explaining this to Philip, but it doesn't seem to ease his burden, and that frustrates her. Aside from being there for him, from hugging him and assuring him that everything is going to be all right, her arsenal to defend him is empty, and that makes her feel despondent.

She reaches for her phone, which is balanced on the side of the sink, and opens WhatsApp.

> Hello darling. All OK here. I've had a good day with the boat. I had a very successful outing and now feel much more capable! So you don't need to worry about me. I'm fine. Can't wait for you to come back. Love, me xxxx

She sees from the blue ticks that he's seen it, and she waits a minute for him to reply, but he doesn't. This bothers her, even though she knows it shouldn't. He's probably out with the crew, making polite small talk with cabin crew fifteen years his junior, and unable to reply. She knows how it goes.

She puts her phone back down and slips further into the bubbles until they encase her ears. Their pop and crackle and the gentle rhythm of the dripping sink tap lull her into a kind of slumber. It's then she allows herself to relax completely, to abandon both her hatred for her mutinous body and her deep-rooted fear that her decision to take a break from the only career she's ever known is a mistake. For a brief moment in time, she is secure, safe, comforted, even joyful. She wallows in it for as long as it stays warm, the heat seeming to keep the real world at bay.

It doesn't last, of course. No respite ever does. When the chill in the air starts to sting her skin, she hauls herself up and gets out of the bath, grabbing her towel from a rail hanging off a non-functioning radiator. It is when she's drying her hair that she realises her mistake. She has been congratulating herself all afternoon about her amazing stewardship of the boat, and yet she's done something both incredibly stupid and incredibly amateur. She's left the key in the engine.

Thefts are very common on the river. Opportunistic thieves, she's been told, have been known to saw outboard engines off boats. But she's gone and made it even easier for them, by leaving the key in it. What a bloody stupid thing to do, she thinks. She will have to go out there now and get it. And what if it's not there? How will she explain that to Phil? They're counting every penny at the moment as it is.

Meredith yanks on her jeans, a T-shirt, some shoes and a jumper, grabs the house keys and a torch and runs out of the front door, slamming it behind her. Then she takes a moment to turn on the torch, because they still haven't fixed any of the outside lighting, and she walks towards the mooring carefully, because it's been raining, and the crazy paving is slippery.

As she approaches the mooring, she can see, even without the torch, that the boat is still there. Relief floods through her. She's got away with it. She still needs to board the boat to retrieve the key, of course, so she walks up to it, shining her torch around her as she goes: there's the statue of the girl with flowers in her hair; there's the overgrown formal garden; there's the mouldering gazebo; there's the boat...

Adrenaline shoots through her. Because although the boat is still there, it is not as she left it. There's writing spray painted along the nearside, huge bright red capital letters.

LEAVE HERE NOW.

Meredith shakes with fear. She feels like she's being watched. Whoever did this obviously came onto the island, and they could still be here, couldn't they? They could be hiding in the bushes, laughing.

She desperately wants to flee back into the house and lock the door behind her, but before she does that, she needs to get the key. She scrambles onto the boat, almost losing her balance and tumbling into the water, but saving herself with her right arm, which hits the rear of the boat with a jolt. She takes a few sharp breaths to recover, then shines her torch on the engine. *It's still there,* she thinks. *Thank God*. She snatches the key, shoves it in her jeans pocket, hauls herself onto the bank and runs back along the path, as fast as she dares.

When she reaches the door, she pulls out the large metal key from her other pocket and fumbles with the lock, her fear apparently cutting the connection between her brain and her head. She exhales loudly when she finally manages to turn it, and shoves the door open so hard, it slams into the wood panelling behind it with a loud thud and a splinter. Then she runs inside and slams the door closed behind her and turns on every light she can find, in every single room. When that's done, she retrieves her phone from the bathroom, walks into their bedroom, shuts the door, checks the curtain is pulled right across and dives under their bedding.

It's here, hiding like a child taking refuge from a monster under their bed, that Meredith finally cries, acknowledging her fear, a fear that has been growing in her since they first moved into May Day House, and which now seems to have become her constant bedfellow.

Bit by bit, she thinks, *day by day, this dream is becoming a nightmare.*

10

ELLEN

December 1943

'Could you hand me the glue?'

Ellen places the coloured strip of paper she's holding down on a nearby table and passes the tube of glue they borrowed from the captain's office to Rebecca.

'Do you think we've enough paper?' Rebecca asks the man who's sitting beside her. He's David Boyd, one of the patients from ward four who have been tasked with organising the Christmas party. The doctors have given him and his ward-mates the job of organising extra-curricular entertainment for the hospital, a move, Ellen has been told, to encourage them to think as part of a team again, as part of a military unit. This has echoes of Dr Lovell's work in Egypt, and she's delighted to see it in action.

'I should jolly well hope so. The chap at the stationery shop told me I'd cleaned him out of red and green.'

'We could always use newspaper if we run out,' says Ellen, feeding a strip of paper through the chain they've made and gluing its sides so it stays put.

'Yes, there's plenty of that about,' says David. 'They keep bringing us the papers every day, but none of us want to read them. Too much… just too much,' he says, his voice trailing off.

'I think we should burn them to keep warm,' says Harry, who's sitting across the table from Ellen. He's got paper chains strung around his neck.

'It's always very warm downstairs,' says Ellen, thinking of those long stifling shifts in ward one with the men receiving insulin treatment.

'Well, it's not up here. They make us keep the windows open to keep us alert, or healthy, or something else batty. As if we weren't batty enough.'

There's an awkward silence, before David breaks it.

'So, what music shall we have at the "do"?' he asks.

'There's a piano in the old drawing room,' says Rebecca. 'Although I make a dreadful din when I try to play.'

'Excellent. I'll have a go,' says Harry.

'You can play?' says Ellen.

'Tolerably, yes.'

'Don't you believe a word of it. I hear Harry here was a music scholar at his school. He's quite the whizz kid.'

Harry raises an eyebrow and carries on cutting and gluing paper.

'Well, that settles it, then. And I believe there's a gramophone somewhere too. We could beg, borrow or steal some records to dance to.'

'Excellent,' says Harry. 'I am looking forward to it.'

'I sing,' says Ellen, before she can stop herself. 'A little.'

'Do you? How wonderful. We must duet together.'

'Well I…'

'Don't be bashful, now,' says David. 'It's all for a good cause. Your job is to make us well, isn't it? Well, what we all need right now is some joy, a time to dance, a time to live. So you should jolly well sing for us. Shouldn't she, Lieutenant Hanson?'

'Absolutely she should,' says Rebecca.

'Fine. I shall,' she says, blushing. 'On your own heads be it if I sound like a frog.'

'I am perfectly sure you don't,' says Rebecca. 'Now, I think Lieutenant Quinn and I need to go and get our beauty sleep. But before we do, I believe there's a tree arriving by boat sometime around now?'

Harry checks his watch.

'Yes, it's due in about ten minutes. Thank you for reminding me, I'd quite forgotten.'

'You'll need an escort to go down to the dock. Lieutenant Quinn, why don't you go? You haven't been outside so far today.'

Ellen is torn between her joy at this granting of time alone with Harry, and fear she might give that joy away.

'Of course. Flying Officer Hennessey, will you come with me?'

'Absolutely,' he replies, removing his paper chain necklaces and placing them carefully on the table.

* * *

'What sort of music do you usually sing?' asks Harry as he holds the front door open for Ellen.

'Oh, church music mostly. I'm Catholic, you see. I was in a choir. But now... anything, anything that takes my fancy.'

'It's a wonderful escape, music, isn't it?'

'Yes, it is,' says Ellen, although her mind is plagued by the memory of a hand where it shouldn't be, and the feeling of hot, rancid breath on her neck. She mustn't blame the music, though. It's not to blame for man's ills. She still loves singing, even though those memories bring her pain.

'You look thoughtful.'

'Yes.' Ellen has no idea what else to say. She hasn't told anyone about what happened, and she definitely doesn't want to share it with a patient, even a patient she has feelings for.

'Care to share those thoughts?'

'Not really.' She hates being rude, so she tries to avoid looking at him as she says it.

'I'm sorry... I didn't mean to overstep a line. I just want to know... more about you.'

Ellen meets his gaze then and feels the colour rising in her face. She desperately wants to know more about him, too.

'What about if I share mine?' he says, his walking pace slowing to a crawl.

'If you like,' she says, fidgeting with her cape to try to distract her mind and her body from the way she's feeling.

'When my mind is full of the darkness, Lieutenant Quinn, full of the horror, I think of music. And if I can, I play music, to allow myself to get lost in it.'

'Oh yes, it has immense power,' she says as they reach the dock. The boat hasn't arrived yet, although she can see a van has drawn up in the car park opposite, and the driver has just opened its back doors to reveal a fir tree inside. Brian is waiting in the boat beside the towpath, ready to ferry it across. Ellen notices he's with a young man, who she presumes is his son.

'Yes. Although it still can't quite blot out the memory of my friend Oliver screaming for his mother over the radio as his plane plummeted to earth trailing smoke,' he says, his gaze caught by two swans which are sailing by.

'I'm so sorry.'

'It's perfectly all right. It's war. People see these things every day. But not everyone ends up here, in the funny farm, do they?'

'Don't call it that. It's a hospital. We will make you well again.'

'Will you? I mean no disrespect, Quinn, but what treatment have I received so far? A few sessions where a chap has tried to make me cry, and now we are to organise a Christmas party, like a pack of Boy Scouts.'

'Have they said what else they might do?'

'Nothing so far. Mumblings about some sort of ether therapy, although I don't know what that entails. I can't see any of it making me "better", anyway. I am constitutionally neurotic, as I'm sure they say behind my back.'

Ellen's eyes snap up.

'What on earth do you mean?'

'My mother was insane. Neurotic. I don't know what medics would call it officially. But she was taken into a mental hospital when I was a boy. She never came out again.'

'How dreadful. For you and for her.'

'Yes.' They stand in silence for a moment, watching the driver of the van manoeuvre the Christmas tree into the boat.

'Flying Officer Hennessey, one thing I do know is that the doctors here do not treat people they don't believe can be helped. They issue a medical discharge to those who they believe are beyond hope. You're here because they can treat you.'

'Perhaps. Or maybe my training makes me too expensive to discard?'

'Come now. Don't be like that,' says Ellen as Brian pushes the boat off the far bank. 'That's not fighting talk.'

'Maybe I'm not the fighting kind,' he replies, staring down at his feet. Ellen wants to respond, but Brian is too close now, and he might hear what she has to say.

'There yer are, Lieutenant Quinn,' Brian calls as he rows across. 'Yer should see the tree Neil and I have for yer. A right bobby dazzler.'

'Thank you, Brian,' she says. She turns and sees Harry has pulled himself up and puffed out his chest. He is wearing his mask once more. 'We can't wait to see it.'

* * *

Ellen hears the familiar chords and is instantly back in the church at the top of the hill, the building she visited at least twice a week throughout her childhood, driven by discipline, fear and shame and, she now thinks, pathetically little faith. The nave is candlelit, the choir stalls full, and she is about to sing her solo. She takes a deep breath and looks into the crowd, keen to pick out Mammy, who's wearing her best hat and a smile as broad as the high street. When she sees her she feels reassured, and when she opens her mouth and sings, the note she hits is strong and pure.

'Once in Royal David's City
Stood a lowly cattle shed...'

The congregation listen to the familiar carol echoing off the ancient stone building's walls, each word carrying with it the weight of nostalgia, of the hope that this year will be different, this year will be perfect.

'...where a mother laid her baby
In a manger for his bed.

Mary was that mother mild,
Jesus Christ, her little child.'

When everyone around the piano joins in with the second verse, Ellen is jolted back into 1943. She looks from face to face, taking in the nursing staff, the admin and support staff, one or two of the more junior doctors who've decided to attend the party and, of course, the patients. She can see the effect the familiar words and music has had on all of them. They've been reminded of the lives they led before the war, and of the hope they all have that they will also have lives once it ends. Doing so, she knows, is at the same time both incredibly painful and vital for their survival.

When they finish their carols there's a loud burst of applause and even some whooping from the back. Ellen smiles broadly and does a little curtsey, and Harry turns round on the piano stool and nods his head.

'More! More!'

'No, I think Quinn deserves a break,' says Harry, standing up from the piano. 'Shall we put on a record?'

'Good idea.'

Ellen walks away from the piano towards a table next to the Christmas tree, where the organising committee have assembled what treats they have managed to scrounge from the kitchen and from their ration books, alongside a bowl of punch which she knows is laced with cheap brandy. She'd never normally be allowed to eat food provided for the patients, but tonight is different. She is off duty and in civilian clothes. In fact, she's wearing the smart dress she packed and thought she'd never need to wear.

'That was really very lovely,' says Harry, arriving at her side and leaning over to spoon himself some punch.

'Thank you. It was probably a bit too melancholy, but I do love it.'

'It was joyful. Exactly what we need. And anyway, I think the boys have some more upbeat music in hand.'

Ellen spins round and sees David leaning over the gramophone. Seconds later, a familiar song fills the room, and several of the men get up to dance, either with each other – the punch having lubricated usually rigid social norms – or with administration or nursing staff they have managed to persuade to take part.

'Will you join me?' says Harry, putting his drink down and holding out his hand as Anne Shelton begins to sing 'Silver Wings In The Moonlight'. Ellen wonders whether it might be safer to decline, given how uncontrolled she is around him, but notes the room is full of normally very unhappy people making merry, and it seems churlish to do so.

'Yes. I will.'

'Excellent,' he says, and she allows him to take her hand and lead her into the centre of the room, into the maelstrom of bodies letting the music take control. When he pulls her closer, she finds herself momentarily winded. The proximity of Harry's face, his cheek next to hers, is intoxicating.

'Are you feeling unwell, Quinn?' he asks as they begin to move slowly around the floor, their hips and feet falling in time.

'No, I'm fine, thank you,' she replies, trying to take deep breaths to recover her composure. The truth is that she is actually very well indeed, better than she has felt in a long time. Like the patients here, she has her own mental scars, and some days she feels like they will never heal.

But right now, in this room, listening to this music with this man, she feels superhuman.

11

MEREDITH

December 2013

As soon as Meredith wakes – drowsy, and with yesterday's headache still making its presence felt – she senses something is wrong.

Then she hears it. It's a man's voice, calling for help. And what's more, it sounds like Philip. Has he come back early from work, unannounced? But how can that be? Isn't he in New York? Maybe he's ill, she thinks. But if so, why hasn't he called her and asked her to bring the boat? *Oh my God*, has he fallen in the water?

She throws back the covers and runs over to the window in her bare feet. She yanks the curtains open to see if she can spot him, and her heart sinks. It's 7 a.m. and December's lackadaisical sun has not yet risen, but the twilight is enough to confirm that thick fog has smothered the island and the river beyond.

'*Help, help.*'

He sounds desperate. But how will she find him in the fog?

She doesn't have time to think about it, however, so she grabs some clothes from the floor and pulls them on, locates her coat and trainers and sprints out of the front door.

'I can hear you,' she shouts. 'I'm coming.'

He calls for her again, but the fog is disorientating. Which side of the island should she try first? She decides to walk along the perimeter of the island to see if she can track him down. She works as quickly as she can, clinging to trees to stop herself from falling into the fast-moving water.

Then she spots movement in the reeds. It's something dark.

Is that him? She peers closer.

Something flies at her. She shrieks.

But it's just a moorhen, probably more spooked by her than she is by it.

'Help, help.'

Is it actually Philip? Now that she is closer to the voice, he sounds younger, maybe, than her husband. But whether it's him or not, there's no doubting this man needs her help.

All of a sudden, the voice sounds like it's coming from the other side of the island. Meredith sprints back across the island, passing the statue of the girl, transformed into a looming spectre in the dark hour before the dawn. When she reaches the other side of the island, she discovers she's next to their boat.

'Help, help.'

She's closer to him now, she thinks, but she still can't see him. And then she decides to act. She leaps into the boat before she can change her mind, pulls out her keys and inserts the key. Within seconds she's untied the ropes and fired up the engine, her earlier trepidation about such things now forgotten.

'I'm coming,' she shouts over the engine's roar. 'Where are you?'

But he doesn't respond, and Meredith fears she's too late. She speeds up as much as she dares and scans the water on either side. The fog is lifting a little now, and the tendrils it has left behind on the surface resemble will-o'-the-wisps. She slows down and watches them rising and dissipating like smoke.

Then she hears the roar.

She knows what it is. It's the weir, which is about four hundred metres downstream of the island. Even in the summer it generates a constant background hum, but in the winter when the river's full and fast, it's deafening up close. Meredith can't see it, but she knows it can't be far away, and she also knows she needs to get away from it as quickly as she can. She's heard that a young man, a keen canoeist, died there just last winter.

She turns the tiller anti-clockwise to put the boat in reverse.

Nothing happens. In fact, the engine has stopped completely. She can no longer hear it running. And the boat is surging forwards under its own steam, the current providing all the propulsion it needs.

She must be almost at the weir. *Shit, shit, shit.*

She reaches into her pocket for her phone and realises she hasn't brought it. She can't call for help. Not by phone, anyway.

It is her turn to shout.

'*Hellllppp!*' she yells. '*Help me!*'

She wishes desperately that she could manifest the emergency oars they've discussed buying and keeping in the boat.

A minute passes, and she decides to lean over and try to paddle using her arms. When her fingers hit the water they are immediately numb, but she doesn't care.

'*Hellllppp!*' she screams into the grey swirling void. '*Help me!*'

She looks up and can just make out the shape of the weir posts ahead of her. She has seconds before the boat either collides with them at speed, or forces its way through to the gates, and then down into the tumbling maelstrom on the other side.

'*Hellllppp!*'

And then she hears the motor.

She wonders briefly if it might be a car on the road beside the towpath, but then it gets louder and louder and she is finally able to believe help might be coming.

'Where are you?' a man shouts.

'Over here!' she shouts back, before realising that in the fog, that's a fairly ridiculous thing to say. 'By the weir…'

'OK. I'm coming,' he replies. She doesn't stop trying to paddle, though, because the weir posts are becoming clearer every second.

It feels like forever, but it's probably just a minute before Meredith makes out the outline of a boat coming towards her. She stops paddling, her hands and arms no longer feeling like parts of her body. As the boat finally comes into view, she sees it's someone she recognises. It's Euan.

They pay him and his dad to take Philip on and off the island. He's in his early twenties and being trained in the family business. As well as acting as river taxi drivers, they also operate the official river ferry, a cafe and a boat chandlery and hire business.

'Hang on, I've got you,' he says, bringing his boat alongside and grabbing hold of a rope that runs along its edge. Meredith doesn't move or speak as he ties the boats together and kicks his engine into life, moving them well away from what feels like the dragon's lair.

A minute or so later, Euan takes his coat off and throws it to Meredith.

'Put that on, you must be freezing,' he says.

Meredith nods and does so. The coat feels like a warm hug. She realises her body was so shocked it had blocked out the pain and the cold, but now she's warming up again, she feels it. The ache in her hands is more of a thud and her body is shaking violently.

'Right, let's get you inside the shop and we'll warm you up.'

Meredith looks to the right and sees the slipway at the chandlery appearing into view. It's then she realises that the man who'd been calling to her must still be out there. She can't abandon him now, not now she's safe.

'Did you find the other person who was shouting for help?' she says, her teeth chattering. 'He was calling out.'

Euan looks confused. 'A man? No. Was he with you?'

'No, I was trying to find him. He was yelling.'

'I only heard you,' he says. 'I was out checking on the boats. I got into the launch as soon as I heard you. I didn't hear anyone else.'

'We should go and look for him.'

'I'm sorry... Meredith, is it? I remember you coming into the shop. I'm sorry, but I think my priority is getting you inside and checked over. You look freezing. I'll call the police and they can alert the river search people, to look for this man. I volunteer with them sometimes. They're very good. OK?'

Meredith nods with reluctance. She doesn't want to abandon him, but she is feeling very cold and very weak and even she knows going out again now would be a terrible idea.

* * *

It's an hour later and she's sitting on a stool by the Christmas tree in the chandlery, wearing one of the warm coats they sell to boaters. She's clutching a hot mug of tea from the cafe kitchen.

'There was water in the petrol tank,' says Euan's father, Tom, entering the shop. He's been taking a look at her boat, trying to work out why it cut out.

'How did it get there? Is it my fault?' she asks.

'It's impossible to say. Have you refilled the tank since you bought it? Maybe some water got in then?'

Meredith shakes her head. 'Honestly, I don't know. Phil might have?'

'Look, if you leave it with me today, I'll clean it out for you. And also see if I can scrub that graffiti off?'

She stares at her tea, not wanting to engage in conversation about how they seem to be hated by almost all of their neighbours.

'Thank you. I haven't had time yet to...'

'Not everyone around here is like that, you know,' he says, and she looks up at him. 'I mean, I'm not pretending that we're delighted about your plans. I've got to be honest with you – if you're successful, your boat hire will take business from us. But I don't wish you harm. You've bought the house. You're just as welcome as anyone to try to make a go of things. That's my view, anyway.'

'Thank you.'

'Don't be. Look, shall I get Euan to take you home? And you've got the rowing boat still, to take you across the mainland?'

'Yes please. And yes, I do.'

'Well, then. I'll deliver the boat back sometime tomorrow,' he says as Euan comes back into the shop from the cafe, where he's been waiting, getting it ready to open for breakfast.

'I can't thank you enough. Either of you.'

'Don't be daft,' says Euan. 'Anyone would have done it.'

'Did the police call back, about the man?' she asks.

'They did. They couldn't find anyone, even though the fog has lifted now.'

Meredith raises her eyebrows, her face a picture of confusion.

'There was definitely someone. I heard him. Multiple times.'

'Yes, well, sadly he's not there any more,' says Tom. 'They might find him by the lock. That's happened a few times. I found a body there once, when I was taking a boat for a test run.' There's an awkward silence, during which his eyes glisten red. 'I'm just glad I didn't have to do it this time.'

* * *

After Meredith is ferried back to the house, her first instinct is to hibernate. She needs some time to herself to think and, perhaps, heal. So instead of heading to one of the rooms to continue the unending task of clearing and cleaning, she heads to bed with a hot water bottle. She picks up the notebook she found in the room upstairs from her bedside table and continues reading.

12

ELLEN

Christmas Day, 1943

Dear Mammy,

Merry Christmas! It's evening here, and I'm about to go to bed. I had a reasonable day, and managed to be jolly, although it feels so strange to be celebrating such an important day away from home, even though of course this isn't the first time I've had to do it.

Despite where they are, and the rain that's falling outside, I think we have made the day as special as we can for the patients. This morning, one of the orderlies donned a Father Christmas costume and we distributed a small gift to each of the men, and lunch was delicious roast chicken, a real treat in times like these. In the afternoon, the men played games. I joined in with charades. I have such fond memories of us all playing that by the fireside after lunch. You'd have been proud of my efforts. I managed to convey A Christmas Carol *using only gestures.*

But Mammy, the real reason I'm writing to you today is that I need your advice. There are some things a girl needs her mammy for, and this is definitely one of those times. And you are also the only one I can tell.

I feel like I'm going mad. I feel – I don't know how to describe how I feel, but I'll try – fizzy? And that fizzy-ness threatens to burst forth at any moment. And

I'm sure you can guess that this is about a boy. Well, a man, I suppose. Neither of us are children any more. But Mammy, it's like every song I've ever heard and every love poem I've ever read, and like joining a club I didn't believe actually existed. If you were here, I think you'd probably tell me to be sensible and to think clearly, to focus on my job and the fact that relationships with patients are not allowed, and you'd definitely be right.

And yet, it's so hard. It has taken every inch of training and professionalism I can muster to keep myself from reaching out for him when I pass him in the corridor, from taking his hand when I'm at work beside his bed. I'm astonished that I can feel this way. I know I sound like a silly schoolgirl, and perhaps in many ways I am. But actually, I have no idea what silly school girls sound like, because as you know, I spent most of my youth hiding in plain sight, trying to be as studious and sensible as possible, so as not to attract anyone's attention. Silly girls, you see, get seen. That's what Daddy says, isn't it?

And Mammy, I want to tell you something else. Something I never told you, and when I tell you, I think you'll understand why. It will help explain why I left Ireland.

It was Daddy who made me join the church choir. Do you remember? He said my voice had been a gift from the Almighty and I should pay it back to him in song. Father Brennan was keen to have me, you see. In fact, you'll recall he sat me right opposite him on the front row of the choir stalls when I joined, so he could make sure I was paying attention to his sermons and not talking during the Mass.

And I was good, as you know; I was a good learner and well behaved with it, and I progressed well. By thirteen I was head chorister, and you know I was pleased as punch with that. I loved singing, I loved my friends in the choir, I loved choral music, and I loved the responsibility I had in the service.

But then the father approached me about becoming an acolyte. I didn't want to leave the choir at all, even if it was to go and help with the preparation of the Mass and all that comes with it, but Daddy told me I had to, that being asked to be an acolyte was a huge honour. I was given white robes to wear with a little rope around my waist. I'd loved my blue choir robes with their stiff white ruff. I felt ugly in the new ones and everyone stared at me during the service, so hard that my face glowed red and sailors could probably have used me to help them avoid dangerous rocks.

Father Brennan saw my discomfort and he offered to counsel me – to impart his experience, to make me a better acolyte, and perhaps to ready me for a life in God's service, if he willed it. Daddy agreed that it sounded like a wonderful idea, and so off I went, every Saturday evening to the parish house.

It started off reasonably well, I suppose. We read the bible together and he offered me some biscuits and he told me I was a good girl and then sent me home. That was the first week.

In the second week, he told me that he was sometimes lonely, and asked if I felt the same. Well I was an awkward teenage girl, so of course I was lonely, and I told him so. He patted me on the knee, gave me some biscuits and sent me home.

The next week, we read our bibles, talked about our Lord, had hot chocolate and biscuits, and then he sent me home without asking about my loneliness. That made me feel a bit sad.

In the fourth week, we read the bible, he offered me biscuits and hot chocolate and then he ran his hand up my leg, stopping just before he reached my underwear. My face burned so bright then I felt I might combust. Then he sent me home.

I didn't want to go the next week. I tried to tell Daddy that I had my monthlies and I felt unwell, but he told me I could not let Father Brennan down, and he walked me to the parish house personally.

I think you can imagine what happened that week. I am unable to remember the details, thank God, because I have blotted out almost all of it. It's the shame that lingers, however. And what's worse is that I didn't tell anyone, not even Daddy, because I felt that it must have been my fault, that I'd somehow bewitched the father with my terrible Eve-like, fallen ways.

My weekly meetings with Father Brennan continued until I left Ireland to start nursing training.

I know Daddy is still angry that I lied about going to Dublin, when I meant to travel to England all along. He wants me to live at home and look after my younger siblings and marry a Catholic Irish man, and I do not want to do any of those things. I have seen the life of a housewife in Ireland, and I do not want it. And I'm old enough now to say if that makes me wicked, sobeit.

There is so much more to say, but I have run out of time. Rebecca will be here shortly and I don't want her seeing this.

Ever yours, x

13

MEREDITH

Christmas Day 2013

Meredith is fumbling with the buttons of her coat. It's so cold outside that her hands have frozen during the short walk from the car to the pub. Forecasters say it might snow. The old her would have embraced that possibility with the glee of a child, but the emotional rollercoaster she's been on for what feels like years has dulled her enthusiasm. Now, she just knows that the house will be freezing, and so will she be.

'Merry Christmas! Shall I take that?' says the waiter, who has been waiting patiently for her to remove her coat.

'You too. Yes, thank you.'

Meredith's spirits rise as she feels the warmth of the restaurant. They've just had a festive tipple with Philip's parents – although festive is rather pushing it – but didn't stay for lunch, because they find hosting too stressful in their small flat. Meredith is quietly pleased, and Philip doesn't seem to mind. And now they are here, and not in their freezing house. This is all Philip's idea, and it's a good, albeit pricey one. He felt making Christmas lunch in their ancient kitchen would be a very stressful undertaking, and that they both need cheering up, and he's right, of course. They've been having a hell of a time.

'Come this way.'

They follow the waiter down a corridor and into a large dining room lined with teal wallpaper dotted with bright pink birds and topped with a vaulted glass roof. Quite like their plans for the orangery, Meredith thinks, noting the similarity with an irony that weighs heavily.

'Here,' says the man, pointing to a table for two against the far wall.

'Excellent. Thank you,' says Phil, taking a seat as the waiter holds the chair out for Meredith, who smiles and sits down. 'Well, this is lovely, isn't it?'

Instead of admiring the room, Meredith examines her husband. He's looking particularly handsome today. He's clean-shaven, wearing one of his best shirts, and he looks every inch the man she married. And yet she can't shake the feeling that something has shifted in him. He's been exercising more than ever – punishing long runs – and she often finds him out of bed when she wakes in the morning. Last week, she'd found him outside in the garden, staring at the river, long before dawn.

'Yes, it's charming,' she replies as a waiter approaches the table and hands them menus on stiff white card.

'Well this is definitely better than beans on toast at home,' says Philip with a forced laugh. Meredith tries to do the same, but she can tell that neither of them thinks their situation is actually funny.

'Definitely,' she says, scanning the menu and making a snap decision to skip a starter and just order the vegetarian main course. She hasn't been feeling hungry recently, and she feels another headache coming on. She can't face a full roast.

'You look lovely,' he says. She's wearing make-up for the first time in several weeks. The work has been so physical, she has spent almost every day in her most scruffy clothes and make-up has seemed irrelevant. But today she felt she should make an effort, because she knows that Philip probably misses the put-together, glossy Merry whose blow-dried hair and dry-cleaned suits used to swish out of the front door at 7 a.m. every morning.

'Thanks,' she says, smiling as the waiter comes over and takes their order from the Christmas Day set menu.

'No starter, Merry?' Philip says when the waiter has left the table.

'No. Sorry. I'm feeling a little off colour.'

'Oh darling. That's not good. Is there anything I can do? Should we leave?'

'No, no, I'll be fine. I'm just tired, I think. There's been a lot going on.'

They sit in silence for a minute, drinking the water the waiter has poured into their glasses.

'So, tell me... what have I missed while I've been away?' Philip asks. He has just got back from a three-day trip to Seoul.

'It was quiet.'

'Well, that's better than...'

'Better than almost drowning by the weir?'

'Yes, definitely better than that.'

It's almost a fortnight since Euan rescued Meredith in the fog. She called Philip afterwards, of course, and he flew home early. He was given a few days of compassionate leave afterwards to stay at home with her, time enough for her adrenaline to subside and for her to restore some equilibrium. She's still not sleeping properly, though.

'Merry, I've been thinking about what happened to you a lot,' he says, as the waiter arrives and pours red wine into their glasses.

'Me too,' she says, and there's a pause as they wait for the waiter to move back out of earshot.

'It's just... after Stuart... I know how dangerous the river is. And we're surrounded by it. I think we need to get you more boat lessons.'

'It's OK, I'm fine with the boat now,' she says, not wanting to mention Damon's lesson, in case it angers Philip, who clearly doesn't like him or his fellow boat dwellers. 'And it wasn't my fault I ended up there, Phil. There was water in the engine. And that wasn't me.'

'Yes. I know. But I think I should take you out a few times and show you everything I know.'

'OK.'

'And I'm also worried that you're too isolated. You don't seem to be in contact with your old friends any more. You need support when I'm not around.'

'We've been through this, Phil. They let me down. They weren't there for me when it mattered. I don't need friends like those. And anyway, I have a new friend, as you know. Holly.'

'Yes. And that's good. But old friends are still—'

'Enough, Phil.'

'OK. Fine. But the other thing is... Your near miss on the river... It's made me realise how unprepared we are for one of us dying or getting ill. I was talking to a colleague and he recommended a great firm in Weybridge who could draw up a will and some powers of attorney for us, you know, so that we can make decisions for each other, should the worst happen.'

Meredith can't look him in the eye. She's raging. They are massively in debt, their planning permission is hanging in the balance and she's physically exhausted from the work she's been doing on the house, and here he is, wanting to secure his bloody inheritance?

'Am I just a cash cow to you?' she says, her voice low but her bitterness emphatically clear. Until she took her career break, her income had far surpassed his, and of course her parents' untimely deaths had meant a sizeable inheritance. Most of it is tied up in the house, however, and that is something she needs to talk to him about, too. 'I nearly died, Phil, and you're more worried about the bloody money?'

'Darling, no, that's not what this is about. I mean, you're my wife, I'd inherit anyway, wouldn't I?' She's still steaming, but also admits, privately, that he has a point. 'And it could be me too, right? I could have an accident at work or something and I want you to be secure. And I want to make sure that if I have a stroke or whatever and I'm not competent to make my own decisions, you're able to make them for me.'

'Phil, we are both still relatively young. What are the chances of that happening?'

He shrugs.

'I don't know. Low, I suppose. But it's solid advice. Martin Lewis from MoneySavingExpert says we should all do a power of attorney.'

Meredith raises an eyebrow. Philip worships Martin Lewis. Or Saint Martin, as she calls him in her head.

'Oh, right,' she says.

'Look, I know this sounds mad. But what if Euan hadn't got to you quick enough, and you'd survived but had terrible injuries, and were on life support? That could have happened. And I would want to know what you wanted, and be able to make those decisions for you. That horrible incident just focused things for me. I feel like we need to do this.'

Meredith analyses his expression. *He looks moved*, she thinks; *upset*, even. Perhaps he really is worried about what might have been. And he's right, of course, that they should have a will, and powers of attorney are always advised, aren't they, by anyone with any sense. Is she making too much of this? Perhaps, she reasons, she should just agree to this, let it go, so she can move on and focus on what she really wants to discuss this evening.

'OK, Phil, fine. Call up the solicitor and make us an appointment.'

She sees his spirits lift, relieved no doubt that she isn't going to spend the rest of a very pricey meal angry.

'I will,' says Phil, pausing as the waiter brings their food, checks whether they need more drinks or sauces, and leaves. 'Sorry, Merry, I didn't mean to upset you. I think that came across wrong. This last trip was really exhausting, and I think I spent too long by myself worrying about stuff, you know... the house, our finances, your safety. I mean, we still don't know who vandalised the boat. I hate having to leave you alone there so much.'

Finally, they are talking about how this impacts on her, and Meredith is relieved. She hates being alone on the island now too, but she knows that it won't help Philip's state of mind if she says so.

'It's your job, Phil. And I knew I'd be alone a lot when we took on the project. It's OK,' she says.

'But you look exhausted, Merry. And the whole idea of this career break was for you to rest, to recover from the miscarriages... To get yourself back a bit.'

'I'm trying. But it'll take time. I can't just... bounce back.'

'I know that, darling,' he says, picking up a roast potato with his fork. 'I'm not expecting you to. I just feel guilty, that's all, about what you're shouldering. I mean, if I'd been there when you heard that man calling for help, I'd have gone out in the boat, wouldn't I? Jesus, I do wish you hadn't gone out.'

Meredith meets his gaze. Her husband's eyes are wet. They haven't spoken much about the incident since it happened. He has been afraid, she suspects, that making her relive it might upset her, and send her spiralling down. He knows how damaged she has been, how hard she has found it to pull herself out of the darkness before.

'I know. I'm sorry. But I couldn't just leave him. He sounded desperate.'

'It was definitely a man, then? And not someone you know?'

'I don't know. I thought at first it was you. But it obviously wasn't.'

'But it sounded a bit like me?'

Meredith shrugs.

'Maybe younger. I'm not sure.'

'Hmmm,' says Philip, exhaling loudly. 'There's just something odd about it. Why didn't the emergency services find anyone? Or a body? And why didn't he say anything else, other than help? It just feels... fishy to me.'

'Do you mean you think someone was trying to lure me to my death?' says Meredith, quizzically.

'I don't know,' says Philip, chewing. 'Maybe?'

They eat in silence for a minute, both contemplating what he's just said.

'No. No. That's just not possible. No one would do that,' Meredith says, picking up her wine glass and swallowing hard. 'They might not want us to work on the house, but they don't want us *dead*, do they?'

'Yes, I'm sure you're right,' he says, but she's no longer listening. Instead, she can hear that voice she'd heard, clear, insistent, desperate. She can remember how she chased it across the island, how she followed it in the boat, disregarding her own safety. Has someone really done that to her? Someone who'd been safe at the time, on a boat or on land? But the man had sounded real, and serious, and desperate. Could someone really have faked that?

'I wish we could pay for more help,' says Philip.

'We've got the roofers booked to come in next month,' she says, hoping this is relevant.

Philip makes a face.

'That's not the sort of help I was meaning. I mean helping you to clear, decorate, deal with the admin. And to just be with you when I'm at work. I don't like the thought of you there alone at night. Anyone could have graffitied the boat, or pretended to be in trouble in the water. I mean, it could be that man, Damon, couldn't it? He and his homeless, drugged-up boat-living mates probably enjoy making posh people scared.'

'Phil! God, you have something against those boat dwellers, don't you? Don't be ridiculous. Why would he want us to leave? He's not on the bloody residents' committee, and he's not going to be affected by our business, is he? All he's done so far is fix our water pump.'

Could he actually be jealous? Well, that would be a first.

'I suppose not.' Philip looks chastened. 'But maybe it's someone else from the local area, who doesn't want us to develop the house?'

Meredith raises an eyebrow. 'Haven't they already done enough?'

They'd received a letter in late November telling them that their planning application for May Day House had been 'called in', meaning that it would be decided by the councillors sitting on the council planning committee, and not by the planning officer they'd been assigned for their case. The hearing date is set for January. They're both deeply worried about the outcome.

'Yeah, I suppose so. I don't know. Maybe they think we have stuff to steal? But what we do know is someone definitely came onto the island and defaced the boat. And it's possible they also, best case, tried to scare the hell out of you in the fog. It's worrying, darling. I can barely sleep when I'm away for worrying about it. I think we should get cameras. I'll order a couple.'

'OK. If you like.'

'And I have another idea.'

'Oh yes?'

'I think we should get a dog.'

14

ELLEN

29 December 1943

It's 2 a.m. Ellen is behind a desk in the corridor, updating notes after her most recent check on her sleeping patients, when the sirens start.

She hasn't heard them for a long time. She left for Egypt in the autumn of 1940, so she'd been spared the vast majority of the Blitz in the capital. And she knows that the skies have been relatively quiet around here for the past few years. Or at least they were until a couple of weeks ago, when a few German bombers aiming for London dropped their load on the small, sedate, inconsequential village of Westcott in Surrey. Six children and four adults died that night, all annihilated in their beds.

The events of that horrible night less than twenty miles away from May Day House shook everyone on the island, Ellen included. They know there is a war on, of course they do, but the absence of the Luftwaffe over London for so long has lulled them into a false sense of security, into a feeling that the war is *out there*, and not *here*. Their patients, of course, rely on this. It's the war that put them in here, after all. May Day House was chosen because it offered their patients a breather, a chance to recover far away from the front. But as the air raid sirens from nearby Weybridge and Walton scream their warnings and patients and staff at May Day are awoken, it's clear that for tonight at least, the war will be paying them another visit.

'Lieutenant Quinn,' shouts Captain Huntingford, pulling a woollen outdoor coat over striped cotton pyjamas as she runs down the stairs and towards Ellen's desk. 'We need to initiate the emergency procedure. I'll make sure the other staff are up and doing their jobs. Can you get started on moving everyone on this floor down to the cellar?'

The cellar is their designated bomb shelter. Ellen has only been down there once, to retrieve a box of new dressings. It's being used partly as a storage room, and it's roughly twice the size of a sitting room in the average semi-detached house. She can't imagine how they'll fit all the men down there, even those who are not too drugged to move. But she's in the army, so she does as she's told.

She stands up and runs into the ward immediately to her right and begins shaking those awake who are still sleeping, urging them, as calmly but as firmly as she can, to make their way downstairs.

'Keep moving. All the way down to the cellar. Keep moving, men,' shouts Captain Huntingford from the stairwell.

Ellen is grateful that the wards she's in charge of tonight are full of men who are conscious. Her roommate Rebecca is on night duty looking after those undergoing insulin treatment, and she has no idea how they are going to move them. *If* they are going to move them.

She's moving into the final ward – four, which is Harry's – when she hears the unmistakable rumble of aircraft engines. *This isn't a false alarm then*, she thinks. *They really are coming.* She feels her stomach tense and adrenaline surges through her body. Fortunately, the men in ward four, Harry included, have been woken by the commotion outside, because Ellen is no longer capable of pretending to be calm. Four men run past her and down the stairs. Harry, meanwhile, is sitting on his bed putting on his shoes.

'Come quickly, everyone. Come downstairs where it's safe,' she shouts, not taking her eyes off Harry, who is still trying to do up his laces.

'*Come on*, Flying Officer Hennessey,' she says, sitting down on the bed next to him and grabbing him by the arm. 'We have to go. Now.'

But he won't move. And he won't meet her eye.

'Flying Officer Hennessey. *Harry*. Please. We have to go. The bombers are coming.'

She can hear the distant but unmistakable sound of explosions. Where are they dropping them? How far away are they? Are they bombing the aircraft factory at Brooklands? That would make sense. Those poor, poor people, she thinks. They still haven't got over the raid there in 1940 which killed ninety and injured hundreds more. She prays that, given that it's late, not many people are on shift, and there was enough warning this time for the employees who are there to take shelter.

'Harry!' She yanks at his arm, and his head turns slowly to face hers. He is oddly expressionless. She realises that he's not truly conscious. This happens to patients at May Day sometimes. They can alternate between being hyper-alert and numb, almost asleep. 'Harry!' she yells, and he blinks and moves to stand. *Thank God*, she thinks. *We can get going.*

As they walk slowly to the door and along the corridor, with Ellen holding Harry's arm and pulling him along, she hears the rumble of more aircraft engines. They're getting louder. So they haven't turned around for home yet, she thinks. Or perhaps this is a different wave, heading for London?

'Harry,' she says, trying to steer him in the direction of the staircase. 'We need to get below. Now.'

As they reach the ground floor, the aircraft sound like they're overhead. The deadly whine is unyielding, and Ellen is no longer able to dissemble.

She is no longer a well-trained, experienced army nurse. Instead, she is a damaged and petrified woman locked in a stinking, burning metal container that is sinking to the bottom of the Channel, just yards from the French shore. She has long abandoned her patients, who are either dead or dying, and is simply screaming for help, clawing at the small port hole which is her only source of light. The water is coming up beyond it now, and she knows she has little time left. 'Help me!' she screams, thrashing away at the side of the ship. 'I'm in here! Help me!'

'Lieutenant Quinn! Ellen… Ellen,' says a familiar voice, and Ellen finds herself returning slowly from her own personal experience of hell, back to the present. 'Ellen, it's Rebecca. Are you all right? We need to get you downstairs.'

Ellen opens her eyes, surprised to find them closed, and realises that she's still on the ground floor of May Day House, with a numb, stationary Harry still on her arm. The aircraft are still overhead. Ellen nods, because she's not sure she can form words, and follows Rebecca down the corridor and through the door that leads to the basement.

Ellen peers down the small flight of steps that leads to the cellar and sees that it's so full; men are sitting on the steps, some of them almost on top of each other. As she takes the scene in, the brick walls lit by caged bare bulbs seem to close in on her, threatening to steal her breath.

She has to get out of here. Now.

She turns and runs, letting go of Harry's arm as she does so.

'Ellen! Ellen!' Rebecca shouts over the roar of the planes as she runs after her down the corridor and towards the front door. Ellen doesn't stop. She needs to get out of here.

She turns the key in the front door and pulls it open, making it through a millisecond before Rebecca, who follows her outside. Ellen sprints down the path towards the boat dock and pauses when she's clear of the house, clear of the small airless room downstairs which is full of bodies. Then she breathes deeply and looks up at the stars. It's a full moon tonight. A bomber's moon.

'Ellen, thank God,' says Rebecca, panting. 'Look, we can't stay here. We've got to take cover. And we have to get back to our patients.'

But Ellen doesn't want to go inside. Instead, she looks up once more and sees the underside of a bomber overhead, momentarily lit up by searchlights.

'Ellen? We need to go.'

Her words, however, are drowned out by an unmistakable whistling. And then there is a flash of bright light, a huge blast that moves both air and objects. Both women are lobbed into the ground.

* * *

'Lieutenant Quinn? Lieutenant Hanson?'

Ellen registers the voice, which is Brian's. He's calling for them. She tries to reply but only a small moan emerges. Then she tries to move her arm and discovers that everything hurts. And she can't move, anyway. Her brain seems to be disconnected from her body.

'*There's a fire*! Someone call the emergency services. Now!'

Ellen hears a man say something urgently in response, and then hears the front door slam several times. She assumes this means that quite a few other people from the hospital – staff and possibly even some patients – are also outside now.

What's on fire? The blast that threw her down into the dirt was close, definitely. Had it hit the house?

Oh no, she thinks. Harry. *Harry is still in there. Is Harry hurt*?

Ellen takes a deep breath and tries to roll herself over onto her front. It hurts like hell, but she manages it. Then she pulls her arms towards her and pushes up, screaming in pain as she does so.

'There's someone over here,' shouts a man. She recognises his voice. It's Neil, Brian's son. Several sets of footsteps come towards her.

'It's them. They're here,' he says. His hands sweep over her, pulling off heavy things from her legs and checking for injuries.

Then she hears groaning nearby.

'Lieutenant Hanson. Can you hear me?' says a voice Ellen recognises as Captain Huntingford's.

'Urghmmm…'

Rebecca is still alive, then. *Thank God*, thinks Ellen. After all, it's her fault they're out here. If Rebecca was dead, it would be her fault.

'How does Lieutenant Quinn look?' asks the captain.

'I dunno. She's breathing. Seems to be in a lot of pain.'

'Yes. Lieutenant Hanson is complaining of pain to her wrist,' says the nurse. 'But both are responsive. Let's get them on stretchers and carry them into the house.'

The next few minutes are mostly obliterated by intense pain, but Ellen is awake enough to open her eyes briefly when she's on the stretcher. She sees flames leaping from the roof of the shed Brian uses for his gardening equipment, licking their way up the trunk of a beech tree nearby. There's a group of people gathered around the fire, throwing buckets of water at the flames. It's showing no sign of abating. She doesn't know if there's a pump or a hose anywhere, and she wonders whether there is such a thing as a fire boat.

As she's hauled up the front steps and into the house, Ellen allows her eyes to close again. She's exhausted and in a whole world of pain. It's only when she's being carried up the stairs that a familiar name rouses her.

'Flying Officer Hennessey, we really have to get you back to your room,' says one of the junior nurses.

'No, no, no,' wails Harry. He sounds as if he's crying.

'If you can't walk by yourself, I'll have to ask the doctor to sedate you.'

'No, no, no.'

'You only have yourself to blame,' the nurse says, and then Ellen hears scuffling. As she's carried down the corridor into her room, she can still hear Harry's screams.

* * *

It is much later. Ellen isn't even sure how long it's been, but it has definitely been at least twelve hours – perhaps even more – since she and Rebecca were rescued from amongst the detritus in the bomb-damaged garden. Daylight is squinting past the blackout curtains at their window. They're back in their own room but being nursed by their colleagues as if they're on a ward. There are no free beds in May Day, so this is the best solution the medics can come up with.

Ellen pulls herself up a little with a great deal of difficulty and looks across at Rebecca's bed. Of the two of them, Ellen seems to have come off worse. Her right arm is in a sling, her ankle is swollen, and her face is badly bruised. Rebecca, meanwhile, has a sprained wrist and some small cuts. Aside from that, they are incredibly lucky. The bomb fell less than forty feet from where they were standing. If Ellen hadn't run towards the boat dock, they might not have survived.

'Are you awake, Becs?'

There's movement in the bed, and Rebecca turns to face Ellen.

'Yep. Every position I try hurts.'

'Same.'

There's an awkward silence. Ellen feels extremely guilty, because she's the reason they are both in this mess. However, she can't work out how to apologise without owning up to the darkness that overtook her just before the blast. She lost her mind there temporarily, and doing so makes her no saner than the men she's supposed to be treating. And that makes her feel ashamed.

'Do you want to tell me what happened last night?' asks Rebecca, as if she has been privy to Ellen's private thoughts. 'I promise it won't go any further.' Ellen bites her lip. She wants to be honest, but she also fears what might happen if she is. 'Look, Ellen, I almost died going after you. You owe me the truth, I reckon.'

She has a point, thinks Ellen. And so she decides to do as she asks.

'I was on the *Maid of Kent*,' she says.

'Oh.' She knows Rebecca will have heard about the *Maid of Kent*. It was a hospital ship that was bombed just outside Dieppe in May 1940. The port had been designated a hospital base and was completely undefended when enemy bombers unloaded their cargo onto the ships below. At the time of the raid, the ship had been covered in an enormous red and white cross printed onto canvas. There could have been no doubt what its purpose was.

'I was in one of the wards below the waterline when the bombs hit.'

'I see.'

'We didn't stand a chance.' Ellen remembers the sound of the bombers overhead, of the whistling and then the enormous explosions that had rocked the ship. 'A bomb dropped straight down the funnel, you know. The others landed in the engine room, the afterdeck, and one of them hit the galley. The ship began to break up immediately. There was water...' And it had been freezing, despite the searing heat from the fires that had taken hold. Ellen remembers the smell of burning flesh and oil, and the screams of the men who were soon to drown. She will never be able to forget them.

'How did you get out?'

'Someone put a gangplank over from the quayside and smashed a porthole. They were able to rescue the few of us who'd managed to climb up.' Ellen swallows hard when she thinks of what, or even who, she must have stood on to get herself up there.

'Oh, Ellen.'

'It doesn't excuse how I reacted last night, Becs, I know that. I'm a nurse. An army nurse. There are high standards for good reason and I know I didn't meet them. I'm sorry.'

Rebecca sits up further and takes an audible breath.

'Don't be ridiculous, Ellen. We both work here. We know, more than anyone, perhaps, the damage that sort of trauma does to a person. We see it every day. Why should it be different for you?'

'But I haven't fought. I simply got caught in the crossfire.'

'You almost died.'

'Yes.' Ellen remembers the minutes and hours after the attack, when a flood of adrenaline had helped her tend the terrible burn wounds of the injured. She had not received any medical treatment herself until much later, when she'd realised she had cuts all over her body. 'I'm so sorry, Becs, about last night. It was the noise of the aircraft. It took me back. I felt like I was there. I couldn't face being underground.'

'I understand.'

'Will you tell the others?' she asks, her voice strangulated. She fears dismissal more than anything. She doesn't know where else she'd go, and this job gives her a reason to keep living. And then there is Harry.

'Tell them what?'

'About how I reacted.'

'Heavens, Ellen, they should know what you've been through. Don't you think?'

'I don't mind them knowing that. It's on my record. But please... Please don't tell them why I was outside last night. Please.'

'Ellen Quinn, do you not know by now that we're friends? If you don't want me to tell them, I won't. But I do worry about you. You need to talk about it. Maybe with one of the doctors here. They could help you, perhaps.'

Ellen thinks about the insulin comas and the electric shock machine and the tears and screams she's heard coming from locked rooms, and she decides that she absolutely does not want to seek treatment at May Day House. But she doesn't say this.

'But I'm a woman. They don't treat women.'

'That's true,' says Rebecca. 'But will you promise me that if you ever feel like that again, you'll come to me for help?'

'Yes. I promise.'

They lie in silence for a while. Ellen wonders what Rebecca is really thinking. Does she believe she's mad? Perhaps, and that's a disturbing thought.

But then Ellen remembers something else that disturbs her. *Harry*.

She remembers his screams as they tried to get him back to his ward, and his absolute refusal to do so. They were doing something to him, weren't they? And if so, what did they do?

As soon as she is able to get out of bed, she resolves to find out.

15

MEREDITH

10 January 2014

It's still dark when Meredith is woken up by growling. She turns over and checks the clock beside her bed. It's 6 a.m.

'*Poppy*. Poppy, love. It's too early,' she mutters, swinging her legs over the side of the bed and grabbing her dressing gown from a chair. It's utterly freezing, and she knows she's going to have to go outside and wait with the dog while she empties her bladder.

They've had Poppy for only a few days. She's an eight-year-old Labrador cross Collie and they got her from the local rescue, her last owner having recently died. She's not exactly a German Shepherd and Meredith doubts that any intruder would find her at all frightening, but she does bark when she sees or hears people, and her company is reassuring. She finds herself talking to the dog when she's making dinner or brushing her teeth, and Poppy follows her around like a shadow.

Meredith slips on her trainers and pulls the front door shut behind her, before realising that she's left her phone, and therefore her torch, inside. She considers going back for it, but as her eyes adjust, she sees that it's unexpectedly bright out. The moon is full and the sky is clear, and the icy paving stones and the statue of the garlanded girl at the centre of the old rose garden glitter like they're studded with diamonds.

'Off you go then, Poppy. Do your business.'

But Poppy, who has already taken to lolloping off down the path without a backward glance when she's allowed outside, refuses to budge. Instead of running off, in fact, she moves closer to Meredith, almost sitting down on her feet.

'Poppy, *get on with you*. Get it over and done with and then we can get back inside and put a fire in.'

Poppy growls once more, and now that she's more awake, Meredith realises what's bothering her. So far, the dog has woken her up with a whine or a nudge every morning. Not a growl. She only growls when there are people about, Meredith thinks. She can feel her heart beating faster, responding to her fear. Had the people who'd graffitied the boat come back? Were they planning something else? She scans the garden quickly, looking for where someone might be hiding. The only place they could sensibly hide on this part of the island would be the dense trees that line the water.

'Poppy, come with me girl.' Meredith pulls her by her collar, but the dog needs little persuading, determined as she is to remain within a hair's breadth of her owner's legs. She stays with her as Meredith strides towards the boat dock. When she reaches it, she walks alongside the trees that mark the edge of the island, stopping every ten paces or so to listen for breathing, for speaking, even for laughter. And yet every time she stops, she can only hear her own ragged breaths. And Poppy does not growl again, even when they disturb a Canada goose that had been sleeping on the bank. When Meredith completes the semi-circle around the downstream part of the island and returns to the front of the house, she concludes there is no one hiding on this side of the house.

She is going to have to walk around the back.

It's not a place she likes to linger. The paving is uneven, the old kitchen garden is still a wilderness, the pump house is full of spiders and gives her the creeps, and most of the courtyard is in shade even on a sunny day. Still, she has no choice. She won't be able to relax until she knows for certain there's no one there who shouldn't be.

Meredith pulls the cord of her dressing gown tighter, takes a deep breath and sets off around the perimeter of the house, past the drawing room's large bay windows, the garden store which Graham avails himself of once every fortnight on average, despite their attempts to persuade him otherwise, and the high glazed window of the scullery.

When Meredith and Poppy turn the corner and walk onto the patio that runs along the rear of the house, she wishes desperately that Philip had found time on his last days off to install the security cameras he'd ordered. It's incredibly dark here, despite the light of the moon. The shadow of the house feels like it's swallowing her whole. Her every instinct is screaming at her to turn and run, but her rational brain, the one that did so well in male-dominated boardrooms for so many years, tells her to stay. All she needs to do now is finish the search, reassure herself that she is indeed alone on the island, and then she can return to the house for a well-earned coffee and Poppy can have her breakfast.

Meredith waits a few moments for her eyes to adjust to the relative gloom and tries to think rationally. If anyone's here, they're either going to be lying behind the raised vegetable beds, or in the boiler house, she thinks. They can't be down the well, as it's covered with metal mesh, and there are far fewer trees on this side, and she can see through them all.

'Come on, Pops. Let's do the veg patch first.'

The dog does as she's asked and follows Meredith as they begin to walk around the two raised beds. Or at least they are until Meredith's foot hits something large and solid and she tumbles down, just managing to save herself with her arms, which take the worst of the impact.

'Ooof,' she says as all the air is forced from her lungs. She lies there for a moment, entirely still, shocked at how quickly everything came tumbling down. But then the dog is worried about her, sniffing her head and nudging her arm.

'It's all right, girl, I'm OK. Just winded and bruised,' she says, successfully pushing herself up to a sitting position and taking several deep, slightly painful breaths, reassuring herself that her body is still functioning. She looks around her and discovers she's tripped over the branch of a tree which had fallen in December. They've not got around to dealing with it yet. 'And a bit embarrassed, frankly,' she says to Poppy, whose muzzle is now draped over her leg. 'Silly Meredith, eh? I should have brought a torch...'

Poppy suddenly wrenches her head away from Meredith's ministrations, stands up and emits a long, deep growl. The dog is staring at the boiler house and looking back at Meredith every few seconds, as if she's trying to tell her something.

'OK girl, OK. I get the message. Let's... go and see,' says Meredith, her muscles screaming at her as she pulls herself up to standing, but her fear is apparently subdued by her pain. The sheer quantity of adrenaline surging through her veins means she feels ready for anything, and given that she'd found no cause for Poppy's growls on the other side of the house, she seriously doubts she'll find any here either.

And yet her throat tightens as they approach the outhouse. They don't have a lock for the door, and it's slightly open. Had she left it like that? Had Philip? She can't remember. The pump has been working ever since Damon fixed it when they moved in, and the boiler is past saving. Perhaps the wind has blown it open.

She walks up to it and pushes it open even further. It falls back against the wall outside with a bang. Philip has clearly had the WD40 out on the previously stiff hinge, she thinks, laughing a little at the frisson of fear that had passed through her when the door had hit the wall.

'What am I like, Pops?' she says, reaching for the light switch on the inside wall and flicking it down. The bulb springs to life, and Meredith sees with relief that the room is empty of human life.

It's when she's turned the light back off and is making sure the door is actually shut this time that she sees him.

First, a flash of grey. Then two legs, clad in something dark, walking slowly towards the front of the house. Her whole body tenses and for a brief moment, she's unable to move. And then in another instant she's unfrozen and running as fast as she can in his wake, Poppy still at her heels.

'Hello! Stop!' she screams between deep, rasping breaths. 'I can see you! I know you're there!'

Her eyes track the man across the garden, towards the boat dock. She's closing on him now, taking long leaping strides, vaulting flower beds, fallen branches and hibernating shrubs. Then her footing falters and she stumbles. She saves herself by grabbing hold of a tree. A second later, when she's regained her balance and is running once more, she sprints up to the riverside, her lungs burning.

She scans around, looking at both the water and the land, but he's nowhere to be seen.

She's lost him.

How is that even possible? He was *just here*. In between desperate gasps for air, she walks slowly around the edge of the island, checking the water for a swimmer, checking the trees for hiding places, checking for boats. Nothing.

'Pops. Can you see anything, Pops? Can you see him?' she says, urging the dog to detect a scent, to growl as she did before, to give the man's location away. But Poppy remains panting by her side, apparently uninterested now in anything other than when her owner might provide a bowl of water and her breakfast.

As Meredith turns and walks back to the house, she feels a growing sense of unease. If he isn't on the island, and he hasn't escaped it by boat, there are only two options. Either there's another hiding place here she hasn't considered – or he wasn't actually human.

* * *

'Are you really sure? Was it really a person? Not a trick of the light, or something?'

It's 10 a.m. and Meredith and Holly are in the kitchen at May Day House. Meredith texted her soon after the incident in the garden and was delighted when she offered to come over and keep her company. Her nerves are still on edge. She feels differently about the house this morning; where she previously felt relaxed and at ease, she now feels jumpy, like she's being watched. Holly's company is a welcoming, soothing balm.

'I *think* so,' replies Meredith, her earlier certainty that she'd seen a man running across the island fading a little. 'I mean, it was early...'

'Was it dark?'

'The sun hadn't risen, but the moon was bright.'

'But it still wasn't daylight. Twilight can play tricks on you.'

'Ye-es.' Meredith is trying hard to convince herself that what she saw was a mirage, and her tone reflects her thought process.

'Oh, Merry, it's shit, what you've been through. That graffiti, losing control of your boat in the fog, being alone so much of the time, and now this. It's not surprising you're seeing things, is it?'

Meredith stares at her mug of freshly brewed coffee, which she's hugging with both hands. 'No, I suppose not.' Her mind is full of thoughts, and not just about the strange figure she saw in the garden. She's thinking, as she often does, about her parents.

She misses them desperately, her father in particular, and especially when she's struggling with something. What would he say to her now? Keep on going, most likely. Yes. *Keep on going, girl, and ignore the bumps along the road. Keep on doing the things you believe in.* He was a practical man, her father, definitely not driven to flights of fancy. He'd been born into money and had essentially fallen into managing the family firm of solicitors, but in his spare time he'd always been making something, doing something practical. He had told her when he was approaching retirement that he'd always wished he'd been bold enough to turn his back on the law, to say no to his parents, and to plough his own furrow. As a result, he had always encouraged her to follow her dreams. He would have made an excellent professional craftsman. He was practical, not overly emotional, but very kind. He would definitely have laughed at her attempts at DIY around the house, but he would've cheered her on, too. And he would have loved May Day Island, and all that it represented. *Oh Dad*, Meredith thinks. *Why did you have to leave me so early? Just when I need you the most?*

'What is it, Merry?' Holly asks.

Her face has obviously been telling its own story, thinks Meredith. She takes a custard cream out of the open pack on the table and sits back in her seat.

'It's not just that recent stuff I'm dealing with,' says Meredith. 'I've had... a really, really bad few years.'

'Do you want to talk about it?'

Meredith takes a bite from her biscuit.

'Yes. Why not,' she says, chewing. 'My mind feels so full, I'm surprised you can't actually see it.'

'You do look like a woman with lots going on,' says Holly, pulling up a chair. 'Tell me what's up. Maybe I can help.'

Meredith raises an eyebrow.

'I doubt it. Do you have a cure for grief?' Her friend looks chastened. 'Look, I'm sorry, I don't want to make you feel bad. That's why I don't talk about this stuff with people. They just end up feeling awkward.'

Holly helps herself to a biscuit and smiles.

'I won't look awkward, I promise. I've been through a fair amount of grief myself, anyway.'

'I'm sorry.'

'It's OK. My mum died a decade ago. Dad died a couple of years ago. He had cancer. I cared for him until the end.'

Meredith stops eating.

'I'm so sorry, Holly, that's awful.'

'It was pretty shit at the time, yeah.'

'I probably sound really conceited, don't I? Like I'm the only person ever to go through grief.'

'No, you don't. And anyway, everyone always feels like that. Every person's experience of grief is unique.'

Meredith takes a sip of coffee.

'I guess so.'

'All I meant to say was, if you want to share, feel free. I've been through stuff, and you never know – talking about it might help.'

'Yes,' says Meredith, taking a deep breath. 'Yes. So... My parents died. Together. Without any warning. In a car crash.'

There's a momentary pause. Meredith sees Holly blink.

'Oh God. That's awful. When? Where? How old were you?'

'It was almost two years ago now. Can't believe it's been that long, to be honest. They were driving around Scotland in an RV, part of the big retirement adventure they'd been planning for years. The RV ended up stuck in some trees down a steep slope... Police couldn't tell us how it'd happened. It was late, it was dark, it was a quiet road... They don't know if any other vehicle was involved. But I just keep thinking about it, about how they must have felt when they'd hit and bust through the barrier, whether they were still alive when they hit the trees... how long they were alive for... whether they were in pain.'

'Jesus, that's awful.'

'Yes, what did I tell you? No one knows what to say when I tell them that.'

'So when you said you bought this place with your parents' money... it was with your inheritance?'

'Yes.'

'Wow.'

'Yes. Phil and I, we were doing fine financially, but we'd never have had the money for this sort of project without my parents' savings. I'm an only child, you see, so all the money came to me. And you know, after all the trouble we had trying to conceive, this felt like the new start we needed.'

'You're trying for a baby?'

Meredith gives a wan smile.

'Well, we were. We tried very hard, in fact. We ended up with IVF, and I even got pregnant a couple of times. But I miscarried. Never got beyond sixteen weeks. And I just... it was driving me to the brink, you know? I was exhausted, mentally and physically. So we've stopped trying, at least for now. This place, this house, I suppose is... a replacement dream. Something else to focus on.'

Meredith examines her new friend's expression. She wonders whether sharing her scars is the right thing to do. Will Holly avoid her in future, keen not to have to listen to these stories? Maybe. She lost several friends when they were doing IVF. Some of them just couldn't cope with the fact that she couldn't cope.

'Well, that sounds entirely sensible to me,' says Holly. 'I have no experience of IVF, but I do have experience of mental health struggles. It got very bad after Dad died. I was pretty... lost there, for a while. But I eventually pulled myself out of it, with the help of some pills from the doctor, a good friend and exercise. Specifically wild swimming. That's when I took it up, you know. And it worked like magic.'

Meredith puts her mug down.

'I'm so sorry to hear that it was so bad for you. I completely sympathise. And I'm so glad you found something that works for you.'

'Yes, it was a complete surprise for me, too. I've always loved running and walking, but I hated swimming at school. I was disgusted by the horrible chemical bath they used to make us wade through and the way the chlorine made my eyes sting. But swimming in the river, a place I have always loved... Well, it works, somehow. And it's not just the exercise, it's the cold. It shocks you, numbs you, reboots you, exhilarates you.' Holly puts her coffee down. 'Do you know something – you should try it.'

Meredith picks her coffee back up and takes a sip, hiding behind the mug, keen for Holly not to see her doubtful expression.

'I'm not a very good swimmer,' she says.

'Even more reason to do it, then. You're living by the water. You need to know how to swim confidently.'

Meredith puts the mug down.

'I know,' she says with a grimace. 'I do really. But I'm a bit... frightened of it, to be honest. What happened to Stuart has made me wary.'

'I get that, Merry. But he jumped in from a bridge. You would be going in from the side and staying close to the edge. The river's only really dangerous if it's in flood, or you're stupid.'

Why not? she thinks. *What have I got to lose?*

'OK, then. You win.'

'Brilliant. Let's finish these cuppas, and we can go to mine to get my stuff. I haven't swum yet today.'

'Today? Now?'

'Yes, why not? No moment like the present, is there? And you've had one hell of a morning. You need something to sweep it all away.'

* * *

It's so cold, Meredith can see her own breath every time she exhales. She's incredibly glad of the wetsuit Holly's leant her.

'Time to disrobe, Merry.'

She glances across at Holly, who unzips her Dryrobe and stands outdoors in three degrees Celsius wearing just a pink swimming costume, looking for all the world as if she's about to sunbathe in Cyprus in July.

'Really?' Meredith says, pleading, looking down at Poppy, who's sitting by her feet, and looks just as doubtful about the predicament her owner has found herself in.

'Really. Come on. Just do it. Don't think about it too much.'

Meredith exhales with force and pulls the zip down. The Dryrobe she's borrowed tumbles down around her feet.

'Right. Great. Well done. Now, let's get in the water quickly. You don't want to hang around too long.'

Yeah, no shit Sherlock, Meredith thinks. *I'm freezing my arse off here*. She looks down at the muddy, fast-moving water next to the bank.

'Is it clean enough to swim in? You hear these stories...'

'Yeah. I mean, it's a bit grim up in central London, but around here it's not too bad. I've never got ill from it, anyway.'

Despite her friend's reassurance, she considers running as fast as she can to get away from this moment. And yet something stops her, and she dips a toe in. It's so cold her nerves can't really process it. It just feels shocking. Then she hears a splash and sees that Holly is in the river next to her and swimming, her arms making rapid circles, her face pink, her eyes bright. Then Poppy follows, her four legs paddling like mad beneath the water.

'Come on, slow coach. Come on.'

Bloody hell, Meredith thinks. *After all I've been through, what can a bit of cold water do to me?*

She steps in with her right foot first, feeling it make contact with the soft silty bottom of the river, which is about half a metre deep right by the edge. Then her other foot enters the water and she stands still for a moment, frozen, both literally and metaphorically.

'Come on. You need to get your shoulders under.'

Meredith nods, turns so that her back is facing the river, and lets herself fall backwards. She shrieks as the icy water envelops her, and then her arms and legs begin moving automatically, remembering the swimming lessons of her youth. She turns onto her front and kicks madly.

'Stay near the side. The flow is too fast in the centre,' says Holly, who is beside her. 'If you get in the really fast water, you can get this thing called flush drowning, where you keep spinning and can't get out. So, stay in the shallows.'

'You sound like you've got experience of that,' says Meredith, her teeth chattering, despite the wetsuit.

'Ha, sadly, yes. I was lucky to survive it. Someone threw me a life buoy and pulled me in.'

'Wow. That must have been scary.'

'Yep. So stay on the edges. But you're doing well. Keep kicking.'

'Should I do breaststroke?'

'Up to you. Just keep safe. I swim all year, but I avoid the crazy-fast water, when the river's red boarded. If you do fall into it by mistake, by the way – people do, all the time – don't fight it. You need to float and raise your arm to attract attention. The river is always busy. There's always somebody about.'

'Noted.'

'But you'll be fine. Stay close to the edge and just keep moving. You'll start to feel warm soon, believe it or not.'

Meredith does as she tells her, with Poppy by her side. As she does so, she examines her surroundings. There's ice hanging off the bare branches of the willow nearby, gulls are flying overhead and there are ducks swimming only a few metres away.

Suddenly, she begins to laugh. It starts small, just a chuckle, but then becomes a full belly laugh, and as she's laughing, the morning's stresses and strains and, frankly, the stress she's been feeling for months, seem to tumble out of her.

'There you go. What did I tell you?' says Holly, who's now doing backstroke upstream.

Meredith feels warmth spreading up from her feet, and within seconds her body is almost entirely numb. Except it can't be numb, she thinks, because she's so full of feeling, so full of joy.

'Thank you, Holly, thank you,' she says, grinning at two passing swans. 'Thank you so much for showing me how to do this.'

16

ELLEN

2 January 1944

'That's it, Lieutenant Quinn. One step at a time. You're doing really well.'

It's four days since the bomb fell on May Day Island, and the first time Ellen's been outside since then. She has extensive bruising, a sprained wrist and ankle and something akin to whiplash, but nothing more serious, and she's incredibly grateful for that. Rebecca is also feeling a lot better and is already sitting out beside the gazebo on the far side of the island in a deckchair, soaking up the weak winter sun. Captain Huntingford meanwhile is beside Ellen, helping her to convince her rebellious muscles to function normally and walk down the front steps. It was her idea that the two nurses should come outside.

'Fresh air will do you both good,' she'd said earlier that morning. 'It's a lovely day out there. Cool, crisp and clear. You both need to get out into it. There are blankets by the gazebo.' Ellen makes it to the bottom of the front steps and pauses to get her breath back. 'Well done, Lieutenant Quinn. Can you make your way across by yourself, do you think? I need to get back to ward duties.'

'Yes, I'll be perfectly fine, thank you,' replies Ellen, grateful that the senior nurse is leaving her. Captain Huntingford has been very kind and attentive since she and Rebecca were injured, but her style is rather dry and Ellen always feels as if she's being told off for being naughty at school. She welcomes an opportunity to be outside, away from her stiff ministrations.

'Very well. I shall come back to help you up in about an hour,' replies the matron, before walking back up the steps and closing the heavy oak door behind her.

Ellen breathes a sigh of relief and takes in her surroundings. It's certainly cold, and she's glad of the woollen coat she's been given to wear over her uniform. However, the sun is out and the sky is the most divine shade of blue. If it weren't for the skeletal trees and the dead roses around her, she could almost persuade herself it was a cool summer dawn.

It's then that she notices the group gathered to the right, next to the burned tree, the destroyed shed and the large crater, all the work of that single stray German bomb. She can make out Brian, their ferryman and caretaker, a teenage boy and several of the patients, who are all wearing slacks, shirts and heavy woollen V-neck jumpers. They are piling up objects from the crater and the broken shed – ready, she assumes, for ferrying over to the mainland for disposal. She decides to walk over to take a look, and to say thank you to Brian for finding her and helping her on the night of the air raid.

'Brian, hello,' she says, as she takes a few more tentative steps in his direction, before stopping with some relief.

'Oh hello, Lieutenant Quinn. How wonderful to see yer out and about. And Lieutenant Hanson. I see she's over there enjoying the sunshine.'

'Yes,' she answers, glancing at her friend, who is reading a novel. 'We're both feeling much better. And we have a lot to thank you for, Brian. You found us and made sure we had the help we needed. We are ever so grateful for that.'

'Don't be silly, lovey, I just did what anyone would do.'

'And I understand I have you to thank, Neil, for helping recover me from the garden after the bombing?' she says, looking over at Brian's son. Neil is around three inches shorter than his father, brown haired and bespectacled. He's avoiding her gaze by examining his feet, but lifts his head up briefly to address her.

'Hello, Lieutenant Quinn,' he says in a voice which doesn't quite know its register. 'Yes, that was me. I stay over here quite a few nights now, with Dad. When it's easier than going home.'

'Thank you so much. I was very glad you were there.'

Neil's face begins to colour.

'What are you up to today, Brian?' Ellen asks, sensing that Neil doesn't want to talk.

'Oh, we're just tidying up the bomb site with the help of some of the patients, so it's ready for filling in.'

'Excellent. Wonderful work,' says Ellen, smiling, hoping the young man can hear it in her voice. She has a great deal of sympathy with those who are shy with strangers. She used to be that way, too. 'It was a horrible night. A good thing to remove the evidence of it, I think.'

'Jolly nice to be appreciated,' says a familiar voice. Harry's voice. Her heart swells. She's been so worried about him.

Ellen looks over at the group of patients and sees him, propping himself up with a large wooden broom. She examines his face and body for any sign of the mental disturbance he was experiencing on the night of the bombing, but he looks perfectly fine. Better than that, even. There is colour in his cheeks, his smile is broad, and he has rolled his sleeves up to his elbows, showcasing the defined flexors in his arms. Ellen takes these in and feels heat rising through her body. In fact, she's fairly sure that she's blushing, and she brings her hands to her face to try to hide it.

'Oh hello, Flying Officer Hennessey. I didn't see you there.'

'I'll try not to take that as a slight.' He's smiling, but there's a tendon in his jaw that flickers every so often, and it's doing it now.

'I promise you I'm so fixated on trying to walk and not falling over that I simply didn't see you.'

'Yes, of course, I'm only making fun.'

'Flying Officer Hennessey was just telling me about the rose garden at his parents' home,' says Brian, noticing their discomfort. 'We are planning to replant this area after we've filled it back in. It turns out he's quite the horticulturalist. He has lots of useful tips.'

'Did he indeed,' says Ellen. 'I'll be sure to ask him when I have my own garden.'

'Brian is being too kind,' says Harry. 'I'm just doing as he tells me. And I'm only here on doctor's orders. We all are. Apparently doing useful work will aid our recovery.'

Ellen smiles and decides it's time to walk away. Talking to Harry with an audience is excruciating, and anyway, she should be content, she thinks, to find him well. She knows they can take their relationship no further. Even if her beloved job wouldn't be at risk if their relationship was revealed, she very much doubts his well-to-do, protestant, English family would welcome an Irish Catholic into their ranks.

She takes a few steps towards the gazebo before her foot finds the uneven edge of a paving stone. She grasps the air with her fists in a vain attempt to save herself, before tumbling forwards, landing on the hard surface with a thud.

'Lieutenant Quinn!' shouts Harry, running towards her. 'Are you all right? Can I help you up?'

Ellen assesses the damage, reflecting that it's the second time in a week that she's been rendered an inelegant sprawling mess on the ground. It's becoming a habit, she thinks, wryly. She can still move her limbs though, which is a blessing. More bruising, then, but nothing worse. Thank God.

Harry is holding out his hand, offering to help her get up.

'Thank you, that would be very helpful,' she says, accepting his hand and trying to smile in an attempt to mask her dented pride.

'Why don't I take you over to the gazebo to join Lieutenant Hanson?' he says, releasing her hand slowly and looking at Brian, seeking his approval.

'Yes, why don't you do that, lad,' he says. 'Be careful with her. She's accident prone, that one.'

Ellen tries to laugh, but her ribs are bruised and it hurts. She's been clumsy since childhood, and she's accustomed to people laughing at her. But she notices Harry isn't laughing either, and she's immensely grateful for that.

'Would you like to take my arm to steady yourself, Lieutenant Quinn?'

As she does so her hand brushes the bare skin on his forearms, and she feels a flash of electricity at her core. *Heavens*, she thinks. *So, this is what it is. This is what the priests told me I shouldn't do.*

'Thank you... yes,' she says, struggling to get the words out. She walks slowly, almost shuffling, partly because her whole body aches, and partly because she wants to make this moment last as long as she possibly can.

'I'm glad I bumped into you, Ellen,' he says, using her real name now they are out of anyone else's earshot. 'I wanted to apologise. For my behaviour. On the night of the air raid. It was... inexcusable. It wasn't me. I don't know how to explain it. It's like another person takes hold of me.'

'You really don't have to apologise.'

'I do.'

'No, you don't,' she says, pausing to rest about ten feet from the gazebo, where Rebecca is still engrossed in a novel. 'You don't, because I also acted out of character that night.'

'No, you didn't. You were evacuating people. You were doing your job.'

'Yes, I was... until I wasn't.'

'What do you mean?'

'I mean, I got to the steps that lead down to the basement, and I couldn't go down there. I fled, ran outside. That's why I was out here when the bomb fell. Rebecca was chasing after me.'

'Ah, I see.'

'Do you?'

Harry locks his eyes on hers and refuses to let go.

'Of course. Ellen, have you seen and heard things in this war that refuse to leave you?'

'Yes.'

'So have I. And that is why I'm here.'

'I am so ashamed. I'm a nurse. I'm supposed to be helping you.'

'You cannot control what your brain decides to do with the horrors it's seen, Ellen. I know that more than many.'

'I was on the *Maid of Kent*.'

There's a short silence, during which Ellen tries to focus on the chatter of the gardening team and on the sound of a barge making its way towards Kingston, and not on Harry's expression. She really should not be sharing her history with her patient.

'Oh, my darling girl.'

Ellen looks into his eyes for a moment and feels like he's glimpsing her soul. The magnetic pull between them threatens to overpower her. She breaks eye contact almost immediately, because it's all too much, too overwhelming. She feels that he is about to reach out and touch her face, and her cheek is almost burning with anticipation.

But he doesn't. He doesn't touch her. And he doesn't say anything, either. She returns her gaze to his face. His expression is hard to read.

'Harry?'

'I want to, Ellen... but I can't. We can't.' He looks like he's in pain. 'I want to, so much. I feel something for you I couldn't even imagine before I came here. But I can't.'

'Are you going to tell me that your loyalty is to the Air Force, Flying Officer Hennessey?'

Ellen starts walking away towards Rebecca, angry at what feels like a rejection.

'Don't go,' he says, grabbing hold of her hand. Ellen looks over at her friend at the gazebo, wondering if she has heard. Rebecca looks up at them for a moment, before returning her attention to her book. Ellen snatches her hand away.

'What if we...' she whispers. 'What if we... could wait... until after the war?' As she says this, Ellen knows there is absolutely no sign of the war ending. The Germans have even started bombing London again. It is far from over. *It might never end*, she thinks.

Harry looks like he might be about to cry.

'I'm married, Ellen.'

She feels as if she's been blindsided. Of all the things she had imagined he might say at this moment, she had never imagined this.

'You can't be. You'd have told me. Someone would have told me,' she says, flailing around, no longer able to control her body's reaction to this emotional assault. Why hadn't she seen this in his notes? Harry takes both her hands to steady her.

'I am. I married more than five years ago, Ellen, to a woman I thought I loved. But now I no longer love her and in all truth, she no longer loves me, but we have a child, and I have a duty towards her and our child that I cannot discharge. As much as I might desperately want to.'

A child. *He has a child.*

'Why didn't you tell me, when we were dancing at the party? I mean... how could you have let me grow to feel the way about you that I do, knowing that we can never be together?'

Harry doesn't answer immediately. It feels to Ellen as if someone has somehow syphoned off all of her hope. She feels herself begin to sink into the darkness, even as she's standing there facing him, in weak winter sunshine.

'Because I am sick and tired of horror, Ellen. In you I see light and I see joy and I see a potential for something pure and extraordinary, and I just couldn't bear to snuff that light out. I'm sorry. It's entirely my fault. I'm a fool... what can I say? I told you as much.'

Suddenly, Ellen cannot bear to be with him any more. She has to get away, to lick her wounds and come to terms with this new, hideous reality. Because he cannot be hers. He will never be hers. She meets his eye and summons all of the strength she has left.

'I must go. Captain Huntingford will be cross if I don't get to my deck chair soon.'

She begins to walk away, and this time he does not reach for her hand.

'See you soon, Lieutenant Quinn,' says Harry, his voice formal and loud, so Rebecca and the other men in the garden can hear him. 'I do hope your recovery is swift.'

Ellen can't bring herself to speak. Instead, she simply nods, and focuses on her step as she approaches the gazebo, refusing to turn back.

17

MEREDITH

15 January 2014

Meredith is woken by an unfamiliar sound.

'Poppy? Pops? Is that you?' The dog's snores, however, confirm that the noise is not coming from her.

'Merry? What is it?' says Philip, stirring from sleep. He sounds groggy, because he arrived back late from a flight the previous night and has only been in bed for five hours.

'Can you hear that?' she asks. 'That sound... it's like somebody's scratching at the window?'

They both listen for a moment.

'Yeah, I can,' he says, and she can almost hear his internal monologue reconciling itself to the fact he's going to have to investigate.

'I'll go.' Meredith swings her legs out of bed, puts on her slippers and walks the short distance to their bedroom window, which has a thick velvet curtain pulled across it. Within seconds, Philip is behind her, tugging on his dressing gown.

'Let me open the curtain,' he says, firmly. 'If there's someone there, I want to be the first person they see.'

Meredith is grateful. She has gone from asleep to hyper-alert in a matter of seconds, and her nerves aren't so much on edge as tumbling into the abyss.

Philip yanks the curtains open, but there's nothing out there but their dark, frosty garden and the river beyond.

'Nothing,' he says, pulling the curtains back across. Then the scratching noise starts up again.

'It sounds like it's outside our door,' says Meredith.

'Yes,' says Philip, running across the room and pulling their door open. But when they turn on the hallway light, there's nothing there either.

There's silence for a brief moment, and then the scraping and scratching returns.

'It's coming from upstairs,' says Meredith.

'I'll go,' says Philip, putting his slippers on at speed.

'I'll come too,' says Meredith, grabbing her dressing gown from the hook behind the door.

The couple run up the stairs, listening out for the sound as they go. One moment, it seems to be coming from a window, the next, the attic. But then it seems to settle on the first floor, and they set off down the corridor. They come to the first door on the left. The eerie scratching is getting louder.

'This one?' asks Philip. Meredith nods. He jerks the handle and the door swings open. Meredith switches on the light. But there's nothing alive in here, just two old wooden bed frames and some mouldering mattresses.

And anyway, the noise has moved. It's further down the hall. Philip and Meredith progress through the rooms in turn, throwing on the light in each but finding nothing but old furniture, rubbish and generations of dust.

Then they come to the last door. The noise is now louder than ever.

'It's got to be this one,' whispers Meredith, and Philip nods in agreement.

She turns the handle and throws the door open and Philip hits the light switch. It's a child's bedroom, one she's been into briefly once, but decided not to return to any time soon. Meredith catches her breath. Just for a moment, she thinks someone is playing a practical joke on her. Why *this* room? She came to May Day Island to try to get over her desire for a child, after all. There's a small Victorian walnut wardrobe on the right-hand side with its door hanging open; a wooden cot in the left-hand corner that was probably once white but is now a sickly shade of yellow; a pine rocking chair missing several spindles; and sundry children's toys lying on the floor – some tin soldiers, a spinning top, some marbles and a teddy bear that is missing an eye and a fair section of its fur.

'Noth—'

Philip does not have time to get the word out. There's a huge clatter as several objects tumble out of the wardrobe, followed by a flurry of movement as something races behind them, jumps off the pile and then scurries past them and out of the door.

It's a rat. A large one.

'*Jesus*,' shouts Philip. He's taking huge breaths, Meredith notices. He's probably as scared as she is. 'I can't believe one rat can make so much bloody noise.'

'Maybe it's not just one of them?'

Philip nods.

'Yes, you're right. We obviously have a rat problem.'

Great, thinks Meredith. *Another problem to add to our list.*

'I'll call the pest controller when they open,' says Meredith.

'Good plan. And in the meantime... Let's get a bloody coffee...' says Philip, pulling his wife into his arms. 'What a shocking way to wake up, and on such an important morning, too.'

The planning meeting that will decide whether they are able to develop May Day House convenes in just four hours. The fact they've both been scared out of their wits on the morning of the meeting that'll decide their fate is not lost on Meredith. Sometimes, she thinks God is having a laugh at their expense.

'I thought we had a bloody ghost there for a bit,' Philip says, doing his best to laugh. And Meredith does her best to do the same. Because if she tries to find this whole situation funny, her growing suspicions about the figure she saw running across the island might not be so unnerving, she thinks.

Except it doesn't really work. Because that was no rat she saw near the boiler house, she's pretty damn certain of that.

And maybe, she thinks, it's not God who's laughing at them, but something or someone else entirely.

* * *

'What room is it?'

It's four hours later and they're at the council offices in Walton-on-Thames. The meeting of the planning committee is about to start, and Meredith's mouth is dry. They've been waiting for this moment since November. She knows that Elinor and the other members of the local residents' committee have the date in their diaries too, keen to see whether their indignant representations have worked.

The consultant she and Philip used to draw up the plans has assured them that the hearing should be a formality; their plans, she has told them, are well within accepted guidelines and necessary to maintain the fabric of an important local building. Meredith, however, is not so sure. And neither, she suspects, is Philip, although he has been talking a good talk for some time, refusing, like her, to accept that their big dream is in danger of ending before it's even really begun. A bit, she thinks, like their individual responses to their collective fear this morning: they had both been petrified by that noise, but they hadn't really spoken about why, not even after they'd found out its cause.

'Room twelve.'

Philip nods. The building is square, was built in the 1960s and has a large courtyard in the middle. He checks the signs and they set off to the right, following the corridor past a row of metal radiators covered in cream peeling paint. They find the room easily and walk into a large rectangular space in which a large oblong table is set up with seats for about sixteen people. Most of these seats are already taken by councillors. A further layer of seating is laid out around the walls of the room for visitors, and Meredith and Philip head for the stretch of these which is not taken, noting that Elinor and her husband are seated along the opposite wall. She is wearing a knee-length figure hugging red dress and pearls, as if she's planning to head off to a wedding reception later. Her husband – the man who had met them at the door when they'd visited the house, but not introduced himself – is wearing a grey suit, a blue striped shirt and a red tie with some kind of crest on it. They are both in conversation with a gaggle of people on either side of them, who Meredith assumes are fellow members of the residents' committee.

'Nice of them to come and support us,' says Philip wryly.

'Spectres at the feast,' says Meredith, taking a seat next to him.

'They might lose, Merry.'

'Yes, they might,' she says, without any actual belief that this statement might be true.

She inhales sharply through her nose and twiddles her thumbs. She has so much nervous energy circulating, and she has no outlet for it. She feels nauseous too, and her palms are sweaty.

Meredith decides to lose herself in her thoughts, to try to take herself away at least momentarily from this uncomfortably full, stuffy room. She considers their journey to this point.

First, of course, there were the miscarriages. She felt like she'd lost a part of herself with each one. And then, her parents' death. Her grief for them was and still is gut-wrenching, anchor-severing, life-changing. And then, when the dust thrown up by that had not so much settled but had at least begun to clear, there had been that glorious sunny day when she'd surprised Philip with the viewing of May Day House. It had been love at first sight for her, the magical island seeming to soothe both her broken heart and her broken body. And then there had been feverish late-night pillow talk about a transformed May Day House, attracting the creative and the wealthy for retreats, bespoke health breaks and perfectly hosted weddings and events. The possibilities had energised her, restored her, and Philip had shared her joy. They'd been more united about their plans for May Day Island than anything; even, she thinks, their hope for a child. Yes, May Day had given them both something to live for, something to look forward to, something to cling to.

And yet in the three months since they took possession of the house, those hopes have dissipated. Slowly at first, but now it seems to Meredith that they fall away in great wads every single day, along with their savings, which are seriously dented. Because no matter how clean and tidy she makes the house, the fabric of it – the plumbing, the electrics, the heating – remain ancient and unsafe.

They'd both seriously underestimated how much money and energy it would cost to bring the house back to life. This aside, they've known all along that without this planning permission, they will not be able to secure a business loan to help them fix these problems and furnish the house to the standard required for visitors. And they certainly know that today's result will either make their dream a reality or signal its end.

Meredith can't bear the thought that it might end, because so much of her is riding on it. Her sanity, for one thing. Her future, too. If she doesn't have the house to focus on, she will have to return to her old job and give up a part of herself she has only just discovered and is actually growing to like. Her father would have loved this part of her. And yes, there have been a few unsettling experiences at the house recently, but she is certain that they're merely a result of her tiredness, some local louts, her already fragile mental state and this viperous local residents' group. She is determined that her body and mind will not succumb and their undoubtedly jealous neighbours won't win. They can't win. They just can't. She won't let her dreams die.

'Are we all present? Good. Let's proceed.'

Meredith looks over at the further end of the oval table and sees a steely-haired woman speaking into a microphone. Her deep, confident voice ushers in quiet, as the visitors sitting against the four walls of the room stop talking to each other and listen.

'Welcome to the council planning committee meeting for January 2014. I'm Sheila Hughes, the chair of the committee. I call everyone's attention to the agenda for this morning, which has been made available to everyone via the council website. Let's turn to the first item…'

Meredith tunes out as the committee discusses absences, substitutions and declarations of interest, and spends twenty minutes debating, and finally giving permission for, the demolition of an old pub to make way for the building of a block of flats. In fact, it's so gloriously irrelevant to her own precarious world that she's lulled into a false sense of security.

'Next on the agenda, we have the proposed development of May Day Island,' says the chair.

Meredith gasps so loudly people look her way, and Philip grabs her hand and clasps it.

'This one has been called in due to objections from the local residents' group. Now, has everyone received a copy of the planning officer's report?' No one says anything, but there's shuffling from all four corners of the room as everyone flips through the documents they've been given. 'Good. Let's get started.'

* * *

The sky is a steely grey, and the waves on the river's surface are being steam-rolled by a strong sweeping wind, denting their peaks. Meredith looks up at the dense clouds and wonders if it might snow. If so, it will be their first snow on the island. And if the local residents' committee has anything to do with it, perhaps also their last.

'Can you hand me the rope?' asks Philip, his voice as icy as the weather. He's not angry with her, of course, but he is undeniably angry. His whole body is alive with it.

'Yes, here you go.'

'Hop in then.'

Meredith does as he asks. As they move away from the bank, the freezing wind whips at her face, blasting her hair into her eyes, nose and mouth. She tugs it aside so she can see how Philip's doing. The current is strong, the result of insistent rain for more than a week, and he's fighting it with every muscle and sinew. His expression is a grimace. She wonders if he sees Elinor's smug, victorious face every time he pulls those oars back; whether he's imagining yanking one oar out and battering her with it. Frankly, Meredith would very much like to do that, too. That woman's crowing expression when the council rejected their plans was so incendiary that Meredith had considered thumping Elinor there and then. There was something about seeing someone delight in your own agony that did that to a person, no matter how passive you might usually be.

As the island mooring nears, Meredith wonders what Philip is thinking. They barely spoke in the car, beyond a few choice expletives and a perfunctory conversation about whether they had enough food in the fridge for lunch. It was clear they were both still too angry and needed time to formulate their thoughts before discussing them.

He'll be feeling dented but defiant, she thinks. How could he not be? That's how she feels, and they are always on the same page on things like this. And yet, he's been so different lately, so strange. It's an unsettling feeling, discovering there are parts of him she neither knows nor understands.

Her personal view is that they've come too far to give up now. It'll take longer, they'll have to adjust their plans a bit and they'll probably have to find other sources of money, but she is certain that they'll still be able to make a go of it. They *must* make a go of it, in fact. Backing out now would be letting that awful woman win.

'Can you hold onto the edge, Merry? I'll get out and tie us up.'

'Sure.'

Philip ties the ropes taut, tests their strength with a jolt, and then holds out his hand to Meredith. She takes it and steadies herself, and by the time she's pulled her coat down and secured her hood, he's already walking towards the house. She follows him along the path, pulling her zip up as high as it will go to try to keep the chill out. It's not the weather for talking out here, and she's quite glad they have enough logs in for a fire. They need to recharge their batteries, she thinks, walking through the door which Philip is holding open for her. Warmth and a comfortable seat will make this conversation much easier. That will make all the difference.

'Shall we go into the sitting room?' she says as soon as she's hung up her coat and made a fuss of Poppy, who came running as soon as she heard the key in the lock. 'I swept out the fireplace yesterday.'

Philip doesn't reply. Meredith assumes he's gone to the toilet and sets about lighting the fire in the sitting room anyway. She kneels down in front of the fireplace and builds a pile of logs, making sure to place a solid buffer of kindling – twigs she's gathered from the garden – beneath, just over the firelighters. She's holding a match to one of these when Philip walks into the room.

'Oh, there you are,' she says. 'Would you like a coffee? And I think we've got some chocolate in the kitchen. I could bring that and we could—'

'I think we should put the island up for sale, Merry.'

Meredith abandons what she's doing and springs up to her feet. Philip's fists are clenching and releasing every second or so, as if he's spoiling for a fight.

'What? We can't. We mustn't. We can't give in to those bastards.'

'We've lost, Merry. We have lost. We can't keep going here. And this house' – he waves his arms around at the room, at its peeling wallpaper, its cobwebbed corners, its disintegrating furniture – 'it's going to destroy us. Can't you see it? Can't you feel it? I mean, you know it much better than me, you've been here the whole time, and I can see the toll it's had on you.'

Meredith walks towards him, because it's clear he doesn't want to come and sit down by the fire.

'What do you mean?' she says, stopping before she gets close enough to touch him. His anger is like a forcefield.

'I mean, you're not well. You've lost weight. You're exhausted, and you're... making strange decisions. You went out in the fog on your own on a wild goose chase, Merry. You could have died. You'd never have done that before. You'd never have taken that sort of risk.'

Meredith fights the clarity of the memories that refuse to be forgotten: the figure of the man in the garden who she'd pursued and lost; the voice that called for help in the mist. Was she imagining things, perhaps? Was she losing her grip on reality? Or was she, perhaps, just getting a grip on reality? Was she just getting braver?

'Don't be ridiculous. I'm fine. I'm just losing weight because I'm doing so much work around here and I can't be bothered to cook. I'm fine. Better than fine. I love this place. You know that.'

Philip shakes his head.

'No, Merry, you're not fine. I love you, I know you, and you're not fine. Something has changed in these past few months, and I don't like it. I thought coming here would make things better, distract you from the grief... but I don't think it's working. We were supposed to spend more time together here, but you don't stop when I get back from work. You spend all of your waking hours cleaning and clearing or buried in that bloody notebook. You're not giving yourself time to heal. This isn't the cure we hoped it would be. And now we have a solid sign that we need to cut our losses and run. We can't get a loan, and we can't fix the house enough to make proper money from it. It's over. We've got to go now.'

Meredith can't believe what she's hearing. This is the man who'd wanted to carry her over the threshold of the house in triumph. How had they come to this, in just three months? How was that possible?

And then she looks more closely at him. There are tears in his eyes. Is it because he thinks their dream is over? Is it because he's genuinely worried about her? Or could it be because he feels he's failed her? *Yes,* she thinks, *that might be it.*

'It's not your fault, Phil.'

He sniffs and wipes his nose with his sleeve.

'Isn't it?'

Meredith moves closer, but something stops her from embracing him. He doesn't look like he wants to be touched.

'No, it isn't.'

'But... all of that money. Your parents' money...'

The money is definitely running out. He's right about that. Their mortgage is several thousand every month, despite the large deposit they put down, and the extra cash they'd earmarked for immediate repair has disappeared on fixing the roof and the water heater. If they're going to have any paying guests, they'll need to refurbish a couple of bedrooms, a bathroom, the kitchen and a sitting room at a bare minimum. She's not sure if they have enough money to pay for that, even if they do it all themselves.

'We haven't lost it,' she says. 'It's in the house. We just need to keep pushing, working. We can submit other plans. We'll get there.'

'Yes, the money is in the house. That's why we need to sell, to get it back, before it's too late.'

Philip looks defeated, and Meredith is so worried about how he must be feeling that she almost misses what he's just said.

'What do you mean, too late?'

A flicker passes through Philip's face. It's gone within a second, but it bothers Meredith, because she's never seen it before. She can usually read her husband very well. What is there he's not telling her?

'I just mean I want us to sell the house before it makes us both ill,' says

Philip after an awkward silence. Then he approaches her with his arms outstretched. She goes along with the hug and rests her head on his shoulder, but it's lucky he can't see her face, because it's telling a very different story. She's confused by what seems like a sudden change of heart, not to mention personality. Where has his fight gone, she wonders. And why is he so worried about her, when she's doing absolutely fine? She's been swimming every day, and each time she plunges into the icy river, she feels her depression lift. He knows this. He goes for a run, and she swims. It's become a new habit.

'Why don't you come and sit by the fire with me,' she says into his ear, and he releases her and follows her to the two armchairs, beyond which the newly ignited fire is now taking well. Poppy comes to join them, curling up at Meredith's feet. They sit in silence for a moment, watching the flames licking their way around the seasoned logs, seeking out vulnerability in their armour. 'I'm worried about you too, as it happens,' she says.

'Me? Why?'

Meredith doesn't look at Philip. Instead, she turns her head and looks out of the window to her right, just in time to see a solitary snowflake floating down on the other side of the glass, coming to rest on the sill beneath.

'You never really wanted to buy this place, did you?' she says, voicing this nagging worry for the first time.

'Don't be ridiculous, Merry. We both signed the deeds. I wouldn't have done that if I didn't mean it.'

'Yes, I know. But you were doing it for me. But I should have thought. It's Stuart, isn't it? Being close to where he died. I can see it's weighing on you.'

'Have I even so much as spoken about him since we moved in here?'

'No. But that's my point. I think it's bottling it up that's eating away at you. Before we moved here, you seemed fine about it. I mean, it's been years. But now you look... like you're struggling with it. Are you feeling guilty about it again? You shouldn't. You weren't there and couldn't stop it. And I've always said, I think these things are better spoken about. If you'd only go to counselling...'

'I can't go to counselling, Merry, you know that. If they diagnose me with anything I'll lose my pilot's licence.'

'Only if you're depressed, Phil, and only temporarily then. You know that. I think it would be worth it for you just to work through how you feel...'

'Merry, seriously, there's nothing to work through. I'm fine. Honestly.'

Philip is smiling at her now, but it isn't quite reaching his eyes.

'OK. Fine. It's not Stuart. Then what is it? The Phil I know would never capitulate to those ridiculous people today. He'd fight them, come up with another plan, keep going.'

'Isn't being worried about you enough?'

He's not telling her the truth, and it's infuriating. She turns to look out of the window again, and she sees that more and more flakes of snow are falling, and that the upper side of the bough of the nearest tree is almost the same colour as the sky.

'We can take another look at the plans for the house, can't we? Get more advice and resubmit,' she says, focusing on the gently falling snow and not her husband's face, which seems new somehow, and genuinely baffling.

'I was looking at our bank account yesterday,' Philip says, leaning down to stroke the dog. 'After our mortgage payment, the bills and the food and stuff, we haven't got much left.'

This is a familiar refrain. Philip has always complained that his salary is too low. The pilot workforce at his airline voted fifteen years ago to accept a far lower salary scale for new joiners. It hadn't been any skin off their nose, of course. They were all right, Jack. But it meant that there were two grades of pilots at the airline, those who'd managed to get in before the change, and those after, and Philip, of course, was one of the latter. His pay would never reach the heights of the captains he flew with, and that fact infuriated him. And then, of course, there was the fact that Meredith had outearned him easily. Given the antisocial hours he flies and the extreme pressures of recurrent training, she knows he feels he's worth more than he's paid.

'It's enough for now. We are coping.'

'But I don't want us to cope. I want us to live. I want us to succeed, to laugh, to enjoy the fruits of our labours. After all we've been through – you in particular, with your mum and dad, and the lost pregnancies… I dunno, Merry, this just doesn't feel like the dream we'd hoped it would be. Does it?'

Meredith tears herself away from the hypnotic, silent falling snow and looks him straight in the eye.

'I don't know what's wrong with you, Phil. Of *course* it is. We always knew it was going to be hard, didn't we? But everything worth having needs work. This is just one stumbling block. It's a big one, yes, but it's not insurmountable. We can do it together. Can't we?'

'We can probably do it eventually, yes. But at what cost to us both, mentally and physically, Merry? Is that worth it?'

Now it's Meredith who's feeling tearful. The very idea that they should give up on their dream feels gut-wrenching to her. She just can't compute it.

'Of course it bloody is. This is our new start. My new start. This is my opportunity to leave the rat race and do something practical, something creative, something my dad would have loved and been proud of. And yes, I have been through hell, but this place is the very opposite of that. Every time I wake up here I look out at the nature that surrounds us, at the peace and tranquillity and the ever-changing view and thank God we bought it.'

'Even when it's freezing cold, the windows leak, you're here alone for days at a time and we have no chance of doing building work for at least six more months, and maybe far longer?'

'Yes. Even then. And anyway, I'm not alone. I have Poppy now.'

'Yes, and she's lovely, but she's not a great guard dog. What if that person comes back and does more than just graffiti the boat? What if whoever was trying to lure you into the river in the fog does something more than just call out?'

'We still don't know it wasn't a real emergency,' she says, and as she says it, doubt leaks further into her mind about what happened that morning. She has clung to the very real fear in that man's voice, but they found no boat, no body, no sign of him afterwards. Might it have been someone wishing her harm? And if so, might that person also have been the figure she saw on the island the other week? She still hasn't told Philip about that. She doesn't want him to think she's seeing things.

'Yes, well. Who knows. But Merry... I know you love this place. I love it too. But I just have this feeling that it's... going to destroy us,' he says, staring at the fire. 'I think we should sell it and move on, find somewhere else to renovate, somewhere else we both can see a future...'

'You can't see a future?' says Meredith, her words catching in her throat.

'No... that's not what I meant.'

'Can you really not see a future here, with me?'

'Of *course* with you, Merry. Just not... here. Not now. Too much has happened.'

'All that's happened is that we've had planning refused. It was our first attempt. There could be many more. Come on, Phil. *Come on*, be with me. Tell me what's really up with you. I love you and I want you to let me in. I can't bear this. This isn't us.'

And with that, Meredith starts to cry. She feels like she's at risk of losing both her husband and her dream, and the thought of that makes her inconsolable. Within seconds, Philip is with her, his arms around her.

'Oh my darling, I'm sorry. Please, don't cry. I didn't mean it,' he says, kissing her cheek, her hair, her neck. 'I honestly didn't. I'm just tired too. And shocked by this morning. I really thought we had it in the bag. I will... recover. We will think of another plan. We will keep the house.'

'Do you really mean that?' she says, pulling away from him. 'Have you changed your mind? You now think we shouldn't sell the house?'

Philip kneels in front of her. He takes both of her hands.

'Yes. I was shocked by today's result, really shocked. But hearing you talk about how you feel about this place – I realise I was mistaken. I read you wrong. I'm sorry, Merry. I didn't mean to cause you pain. I want the very opposite. We *should* keep the house. We'll make it work, somehow. We have to.'

Meredith leans forward, so that their noses are almost touching.

'Listen to me, Phil. Really listen. I am telling you the truth. I want to stay on May Day Island. And I want you to stay with me here, too. You're my best friend. We can face anything together. Anything that life throws at us. OK?'

'OK,' says Philip, leaning in to kiss her. 'Message received and understood.'

Then he takes hold of her arms and pulls her up, lifting her so that her legs are wrapped around him. He turns slightly to steady himself, giving Meredith a view of the garden, which is now draped in ice. As she leans in to kiss him, her right eye sees, just for a split second, a pale face at the window. But then she blinks, and the face is gone.

'What the...?' she says, releasing her grip on him, lowering herself down and running to the window, before scanning the snow-covered garden for any sign of human life. But there isn't any. There are no footprints in the virgin snow, aside from those of a robin perched on a low wall, which seems to be looking straight at her, as if it's wondering who on earth she is, and why she has a right to be on the island too.

'What is it?' says Philip, joining her and slipping his arm around her waist.

'Oh, nothing.' *There's no way I'm going to tell him what I thought I saw now*, she thinks. *He already thinks I'm unstable.* 'I just saw that beautiful robin.'

'Oh. Yes. He looks perky, doesn't he?'

'Yes. And such a beautiful contrast with the snow.' *I didn't see anything*, Meredith thinks. *It was just the snow and a trick of the light.*

'God, I love snow,' says Philip, his voice so much lighter. They are back on track. This chat has really helped. 'It brings out the child in me. Shall we go out and roll around in it like little kids?'

'Yes, why not,' says Meredith, forcing down her instinctive fear. Because she refuses to be frightened. She loves this place, and she loves Phil. And her dreams are still within her reach.

Yes, she thinks. *I refuse to be frightened by anything.*

18

ELLEN

5 January 1944

It's a bright, cold January morning, the kind that draws people outside to worship a teasing sun. Ellen is one such person. She's standing at the bottom of the front steps of May Day House, her eyes closed, the gentle warmth seeping into her skin.

She's praying it will heal her, both inside and out. It's nearly ten days since the bombing, but less than a week since Harry told her about his wife. Her bruises are still colourful, but her whiplashed muscles have finally let go, and she is much more mobile. Her emotional injuries, on the other hand – the damage to her heart, her soul and her armoury of hope – will take far longer to heal.

Rebecca returned to her duties this morning, and Ellen will do the same tomorrow. The sight of such glorious weather on her final day of recovery has persuaded her to don her woollen cape and some leather gloves so that she can wander around the grounds, spotting the first signs of spring. And there are plenty: in the flower bed to her right, she can see shoots of crocuses breaking the soil; the fragile first snowdrops are flowering beside the water's edge; short darts of bright green beneath the trees signal the eventual arrival of crowds of daffodils. Spring is her favourite season, and although it is still some way off, these signs of the glory that awaits them is the tonic she desperately needs. She needs to believe that things will get better, that her soul's dark night will end eventually.

She strolls around the perimeter of the island, stopping to enjoy the serenity of a solitary swan at the side of the house, before reaching the back. It's here she finds Brian. He's just coming out of the pump house.

'Oh, hello, Lieutenant Quinn,' he says. 'Nice to see yer out again. How are yer getting on?'

'Much better, thank you. How are things with you?'

'Well, I'd be better if we could fix the pump. I've been at it for ages this morning and I still can't get it to do my bidding.'

'Oh. We don't have any water?'

'Well, we have some reserves in the tank, but we'll run out soon if we don't kick it back to life. I've put a call in to an engineer in Guildford, but he says he won't be able to get here until tomorrow.'

'So we could be without water tonight?' Ellen is thinking about the knock-on impact for the patients and the nursing staff. She experienced water shortages when she was in Egypt, and it made her role so much harder. Cleanliness is such a vital part of their work.

'Well, running water, anyway. We have the well, as yer know,' he says, pointing to the circular brick well with the tiled roof behind her. 'If we need to, we'll have to do it the old-fashioned way.'

'Oh. That sounds like hard work.'

'Yer, it will be. But needs must.'

Ellen considers telling Brian that she has a passing acquaintance with water pumps, from her time in Cairo, but reasons that her scant knowledge will be nothing compared to his own experience, and so thinks better of it.

'Well, good luck with it.'

'Enjoy the walk, Lieutenant Quinn.'

'Thank you.'

Ellen continues walking around the side of the house until she reaches the area where the bomb fell. She spots Neil, Brian's son, who's getting rid of the last remnants of the old shed.

'Hello,' she says as she approaches, keen not to startle the teenager, who seems very involved with his work. Despite her forewarning, he turns sharply and seems to do a little jump. 'Oh, I'm sorry. I know you're busy...'

'No, it's all right, miss,' he says, his face the colour of beetroot. Bless him, he's a shy one, thinks Ellen.

'You're doing a great job, Neil.'

'Thank you, miss,' he says, staring down at the ground.

'Well, I'll head off and leave you in peace,' she says, feeling about as awkward as he is.

'Right you are,' says Neil. 'Mind how you go, miss, over the uneven ground... and don't stay out too long. They say it might snow later.'

Ellen looks at the sky, which is still cobalt blue.

'Are you sure?'

'Yes, Dad heard it on the wireless.'

'Goodness. Well, thank you, I'll make sure I'm inside long before any clouds come our way.'

* * *

As much as Ellen had doubted it, Neil's forecast proves to be correct. The sky turns steely grey by mid-afternoon, and by early evening a thick layer of snow has settled over the island. She spends the afternoon reading and writing in her room, watching the flakes fall and the winds cast them into flurries, before deciding, as the light fades, that it is time to re-engage with the world. She is hungry, and it's supper time. She will go downstairs, she decides, rather than eating in her room tonight.

'Ellen, how wonderful to see you,' says Rebecca, the very minute she enters the staff dining room.

'And you too,' she says, embracing her friend. 'How was your first day back on the job?'

'Go and get your food, and I'll tell you.'

Ellen does as she asks. She goes up to the servery hatch and is presented with tonight's meal, which is some kind of pie – *cottage pie*, she thinks, with the meat eked out with the help of a great deal of root vegetables – and a side of cabbage. *When the war's over,* she thinks – *no*, if the war is ever over, she corrects herself – *I will* never *eat cabbage again.*

'So, tell me everything,' she says to her friend as she returns to the table and takes a seat next to a couple of male orderlies and several of the cleaning staff, who are all engaged in rapt conversation about the weather. Snow is always a cause for excitement to the British, she thinks.

'Oh, it was fine, mostly. Tiring. I'm exhausted now. But it's so much harder because of the water problems.'

'Oh, so Brian didn't manage to get it started again, then?'

'No, sadly. We shall have to wait until tomorrow, I think. In the meantime, we're on a roster at the well. We need enough water for bed baths and other ablutions tonight at the very least. And for drinking water too, of course.'

Oh, what the hell, Ellen thinks. *In for a penny, and all that.*

'You know, we used to have a water pump in Cairo. I had to help maintain it on occasion. I could have a look, perhaps?'

'Golly, Lieutenant Quinn, you are full of surprises.'

Ellen's eyes sparkle.

'I can't promise anything. I know almost nothing. But... I aim to please.'

'Well, if you could fix it you'd be in everyone's good books, let me tell you. Brian and Neil did the best they could and a couple of the other staff had a go in their breaks, but at the moment we are literally filling buckets. Any magic you can provide would be most welcome. But wrap up warm. It's Baltic out there.'

* * *

Ellen is wearing her woollen cape and a borrowed hat, scarf and gloves, but the icy wind finds its way in as soon as she walks out of the kitchen door. It's still snowing. The flakes seem bigger now, and they're filling crevices, piling up in corners, cementing canopies of leaves. She feels like she's being plunged into icy cold water.

As she runs towards the pump house, one of the hospital orderlies, a young man called Michael, scurries in the opposite direction carrying a bucket of water. He tries to smile in greeting but it turns out to be more of a grimace. She doesn't blame him. She hears the door of the kitchen slam behind him as she runs to the pump house, pulls the door open and lets it fall shut behind her. She sighs with relief that she is at least temporarily able to step out of the snow.

'Who's that?' says a very familiar voice.

'Heavens...' she says, walking down the corridor and into the pump room. 'Harry... What on earth are you doing here? Why aren't you inside?'

They are alone. She doesn't know how to deal with this. She has been relying on others being around to save her from herself.

'I really should be asking the same of you,' he says, standing up and wiping his hands with a cloth.

'I'm here to try to fix the pump.'

'And so am I. My family had one of these.'

'At your stately home?' she says with one eyebrow firmly raised. She decides she will try to be difficult, prickly, anything to get him to keep his distance.

'Yes, Ellen, at my stately home.'

'How charming.'

'Not really. It was for an old lake, which housed mostly dead fish, and the pump house provided a home to a colony of spiders. But I still preferred playing around with the pump more than I did spending time with my father. So, tell me, how do you know about water pumps?'

'Well, I worked in a field hospital in Egypt for a while, and we had one there that brought water up from a deep well. It was the only way we could keep our patients clean and hydrated. We all got very proficient at fixing it.'

'I see.'

'So, what have you found so far?' she says, determined to keep this professional, perfunctory. She cannot risk it turning out any other way.

'Well, I've checked the pipes, and there are no leaks. And the pressure gauge looks OK.'

'Have you tried the pressure switch?'

'No, that's a new one on me,' he says, with just a touch of umbrage. 'Why don't you have a look?'

'Have you got a screwdriver?' she asks.

Harry reaches into a box behind him and hands her one.

'Brian left his tools here earlier.'

'Good,' she says, kneeling down in front of the pump, Harry just a few inches to her left, leaning against the wall. Then she takes the screwdriver and bangs its handle sharply against a tube which sits just below the pressure switch. A second later, there's a spark and the pump springs briefly back to life, before spluttering and returning to silence.

'That was it. What did you do?'

'Hitting it causes the electrical contacts to knock together. I've basically just confirmed we need a new pressure switch. And unfortunately,' she says, standing up again, 'we don't have one of those.'

'Ah,' says Harry. 'That is a problem.'

They stand there in silence for a moment, listening to the wind whistle around the pump house. Ellen realises that she's no longer cold, despite the fact the pump house has no heating. She tries not to think about what that might mean.

'But maybe...' A shadow of a memory flickers, and suddenly Ellen knows what to do. 'I think we had something happen like this in Egypt and we did some kind of temporary fix. The pressure switch isn't working because the contacts are burned. But if we can file them, we might be able to make it work again, at least temporarily...'

'Right. So how do we file them?'

'Does Brian have a metal file in his kit?'

Harry turns around, bends down and rifles through the tool kit, emerging a minute or so later with a small abrasive sheet of metal.

'Yes, that might do it,' she says, taking it from him. Harry picks up his torch and shines it at the pump. Ellen sits down and removes the switch and peers behind it. She can clearly see that the contacts are burned. She leans in and files each one gently, hoping desperately that she doesn't break them completely in the process. When she's satisfied she's done as much as she can, she hands the file back to Harry and replaces the cover.

'Right,' she says, standing up and brushing dust off her cape and skirt. 'I reckon that might do it, at least until tomorrow. Shall we see?'

'I'll try turning it on,' says Harry.

Ellen nods and holds her breath. If this hasn't fixed it, then she's out of ideas. Harry flicks the switch. Nothing happens. Her heart sinks. But then there's a clunk and a chug and the machine's parts start to turn, slowly at first before gaining speed and rhythm. They can hear the tank refilling.

'You beauty,' he says, grinning at Ellen, who is doing her own, somewhat restrained, victory dance. 'You did it,' he says, stepping towards her and gathering her in his arms. 'You clever woman.'

And that's enough for Ellen. No one has ever told her she is clever, for a start, and more than that, she has never felt this alive near someone, never felt this level of joy.

All of her determination is undone. And whether it's that or just his beauty or his smell or this strange, intangible magic that encircles them that makes her do it, she doesn't know, but she does it anyway. She's kissing him, and he's kissing her back. And it doesn't matter that it's freezing cold or that the room is lit by one bare lightbulb or that they are sharing the space with God knows how many insects and rodents, this room is, just for tonight, the centre of the world for them both. Nothing else matters. Not even his wife.

'Are you sure, Ellen? Are you sure you want this?' he asks, his breath a tropical breeze on her skin. 'I can't marry you… I can't…'

'Yes,' she replies, more certain of this than anything. 'Yes.'

19

MEREDITH

18 January 2014

It's 10 a.m., and Meredith is in bed. She got up earlier to let Poppy out and grab some coffee from the kitchen, but it's still incredibly cold and the snow has turned to rain, so she's retreated to her bed, which is the only place in the house where she can be properly warm.

The truth is, though, it's not just about the warmth. It's also because her bed feels like a place of safety, somewhere she can hide from the world. She's still heavily bruised by the council's rejection of their renovation plans, and, frankly, from Philip's uncharacteristic response to it. His announcement that he wanted to sell the house had blindsided her, and his apparent change of heart soon afterwards still makes her uneasy.

He was home for a couple of days after that dreadful council meeting. He'd managed a brief moment of frivolity out in the snow, but mostly he'd spent his time on the island outside, tinkering with the boat, going for long runs along the towpath and garrotting weeds and trees that were unfortunate enough to be in his path. It was clear he needed space and somewhere safe to vent his anger and frustration. When he was with her he'd managed to smile and sound excited about the challenges that lay ahead, which now seemed set to include a revision of their plans for the house and a small-scale, focused restoration of a few rooms to let out on Airbnb, just to tide them over. However, she'd caught sight of his face when he didn't know she was looking a couple of times, and he'd looked far from excited. Frankly, he'd looked frightened.

She has decided to wait and see how he is after this current trip. He's in Kuala Lumpur this time. And so she is alone again, and unsettled. She's hiding in bed, rain hammering down on the roof which she is very thankful they had enough money to make waterproof, wondering how on earth she is going to fill her day. Despite her outward proclamations of determination, the council's decision has dented her enthusiasm for the enormous task she faces. She feels lethargic, her head aches and her every instinct is to retreat into her cocoon to heal. And perhaps, she thinks, that's no bad thing. Everyone needs a duvet day sometimes, don't they?

Determined not to leave her bedroom for the rest of the day except for toileting necessities, letting the dog out and food, she reaches over to her bedside table and checks her phone first. There's a message from Philip, who's about to head out for dinner with the crew. She imagines him in the sunshine, wearing those slightly garish shorts he'd bought for their honeymoon, striding out on the busy streets, heading to his favourite local restaurant, laughing at something one of the other crew has just said. The contrast between his life and hers seems particularly bleak at the moment.

To distract herself, Meredith pulls out the notebook she found upstairs. When she has the time, she reads it voraciously. It's a curious mix of the humdrum – lists like 'stamps, note paper, starch' and diary entries that read: 'Woke up at 6 a.m. ready for my 7 a.m. start. Slept fitfully. Powdered eggs for breakfast,' alongside, of course, the fascinating letters. Meredith assumes the nurse used the notebook to draft them before writing them up on proper paper. It clearly fulfilled many purposes for a busy young nurse who lived a regimented life with little time for navel gazing.

Meredith is slightly jealous of this mystery woman's sense of purpose and drive, although the insight into her childhood and the abuse at the hands of someone she should have been able to trust was truly shocking to read. She wonders if the nurse ever sent that particular letter. Her mother would have been shocked and distressed to read about that priest. Any mother would.

Meredith props herself up with several cushions and opens the notebook where she left off. She flicks through several pages of perfunctory diary entries until she finds a longer one. It describes an air raid on the area, and Meredith is both shocked and surprised to read that a bomb had fallen on the island, and that her mystery nurse was injured. She's relieved to find that there were no serious injuries, however, and she's just reading about her recovery and the clean-up efforts afterwards when her phone rings. Meredith sighs, even though there's no one but the dog to hear her. She doesn't want to engage with the world today.

She picks up her phone and sees that it's Holly. She hasn't seen her since before their planning permission was refused, and she realises that she could really do with talking to a friend about it all. Talking to Philip after his change of heart was like talking to a born-again Christian. He was a little over-zealous, as if he was trying to convince himself of what he was saying. She needs to talk to someone who isn't invested in this place, she thinks. She picks up the phone.

'Hi, Holly.'

'Hey, you. I wanted to say hi, to see how you're getting on, after the council meeting.'

'So you've heard, then?'

'The usual Chinese whispers. But I think I've got the gist.'

'Oh. Right. So yes, it was a disaster. They torpedoed us.'

'I heard. Look, are you free this morning? I could come over?'

Meredith feels her soul and her fatigue lift. She hadn't realised until now how much she needed a friend, and another baptism in the river might be the reboot she needs.

'Yes, that sounds wonderful. I'll see you in a bit.'

* * *

Holly and Meredith are huddled around the fire in May Day House. They're sipping from large mugs of steaming hot tea. Poppy is nestled on the floor between them.

'So, tell me what they said again?'

'They said the house and island were of historic interest and that any development outside the original footprint would risk changing the character of the site.'

'Oh, right.'

'I think it's just that so many locals complained, you know, the members of the residents' committee, and the guys who run the ferry and the boat hire business.'

'Oh, the Stirlings?'

'Yes, them. They're nice people. I mean, Euan saved me, didn't he? And we pay them to take Phil across to the mainland. But they don't want the competition from us trying to hire out boats here. They warned us they'd be objecting. They at least aren't being awful about it.'

'I see.'

'The worst bit was Elinor from the residents' committee's expression afterwards. It was like a parent saying I told you so.'

'*Jesus*, I can just picture her. She's horrible, that woman. She's campaigning to get the lads who live in the boats along the river moved on, you know, although there's nowhere for them to go. They'd be homeless otherwise. And they bought those boats, fair and square. That woman doesn't have a heart.'

'Yep. That sounds like her.'

'Just as well,' says Holly, grinning. 'So, Phil suddenly decided that he wanted to sell the house?'

'Yep. He just came out with it. He said he was worried about money. But we aren't going to be repossessed, or anything. We'll be OK. It'll just take longer and I might have to go back to work.'

'How long do you think it'll take now?'

'Oh, dunno. Maybe several years. Could be a decade. I honestly don't know. We can probably get something small-scale ready to go in a year, maybe. What I do know is I'm not giving up. This is my dream. Our dream. I'm not the sort of person who bails at the first sign of trouble.'

'Good for you,' says Holly, but with a look of concern.

'Thanks,' says Meredith, watching a log turn white, its structure consumed by fire. 'We were hoping to get a business loan off the back of the planning permission, to pay for the refurbishment of the house, to make it ready for weddings, business events, that sort of thing.'

'And without it?'

'Without it, we're looking at just opening up a few rooms for Airbnb guests, doing most of the refurb work ourselves. That would pay enough to stop me having to go back to my old job and we'd be able to afford the bills here. But it's not going to get us the big return we'd hoped for.'

'Do you have the savings left to do it? The smaller-scale work, I mean?'

'Yes, we've got enough left over, some of it from the pot my parents left me.'

'That's good, then.' Then Holly laughs. 'You know, I thought pilots earned a packet. That you'd be able to buy anything you wanted and be a lady of leisure.'

Meredith laughs too, and takes another sip of tea. She savours the warmth.

'Holly… I wanted to talk about something, actually,' she says, clearing her throat. 'Do you remember when you said about people seeing things on the island? Ghostly things?'

'Yep,' says Holly.

'Can you tell me more about that?'

'Oh, you don't want to be listening to local hearsay. It's all a load of bollocks, most probably.'

'Just tell me, Hol. I'd like to know.'

Holly looks at her quizzically. 'You want to hear scary stories about where you live?'

'Yes, well, I might have some of my own to add to the folklore.'

Holly's face snaps round to look straight at Meredith.

'Really?'

'Yes, really. I'll tell you about it in a minute. But before that, tell me yours.'

Holly shifts in her seat.

'OK. Well, back when I was a kid, some of the boys who'd been camping on the island told me they'd been scared witless by something they'd seen in the garden.'

'What was it?'

'They never actually saw anything, they said. But they heard someone walking around when they were in their tent, but when they came out, expecting to find someone, there was no one there. They packed up pretty sharpish after that, I think.'

'Is that the only thing you've heard?'

'No. The only other thing, and I promise the only other one, was more recent. Some guy who berths his posh boat at a marina my friend works at said he swore he'd seen some ghostly face looking out from one of the windows on May Day House.'

'Right,' says Meredith, her mouth suddenly dry.

'But those boys were probably off their heads on cheap cider and ripe for imagining all sorts of things. And that bloke in the boat was probably seeing a weird reflection, or something.'

Meredith nods.

'Yes, maybe.'

'So, don't keep me in suspense... what have you seen?'

'Do you promise you won't tell anyone? I don't want the island getting a reputation. No one will come and stay here if they hear about this, I'm fairly sure of that.'

'I promise.'

'Well. I think I saw a man... a figure of a man, anyway, he was the right shape, but I couldn't make out the details... in the garden.'

'Where?'

'By the pump house. I chased after him. Didn't see him up close. But he got ahead of me and seemed to disappear.'

'Oh. Could he have got into a boat? Or the water?'

'Maybe. But I didn't see anything. There was nothing in the water.'

'You can't be on all sides of the island at the same time, though, can you?'

'No, that's true... but I did look around pretty thoroughly.'

'He might just be a local chancer, though, right?'

'Yes, he might have been.'

Meredith ponders this. Could he have been a teenager looking for something to steal, or something to graffiti? *It's possible,* she thinks. *Possible.*

'Is that all?' asks Holly, her whole face a question.

'No. But I haven't seen anything else. I've just... heard things.'

'Like what?'

'Did I tell you about the man calling for help in the fog?'

'The time you had to be rescued by the Stirlings? Oh yes, I remember that.'

'Well, they never found anyone, did they? They never found the man who needed help.'

'So you think it was... a ghost?'

Meredith stifles a laugh. 'Yes, I know how mad that sounds.'

'A little, Merry, I can't lie,' says Holly, smiling. 'But I understand why you might think that.'

'Yes, it's just... odd.'

'Do you think there's a chance you might just be unsettled, you know, after the graffiti on your boat? And those rats you were telling me about?'

'Yeah. Yes. Maybe.'

Sitting here in the warmth with her friend and with her lovely dog at her feet, Meredith finds it hard to evoke the creeping, evolving fear she's been feeling over the past couple of months. Could it just be her imagination, she wonders, melding with her anxiety and the latent grief she hasn't really properly addressed? It might be that, mightn't it?

'There you go. I really don't want to think that my mentioning that silly local story about the boys in their tent has led you to think there's anything supernatural here. I don't want that on my conscience. Look, you love this house. And it loves you. There's nothing here to worry about aside from teenagers playing truant, rats, probably lots of bats and a whole lot of spiders. Don't let stupid rumours ruin how you feel about this place, Merry. You've been through so much already.'

Holly's warmth infects Meredith, seeing off the last vestiges of her fear. *Yes*, she thinks, *I've made a mountain out of a molehill here. All I'm dealing with is a collision of my fragile mental health, infuriating circumstances and complete coincidence. And I need to stop this now, before it takes me over*.

'Thanks so much, Hol,' she says, finishing off the remains of her tea. 'Thank you. I feel so much better now.'

20

ELLEN

10 January 1944

'Can you please go and collect Flying Officer Hennessey, Lieutenant Quinn?'

Ellen desperately does not want to be in this room, and she absolutely does not want to go and get Harry, because she knows what's coming. She was present when the doctors – Major Cole and his junior colleague, Captain Joyce – decided to take this particular course of action. She has seen several other patients endure it, and she has no wish to have Harry put through it too. Not that she has a choice, of course. This is the army, and she will do as she's bidden.

Ellen leaves the doctor's office and walks up the stairs to the room Harry shares. She finds him in the middle of the room, seated at a table, playing solitaire. The other men are either sleeping or outside taking some exercise, supervised by one of the orderlies.

'Harry,' she says, quietly, so no one hears her using his Christian name. 'Harry, I've been asked to find you and bring you to Dr Joyce's office.'

'Oh really? Why?' he asks, standing up swiftly and leaning towards her for a kiss, before remembering where he is, and thinking better of it. Ellen looks around to check no one has seen and then blushes, because she would give anything for it to be last night again, for them to be alone and able to touch and possess each other. She has been going about her duties robotically this morning, all the time replaying what happened in her head. Was the heat inside her, the animalistic desire she felt – was still feeling – how other people felt when they were in a relationship? If so, that scares her a little. People usually seem so under control, she thinks; it's quite worrying to think they might all be feeling like her right now, underneath.

She had no idea she was capable of feeling like this. She has shut out men and her body's instincts for such a long time that she'd thought she was destined to be numb forever. But Harry has changed all that. Now her desire for him is consuming every spare moment she has, and every nerve in her body. All she wants is to be with him, all of the time. Just looking at him is making her hungry for a food that until recently she hadn't even known existed. She knows she is now incapable of rational thought. Her thorough, hardworking, segregated mind is outraged by her behaviour, but she's powerless to stop herself.

'They want to do a... therapeutic session with you,' she says, trying to avoid looking directly at him.

Harry knows what this means, and his expression changes from adoration to fear in the time it takes for her to blink.

'Now?' he says, his eyes suddenly alert to danger, as if they're checking for an enemy sniper.

'Yes. I'm afraid so,' she says.

'I will not come, then,' he says, sitting back down at his table, staring at the cards. 'I shan't do as they say.' He resumes playing cards, but his moves are frantic and illogical. The cards are flying across the table and landing in haphazard piles, all rules forgotten.

'Harry...'

She's about to sit opposite him, to try to cajole him, when Dr Joyce enters the room.

'We wondered where you'd got to, Lieutenant Quinn.'

Ellen examines him for any sign he has heard their conversation up to this point but finds none.

'I'm so sorry, Captain Joyce, we were just coming.'

'We were not,' says Harry, now shuffling cards. 'I was not going to come. Lieutenant Quinn here was trying her best to persuade me, however.'

'Come now, Hennessey. You are our patient. We know what's best. And the best thing for you now is more treatment. We've tried a wait and see approach, but we don't feel that your progress is sufficient, so we've decided to up the ante, as it were. We want to make you well.'

'Well?' says Harry, turning his head slowly and glaring at the doctor. 'You are going to make me well? I think that ship sailed long ago, Joyce.'

'We are going to do our level best to ensure that you are well enough to return to your unit and continue fighting this damned war,' says the doctor, taking a few steps towards Harry and using his considerable bulk to loom over him. Harry flinches, and any fight he has seems to seep out of him. 'We need all the pilots we can lay our hands on.'

'Very well,' Harry says, in a voice Ellen doesn't even recognise. He stands up, stumbles slightly and walks through the door and down the corridor, his head hanging loose on his shoulders. The doctor and Ellen follow. She knows she has no choice but to play her part in this afternoon's proceedings, and her stomach lurches. *This is going to be almost impossible to watch,* she thinks. *Impossible to bear.*

'Lieutenant Quinn, please can you prepare him for the drip, please?' says Major Cole, as soon as they are all in the room and the door is shut. Captain Joyce remains silent, taking notes. He's here to learn from this grisly spectacle.

'Please take a seat, Hennessey.'

Harry does as he's told. He sits down in the large static leather chair in the centre of the room, opposite an oak desk, behind which the two doctors sit on two chairs which swivel and creak as they talk and shift their weight, the resulting noise a macabre soundtrack for their task.

This is part of the treatment. Or perhaps, she thinks, *it would be better to call it a game. Anticipation and fear all have a part to play.*

Harry doesn't say a word in mitigation or defence. He also avoids looking directly at Ellen, even when she walks up to him and wipes down the skin on his left hand with iodine.

'I am just preparing the skin for the cannula,' she says, her voice wavering as she takes hold of his hand. 'That's a needle that will go under your skin and allow the medicine to enter your bloodstream.'

Harry nods. Ellen continues, working through the steps methodically, grateful for her training, which is really coming into play now. Without it, she would be weeping at Harry's feet.

Ellen is relieved when the cannula is fitted with minimum ceremony. Then she walks back over to the preparation area, and retrieves the sodium amytal solution, the intravenous giving set, some saline solution and a syringe. She checks the solution's batch number and notes this down carefully in the medicine log beside her. Then she wheels the drip stand beside Harry's seat, hangs up the bag of sodium amytal and runs the saline through the cannula, checking she has placed it correctly. Finally, she jabs the giving set into the drip bag, checking that the tube isn't twisted, pulls the cap off the set and allows the liquid to flow through, before attaching it to the cannula and setting the liquid to drop through at the right pace for an hour-long session. Once she's satisfied that the task is done, she walks back to the preparation area, faces the wall and sets about tidying and cleaning the area. It's only then she allows herself to breathe normally. She had been worried she might cry or shout if she'd opened her mouth when she was so close to Harry.

'Thank you, Lieutenant Quinn. Would you remain here with us please, to monitor the patient?' asks Dr Joyce.

'Of course,' Ellen replies, clearing her throat to try to mask the emotion in her voice.

'Now, Hennessey. You no doubt will have heard about this procedure from the other patients, but for the avoidance of doubt... we are giving you a drug called sodium amytal. It's a barbiturate. It will relax you and help you to talk about experiences you've had which under normal circumstances, you would not mention.' There's a pause. 'It's perfectly all right, Hennessey. Lieutenant Quinn is an army nurse. She has seen this done many times. There is nothing you can say that will shock her.'

Ellen assumes this is in response to a look of horror from Harry, no doubt realising the implication of what is about to happen. *It's one thing sharing a private, passionate moment with someone,* Ellen thinks, *but quite another having one's private horrors shared with that person also, and not at a time of your choosing.* She's heard that this drug is described in some quarters as truth serum. It makes people talk without inhibition. Army psychiatrists have been using it to encourage patients to talk about the horrors they've seen. She's heard things in this room that will stay with her always.

She tries to make herself as small and unobtrusive as she can, hiding in plain sight in the corner, quietly going about her business, with her eyes turned. She wishes desperately she could block her hearing, too.

'The medication will take effect quite quickly. We will begin with some easy questions. Can we start with why you believe you are here?'

Harry's chair squeaks. Ellen imagines him squirming, toying with the idea of bolting.

'Haven't we been over this all before, in the talking sessions?' he says, his voice beginning to slur slightly. The sodium amytal is already starting to work.

'We have, but not with the assistance of this drug, which should make things easier,' says Major Cole. 'We need you to really reconnect with your emotions, Hennessey. We need to do that so we can elicit and expunge your painful memories. Doing this, I promise, will be much less hard work for you than going over and over the same experiences in normal talking therapy.'

He's not telling him the whole truth, thinks Ellen. And Harry knows that, too.

'So, Hennessey. The reason you're here?'

'I have battle exhaustion.'

'And how does that manifest itself?'

'Palpitations. Headaches. Nausea. A numbing of the senses. And I find... I find I cannot fly. I cannot get back in the aircraft.'

'Can you identify an incident that was the cause of this?'

'You know damn well I can.'

Good for you, Harry, thinks Ellen. Even though he's drugged up to his eyeballs, they aren't managing to break his spirit.

'It will be different this time, Harry. The medication we have given you will help you. Can you tell me, then, what happened before these symptoms began?'

'We had a sortie.'

'Go on.'

'We were escorting some American bombers over the Channel, into France.'

'But something went wrong?'

Harry laughs. It's a deep laugh, hoarse, angry.

'Something always goes wrong up there. Our aircraft are patched up after every flight with tape, there's a shortage of parts, the runway gets strafed and we have to dodge potholes at take-off, we don't have enough pilots, the pilots we have aren't trained well enough. And we are all exhausted. We are flying too much, and the odds are against us.'

'And yet we won the Battle of Britain?'

'We did. But it was at a terrible cost. I lost so many of my friends... my men...'

'And this upset you deeply?'

There's a long silence, during which Ellen can hear Captain Joyce scribbling on his notepad.

'Goodness, man, wouldn't it upset you?' says Harry, finally.

'Yes, it certainly would. But not all men who've gone through such a thing end up with battle exhaustion and neurosis, Hennessey.'

'Ah, well, they are not all sons of a lunatic.'

There's another silence, but Ellen senses that this one is from the doctor's side. Harry has told her about his mother but has obviously not told the hospital staff in any of his previous sessions.

'Your mother is in an asylum? There's nothing in your records.'

'No. There wouldn't be. My father would have tried to hide it. He's ashamed.'

'What is her diagnosis?'

'Goodness knows. Hysteria, perhaps? I don't know. No one has ever told me.'

'I see.'

'So you see, you cannot fix me. All of your fancy techniques here, your pointless attempts at re-instilling military discipline in me, in trying to make me feel guilty enough to return to the fray – it is all in vain. I am beyond help.'

'I disagree. Let's go back to what happened – the incident that ignited all of this. I understand you distinguished yourself in the first few years of the war. You shot down several enemy aircraft. In doing that, you must have experienced the loss of many of your fellow pilots.'

'Yes.'

'So why did you suddenly burn out? What was the final straw?'

Harry sighs. He sounds worn down. The drug must be at its full effect now.

'We had a new chap join us. He was very young. Eighteen. I knew his father. He taught me History. He wrote to me when his son came to the unit, asking me to show him the ropes and keep him out of trouble.'

'What was his name?'

'Oliver. Oliver White.'

'That's good. You haven't told us his name before. Go on.'

'He arrived fresh out of training,' says Harry, continuing, Ellen notices, without pause, with a strange energy in his voice. 'He was clean cut, keen, eager to please, but incredibly anxious. He had this tic of running his hands on the back of his head, and his hands shook when he thought you weren't watching. I saw that and I took him for a walk about the airfield. I tried to jolly him up, tell him about the scrapes I'd been in, that sort of thing. I tried to make it sound like a game.'

Harry laughs again, but this time it sounds more like a sob.

'What did you talk about together?'

'He told me about his schooling. How he'd attended the same school as me – he was a don's son, of course – but he'd hated it, just as I had. And then he told me about his mother.'

'I see. What about his mother?'

'She... wasn't well.'

'In what way?'

'She was having some kind of... mental breakdown.'

'And this, I imagine, reminded you of your own mother?'

'Yes. I felt for him. He was, as I say, a lovely chap.'

'Was he a good pilot?'

'He was jittery as hell to start off with, unpredictable, did a couple of nasty landings, but he got better.'

'What happened, then, to this lovely chap?'

'We flew a sortie one morning, as I said.'

There's a long pause before the doctor speaks again.

'How long had this Oliver been with your squadron?'

'He'd been with us for about a fortnight.'

'Long enough, then, to get to know each other?'

'Yes.'

'I heard, from your senior officer, that you took this chap under your wing, rather. Like a big brother, he says, in his report,' says the doctor, shuffling his papers.

'Yes, I suppose that was how it was.'

'So, you were sent up to escort a squadron of bombers.'

'Yes.'

'And then? Come on, Hennessey. Let's get this out in the open. Tell me how it was.'

Ellen hears Harry swallow and then breathe out hard through his nose.

'And then,' he says, almost whispering, 'we were besieged by a swarm of Messerschmitts.'

'It was a dogfight?'

'Yes. They came at us from above, hidden by the sun. We had no time to regroup.'

Ellen hears real fear in Harry's voice, as if he's still there in the moment, being hunted down by the enemy.

'Do you blame yourself for not spotting them?'

'I was the lead pilot up there. I should have called it. I should have. But I don't know... you have to look everywhere, all the time. I don't know.'

Harry sounds agitated.

'And then what happened?'

'They opened fire. They were aiming for the bombers – they are sitting ducks up there, those poor men – but they were trying to get us too, of course, as we are a far greater risk. Far greater.'

'They started to fire?'

Harry swallows so loudly, Ellen can hear him do it.

'Yes. We were all trying to get height, to give ourselves an advantage. I managed to climb up a fair amount. One of the Jerries came at me on the nose. I opened up the machine gun and knocked a few holes in his fuselage.'

'And?'

There's a pause, during which Ellen imagines Harry fighting the drug in his system with all his might. But it's clear he's losing the battle. He keeps talking.

'And I hit him.'

It's then that Ellen hears a noise that sounds like retching, and then gasping, as if Harry is drowning. She turns around, unable to stop herself. She sees tears streaming down his face.

'Don't be concerned, Lieutenant Quinn. He's perfectly fine,' says the doctor, noting her discomfort.

She turns back to face the wall, fighting her own tears. She can't bear to see him in this much pain.

'What happened then, Hennessey?'

'The aircraft I hit lost control.'

'Because you hit it?'

'I... don't know.'

'I see. And then what happened?'

'You know very well what happened, doctor,' says Harry, his voice slightly nasal as a result of his tears.

'Ye-es,' says the doctor in a laid-back drawl. 'But I'd like to hear you tell me, from your perspective, what happened next.'

'The Jerry plane went into a spin, an unrecoverable spin, I think, and as it was going down, it took out one of ours with it.'

'And whose aircraft was it?'

'Damn it, man. It was Oliver's plane. Oliver White's plane. The boy I'd taken under my wing and tried to make feel welcome and promised he'd be safe if he stayed with me. It was a... knockout blow. The Messerschmitt hit his cockpit. He didn't stand a chance.' Harry stops talking and sobs, interspersed with short rasping breaths. 'No chance. None. I didn't mean to... I didn't... It was...'

'That's good, Hennessey. Let it all out.'

And then Harry screams.

For a good minute or two, Ellen and both doctors are bystanders to Harry's grief. It's a full-bodied force, undeniable in its outrageous power. He seems to barely pause for breath. Ellen suspects that his roommates will be able to hear his rage and frustration and anger all the way down the hall. Harry has told her he's heard similar in the past.

'Take my handkerchief,' says Major Cole, finally. 'Wipe yourself up, Hennessey. I want you to tell me what happened after that.'

More? thinks Ellen. *He wants more?*

'I disengaged,' says Harry between staccato breaths. 'I... flew away. From the battle.'

'You deserted?'

'No... no... no-no-no. It was over. The battle. There was nothing further we could do.'

'That's not what we have in our records, Hennessey. We hear that you flew back to base while the fight was very much still on, landed so hard the airframe needed maintenance work, and went AWOL for hours. You were later found in a dark corner of a local pub, almost comatose.'

'No... No-no-no-no...'

'And when you sobered up back at base, you remained mute and immovable, interspersed with bouts of extreme crying. Several days later, the base medical team decided to send you here.'

Harry stops protesting his innocence, although his rasping sobs are still puncturing Ellen's heart. She wishes with all her heart that she could turn around and go and comfort him.

'I think we're almost done here,' says Captain Joyce. 'Lieutenant Quinn, could you please remove the drip, and help the patient to return to his quarters?'

Ellen turns around. Harry is leaning over in the chair with his head in his hands. He's mopping up mucus from his nose with the doctor's sodden handkerchief, and his hands are shaking.

'What did you make of that, Joyce?' Major Cole asks his colleague.

'It was very interesting, sir,' replies Captain Joyce. 'Remarkable how the drug provided an outlet for the patient to relive memories that are so often suppressed.'

'Ye-es. Although it's not really about the recovery of memory. Essentially, it allows for a greater intensity of emotion than during normal therapeutic work. It induces an emotional crisis and collapse. And this helps reset the patient, so to speak.'

Ellen concentrates on performing her role – removing the catheter, stemming any bleeding when the needle is withdrawn, removing the drip and disassembling the equipment – while trying to ignore what the doctors are saying. Their habit of talking about patients while they are still present, as if they are babies, has always infuriated her. *How* dare *they*, she thinks. *How* dare *they do this to Harry.*

'Flying Officer Hennessey,' she says, her voice gentle, her right hand brushing his arm as she pushes the drop stand away. She wants to place her hand on his arm again right away. The connection between them feels magnetic. 'I'm finished here. Shall I help you back to your room?'

Harry doesn't raise his head, but nods briefly. Ellen waits beside his chair for him to rise, but he doesn't make any attempt to stand.

'Come now, Hennessey. The lady can't lift you. *Stand*, man,' says Major Cole, standing up and walking around to the front of the desk so that he towers over Harry. They wait in silence for a moment. 'Could you fetch the wheelchair, Lieutenant Quinn?' asks the doctor, his exasperation clear. 'It looks like we have no choice in the matter.'

By the time Ellen returns with a chair, Captain Joyce and Major Cole have taken hold of one of Harry's arms each.

'Right. On the count of three…' says Major Cole. 'One, two, three…'

Ellen watches in horror as the two men heave Harry into a standing position, his limbs as floppy as a puppet's, before wrenching him upwards and dropping into the wheelchair with the bare minimum of ceremony.

'Thank you, Lieutenant Quinn,' says Major Cole, his face reddening from the effort. 'You may take him now.'

Ellen has to fight the urge to run to Harry, to get him away from these two men as quickly as possible. Instead, she walks quickly, takes the handles of the wheelchair and turns it at speed, pushing him out of the room before the two doctors can say another word.

It's only when she's back in the corridor and the doctor's door has swung shut that she stops, checks that they're alone, runs around to the front of the chair and gathers Harry into her arms. He is limp, but she can feel his heart thrashing through his shirt. And then he begins to sob.

'Oh my darling, oh my darling,' she whispers, her arms running all over his back, as if she's checking he's still intact. 'Oh, my darling. I'm so sorry.'

21

MEREDITH

25 January 2014

It's either the early hours of the morning, or very late at night. Meredith can't be more precise than that, because she's lying in bed, rigid with fear. There is someone in her bedroom.

She saw them as soon as she opened her eyes, a clear dark shape in the corner silhouetted against the white door, even in the half-light seeping through her curtains. She doesn't know if they know she's awake, which is why she's keeping still. She needs time to consider her next move.

I so wish Phil was here, she thinks, her fingers instinctively touching his side of the bed. *Why am I always alone, dealing with these things?*

Her heart thumps in her chest. She wonders what this person wants. Do they want to assault her? Steal from her? She tries to keep breathing deeply, as if she's sleeping. She listens to see if she can hear this person breathing, but she can't detect anything. Are they holding their breath? And then she wonders why Poppy hasn't stirred. After all, she's supposed to be here, protecting her. Or at least, warning her. So why no sound?

I give up, she thinks. *If I don't move soon, I'll go mad.* Meredith lobs the duvet back and launches herself out of bed. The next few seconds are something of a blur. The dog wakes up and starts barking as if possessed;

Meredith surges towards the bedroom door, her head spinning, screaming words she doesn't even recognise; she loses her balance and falls hard on the floor. When she finally pulls herself back up, the figure is gone. In pain from her fall but flooded with adrenaline, Meredith flips on the bedroom and hallway lights, only to see the figure running up the stairs. She bolts after it.

Meredith keeps pace and follows it up to the first floor, where she sees them disappearing into the third room on the right. She runs up to the door and is about to turn the handle and surge in, before she stops herself.

What the hell am I doing? she thinks. *He's in there, isn't he? The intruder. What will he do if I corner him? Has he got a weapon?* She wishes she'd had the forethought to pick up her phone. *What options do I have now? I can't call anyone. I can't shout. Or... can I shout?* She's thinking about saying something, telling them she's outside, that she needs to know who they are and what they want, when Poppy runs up the stairs and joins her. She's still barking, and in fact, she goes completely mad at the door, as if it's her sworn enemy. Her presence emboldens Meredith. *I can do this*, she thinks. *I'll open it.*

She turns the handle quickly and pushes the door open. Poppy stops barking immediately.

What Meredith finds behind it is a scene beyond her wildest imagination.

Unlike all the others on this floor, this room is neither full of ramshackle furniture nor in darkness. In fact, there's a light on. It's an Anglepoise light, and it's shining directly at Meredith. Despite this, she can see the outline of a large high-backed leather chair a few feet in front of her. Behind that is a large desk, and behind that, in front of the windows, is the clear outline of two adults sitting in desk chairs.

She doesn't have time to compute what she's seeing, that it can't possibly be real, that this furniture wasn't in here when she swept the floor last month, that one shady figure in the corner of her bedroom has somehow transmuted into at least two people. In fact, she can't see into the high-backed chair from where she's standing; it might even be three. Instead, she's just caught up in the moment, riveted to the floor by shock and by a force she cannot comprehend.

Then there's a hideous sound, a desperate retching, which reminds Meredith of the sound she made when she'd been fighting the river flow, and about to succumb. Then the light changes slightly, as if the lamp has been moved.

And then there is a scream. It's a scream with power, a pure distillation of overwhelming anxiety and fear.

It jolts Meredith out of her frozen stance. She finds that she can move. And she is absolutely determined to escape this room and this agonising scene, right now. She turns on her heel and runs. Poppy, who has been cowering beneath the doorframe, joins her, and together they flee down the stairs and back into the bedroom.

Once there, she and the dog leap onto the bed and she pulls the covers over them; right over her head, as she'd done as a child, to ward off the monsters that lived beneath her bed. And then she grasps the dog firmly, as if she's clinging to a life raft in a stormy sea, and gradually, her heartbeat slows, and as Poppy's breathing relaxes, so does hers. And eventually her mind releases her from the hellish prison in which it's been confining her, and she falls asleep.

* * *

'Morning, beautiful. I thought we said the dog wouldn't be allowed to sleep on the bed?'

Philip's voice is a balm, and for a second or two, Meredith forgets the horror of the night just gone. She's delighted her husband has returned, so she manages a smile as he leans over to kiss her. But that smile has disappeared before his lips touch hers, and he notices.

'Merry? Are you OK?'

Meredith runs her hand over her forehead as if checking for damage, pulls herself upright and tries to smile again. She takes in her husband; he's still in his uniform, but his face bears the signs of a night flight. His eyes are bloodshot, his laughter lines are deeper and there's a hint of a five o'clock shadow on his chin.

'I'm... I don't know, Phil. I had a horrible experience last night.'

'Are you ill?' He sits down beside her, his tired eyes full of concern.

'I don't know. I don't think so. I'm tired, I think.'

'But you've just woken up.' She detects a note of annoyance in his voice. After all, he hasn't yet made it to bed.

'I know. But I was awake for a lot of last night.'

'Insomnia?'

She pulls her hair out of its topknot and smoothes it down, before pulling it into a ponytail.

'I don't think so. Oh God, Phil, it was so bloody horrible. I was scared out of my wits.'

'You were scared? Was it a nightmare?'

Meredith weighs this up. Had she dreamed it? That would be a relief, if so. And yet it felt so very real.

'I don't know. I woke up at... I don't actually know what time it was... and there was someone in the corner of the bedroom.'

'Are you sure?' Philip leans nearer to her.

'I don't know. It was so dark. I couldn't really see.'

'That must have been frightening.'

Philip pulls Meredith in for a hug, and she yields for a moment, before pulling away and sitting back against her headboard. She feels prickly this morning. *Anyone would,* she thinks, after what she went through.

'I waited for a few moments to see if they'd do anything, but they just stayed there, so in the end I decided to try to scare them, or confront them. I got out of bed, but I fell over and by the time I got to the door, they'd gone. But then when I turned on the hallway light, I saw them running upstairs.'

'Why didn't you call the police?'

Meredith shrugs.

'I don't know. I was just waking up... I was too shocked... It was just a lot to take in. My phone was on the bedside table and I didn't turn the light on to locate it. I just felt I needed to find out who the hell it was, so I followed them.'

'*Upstairs*? God, Merry.'

'I wasn't thinking, was I?' says Meredith, the frustration clear in her voice. 'Obviously I wasn't. What I knew was that someone who shouldn't have been there was in our house and in my bedroom. And then Poppy woke up and went mad, and that sort of energised me, so I ran after them.'

'And then what happened?'

'I saw them disappear into one of the bedrooms on the first floor.'

'One of the ones at the front? The ones with two windows?'

'Yes.'

'I ran up to the door. I almost opened it straight away, but I saw sense for a bit and realised the predicament I was in. And then Poppy ran up to me and was thrashing away at the door like her sworn enemy was inside, and it sort of... galvanised me into action. I turned the handle and pushed the door open.'

'And what did you see?'

Meredith swallows.

'I saw... two men. Maybe three.'

'There were... three men... upstairs in our house?' Philip is looking askance. 'I don't understand. How did they get in? Did you remember to lock the door?'

'Yes. I always do, Phil. But nevertheless, they were there. I saw them. They seemed to be talking to someone who was sitting in a big chair. He had his back to me...'

'They were sitting on our furniture?'

She pauses for a moment. How much should she tell him about what she saw? Will he dismiss her entirely when he finds out what she thinks she's seen? *But no,* she thinks. *He's my partner, my best friend. If he doesn't listen to this story and believe me, who will?*

'They were on furniture that I didn't recognise,' she says, choosing her words carefully. 'And there was a light on, and it was shining on me.'

Philip blinks repeatedly, as if he's trying to see more clearly.

'How do you know you weren't dreaming? You've been reading all sorts of stuff in that notebook, haven't you? All sorts of stuff from when this was a hospital. That's probably enough to set you off. You're vulnerable as it is.'

Meredith thinks about this. A couple of days ago, she did read a letter the nurse had written about witnessing the man she was in love with going through some sort of hideous interrogation. *Could that have made me dream about it?* she wonders. *Could it?* But her experience last night was so visceral, it just can't have been a dream. And she woke up with Poppy in bed with her, didn't she? And Poppy never sleeps in her bed normally. How can she explain that?

'I wasn't,' she says, with slightly less confidence.

'Take me to where it happened,' says Philip, standing up and pacing around the room. 'Show me where these... men... were last night.'

Meredith takes a deep breath and throws off the covers. She finds her dressing gown and slippers and together they walk out of the bedroom, up the stairs and onto the first-floor landing. When she reaches the room in question, she finds the door is still ajar, as she left it last night when she fled.

'This one?' he asks, his voice low. Why is he doing that? Does he think someone's asleep inside?

'Yes,' she replies, and he throws the door open wide.

The scene inside is nothing like she remembers from the previous night. There is no high-backed leather chair, no large wooden desk and no Anglepoise light. Instead, there is a heavy chest of drawers in front of the window, and there are several large packing cases on the floor, most of them empty.

'It wasn't like this,' she says. 'It was... a completely different room.' She examines Philip's expression, but it's hard to read. Maybe it's because we're both tired, she thinks. Perhaps she should have waited to tell him all of this until later. But she also knows that if he doesn't believe her, no one will. 'You do believe me, don't you?' she says, approaching him and pulling him towards her. 'I saw it. And I'm scared, Phil. I'm scared and I'm overwhelmed. I need you to be here for me, to help me while we work this out, together.'

She embraces him, and he reciprocates. She revels in his warmth, in his familiarity and his affection.

It's only afterwards, when they're downstairs and she's making breakfast and he's having a shower, that she registers that he didn't reply.

22

ELLEN

11 January 1944

Ellen's shift is over. She has monitored drips, replaced dressings and completed a stocktake on the drug cabinet, at the captain's request. She is grateful to have been busy. It has helped her to stop thinking, if only for a moment at a time, about the horrible 'therapy' session Harry was subjected to yesterday. That scream... those wretched tears... That session was a window into a part of his soul she knows he would have preferred she hadn't seen. Seeing it had felt more intimate than anything they had done together. In fact, it had felt like a violation.

'You coming?' asks Rebecca. Brian has offered to take some of the staff over to the mainland this evening so that they can visit the pub and feel like average people for a few precious hours.

'No, sorry,' replies Ellen, trying to avoid looking directly at her friend. 'I need to write to Mammy. I've been promising to do so for a good while. Peace and quiet here tonight will mean I've run out of excuses.'

'Fine. So be it,' says Rebecca, her expression reflecting her doubt about this particular excuse. Ellen is grateful, however, that she doesn't press her further.

'Have a lovely time,' says Ellen, watching as her friend races upstairs to change her clothes, before heading out to the boat with the others. Ellen, on the other hand, takes her time filing all the paperwork from the day, and handing over to the nurse for the next shift. By the time she's finished, Rebecca has headed down to the jetty. As soon as she sees her go, Ellen also runs upstairs. Here, she changes into slacks and a shirt, dons her cape and walks down the stairs as quickly and lightly as she can. Then she walks as purposefully as she can through the kitchen and out of the back door, and then, after checking that she's not been observed from one of the upstairs windows, runs through the rain to the pump house, opens the door and walks inside.

'Ellen.'

Harry is sitting in the far corner, his knees bent, his body folded over.

'*Oh, Harry*.'

She rushes over to him and sits down on the cold stone flags beside him. It's then she notices the envelope he's holding in his left hand.

'What's that?'

'It's a letter. From my father,' he replies.

'Oh.'

'Does he write often?'

'He hasn't written to me for months.'

'I see.'

'Do you?' he says, his head dropping onto Ellen's shoulder.

'I imagine it's not a nice letter, from the way you obviously feel about it.'

'You are a wise woman, Quinn.'

They sit in silence for a moment, listening to the rain falling onto the roof, and the distant sound of the swollen river tumbling over the weir.

'Is it bad news?'

'No, no. There is no news. In fact, that's part of the problem. It seems my father is rather keen on there being good news from here. He's very invested in my military career, you see. He has told me, in very definite terms, that I must pull myself together, stop all this nonsense and get back to battle.'

'But doesn't he understand where you...'

'He understands perfectly, apparently. He tells me that my sanity is within my own control, and as a further sweetener, he will disinherit me if I do not recover and return to the skies in short order.'

'Oh, Lord.'

'Yes. I can just imagine his expression as he sat there and wrote that. He will have been smiling at the time, admiring his own cleverness. But of course, as we both know, it simply won't work. I am mad. It cannot be helped, and no financial threats will cure me.'

'Harry, that's not true. I have seen people recover here...'

'My dear, I wholeheartedly wish that would happen to me, but I know it won't. And you were there yesterday, you heard everything, all of the darkness that's in my soul. Did that living nightmare cure me, do you think?' Ellen isn't sure if he's actually asking her a question. If he is, she knows that the answer is far from simple. 'The answer, my dear, is – to save you the trouble of trying to come up with a diplomatic answer – no. I heard an engine backfire on the towpath this morning, and I ran and took cover in the woodshed, and shook like a damned jelly. One of your colleagues had to pull me out.'

'But Harry, it's a process...'

'It's not a damned process that will work for me, darling girl.'

Ellen thinks about her own reaction to the bomb, which sent her fleeing into the garden and away from safety, risking the life of both her and her friend. She knows she is not rid of her own problem. She will never know if the treatments offered at May Day would cure her, because the army is not interested in treating women, even those who almost died in an enemy attack. But she knows how Harry feels, because she also feels like she's sharing her body with a sleeping serpent that rears its ugly head when provoked by goodness knows what. She wants rid of it, but understands Harry's pessimism, too. How on earth could talking, with medication or without, remove this snake from her soul? It's just not possible, she thinks. It can't be.

'Where do they think you are?' she asks Harry, keen to change the subject.

'Oh, they think I've come to service the pump. They don't want a repeat of last time. You?'

'Writing a letter in my room. A group of staff have gone out to the pub in Weybridge tonight. They won't be back for ages.'

'We have a while, then,' says Harry, his hand slipping down Ellen's leg, towards her ankle, where he grazes her bare skin.

'We do,' she says, turning towards him. He raises his head and kisses her, gently at first, and then with more intensity, an intensity she is more than happy to return. She reaches out and puts her hand around his waist, and then along the gentle curves of his back, and, when he pushes her over gently onto the floor, the curves of his buttocks, which she cups and presses firmly into her with a new, addictive rhythm she knows she will remember for the rest of her life.

* * *

Afterwards, they lie in each other's arms, trying to ignore the piercing cold of the floor and the icy, damp air around them. For just a few precious minutes, they are in a world of their own making, a world where it is warm and they are secure, in control of their own destinies, with no battle to return to, and no battle within themselves to fight. It is such a wonderful feeling that Ellen closes her eyes and makes a conscious decision to try to capture it, to store it in her memory vault so that she can revisit it whenever she wants.

'So what will you say, in reply to your father?' asks Ellen, when she has sealed her vault.

'Oh, I shan't reply. I mean, for the love of God, what am I meant to say? Yes of course Father, I shall cease my madness immediately and go back to killing Jerry with alacrity?'

'Good. He doesn't deserve a reply. Although... aren't you worried, about the threat about the money?'

'All I've ever seen, all my life, is people with money being miserable. They have a huge house, lots of land and lots of people who depend on them, and they are still miserable. If he wants to cut me off, then well, so be it. I shall manage.' Ellen wonders how he would really fare, out of the RAF, out in the working world. Not very well, she suspects, her heart heavy with it. 'Or failing that, we're both going to have to run away and join the circus.'

Ellen wants to laugh at Harry's attempt at lightening the mood, but the cold reality of their situation is not something she can find funny. They are prisoners of social convention, of religion, of financial restrictions and, most of all, of their own mental illnesses, of which they are both only too aware. It all feels so desperate.

'Are you cold, darling?' says Harry. Ellen wishes she could say no, but in all honesty, it's freezing in here.

'A little.'

'We had better get moving, then,' he says, sitting up and helping Ellen do the same. They spend a few moments rearranging and replacing their clothing.

'Oh goodness, do we have to?' says Ellen, properly dressed once more, and sitting next to Harry on the floor.

'I am afraid so, Ellen. I am afraid so.'

'When can we be alone together again?' she asks, her head nestling in his neck, seeking out his warmth. 'I can't bear that I have to walk past you every day, or come along to change your sheets, and not touch you, not be with you, how I want to be.'

'I know. And I feel the same. Perhaps I can pretend that the pump needs a part, and that I need some time to fit it.'

'That sounds believable.'

'Yes.'

There's a small pause, and Ellen realises Harry is working himself up to saying something. 'Darling, I don't know if you've heard any gossip amongst the ranks...'

'What about?'

'About... other treatments? I've been told that they plan to give me electro convulsive therapy. They said my response to the sodium amytal was below par. I was apparently supposed to be "cured" by it, you see, and I'm still mad, so this is their latest grand plan.'

Ellen knows exactly what he means. The doctors have been talking to each other about using ECT for some time, and they recently purchased and installed the relevant equipment in one of the rooms on the ground floor. She swallows hard, trying to cover her response, which is one of fear. She observed an ECT session in Cairo. Despite the sedation given to the patient, it had seemed to her to be an act of great violence. She has heard that some patients have even broken bones as a result of the full-strength convulsion it can induce. And there have also been reports of memory loss, of a dulling of the senses, afterwards. She cannot bear the thought of Harry, *her Harry*, being put through it. But what can she do? She's only a junior nurse. The doctors won't listen to her.

'I see,' she says. It's the only response she can manage.

'What do you think? Will it help? What does it involve?' She wants to tell him the truth, that the violent juddering and horrible noises the patient had produced during the session still haunt her dreams. 'They say it has a high efficacy rate. It might cure me.'

Should she tell him? Should she?

'When are they going to do it?' she asks, stalling for time.

'Oh, next week, I think. They said they want to start on Boyd.'

Sergeant Boyd – David – is one of Harry's ward-mates. He is given to fits of crying at all hours of the day and night that could wake the dead. Ellen spent a great deal of her time yesterday comforting him.

'I do hope it works for him,' she says, meaning it, while simultaneously being glad that Harry isn't first. It gives her more time to think. The idea of her wonderful, gentle, vulnerable man enduring something which might dull his senses and his intellect fills her with dread.

'Yes. Me too.'

'Is there something you're not telling me, Ellen?'

Damn it, she thinks. This man reads me like a book.

'I am worried about you, that's all. ECT is… difficult.'

'Harder than sodium amytal?'

She thinks.

'Yes. I suppose so.'

'Oh, Lord.'

They hold each other tightly, as if they have been cast out to sea on a miniscule life raft.

'I'll think of something,' she says, not really believing it, but really, really wanting to, because she has to protect him somehow. She will not let them do this to the man she loves.

23

MEREDITH

31 January 2014

'Do you want some more of that kefir rubbish?' says Philip, doing his best to smile.

'Yes please.'

Meredith and Philip are sitting at the oak table in the kitchen. He's been home twenty-four hours now and has slept well. She's relieved about that. She always tries to avoid talking about anything important when he's just come back from a trip, because he's always exhausted and his mind is still half on the job.

That's why she really wishes she could have told him about what she witnessed upstairs *this* morning, rather than yesterday morning, when they were both ratty and strung out. She tried to speak to him about it yesterday afternoon, but he shut her down, telling her he had some work to do for his upcoming simulator check. She hopes today will be different. She needs to know that he's taking it seriously.

She watches as he stands up and goes to the fridge to pull out the bottle of kefir, finds a clean glass from the cupboard, pours it and puts it down in front of her on the table.

'Coffee too? Cappuccino?' he asks.

'Yes please.'

'I don't know why you like that stuff,' he says, as she takes a sip of kefir. 'It just tastes like off milk to me.'

'I suppose that's what it is,' she replies, smiling.

She watches him as he makes the coffee, following the familiar rhythm of the task in hand, the machine humming as it forces hot water through the grounds and works up steam for the milk.

'Phil?' she says as he's pouring the froth over the dense, fragrant coffee beneath.

'Yep?'

'I want to talk to you about yesterday. About what I saw.'

'Uh-huh,' he says, carrying the cups to the table and placing one beside Meredith. She notices he's forgotten the chocolate that would normally adorn its surface. 'I wanted to talk to you about that, too.'

'That's good,' says Meredith, relieved that they are on the same page. 'I know it must have seemed a lot yesterday, what I told you.'

'You can say that again,' he says, pulling up a chair next to her.

'I know you worry enough as it is, not being able to be around all the time, and I didn't want to make it worse.'

'I see,' he says, lifting his cup and taking a sip.

'But what I saw the night before last... I'm convinced it was real, Phil. I wasn't dreaming it. The door was open to that room, anyway, wasn't it, and it was definitely closed before, like all of the others on that floor. I am certain I was awake, and that I saw someone in our room, and that they ran upstairs.'

'And the other two men in the room?'

Meredith takes a deep breath.

'Yes, I am sure I was awake when I saw them, too. Although they can't have been human, can they? They didn't run back down the stairs. I would have heard them. Phil... I'm wondering whether they might have been... ghosts.'

'Ghosts? Merry, you don't believe in ghosts.'

This was true, of course, before she moved to May Day Island. She had never had any time for ghost stories and had firmly believed only in things that science could prove. But now her scepticism had deserted her.

'I know what I saw.'

'Don't you think you might be reading that notebook too much? It's unhealthy, your obsession with that thing. I wouldn't be surprised if it had caused you to have nightmares.'

Stop it, Phil, she thinks. *Stop making me doubt myself.*

'So you don't believe me?'

There's a long pause while he drinks more of his coffee. Meredith has not yet touched hers.

'I don't know.'

Meredith takes a sharp intake of breath.

'Phil. I'm your wife. I'm your best friend, you're mine. And I'm telling you, with absolute certainty, that I've seen something strange here. And I'm not the only one.'

'What do you mean?'

'Holly told me that some teenagers who camped on the island said they saw something here and were spooked. And a guy in a boat saw someone in a window upstairs...'

'*Jesus*, Merry. Are we taking the word of teenagers, who were probably high on weed, and tipsy day boaters now?' Philip's nostrils are flaring.

'Why are you so angry?' she asks, taking a sip of her coffee, which is so hot it almost burns.

'Because... because you just don't seem to be... yourself at the moment. You don't seem like *you*. It started when you cut all your old friends out of your life. And ever since we moved in here, it's felt like there's some kind of distance between us. We used to be such a team. And now you're listening to stories from random people and I'm hearing about it much later—'

'Holly is not random. She's my friend.' Meredith slams her cup down.

'—and you're believing them. And, you know, going out in the fog on a boat you hardly know how to use, searching for someone who wasn't there. I'm so worried about you, Merry.'

'Bloody hell,' she says, putting her coffee cup down. 'And there I was thinking you would take my side, and believe me, and deal with this thing in this house, whatever it is, together. But I was wrong, clearly.'

'Put yourself in my shoes. If I came and told you that I'd seen a ghost, what would you say?'

'I'd believe you. I have known you for a long time. I'd believe you, and we'd talk it through, and figure out whatever we need to do next, together.' She sees her husband soften slightly.

'I am on your side. I love you more than anything, you know that. And that's why I'm so worried. Because I don't believe in ghosts. I do believe, however, that you've been seeing things, and that throws up all sorts of worrying questions.'

'*Worrying questions*?' Meredith is starting to feel a bit nauseous.

'Yes. Look,' he says, trying to put his arm around her. She pushes him away. 'We both took a bit of a hammering, what with the IVF and the... miscarriages. It was hard on both of us. But I'm beginning to think that it was much harder for you to recover. I mean, of course it was. You had to go through all of that, take all those hormones, deal with the fallout after each miscarriage... It's not surprising, I suppose... Then your parents...'

'Phil – are you really suggesting that the miscarriages and my parents' deaths have... made me go mad?'

Philip takes a gulp of coffee and swallows hard.

'No... no. But I don't think we should rule out some kind of... hallucination, or maybe vivid dreams? Stress can do that. So can... mould spores. I read about that once...'

'Bloody hell. You really think I'm making it up.' Meredith considers getting up and walking out to try to contain her rage, but realises that she's so furious, she will stay where she is, and let him have it.

'Not making it up, exactly. I absolutely believe you saw what you saw. It's just why you saw it that I'm disputing. Shall I make an appointment with Dr Ahmed again? She might be able to help.'

Dr Ahmed is a psychiatrist. Philip had persuaded Meredith to see her privately after her parents had died. He had insisted that she see 'the best', and not rely on their GP. She'd done it to appease him and had even taken the anti-depressants she'd given her for a short while. She had been a kind woman who clearly knew her stuff, but Meredith had come to the conclusion that her expertise was really for people with genuine mental health issues like schizophrenia, not people suffering the common but life-changing effects of gut-wrenching grief.

'I don't need to see her.'

'Merry... I think really...'

'I *don't*. I will not see a psychiatrist for something I actually saw. For something I actually experienced. I am *not* mad.'

'You aren't listening to me...'

'No, it's you who isn't listening to me. I saw an actual ghost. Several ghosts, actually. There is something going on in this house. And do you know what? I don't give a shit that you don't believe me.'

'Merry...'

'No. I'm not going to sit here and listen to you come up with all this bollocks about my grief making me imagine things. I'm going out now, to see someone who will listen to me and take me seriously.'

'Where are you going?' he says, his eyes widening.

'To see Holly. I'll be a while,' she says, walking out of the room at speed, and into the hallway to find her coat and shoes.

'Be careful on the river... it was mega fast when I got back yesterday,' he shouts after her, like a mother reminding their child to pack their PE kit.

'I know, Phil. I live here a hell of a lot more than you do,' she shouts as she pulls her shoes on, walks to the door, opens it and slams it behind her, leaving the hurtful statement which she had absolutely intended hanging in the air.

Once outside, she is not surprised to discover that it's still raining. It seems like weeks since she last saw the sun. The ground beneath her feet is yielding with every step. She pulls the hood up on her coat to keep the worst of the weather at bay and sets to work untying the boat, which has at least two inches of rainwater sitting at the bottom of it. She makes a mental note to look into some sort of cover to stop it getting so saturated.

When the engine kicks into life and she pushes the boat off into the stream, she's unnerved by the lack of progress she's making through the water, despite the fact she's got the engine at full power. *This is like swimming through treacle*, she thinks, and is grateful when she reaches the other bank and is able to disembark.

The insistent, incessant rain becomes more like drizzle when she reaches Holly's place. She walks up the front steps and knocks on her door, praying that she's in. She wishes she'd texted in advance, but also realises that once she'd told Phil she was coming here, she was committed to doing so. If Holly isn't in, she'll have to go to the shops. Or maybe go to see Damon? She remembers his cosy red boat and his warm welcome. It's a reassuring thought.

It's been a minute or two, and there's been no answer. Meredith peers through the glass in Holly's front door and sees no sign of any life. She's about to admit defeat and head towards Damon's boat when she hears a door close inside, and footsteps walk down the corridor and into Holly's living room.

Meredith smiles broadly at her friend, who returns her smile and unlocks her front door.

'Come in, come in. It's pissing it down.' She does as she's bidden and walks through into Holly's cosy living room and kitchen. 'Give me your coat, I'll hang it up by the boiler. Should help dry it out.'

Meredith pulls her coat out and hands it over before walking over to Holly's bar and taking a seat on a stool, just before Holly returns from her trip to the utility room.

'I'm so sorry to pop in unannounced,' says Meredith. 'I've had a row with Phil and you were the first person I thought of.'

'Then I am honoured,' says Holly, walking swiftly in the direction of her kitchen, where she finds two large wine glasses. 'Sounds like you need a drink. White or red?'

Meredith never usually drinks in the morning, but her current mood is so contrary that she doesn't care.

'I'd love one. White. Thanks.'

Holly opens her fridge and pulls out a half-drunk bottle of white wine and pours two large glasses. She hands one to Meredith.

'So, tell me. What happened?' Meredith swallows a swig of wine and tells Holly everything: about the strange things she's seen and heard at the house; about the notebook which described a similar scene to the one she saw in the bedroom in May Day House; about the profound impact of her repeated miscarriages and her grief for her parents; about Philip's refusal to believe her and his insulting assumption about her mental state; about his insistence she see a psychiatrist.

'Bloody hell. I see why you walked out. I'd have done the same,' Holly says.

'I'm so relieved to hear you say that,' says Meredith, taking another sip of wine.

'I think anyone would say the same. I mean, you've been through so bloody much, you spend so much time alone and you've worked so damned hard on that place all by yourself, and you tell him about something really profound that happened to you, and he dismisses it and basically accuses you of being mad? I'd be apoplectic.'

'Yes. Well, I was. I've never walked out on him like that before.'

'About time, if you ask me. He's being tone deaf. And after all you've been through. Is this new for him? I mean, was he supportive before, after your parents died? And after you lost your pregnancies?'

Meredith remembers his arm shielding her from the gaze of strangers in strip-lit hallways; bringing her food in bed, insisting that she eat; calling her employer for her and telling them, in no uncertain terms, that she needed a break, that she needed time to recover.

'Yes. He was.'

'So what's changed?' says Holly, sitting down opposite her and cradling her wine glass.

Meredith thinks.

'Well, it's been a gradual thing, ever since we moved to the island, I suppose. It all started off as a big adventure, but Phil has been so worried about money, especially because I'm not working, and his income isn't that great...'

'I remember you saying that before. I've got to say, that doesn't sound right to me. I know that pilots don't earn what they used to, but still – have you checked that?'

Meredith frowns.

'How would I do that? And why?' she says, before the doubt Holly has just injected into the conversation starts to seep in. 'Oh, I see. You think he's lying to me about how much he's making?'

Holly puts her glass down and looks her friend in the eye.

'I'm not saying that it's for a bad reason. Maybe he's saving up for something you don't know about? Or putting extra into a pension? It just didn't ring true to me, that's all.'

Bloody hell, thinks Meredith. As the alcohol spreads warmth through her veins, she wonders whether Holly could be right. Could her husband, the man she trusts above all else, be lying to her? And if so, why?

'I suppose he might be. It's not... impossible. But I just can't quite...'

'Look, he might not be. Maybe pilots really are paid peanuts these days.'

'Hmm,' says Meredith, still processing this new idea. 'He has seemed... very concerned about our finances for a while now. He took me out for lunch on Christmas Day and he was going on about wills and powers of attorney, as if we were both already decrepit.'

Holly's ears almost visibly prick up.

'Power of attorney? At your age? That's... weird.'

'He said it was so that we could make decisions about healthcare and things, if anything happened to one of us. I think maybe he was spooked by the time I almost went over the weir. That spooked me too, frankly.'

'Yes, fair enough. But... I dunno, Merry, there seems something wrong about all this. Something a bit strange.'

Meredith feels her stomach churn as an intensely unwelcome thought enters her mind.

'Oh Jesus,' Holly says, taking another mouthful of wine. 'You don't think he... no,' she says, as if answering her own question.

'I don't think he... what?'

'You don't think he... is trying to get you... sectioned?' she says, gulping down a large mouthful of wine.

'Blimey, Holly, that's a bit... a bit... dark.'

'Yes, I know. Sorry, it's probably the wine.'

Meredith doesn't reply for a moment. She's letting Holly's suggestion sink in.

'But why are you even thinking that? What has made you make that leap?' Meredith says, starting to feel a bit sick.

'I suppose the money thing, and then his insistence about you seeing that shrink... even though you don't want to. But, you know, it's nuts, isn't it? Nuts. I'm talking rubbish. It's pretty extreme, isn't it? I mean, why would he do that to you?'

'Maybe he wants to take control of all of our money?' says Meredith, the very thought of this sending a shot of ice run through her veins.

'He's got your assets, though. You're married. You share everything, don't you?'

'True. But pretty much all of it is in the house.'

'...which he wants to sell. And you don't.'

Meredith nods slowly.

'Yes, he does. But why would he need to go to such extreme lengths to get the money? Couldn't he just beg me? Explain how much he's worried about running out of cash? I mean, this whole idea of having me declared lacking in capacity is just... God, it is madness. Sorry. That's the wrong wording.'

'No, I agree, it does seem that way. It's a bit too out there, isn't it.'

They sit sipping their wine for a minute, both trying to come to terms with the serious nature of what they've just discussed.

'There is one other possibility,' says Holly, refilling her glass.

'What?'

'Well... couldn't he be having an affair? Maybe he's decided he wants to get out of your marriage, and he's been stuffing money away for a bit so that he can leave?'

'No. No, that's...' says Meredith instinctively. Philip may be many things, she thinks, but he is not a cheater. And despite everything they've been through, all of their shared grief, divorce has never once crossed her mind.

'And maybe he wants more than a half share of the house?' says Holly, knocking back more of her wine.

'That can't be it. It can't,' says Meredith, her head starting to swim. 'He wouldn't do that to me. I know everything about him. He knows everything about me. I'd know if he was doing that.'

'Some people are really good liars,' says Holly. 'My friend Andrea was with her girlfriend for three years before she found out she'd been in jail for a spell, *and* that she had two kids. The thing is...'

Meredith nods politely but isn't listening. Part of her really wants to be distracted by Andrea's sad tale, but the other part is trying to make sense of these new ideas. Could Philip really be hiding something from her? Could there be something dark, something macabre, almost, behind his insistence that she's seeing things, and needs to see a specialist? Or is it simply that the stress of the refurbishment they're attempting, and the failed planning permission, is taking its toll on them both?

Yes, she thinks, finishing her glass of wine and resolving not to have another – *yes*, that must be it. All of the other suggestions they've been talking about sound fantastical, like they're the plot of a Netflix thriller. Philip is just being caring, as he always is, and when she thinks about it, she is asking him to believe a lot on faith. If she puts herself in his shoes, she can see that the ghosts she's seen sound... ridiculous. She mustn't let her mind run away with her; after all, that's exactly what he thinks has happened to her, isn't it? She must try to remain calm and logical.

'I think I should probably go home now,' she says about twenty minutes later, when Holly has finished talking about Andrea and has now moved on to the great evil of the local residents' committee and their ridiculous planning decisions.

'Are you sure, lovely? You can stay all day if you like,' says Holly, lifting up what Meredith thinks must be her fourth glass of wine.

'Yes, I'm sure,' replies Meredith, taking a swig of water from a glass she's just poured, in an attempt to take some of the boozy smell off her breath. Although she doubts he will be fooled. 'I need to talk to Phil.'

* * *

'Merry? Is that you?'

'Yes, it's me,' she replies, closing the door behind her and following the sound of Philip's voice to the living room, where she finds him in the process of stripping wallpaper, something he's been promising to do for weeks.

'Thank God you're back, I was so worried about you going out in the boat by yourself,' he says, putting down his tools and walking towards her. *Good*, she thinks. *He's calmed down*. He opens his arm for a hug and she yields and falls into it, breathing in the scent of shower gel, coffee and wallpaper paste.

'I'm sorry,' she says, her desire to be close to him again overriding any desire for him to acknowledge her experiences. *He'll come around to it soon*, she thinks. *It's a lot to ask*.

'I'm sorry, too,' he says, sniffing her head. It's something he's done ever since she's known him. She supposes he does it to check she's still 'her'. *Well, I'm definitely still me*, she thinks. Despite everything.

'Have you been drinking?'

'Yes. Holly had wine in, and we had some.'

'You never drink during the day.'

'I do, when there's reason to.'

Philip releases her.

'You've changed, Merry. I don't recognise you sometimes, now. It's... disturbing.'

'For God's sake. I've had a couple of glasses of wine. What's wrong with that? Are you going to call the police on me, or something? Or, I don't know, *the doctor*?'

'Stop it. I'm just worried about you. You tell me you've seen things, you know, re-enactments of stuff you've been reading about, or whatever, and you went out into the fog following a man's voice which may or may not have been real...'

Meredith's hackles rise.

'How *dare* you.'

'I'm only telling you how it all looks from my perspective.'

'A man called out, and I followed him, I went to help him. It was a real voice. At first, I thought it was you. *Jesus*, Phil. Why aren't you on my side any more? Why are you so obsessed with money? Has something happened? Is there something you're not telling me?'

He shoots a look at her she's never seen before, and it chills her to the bone. She knows, instantly, that he's definitely hiding something.

'I'm not going to talk to you any more, until you've sobered up,' he says, walking towards the door. He's got his hand on the handle and is about to walk through it when he stops and turns. 'Oh, and by the way. I've made an appointment with Dr Ahmed for you. I'm home for it. I'll take you. It's in a fortnight.'

24

ELLEN

7 February 1944

Dear Mammy,

I'm sorry I haven't been a better correspondent. My job here has kept me almost entirely occupied; when I'm not on duty I am either eating or asleep, and even if I try to carve out a few moments to read or write letters in the evening, I often find I wake up several hours later with my head resting on the page.

The doctors here are starting to abandon the insulin treatment they previously preferred (and which we nurses all hated, due to the workload attached and the risk to our patients) and are now moving onto methods that seem to me to treat the men like animals. Honestly, Mammy, I saw cattle in the fields behind our house treated better than the men here. All that talk of following the methods Dr Lovell used in Cairo has come to nothing.

It seems to me (and Lord knows, I'm not allowed to have an actual opinion here) that they are becoming desperate. They are undoubtedly under pressure from higher-ups to send men back to fight. But having read about the recent German surrender to the Russians in Stalingrad, it does feel like the tide in Europe is turning. And if so, do they really need these soldiers so much that they are prepared to induce violence spasms and fits, which might actually damage their brains? Sometimes, I worry they are doing it for sport…

'Ellen, there you are.' Rebecca has appeared at the door, slightly out of breath. 'Ellen, I think you need to come down now.'

'But I'm not on duty. I only got off an hour ago.'

'I know that,' says Rebecca, her weight shifting from one foot to the other as she does so, 'but… Boyd has just come back from his ECT.'

Ellen snaps her notebook shut and puts it in the drawer of her bedside table.

'How is he?' she asks, knowing full-well what Rebecca will say.

'He's… groggy. He's vomited a few times.'

'Do you need me to sit with him?'

'It's not Boyd I need you for.'

And the penny drops.

'Harry?'

'Yes. I've seen how he responds to you. He trusts you. The thing is, he hasn't taken it well. He can see how Boyd has reacted and I think he managed to get hold of one of the textbooks the doctors left on the nursing station, so that we can read up on the procedure. He's… very panicked.'

'Oh Lord.'

Ellen scrabbles around for her shoes, pulls on her uniform and is ready within a minute. She follows Rebecca down the hallway and the stairs. She expects to be taken to Harry's ward, but is surprised when her friend opens another door. It's the door to a bathroom. Ellen walks inside and Rebecca leaves, closing the door behind her.

For a brief moment, Ellen thinks Rebecca has made a mistake. Harry isn't in here, she thinks. But then she hears quiet sobbing, and walks over to the far left corner, where the roll-top bath meets the wall. Harry is wedged between them, his head bowed, his body shuddering.

'My darling… Harry… It's me. Ellen.'

It takes Harry a good few seconds before he shows any sign of hearing her, and when he does respond it's very gradual. The shaking in his hands reduces first, and then his head and upper body rise gradually, as if they're being cranked by hand.

'Ellen,' he says, his voice a crackle.

'Harry, my love, I'm here. *I'm here*,' she says, locking the bathroom door and getting down onto the floor in front of him.

'I'm sorry, Ellen.'

'What on earth for?'

'For being mad.'

Ellen wishes she was strong enough to scoop Harry out of the crevice he's wedged himself into and to hold him tightly, and then to tell him, repeatedly, that he is not mad, that he is just injured: injured by war, injured by evil, injured by the terrible things humans are capable of. But she isn't, so she just grasps the part of him she can reach – his legs – and holds them tight, as if her arms are the only thing saving him from falling.

'I'm here, Harry. I'm here. It'll be fine, I promise. It'll all be fine.'

A few minutes later, when Ellen's legs and arms are beginning to feel numb but her grip is still firm, Harry lifts his head upright and looks directly at her.

'They say I'm booked in for ECT on Thursday. I can't go through that, Ellen. I can't go through what Boyd went through. I would not survive it.' Then he shuffles himself out of the gap and into Ellen's arms, where he begins to sob once more.

'I know darling, I know,' she replies, stroking his head and his back rhythmically, in an attempt to soothe both Harry and herself, because she remembers far too clearly the concerns raised about ECT in those medical textbooks: 'potential for amnesia', 'impaired mental functioning' and 'a recommendation against the use of convulsions for patients engaged in intellectual work.' *No,* she thinks. No. *He will not go through this*. 'I'll make sure it doesn't happen,' she says, continuing to stroke him as he cries.

'How?'

'I'm going to speak to them. To reason with them. I'm going to telegraph Dr Lovell to ask him to intervene. And then I'm going to speak to the doctors.'

Ellen resolves to do everything she can to help Harry, whatever the army might think about it.

When she returns to her room, she finishes her letter to Mammy, giving her an account of the day's events, before drafting a telegram she will ask Brian to send urgently on her behalf.

25

MEREDITH

8 February 2014

It's still dark, but Meredith can't get back to sleep. Her head's aching and her brain isn't yet ready for the literary novel she's been trying but failing to get into for weeks, so she picks up the notebook she found in the room upstairs, keen to read the next letter.

It seems the mystery nurse is desperately worried about the soldier she's in love with. He's due to have ECT treatment soon. Despite the fact it's decades later, Meredith feels anxious on his behalf. She's about to turn the page, eager to find out what happens next, when her phone bleeps. It's a message notification, which is unexpected as she has almost all calls and texts blocked until 7 a.m. This means it can only be urgent. She fumbles on her dressing table and pulls it towards her with trepidation, and the preview on the home page does nothing to calm her.

> Flood Warning: There is a flood warning in place for the River Thames between Chertsey Lock and Shepperton Lock. Flooding of property is possible.

Meredith opens the message in full and clicks the link inside, which contains advice from the Environment Agency about how to prepare. The list includes moving all valuable and important items from ground level, putting sandbags or stoppers in front of air bricks and making sure that you have enough drinking water, should the groundwater supply become contaminated.

Oh my God, she thinks. *Just how bad is this? It says flooding is possible. How possible?* She instinctively turns over to Philip's side of the bed to tell him and ask his advice, but he's not there. Of course, she remembers. He left very early this morning for Osaka. He won't be back for four days. As so often seems to be the case, she's on her own with this one. Although, not absolutely on her own, she thinks. She opens up the messaging app and sends Holly a text.

> Help! Got the Flood Warning text. Tell me – is this bad? Do I need to buy an ark?

Holly replies quickly.

> Hey hon, yes, got the same. This is definitely one to take seriously. We get quite a few flood alerts most winters but warnings are a lot more worrying. It only says property flooding is possible but not definite, which is good, but you still need to take it seriously and prepare. Is Phil with you?

> No. He's not back for four days.

> Oh, crap, that's not good. Do you want me to come and help?

Meredith really wants to say yes, but she knows that Holly will have her own preparation to do – after all, she also has a house next to the river, and she also doesn't have her own boat. Meredith doesn't fancy trying to take her boat across the river to collect her, if it's as feisty as the flood warning suggests. *No, it's probably safer to stay here and do it alone,* she thinks. She'll call Holly if she needs to. After all, moving important stuff above ground level won't take long – they have pretty much nothing of value.

No, it's OK. I'll manage.

If you're sure. Keep me posted on your progress.
Let me know if you change your mind.

I will. Thanks hon x

Meredith puts her phone down and takes a deep breath as she attempts to formulate a battle plan. Her water, which comes from underground, might be contaminated, or the pump might be flooded and stop working. She can't get over the river to buy more water, but she knows there are a few large plastic water containers around. *I'll fill them up and store them in the house,* she thinks, mentally ticking off the first thing on her brand-new to-do list. Then she decides to walk around the house looking for air bricks. She hasn't got any proper covers for them, however. Would plastic sheeting and duct tape do a reasonable job? It's worth a try. Everything's worth a try. She hasn't got any sandbags, so that's a no, and she'll have a look around and try to put anything on the ground floor that's electronic or valuable higher up, to save them if the flood waters manage to get into the house. She's already made sure that their boat is tied up in a place that should withstand rising water levels.

Meredith pauses, her mind still foggy with sleep, and considers how serious her situation could actually be. Is there really a chance that the river might make it into the house? They'd been given a flood risk map in the searches when they were buying May Day and of course they knew they'd be buying a house with a serious flood risk, but it has stood for so long and, as far as they knew, had avoided any serious flood damage – could that really be about to change? Meredith decides that she will not think about that right now.

She picks up her phone again and sends Philip a message. He won't get it until he lands in Japan this afternoon, but she wants to send it now so he knows she is OK and working on a plan.

They are still cross with each other. They had said only the most perfunctory of goodbyes when he'd come in to see her just before he'd left, waking her. She'd been half-drunk with sleep and had almost reached out to him for a hug, before remembering their argument and putting her arms down firmly by her sides. He'd kissed her on the cheek and said, 'Look after yourself, darling,' and she'd sort of grunted and turned away from him. In truth, she thinks her response was rather childish and she wishes she hadn't let him leave for four days like that, but she can't change it now.

> Morning darling. Hope your flight was OK? Got a text from the EA this morning about a flood warning – did you get similar? Anyway, have read their advice and am putting as much of it as I can into practice. Call me when you can. I'm absolutely fine.

Meredith considers putting 'love you', at the end, her normal sign off, but thinks better of it. She still hasn't forgiven him, and he has yet to apologise. *They'll have to keep talking when he comes back,* she thinks. *It's no good trying to resolve things when they're thousands of miles apart.*

The next few hours are both busy and exhausting. It's still dark for the first couple, so Meredith spends that time placing all power cables and anything that might potentially be of value on tables and chairs, with Poppy following her around like a shadow.

Next, she goes down to the basement to locate the water containers. It's cold down here, as usual, and everything is draped in finely knit cobwebs, some of which could be decades old. The caged bare lightbulb above her head is caked in dust, and casts a yellow hue on the space, which they have still not found time to sort through. She spots the blue water containers in the corner, peeking out from beneath an old tarpaulin and several chairs which are each missing a leg. She walks towards them and is about to haul them out when she sees something unusual. The floor beneath her feet, which is never usually anything other than light brown, is unusually dark. She takes her phone out of her pocket and shines its light on the surface and can clearly see what looks like liquid. She touches it, and it definitely feels wet. She lifts her hand to her face and smells; it has no odour. Is it water? And if so – where is it from? She looks around for an obvious source, but finds none. There are no marks on the ceiling, and there are no other dark patches anywhere else. *Oh well,* she thinks, *that's just another mystery to add to the list. May Day House just keeps on giving.*

When she returns above ground with three containers, dawn is breaking. She takes a quick break to make some coffee and eat a bowl of cereal, before returning to the task in hand. She opens the back door and steps outside for the first time this morning and is immediately struck by the roar from the weir. It's always there in the background, of course, but this morning it's like a diva demanding to be front and centre stage; it is simply impossible to ignore. She imagines the brute force of the water flowing through the gates and shudders. Most of the time, the Thames is like a gentle family pet, a gorgeous, familiar, reassuring presence, but today it feels like a predator.

Keen not to get too overwhelmed by her isolation, her predicament and her task, Meredith stoops down to stroke Poppy and give her a treat, and then keeps moving. She stands by the outside tap and begins filling the containers. It's a boring and lengthy job; each container is about eight times the size of a normal garden watering can, and the water pressure is fairly low. She hopes that doesn't mean the pump is about to break again. She has enough on her plate already.

She's halfway through filling the third container when she spots something in the periphery of her vision. Her eyes dart upwards and for a split second she sees a man's face in one of the first-floor windows. It's definitely a man, although she doesn't really have long enough to really digest his features. And this time, she instinctively feels that he is human.

She sprints back into the house, not caring that the tap is still running. She needs to find this man and ask him why he's in her house. *If I can find him*, she thinks, *I can prove I'm not losing my mind.*

She bolts into the hallway and quickly checks the rooms downstairs – no sign of him here – then runs up the stairs and begins to search each room in turn, opening the doors at speed, as if she's a cop with a loaded gun doing a sweep of a property. And yet all she finds behind door after door are the usual stacks of mothballed furniture and mildewed books. Where has he gone? Could he have possibly made it downstairs before she came back into the house? Surely not. She was in the hallway in seconds, and that definitely wasn't long enough for anyone to run out of any of the upstairs rooms and down into the hallway and through the front door. That's just not possible.

Meredith enters the last room with trepidation. *He has to be in here,* she thinks; he won't have had time to go upstairs, because she'd have heard his footsteps. She kicks the door open.

'Come out. I know you're in here,' she shouts, but there's no answer. 'Don't be ridiculous. I saw you. Come out.'

She stands stock still for a moment, listening out for any breathing sounds, anything that would give the man's location away. But all she can hear is the boom of the weir and the thrashing of her own heart. She opens up all of the boxes and looks inside, behind and below every piece of furniture, but there's no sign of anyone in here. Frustrated, she walks to the window to check on the state of the river.

It's then she realises there's something wrong with the picture. From her viewpoint, she should be able to see their boat moored, attached to a tree to keep it afloat and safe during any flood.

But it's not there.

Is she looking at the wrong side of the island? But no – she can see the wooden mooring through the trees, which winter has stripped of their greenery. There is no boat moored anywhere nearby. Adrenaline floods through her. Their boat is gone.

As she runs back down the stairs, yanks on her shoes and sprints towards the mooring, questions flood her mind. Was it tied up properly? And if it was tied up properly – then has someone deliberately untied it?

And then she realises. The man she saw upstairs must have taken it. *That bloody man, who's violated my home and destroyed my sanity, has stolen my boat,* she thinks, the rage growing inside her. She realises, however, that he can't have gone far, not with the river as fast as it is. *If she has a faster boat, she might be able to catch him,* she thinks, or at least find it wherever he's planning on dumping it.

She pulls out her phone from her pocket.

'Damon? Hi, it's me, Meredith. I'm really sorry to bother you.'

'Oh, hi! I was thinking about you, with the flood warning this morning. What do you need?' She thinks she can hear the roar of the river in the background. No one near the Thames can avoid the sound of it right now.

'You won't believe this, but someone has stolen my bloody boat.'

'Oh shit… Sorry. That's grim.'

'I know, it's all I need. I just can't believe it myself. I was wondering… is there any chance you could pick me up in yours and we could go looking for it? It can't have got far.'

'Oh, wow, yes, sure. I'll be there as quick as I can.'

Meredith rings off, instantly relieved that she has a plan. While she waits for Damon, she walks around the garden, focusing on the water's edge, trying to work out how far the river has risen in the past fortnight. She can see quite clearly that a large chunk of the grassy bank is now submerged, and tree branches that previously skimmed the surface are well below the waterline, the pace of the stream constantly tugging, as if it's desperate to pull the whole tree under.

When she hears a boat engine in the distance, she walks back over to the mooring, which is still just visible. She waves when she spots Damon's boat. Despite its powerful engine, it's clear that it's taking a lot of energy to force the vessel against the stream. Seeing this makes Meredith glad that she didn't attempt to cross the river in her own boat yesterday. These conditions are clearly difficult even for experienced river people.

'Hiya,' he says, when he's near enough to be heard.

'Thanks so much for coming so quickly,' she says, as he pulls the boat in and grabs hold of the dock.

'No bother. Hop in,' he says, holding out his hand to steady her as she jumps on board. As soon they get moving, she regrets not bringing a raincoat. She'd felt fine in the garden, when she'd been walking around searching for the boat or the man she suspects took it, but on board, sitting still, the wind is slicing through her jumper and T-shirt and the rain is pelting down.

'You wet?' Damon says, smiling wryly as the rain starts to lash their faces.

'A bit,' she says.

'Put this on,' he says, throwing her a coat that's sitting by his legs. 'I always carry a spare one. It feels at least five degrees colder on a boat.'

Meredith smiles gratefully and pulls on the large, hooded, padded jacket. It's quite dirty and smells a bit of mildew, but she doesn't care. She warms up quickly and is soon sitting on the opposite side of the boat to Damon, scanning the river for the boat.

'So you think somebody took it?'

'I reckon so.'

Damon nods.

'How long ago? Any idea?'

'I don't know. But when the Stirlings came to collect Phil early this morning to ferry him over for work – we have an arrangement with them, you know – they'd have seen if it wasn't there. So it must be fairly recent. Do you think we've got any chance of catching them up?'

'Dunno. Doubt it. But they can't just hide a boat. They'll have moored it somewhere. Let's see.'

They're making good progress down the river now and are just about to pass Damon's narrow boat. 'Actually, I think a man took it.'

Damon stops scanning the water and turns to look at Meredith.

'A man?'

'I saw him. He was inside the house. I tried to find him but he must've got away before I could get to him.'

'How did he get onto the island?'

Oh God, Meredith thinks. *Why have I been so stupid?*

'I don't know. Maybe he had his own boat?' she says, realising as she says it that this would mean the man had no reason to take her boat.

'Taking two boats would take a long time to do. You'd have to tie them together.'

Meredith wraps her arms across her chest and looks away, embarrassed at her mistake.

'You're right,' she says. 'He couldn't have got onto the island without a boat, could he.'

'It's possible someone did take it,' says Damon, noting her distress. 'Must've been two of them. Theft on the river is really common. People come along in boats, saw off engine locks and ropes and take craft, sometimes even in daylight. It's very possible.'

'If they do that, what do they do with the boats they've stolen?'

'Sometimes they just thrash them around a bit, like a joyride, and then dump them. And sometimes they are stealing them to sell.'

'Can't imagine anyone wanting ours.'

'You'd be surprised,' Damon replies. 'You have a newish, powerful engine.'

They're quiet for a minute, as they continue examining the towpath, slipways and gardens along the river.

'Is this just pointless?' Meredith asks.

Damon slows down.

'Nah. Definitely worth a look. And then there's the hassle of you having to claim on your insurance for a new one... Let's search for a bit longer.'

Meredith nods in agreement, and they keep looking. They pass at least ten live-on boats. Damon waves at one of their occupants.

'That's Tim,' he says. 'He's a nice bloke. Bit square. He's a copper.'

Meredith raises an eyebrow.

'I know what you're thinking. He's a copper, and he lives in an illegal houseboat. How does that work?'

'Yes, pretty much,' she says, slightly embarrassed.

'Yeah, well, there's quite a variety of us here. Housing is so expensive now, even people with proper jobs sometimes end up buying a boat and living here. I know some people call us river gypsies' – Meredith winces – 'but most of us are just honest, hardworking people who can't afford rent. And it's much warmer in a boat than in a tent.'

'I see.'

'I bet you hate looking at our ugly boats though, don't you?' says Damon, with a hint of a smile on his face. 'Don't blame you. I would, too. But it's so expensive to paint them properly and obviously if you haven't much cash in the first place, you can't buy a nice boat. And then it's so expensive to maintain them...'

'Yes, I understand,' says Meredith, keen to get off this rather uncomfortable topic.

'Yeah. It's a tough life, though, definitely. And hard to get out of once you've got into...'

'Look over there! What's that? Is that it?' Meredith has spotted something that she thinks might be her boat. It's obscured by the overhanging branches of a tree, but it's the right colour – grey – and she thinks it looks big enough to be a boat.

'Let's take a closer look.'

Damon turns down the power and steers the boat towards the trees. When they're on top of it, Meredith pulls back some of the branches. Her heart leaps when she sees the familiar engine on the back and the plastic boxes they use as seats. 'Yep, this is it.'

'Blimey, good spot,' says Damon. 'And look, whoever it is has tied it up. It definitely didn't just wash away.'

Meredith sees that someone has tied it around the tree trunk and knotted it securely. Yes, someone doesn't want this to slip its mooring, that's for sure.

'Bloody bastards,' she says.

'Maybe they were planning to come back for it later.'

Meredith looks around then, to see if there are any boats moored nearby who might have seen what happened. However, they're on an uninhabited stretch of the river, and there's no one to be seen, not even a dog walker or runner. *It's not the weather to be outside voluntarily,* she thinks.

'Yes, maybe.'

'Well, let's make sure they can't,' says Damon, making for the bank, where he secures his boat to another tree and hops out. Meredith watches as he unties the other boat and pulls it along the towpath towards her.

'The engine is still on it. That's lucky,' he says as he sets to work tying the two boats to each other. 'Looks like it came through the experience pretty unscathed.'

Meredith smiles. She's genuinely relieved to have it back, even though she wouldn't fancy taking it out on the river until the flood warning has eased. It represents her connection to the outside world, and given what she's been through lately, she thinks she needs that more than ever.

Once Damon has finished his task, they set off slowly upstream. They're against the wind, and it's whipping up waves which are colliding with the prow of the boat, sending showers of icy water over them. They are going much more slowly now, and she can hear that the boat's engine is labouring as it battles to drag almost twice its weight through the surging, swollen stream. She pulls her borrowed coat more tightly around her face and lowers her head so that she's looking down at the boat floor for most of the journey back. She's hugely relieved when she hears Damon reduce the engine's power. She lifts her head and sees that they've reached the island.

'Home sweet home,' he says, trying to keep his voice light, but she can tell that even he has found the boat journey back stressful. The river is no one's friend at the moment. When Damon reaches over from the bank to give her a hand to help her alight, Meredith's mood lifts, and he seems to feel the same, judging by the smile on his face.

'Thank God that's over,' she says, her words echoing what they both feel. 'Thanks so much, Damon, honestly, you're a lifesaver.'

'Like I said, river people stick together.'

They stand in silence for a moment by the swollen riverbank, both so soaked through now, despite their raincoats, that a few more minutes outside won't make any difference.

'Would you like to come in and dry off?' she asks, feeling that she needs to do something to express her gratitude. 'And maybe have a coffee or something?'

'As long as it's an *or something.* I need something strong after that,' he says, following her as she walks towards the house. 'I really don't fancy going back onto the river again right now.'

26

ELLEN

9 February 1944

It is 6 a.m., and that means it's time to get up for her shift, but Ellen cannot muster up the enthusiasm to push her blankets away. She already knows that it's bitterly cold in the house; not as cold as outside, of course, but still chilly, and damp, too. May Day's leaky sash windows have not been able to keep the insistent rain entirely at bay. She doesn't need to open the curtains to know that it's still pouring outside, because the rainfall that's hammering on the roof of the orangery is so loud it sounds like someone's skimming stones on its surface.

She looks over at the other bed and sees that Rebecca has already got up. She's surprised that she didn't stir when she was getting dressed, but then, she's abnormally tired at the moment, and not sleeping well. She'd lain awake for a good few hours last night, wondering whether Dr Lovell had received her telegram yet, and if so, when he'd reply. She has little time. Harry is booked in for ECT tomorrow. She knows that she needs Dr Lovell's backing if she's going to stand any chance of changing the doctors' minds. But will he give it? She's not sure, and even if he does, will his opinion sway the opinions of Major Cole and Captain Joyce? She's even less sure about that.

Ellen's thoughts are interrupted by a knock at the door.

'Yes? Who is it?'

'It's Captain Huntingford,' says the senior nurse, opening the door without further warning. 'Goodness, still not up, I see. Come on, shake a leg. You've been asked to attend a meeting with Major Cole before your shift.'

A bolt of electricity shoots through Ellen.

'Why?' she asks, casting her sheet and blankets aside and reaching for her slippers. She needs to go and wash her face and brush her teeth before she can get changed into her uniform.

'They haven't deigned to tell me, I'm afraid, Lieutenant Quinn. But it does make me wonder. What on earth have you been up to?'

Captain Huntingford's air of suspicion, tinged with disdain, reminds Ellen of her senior school French teacher, who'd mistaken her natural linguistic ability for cheating. She never liked Madame Williams, and she has never particularly warmed to the captain, either. What the senior nurse thinks or doesn't think about her is of no consequence. What lies in store in the doctor's office does, however.

'Nothing, Captain Huntingford. Just my normal duties,' says Ellen as she picks her dressing gown off the hook on the back of the door and puts it on, tying it at her waist.

'Hmmm. Well, whatever the reason might be, please get dressed in double quick time and go down to see Major Cole immediately. I'll expect you at the nurse's station afterwards. We are short-staffed. We couldn't bring back two nurses from day leave yesterday. The river is running too fast for the safe operation of the boat.'

Ellen is not surprised – she's seen how fast the river is flowing – but she is perturbed. The boat is the only connection they have with the outside world, their only source of more food and medicine, and knowing that it's currently out of action makes her feel on edge.

'I see. I'll be there as quickly as I can,' she replies, walking past Captain Huntingford, in the direction of the communal bathroom. The senior nurse's nostrils flare as she passes.

'Very well. I shall see you soonest,' she says, turning on her heel and walking back down the hall.

'Can't wait,' replies Ellen under her breath, closing the bathroom door behind her. It's only then, as she goes through the mechanics of getting ready for her day, that she allows the low-level panic she is now feeling constantly to expand to its full capacity. She has been called to the doctor's office, after all. Alone. It's not a routine meeting. Have they found out about her relationship with Harry? If so, she will certainly be sacked. Or has Dr Lovell been in touch, perhaps? *Maybe,* she thinks, *this is good news?* After all, Dr Lovell is widely regarded by the psychiatric community as a figure of authority.

Ellen leaves the bathroom and walks back into her shared bedroom where she puts on her uniform, making sure that it meets the captain's exacting standards. If this is in any way good news, she doesn't want to spoil it by getting a disciplinary for being shoddily turned out. After a brief check in the mirror, she leaves the safety of her room and walks briskly down the hall and takes the stairs to the first floor. She raps on Major Cole's door, determined not to display her anxiety about what this meeting holds.

'Come in.'

Ellen does as she is asked, shutting the door firmly behind her. When she turns around, she finds both Major Cole and Captain Joyce sitting on the other side of the large rectangular desk, as they had done during Harry's treatment with sodium amytal.

'Take a seat,' says Major Cole, directing her to an upright wooden chair, which is in the same place as the large leather chair they had asked Harry to sit in.

'Lieutenant Quinn,' says Captain Joyce, as soon as Ellen is seated. 'Thank you for coming to see us promptly.' Major Cole shoots a censuring look at Captain Joyce at this point, as if he's in trouble for being off-script.

'Quinn,' says Major Cole, deciding, clearly, that today is not a day for army protocol. 'I have had a telegram, and subsequent phone call, with Lieutenant-Colonel Clarence Lovell.' Ellen's spirits lift. Dr Lovell has responded to her plea for help. *Of course he has,* she thinks. He's a good man. A very well-respected man. They will listen to him. 'Lovell tells me you contacted him asking for his help.'

'Yes. I worked with him in Cairo. I very much enjoyed doing so. I was nursing men who were experiencing mental disturbance after terrible encounters and dreadful injuries. He had a unique way of dealing with them.'

'We know about Lovell's practice and his... theories,' says Major Cole.

'He is very well regarded, I understand,' says Ellen. 'His latest paper on—'

'I do not need you to tell me anything about my own specialism, Lieutenant Quinn. Nothing at all.'

Ellen swallows hard. It's clear that being spoken to, and advised, by a more senior army psychiatrist has bruised the major's ego. Does this mean that he's been told to stop carrying out ECT at May Day House? Perhaps that's it. Perhaps he's furious at being told to stop. The thought buoys her.

'Of course, Major Cole.'

'And yet you clearly feel that you do, Quinn, or you wouldn't have wasted both your time and money sending a telegram to Egypt.'

Her spirits sink. This is not the way she had hoped things might turn out.

'I merely wanted to ask him, sir—'

'Whether our treatment regime here is acceptable? Reasonable? Evidence-based?' Ellen does not know how to respond. Almost anything she says will land her in trouble. So she says nothing, and the doctor doesn't seem to mind. 'Well, Quinn, I can tell you that I don't give a damn what you wanted to ask him. Your opinion here is *not required*.' His voice is so harsh, Ellen sees Captain Joyce flinch. 'The army employs you, Quinn, as a nurse. You are to tend to the men, to keep them comfortable and to administer any medical regimes we, the doctors, see fit. Your role is not to question and it is certainly not to be insubordinate.'

'No, Major. I understand that, Major.'

'Clearly, Quinn, you do not,' he says, annunciating so harshly, he's almost spitting. 'Otherwise, I would not have had the conversation I've just had on the phone, long distance, from Cairo.' There's a brief pause. Ellen wonders whether she is expected to speak. Perhaps she is – but if so, what does he expect her to say? She is intelligent enough to know that saying anything else at this stage would amount to laying her own trap. 'So, you aren't interested in what was said? I am most surprised, Quinn. Most surprised. Because I am told that you are interested in the care of one of your patients in particular. It is him, I understand, that prompted your concern about our use of electric shock treatment...'

'It is about all of the men, sir. My colleagues and I cared for the man who underwent the first ECT session. He was... vacant, sir. He was... slow. It was like his personality had left him.'

'And yet you only called your doctor friend when a particular young man, one Flying Officer Hennessey, was due to undergo the same treatment. Why is that?'

Ellen feels warmth flooding to her cheeks. She daren't look at Major Cole, in case he can detect the guilt in her eyes.

'It is simply that I saw how it was the first time, sir, and I am deeply worried about some of the men... They are vulnerable, sir. They are... ill. They don't have the strength to—'

'They're soldiers, woman! Soldiers. It is our job here to give them the shock they need to snap out of their current condition, rediscover their consciences and their sanity, and return to the fray. That is what we are here for.'

'But Dr Lovell says—'

'Lieutenant-Colonel Clarence Lovell may find his methods work for him in Cairo, but damn it, he is not here. He is *not*. *Here*.' Major Cole pauses. He pulls a handkerchief out of his left jacket pocket and pats his forehead with it. 'But I am. And I find it most irregular that you have tried to intervene in this way. I am suspicious of your motives.'

'I just want the best for the men...'

'Hmmm. As you say. But I don't believe you, Quinn. Joyce, please tell Lieutenant Quinn what is going to happen,' says Major Cole, as if he is ordering tea. Ellen turns her attention to the major's junior colleague, who has remained silent so far. Captain Joyce keeps crossing and uncrossing his legs, as if he's having trouble getting comfortable.

'Major Cole has decided... that your services will no longer be required here at May Day House,' he says, looking down at his notepad.

'But I—'

'Don't argue, girl,' interrupts the major. 'It is not in your best interests to argue. You should be grateful, in fact. I am merely recommending that they move you to another hospital. You will not lose your job, although I firmly believe that the level of disrespect you have shown the doctors here merits it. Unfortunately, we need nurses as much as we need doctors at the moment, and so I have been persuaded simply to have you moved. Joyce, please continue.'

Captain Joyce clears his throat.

'You will be required to return to your room now, and not leave until such a time as transport can be arranged to remove you from the island. You will not speak to any of the patients, or any of the other staff, until you leave.'

'But I—'

'No buts, girl. The time for buts has long gone. Go, pack your things and ready yourself.'

Ellen feels as if she has been winded. She wants to argue back, to tell him about the papers she has read which describe ECT, with its benefits and negatives – which, undoubtedly, he has also read – and to beg to stay, to carry on the work she has been doing, alongside her Harry, her darling Harry. But she knows that it would all be pointless. She did the best she could, the *only* thing she could, to try to save him from undergoing brutal treatment, and this is her punishment. It was a risk she had run, and she had lost.

Ellen stands up slowly, gives Major Cole a cold glare, turns around and walks out of the room. She begins to cry as soon as the door clicks shut behind her, and by the time she reaches her room upstairs, she is sobbing. She puts her hand over her mouth to try to stifle the noise, and throws herself down on her bed, the bed that she'd only left half an hour ago, in what feels now like another lifetime.

* * *

'Can I come in?'

Ellen recognises Captain Huntingford's voice immediately, although it's not the same officious voice she'd used a few hours earlier, when she'd come to tell her she needed to see Major Cole.

'Yes,' replies Ellen, her voice croaky. She pulls herself up to sitting, reaches for her handkerchief and wipes her face to try to make herself slightly more presentable.

'Goodness,' says Captain Huntingford, surveying the scene. Ellen knows she must look a state. She has been crying for a couple of hours now, interspersed with the cathartic beating of her pillow, or hammering of her feet on the floor. She must be red in the face, her eyes must be puffy and her hair is no longer restrained by its regulation bun. She instinctively gets up to go and check it in the mirror. 'Don't bother on my account,' says the senior nurse, sitting down on Ellen's bed. Noting this unusual behaviour, Ellen sits back down. 'I'm told that you are to be transferred.' Ellen nods, worrying that she will start to cry again if she tries to speak.

'Frankly, I think that is a great shame.' Ellen looks at her colleague in surprise. 'I think you have been doing a very good job on the wards. The men like you and trust you.' Ellen sniffs and tries to smile. 'Unlike certain other elements of the medical staff.' Ellen examines Captain Huntingford's expression. *This is definitely not her usual script,* she thinks. 'My brother was at El Alamein,' she says, not missing a beat. 'He survived, but he is not... the same. He was treated by Lieutenant-Colonel Lovell in a military hospital in Cairo. And, I now understand – nursed by you.' Ellen looks up in surprise. 'For what it's worth, Lieutenant Quinn, I think you did the right thing, asking for Lovell to intervene here.' Ellen is dumbfounded. 'Yes, I think it was the right thing.' The senior nurse gets back up and readies herself to leave. 'The doctors here have been told to pause the use of electric shock treatment, pending a review,' she says, as she puts her hand on the door handle. 'I thought you should know.'

Ellen is still digesting her extraordinary words, and the brilliant news within, as she turns the handle.

'I will make sure that food is brought to you regularly, and that you have some books and magazines here also, to pass the time until the river returns to normal,' she says. 'Goodbye, Lieutenant Quinn. Thank you for the excellent care you have provided, to all our patients.'

27

MEREDITH

9 February 2014

'And this is where we plan to hold weddings,' says Meredith. They're standing in the orangery, and she's having to shout so that Damon can hear her over the hammering of the rain on the roof.

'Rii-ght,' he says, taking in the overflowing buckets which are located at random intervals beneath the many cracks in the glass, and the waterfall that's rushing down the tree in the middle, which has long since pushed its way through the glass towards the sky.

'It takes a bit of imagination,' she says, taking a swig from the large gin and tonic she poured herself a few minutes earlier. 'But it's going to be amazing.'

'I can see that,' replies Damon, also swigging gin and tonic. 'You'll need a few bob, though, won't you?'

'Yes. Unfortunately. We've replaced the roof on the main bit of the house with savings, but we needed planning permission for this bit, because we want to demolish it – as you can see, it's absolutely wrecked – and make it bigger so we can fit at least a hundred in here, sitting down.'

'But the buggers at the council turned you down, didn't they?' says Damon, running his hands down the rotten wooden window frames.

'Yep, they did. Not helped by the local residents' association sticking their oar in.'

'Nest of vipers, that lot. They are always trying to get our boats moved on, or scrapped, or whatever. I mean, if they confiscate the boats, where do they think we're going to go? Twats.'

'We're both clearly persona non-grata around here,' says Meredith, walking towards the door that leads into the main house. 'We outlaws should stick together.'

'Yeah, definitely. Persona-non-grata. Whatever that means.' Damon laughs and holds his glass up. Meredith does the same with hers, and they clink together, the high-pitched chime produced by the two Edinburgh crystal tumblers – a wedding present from her parents – cutting momentarily through the roar of the rain.

'Where's Phil at the moment?' Damon asks as they walk through to the kitchen.

'Oh, he's on a four-day trip. Won't be back for three more days,' says Meredith, opening her fridge door. 'Do you fancy lunch? I can put something together.'

'Yeah, that'd be great,' he replies, taking a seat at the table.

'Anything you don't eat?'

'Nah, I'm an omnivore. Whatever you have is fine by me.' Meredith nods and pulls out the ingredients for a homemade pasta sauce. 'Must be hard for you, spending so much time here by yourself.'

'Yes, I suppose,' she says, peeling an onion. 'But I'm kind of used to it now. He's always been away for days at a time, ever since we met.'

'Yeah, but you haven't always lived on an island, have you?'

Meredith laughs.

'No, that's true. And I used to work full-time, so I had a lot to keep me busy. But now it's just me and Poppy,' she says, giving the dog a stroke as she passes by, in search of her water bowl, 'and a *whole* lot of DIY.'

'You can say that again. Honestly, I don't know how you do it.'

'I'm not sure how I do it, either,' says Meredith, slicing through the onion. 'You know, I'm not even sure I do? Sometimes, I don't think I'm keeping it together at all.' She pauses for a moment. 'Not at all.'

'We all have days like that.'

'Yes, I know. But I bet you haven't started seeing things?'

There's a beat, during which Meredith keeps chopping, as if by doing so she will somehow slice through the awkwardness which is hanging in the air.

'Like, what things?' Damon says, getting up and helping himself to more gin from the sideboard and tonic water from the fridge. 'A top up?' he says, hovering over Meredith's glass.

'Yes please. And I mean... ghosts. *That* sort of seeing things. The whole *Woman in Black* shmoo. Apparitions. Noises. The whole caboodle.' Meredith empties the chopped onion into a frying pan and turns on the heat.

'Well, this conversation has taken an unexpected turn,' says Damon, sitting back down and taking another sip of his drink.

'You don't believe in ghosts?'

'Nah. Well, I've never seen one, anyway.'

'You haven't heard the rumours about this place?'

'Oh, yeah, I've heard 'em. When I was a kid, we used to tell each other stories to try to scare the shit out of each other. We'd dare our mates to go onto the island and spend the night there, stuff like that. But it was just kids being kids. We never saw anything. Well, I didn't, anyway.'

'Lucky you,' says Meredith, taking a pepper out of the fridge and beginning to slice it.

'So, you've seen stuff here? Really?'

'Yep,' she replies, drinking some more of her gin and tonic. 'Well, at least I think I have. I saw someone in the garden, but I couldn't find any trace of them. And then I heard a voice, what sounded like a young man, calling for help in the fog. And then, the *pièce de résistance*, I saw three men in an upstairs room.'

'Bloody hell. Three men?'

'Yep. And they looked like they were from World War II.'

Damon whistles.

'Shit. That's quite out there,' he says. 'Doesn't it make you want to just sell up and leave this place behind, that sort of thing? I don't think I'd want to continue living here after that.'

'You know, honestly, despite everything I've been through, I have never once considered leaving this place. Isn't that funny? It's like, deep down, I know this house and I belong together. That we're linked in some way, and that these ghosts, if that's what they are, they're separate, transient. I have felt at home here on May Day ever since I first saw it. It drew me in immediately. I don't ever want to leave.'

'Fair enough. Can't argue with that,' says Damon, putting his glass down so hard, it seems to slap the table. He's getting quite drunk now, Meredith thinks. And come to think of it, she realises, *so am I.*

'Phil, mind you – he does want to sell now, apparently. I can't quite believe it, but there it is. We've argued about it. We almost never argue. Or at least, we didn't used to. It was… grim. It's like he's… lost the love.' *Both for this house and for me,* thinks Meredith.

There's a brief pause, during which she turns on the extractor fan on the wall.

'Do you know about the island's history, in the Second World War?' *Bless him for noticing my discomfort and changing the subject,* she thinks.

'Yes. It was a military hospital,' she says, tipping the peppers into the pan.

'I don't know much, but I have heard that soldiers used to come here to recuperate and stuff.'

'Yes, that's all I knew. But then I found a notebook, hidden in a drawer upstairs,' she says as she reaches for a tin of tomatoes from one of the cupboards. 'I think it's by a nurse who worked here. No name, but she seems to have been an army nurse. She was looking after soldiers with mental illnesses. What we'd call post-traumatic stress.'

'Oh?'

'From what I can tell, some of the treatment was pretty brutal, although there isn't much detail. There are some letters in it, though, and they're fascinating. It seems she fell in love with one of the patients. He was about to have ECT treatment – electric shock – but I don't know what happened next, because I haven't had time to read any more yet.'

'Look, please don't take this the wrong way,' says Damon, getting up and coming to stand next to her by the hob, clutching his drink to his chest. 'But is it possible that reading this stuff has set you off – you know, given you weird dreams? And that you were asleep when you saw those things, in the house?'

Meredith feels colour rise to her cheeks, and not just because of the alcohol that she's consumed. She knows that she sounds mad. And it really bothers her that Damon, this friendly guy who's helped her out, and who's just getting to know her, thinks that about her. What if he tells everyone in the area what she's just told him? Suddenly, she feels very vulnerable. And without warning, she starts to cry. She engages in a flurry of activity to try to hide it – grabbing a tin of tomatoes and wrenching it open, before emptying it into the pan, sending red globules of sauce flying over the kitchen surface and her own jumper – but her efforts are fruitless.

'Oh, mate, please don't cry,' says Damon, looking around for the kitchen roll, finding it, snatching off a piece and handing it to Meredith. She dabs her eyes and then tries, fruitlessly, to remove the sauce from her clothes with it. 'I'm sorry, I didn't mean to trash what you've been through. I mean, what do I know? I've seen all kinds of shit. Once, when I'd done mushrooms, I even thought I could fly.'

Meredith tries to smile, then grabs a clean cloth from beside the sink and runs it under the tap, before dabbing it over her jumper.

'No, I'm sorry,' she says. 'How pathetic. If I can't even cope with someone doubting me, quite reasonably, what the hell is wrong with me? And Christ, just listen to me... It's no surprise that Phil thinks I'm losing my mind.'

'Phil thinks what?' says Damon.

'He thinks I'm losing it. These things I've seen... He wants me to... see a psychiatrist. He's even made an appointment.'

'Seriously?'

'Yes, seriously. He thinks, you know, that all of the grief I've had to deal with... My parents died, you see... Plus the trouble we've had here since we bought the house – the planning permission, the money worries, the damage to our boat, and then the theft of the boat – he thinks that it's tipped me over the edge.'

'What do you think about that?'

'I'm furious. Holly, my friend – do you know her?'

'Holly? Oh yeah, I do, I think. In her thirties? Lives just off the towpath? Teaches yoga?'

'Yes, her. She's nice. We're friends. Anyway, we were talking about this the other day and it really made me think.'

'About that?'

'Well...' Meredith wonders momentarily about whether making this admission is the right thing to do – after all, she's not sure how good Damon is at keeping secrets – but a combination of the alcohol, the morning's stress and the simmering anger at Philip's disbelief makes her throw this idea aside. 'You know... maybe, that he might be trying to... have me committed. Declared unfit, you know? So he has control of my money.'

'Bloody hell, that's quite...' says Damon, rubbing his right hand over his forehead and sweeping it over his hair. 'That's quite an idea, isn't it?'

'Yes,' replied Meredith, glugging back her gin and tonic, desperate to do something to mask how uncomfortable this conversation is making her feel. Then she fills the kettle with water, puts it on and grabs a saucepan for the pasta.

'What did you think about that?'

'I think... that it's far-fetched,' says Meredith, taking a small pack of fusilli out of a cupboard and emptying half of it into the saucepan. She takes a wooden spoon out of the cutlery drawer, stirs the pasta to prevent it sticking, and then places it back down on the counter. 'But you know... it's been niggling at me.'

'What – you reckon there's something to it?'

'I don't know. Part of me is certain there isn't. But you know, it's all so... strange. Him changing his mind about the house, wanting to sell, and then being so determined to get me to a psychiatrist... it doesn't add up. Something's wrong.' She carries on stirring the pasta, far more than it actually needs, and as the water starts to boil, feels tears well up, and within a few seconds, she's crying again, loudly, overtly, embarrassingly. *Shit*, she thinks. *Shit.*

Damon doesn't say anything, but he leans past her, turns both hob rings off, and draws her in for an embrace. She stands there, crying into his shoulder, for longer than she suspects either of them is comfortable with.

'Blimey, you've been having a crap time,' he says, finally. 'Look, come and take a seat.'

'What about lunch?'

'It can wait. Come and sit. Let's talk about this. It seems to me that that's what you need.'

Meredith does as he suggests and takes a seat at the long oak table.

'Sorry,' she says, wiping her eyes with her hands. 'I'm so sorry. What a bloody mess.'

'Don't be,' says Damon, sitting down next to her. 'Now look. You've had a hell of a lot to deal with, it seems to me.'

'Yes.'

'And you've been working here by yourself, for days at a time.'

'Yes.'

'And then you were turned down for planning permission, and you fell out with Phil about money, and selling the house.'

'Yes, but...'

'I can see Phil's side, a bit. I mean, you've had a lot to deal with. Maybe these things you've been seeing. You know, maybe you are, what's the word...'

'Hallucinating? I know. I get that. But I'm not. Seriously. The dog saw the same things I saw.'

'Did she? Every time?'

Meredith thinks. Perhaps not every time? Last time, when Meredith had seen that figure in her bedroom, she hadn't stirred, had she? Not for ages.

'I suppose not. But, do people really see apparitions when they're grieving, or stressed? Full-figure ones, whole scenes? Because I've been doing some research, and I don't think so.'

'Yeah, I was wondering about that.'

'And this psychiatrist... He's made me a bloody appointment. Like I'm a child. I don't know... it's like...'

'Merry – a thought just occurred to me, and honestly, you can make of it what you want, but...'

'...but?'

'I've had experiences like yours when I've taken drugs.'

'I don't take drugs, though. I never have.'

Meredith blinks furiously to try to stop herself from crying.

'Right, yeah, I'm not surprised. You don't seem the type,' he says, and she raises an eyebrow in protest. 'You just don't, Merry. That's not a judgement or whatever. But yeah, I was wondering whether there's any chance that you're taking them and... not knowing that you are?'

She sits back in her seat and blows a stream of air up towards her eyes.

'Like I'm taking them in my sleep, or something?'

'Nah. I meant...'

And then the penny drops.

'You mean, you think Phil might be... buying them and giving them to me? What, in my tea?' Damon says nothing, his fingers thrumming on his now empty glass. 'Jesus. I mean, there's dark, and then there's...'

Two conflicting emotions erupt in her simultaneously at that moment.

One, anger: how can this man she hardly knows be making this hideous accusation about her husband? And the other, fear: what if, by some chance, this man is actually right?

28

ELLEN

10 February 1944

Ellen has been confined to her room for twenty-four hours. She's playing her tenth round of solitaire of the morning, and it is rapidly losing any semblance of appeal. She has also started and abandoned two novels, done the crossword and practically memorised the rest of the newspaper, including the obituaries. Occasionally, she gets up and walks to the window and stares out, monitoring the river for any sign that the force of the flow is letting up.

It's not, however. Not even close. *In fact, if anything,* she thinks, *it's getting worse, even though the pouring rain has now given way to drizzle.* There are puddles forming on the lawn, and she keeps catching sight of sundry, incongruous items – fence panels, plant pots, waste bins – being carried down the river, as if it's a hunter showing off its prizes.

There's a knock at the door.

'Come in,' she says, immensely glad of any interruption that alleviates both her boredom and her thoughts.

'It's only me,' says Rebecca, and her heart sinks a little. She's been hoping that Harry might find a way to come and find her here, although she knows it would be hard for him to get away and sneak in without being seen. He must know by now that she's being moved, and she hopes he will also have found out why. Her heart aches with the immense pain of knowing that she's going to be taken away from him, but she is still incredibly relieved that he will be spared the electric shock treatment. Making sure he's safe is the only thing that matters.

She will bear the pain of moving, knowing that he will be all right. She cannot let her love for him cloud that. Because she can't have him, can she? He's married. They will have to be parted sooner or later, whether it's the war, or the end of the war, that does it. And this way, perhaps, is the best way. She would never have found the strength to leave him by herself.

'Oh, hello, Bec,' says Ellen, doing her best to look pleased at her friend's arrival.

'Hello, you,' says Rebecca. 'I've brought you a new magazine,' she says, walking to Ellen's bed and handing it to her. 'You must be bored to death up here.'

'Thank you. You could say that.'

'The captain is going spare downstairs,' says Rebecca, sitting down on the bed. 'She's telling everyone we're severely short-staffed. Particularly when she's near the doctors…'

Ellen tries to smile, glad at least that someone is missing her.

'Any sign of them being able to bring the other nurses over the river yet?' she asks, although she's already certain what the answer will be.

'No, not yet. The river seems to be getting worse, if anything. You're going to be stuck up here for a while yet. Sorry, lovey. How are you bearing up? You were awake early this morning.'

'Not great, to be honest. A mixture of boredom, frustration, anger and sadness. I can't believe I'm going to have to leave here. Especially now…'

'It must be so hard to leave him.'

Ellen's eyes dart upwards.

'You know?'

'Oh, Ellen. You don't even have to say it. I can tell, just by how you are with each other.'

'I am sure you don't approve…'

'Don't be silly. It's not about my approval. I'm not a prude, and I live in the real world. I know how things go. I know what love feels like. I just don't want you to be hurt. He's married, isn't he? And he's not going to divorce her. He can't. He's too honourable.'

Ellen nods, swallowing hard to try to hold her emotions in check.

'I know that. All of that. And I don't disagree. But it's so hard, Bec. It's so hard to feel that way about someone and to hide it, to deny it. It's like a kind of madness. And I know the irony of saying that, here.'

'I quite understand. I've been similarly mad in my time.' Ellen sees that her friend also has tears in her eyes, although she senses she doesn't want her to delve deeper. 'He knows everything, by the way. I told Harry myself this morning. I wanted to make sure he heard it right, and he understood why you're being sent away.'

'Goodness. Thank you, Bec. Thank you. I wasn't sure if anyone would tell him. I didn't want to ask you. I didn't want to get you in trouble.'

'Don't be daft. Of course I was going to tell him.'

'Well, thank you. For everything. I'm going to miss you, you know, when I go.'

'Do you know where they'll send you?'

Ellen shakes her head.

'Not yet. Not a dicky bird. Part of me hopes they'll send me back to Egypt, back to Dr Lovell. I can't stay near Harry, it would be too painful. And I want to keep doing good.'

'Well, missy, wherever they send you, you make sure you keep in touch,' says Rebecca, standing up and brushing down her skirt. 'When this is all over, you can come and stay with my family in Gloucestershire. Mother does a mean roast beef joint.'

'I will. Of course I will. And anyway, I'm not going yet. I'll still be here when you finish your shift tonight. I could be here for a week, at this rate.'

'Excellent. Now, enjoy the magazine. There's something on page twenty I think you'll like particularly,' says Rebecca with a wink, before opening and closing the door.

As soon as her friend has gone, Ellen opens the magazine and turns to the page in question. She is surprised to find a handwritten note slipped in between the pages.

It reads:

Dearest E,

R told me the news today. I couldn't believe it, and I am beside myself, thinking of you stuck up there, so close and yet so far away. I can't bear it. I know, my darling, that you put your career on the line for mad old me, and for that I am astonishingly, eternally grateful.

Look, damn it, I refuse to let them send you away without seeing you one last time. Will you meet me in the pump house at 11 p.m. tonight, so that we can say our proper goodbyes? R will be on duty in the hall, and I know that she will not tell a soul.

With all my love, always,

Me x

Ellen sits back against the bedhead and holds the note against her heart. Just the knowledge that Harry has also held it gives her comfort. She closes her eyes, says a prayer for forgiveness, and counts down the hours until she can see Harry for one final time.

29

MEREDITH

9 February 2014

'Are you sure about this?' asks Damon.

'Absolutely,' replies Meredith, wobbling slightly as she walks down the steps to the cellar. She needs to know that these things she's been thinking about Philip aren't true. She has to search everywhere, so that she knows he's in the clear.

She's already searched his bedside table – nothing there but eye blinds, ear plugs and moisturiser, the standard toolkit of the long-haul pilot – and through the bathroom cupboards, although she sincerely doubts that he'd hide anything there, as she goes there looking for things far more often than he does. This is the only other place that she can think of where Philip has been spending time alone recently, sorting through stuff they inherited with the house, to see if there's anything worth selling. So far, he's found some silver plates and a couple of bits of porcelain amongst the detritus, which sold on eBay for a few hundred quid.

Meredith flicks the light switch and gasps. The small damp patch she'd spotted on her previous visit has grown into a small pond.

'I'm assuming that wasn't there before?' says Damon.

'Yes. When I last came in here, it was a bit damp. I thought something was leaking from above, but... obviously not, unless it's a huge leak?'

'Nah, that's the water table rising. We should check the flood alert status when we get back up and have signal. That's a bit... worrying.'

'Have you seen this before?'

'Well, obviously I don't have a basement,' he says with a half laugh, 'but I do know that when this area floods, it's not just the river breaking its banks that does it. It comes up through the ground. Like this.'

'Oh.'

'Do you have anything down here that's valuable, that you need to keep safe?'

Meredith examines the piles of old boxes, sheets, broken plastic buckets and gardening equipment.

'I don't think so. Phil's been going through it. It was all here before we moved in.'

'Good, because I suspect it'll all be pretty damp, pretty soon.'

Meredith feels a twinge of fear. She imagines the water rising through the floor at speed, forcing the contents up towards the ceiling, blocking out the light.

'Shall we go up and check it?' she says, her heart rate rising. 'I can't believe he'd put anything in here.' In fact, Meredith can't quite believe she's spent so long looking for something she is now 100 per cent certain will never be found. Because the idea of Philip deliberately drugging her is so outlandish, it's like it's also a hallucination.

'Yeah. After you,' he says, following her back up the stairs into the hallway. When they reach the top, Meredith's phone beeps. She pulls it out and looks at it, thinking that it'll be Philip, letting her know that he's heading back to the airport for the flight home. But it isn't.

'Shit,' says Damon, who's also looking at his phone.

Flood Warning: Chertsey Lock to Sunbury Lock. River levels are high, and some property flooding is expected. Be prepared. Call Floodline for advice.

'Oh God,' says Meredith. 'Does that mean what I think it means?'

'Yeah, I think so. But don't panic.' Meredith's mouth twitches. 'Look, I know I sound like something out of Dad's army, but honestly, usually they just mean that water will creep up gardens and *might* do things like flooding basements like yours. But nothing else.'

'OK,' says Meredith, who is starting to pace. All of her earlier, warm drunkenness seems to have deserted her.

'Look, let's go back into the kitchen, I'll make you a cup of tea, and then we can talk about next steps.'

'Right,' she answers, dazed. She follows him into the kitchen and sits down at the table, while he buzzes around filling the kettle and then opening random kitchen doors. 'Mugs are in the cupboard above the sink,' she says, her head in her hands on the table. 'Tea bags are in the one to the right of it.'

'Right you are,' he replies. As he goes about his task, she pulls out her phone and sends Philip a text.

> Flood alert just became a flood warning. Sounds a bit scary, but don't worry, Damon – you know, the guy who fixed our pump – is here and helping. I'll be fine.

It's the first time she's mentioned Damon to Philip. She didn't tell him about the boating lessons Damon gave her, because it was obvious Philip didn't approve of boat dwellers, judging by their first meeting. She reckons, though, that he'll probably be reassured she has someone around to assist. He hates leaving her on her own.

'Here you go,' Damon says, placing a mug of tea next to her. She sits up and runs her hands down her face. 'Hope it's OK. It's pretty strong.'

'Thank you. I need it,' she says, picking it up and taking a gulp.

'So, this flood warning,' he says, sitting down next to her with his own cup of tea. 'The main thing is the stuff you've already done. You need to take things that are precious off the floor, secure your boat, and try to block up any ventilation bricks.'

'Yes. They mentioned sandbags too, but I don't have any of those.'

'Don't worry about that. The house is up a couple of feet from the ground, that's why there are steps up to the front. You should be grand. You won't need those.'

'OK. Are you sure?'

'Merry, I'm not a time traveller, but I've lived here a long time, and this house has never flooded since I've been here.'

'I believe you.'

She sits back and cradles her tea.

'Shit, I wish Phil was home,' she says.

'Yeah, it's crap. Look...' he says, putting his mug down. 'Do you want me to stay? I mean, I can bed down in your living room, or one of the rooms upstairs. If it makes you feel better?'

The relief shows on Meredith's face.

'Thank you, that would be amazing,' she says, really meaning it.

Her phone beeps again. She checks it. It's from Philip.

> Damon's there? Living on a boat Damon? Why is he there?

'Just don't put me in the haunted bedroom.' Damon grins, and Meredith smiles in return, in an attempt to mask her unease at Philip's reaction. She hates his irrational hatred of the boat people. She types a quick reply.

> I called him because someone stole our boat and I wanted to try to find it. I didn't want to worry you about it. He took me down the river. We found ours, brought it back and tied it securely. He's going to help me prepare the house for possible flooding. He's being really nice.

'Who's that you're messaging?' asks Damon.

'Oh, just Holly,' lies Meredith.

'Oh, sound. Is she worried too?'

'Seems fine,' she says, quickly, locking her phone and putting it in her back pocket. 'Look, I was making you lunch,' she says, realising that it's almost two in the afternoon, and she started cooking several hours ago.

'Oh, eating's overrated.'

'Don't be silly. I'll get back to it. The sauce will be fine, at least.'

Meredith stands back up and walks over to the hob. She turns the heat back on and checks the pasta, which is congealed and cold. She decides to make another batch, so empties the remaining water in the sink, dumps the pasta and starts again.

'Honestly, I'm just so glad you're here,' she says, feeling more in her stride. 'It makes me feel so much better.'

'Don't mention it. It's nice to be somewhere with a working hot water system and proper electricity, to be honest.'

'Glad to be of service,' she says, putting more pasta on to boil. 'And I'm sorry that you've had to listen to my angst all day. I'm guessing you had more fun things to do.'

'Nah, not really.'

'Well, good.'

She leaves Damon scrolling through his social media while she finds plates, cutlery, a large chunk of cheddar and the salt and pepper. She lays them on the table a few minutes later, when the pasta is reaching al dente.

'What would you like to drink?' she asks. 'More gin and tonic? Another tea? Something else?'

'I think I could do with a glass of water, to be honest,' he says, putting his phone down. 'I might say yes to a beer or something later, mind you. But water would be great for now.'

'Good idea.'

Meredith opens a cupboard near the window that overlooks the back of the house. It's where they store the sundry items – their cafetiere, the measuring jug, the juicer, the grater – along with their everyday drinking glasses. She chooses two water glasses, snatches the grater, because she'll be needing that later, and then is about to shut the door when something unusual catches her eye.

'What the…?' she says, as she eyes a small plastic bag just visible behind a box of coffee papers on the second shelf. She doesn't recognise it. She pulls it out.

'Let me look at that,' says Damon walking over to where she's standing and gently taking the bag from her. He opens it up – it's one of those bags with a press seal at the top – and sniffs it, before dipping a finger in and tasting a small amount. 'Hmm,' he says. 'That's not sugar.'

'Then what...?' says Meredith, her head beginning to spin.

'I'd say that's a drug. It was bitter. If I had to put money on it, I'd say it was ketamine.'

* * *

'I still can't believe it.' It's two hours later, and Meredith and Damon are sitting in front of the fireplace in the front room of May Day House, sipping red wine from a bottle that is now half empty. A fire is blazing, its heat gradually warming the damp, frigid air in the room. The only other light is coming from a tall standard lamp in the corner. 'I just... can't.'

'Yeah, I know. It's a lot to take in.'

Damon has been telling Meredith about ketamine, and how it can make you feel confused, alter your perception of time, and even make you hallucinate. He seems to know what he's talking about, and she knows that if this theory proves to be true, and Philip really has been secretly dosing her up with the drug somehow, it explains an awful lot. It would certainly explain the ghosts – visions, hallucinations, she doesn't know what to call them – that she's been having. But even given that, she just can't reconcile Damon's suggestion with the man she knows, the man she married, the man she loves.

'But how would he have given it to me?'

'I dunno. Food? Drink? Is there something you drink that he doesn't?'

There's my kefir, she thinks. *I'm the only one to drink that. But surely not...*

There's a long silence. Then Damon speaks.

'Look, I think I should tell you something.'

These words hit Meredith like an icy blast.

'Go on,' she says, her throat tightening, so she struggles to get the words out.

'I know Phil, from before. I knew him when we were kids.'

'Did you?' Meredith's head snaps around, so that she is looking directly at Damon. He isn't looking at her, though, he's looking straight at the fire. She remembers how frosty the atmosphere had been when they'd met at the pump house when they'd just moved in. They hadn't acted like old friends. In fact, they hadn't even seemed to know each other. 'Why didn't you say?'

'We fell out, you could say.'

'When? Why?'

'Look, if I tell you this, you have to remember it was a long time ago, OK? People change. That's why I didn't say anything to you before. But it occurs to me that it might... explain things a bit.'

'Go on,' she says, her stomach starting to churn.

'So, yeah. A group of us used to hang out together around here after school and at weekends, Phil and Stuart included. Mostly we would just sit around listening to music, smoking roll ups and drinking cheap cider, and in the summer we'd swim and egg each other to come onto May Day Island, that sort of thing.' Meredith pulls herself up in her seat and puts her wine down. The mention of swimming in the river has sent shivers down her spine, because of course, she knows how Stuart died. 'You know how teenagers are, don't you? We were always searching for the new thrill. The old thrills didn't quite do it any more. So eventually, we transitioned from cheap booze and fags to drugs. Slowly at first – it started with weed, which I managed to buy off some guy who hung around the gates at school. I enjoyed it. We all did. We were so chilled out, we laughed loads, it was ace. We even took ecstasy once, but we only managed to buy the one and we shared it between at least six of us, so we felt absolutely nothing. It was probably made from talcum powder anyway.' Damon laughs at this, but Meredith is struggling to find it funny. As far as she was aware, Philip had never touched drugs at all. 'But it wasn't enough for Phil. I'd noticed how he'd always smoke more intensely than the rest of us, roll himself a bigger one. The rest of us were having a laugh, but it became a bit of an obsession for him. Anyway... one day, he came and met us, all excited. He'd told us he'd met a guy at his job – he worked as a... what was it...?'

'As a waiter in a pub?' This part of Philip's story, she did know. He'd worked there in the school and university holidays.

'Yeah, that's right. Some guy he worked with had managed to get hold of some cocaine. Phil'd spent his wages on enough for all of us. We were all flat broke, you know, and used to weed, so it came as a bit of a shock.

But we did it, of course we did. We didn't want to lose face. And it was... wild. At the beginning, I felt like I could do anything, you know, anything I set my mind to. It was like the biggest adrenaline rush you could ever have. It was... mad. And Stuart, oh God, he was beyond high. He was usually one of the quiet ones, you know? Not one to speak much, not one to do anything wild. He was in his brother's shadow a lot. But when he took the coke, he was like a different person. It was his idea to go to the bridge. And we all went with him.'

'Wait... Phil was there? When Stuart went into the water?'

'Yeah. Didn't he tell you?'

'No. He told me he wasn't there, and that's why he feels guilty. That he couldn't save him, because he wasn't around to...'

'He was there all right.'

Meredith feels her stomach flip. Surely this can't be true. Surely? Philip can't have been lying to her all this time?

'Oh yeah, he was definitely there. Anyway, we all climbed up onto the bridge that goes over to Desborough Island. Do you know it?' Meredith nods, and swallows hard, trying to keep as calm as she can. 'Yeah, well, as I say, Stuart was high. Very, very high. And he said that he wanted us all to jump off the bridge into the river. It's a famous spot for that, that bridge. Loads of kids do it every year, still do. But we'd never done it. Not mad enough, maybe. But that day, Stuart wanted us to. We all went up there, and even though we were high as kites, everyone except Stuart was having second thoughts. I remember looking over the side and the river seemed a long way down. I mean, it is, it's got to be at least a twenty-five-foot drop. But we all tried to laugh it off, cracked some jokes, took the piss out of each other, all the usual stuff you'd expect from a bunch of lads. I remember Phil saying he didn't fancy it, and Stuart telling him that he was a poof. I know that's not PC... but that's what we used to say. It was the nineties. Anyway, Stuart, before we knew it, he'd jumped up on the side of the bridge, and he was just standing there for the briefest of moments, like a millisecond, balanced like a tightrope walker... and then, he was gone.'

'Was he dead when he... surfaced?' asks Meredith, piecing together this new story with the version Philip had told her.

'I don't know. Honestly, I don't know when he died, exactly. We all ran down to the riverbank when we saw that he wasn't moving. We thought he was joking, at first. He could be a joker. But then the seconds went by and he didn't move. Despite the drugs in our system, we all sobered up pretty quickly then. I threw myself into the water and swam over as quickly as I could. I turned him over and I put my ear to his mouth to see if he was breathing. But… he wasn't.'

'Oh, God.'

'Sorry, Merry, I know this is a horrible story. I know it is. But I wanted you to know it, know what happened, because… I think you deserve the truth. After Stuart died, well, our group fell apart, more or less. Phil still came for a bit, though, and always with drugs he'd bought. It was definitely more about the drugs than it was about any friendship we had. He was broken, after his brother died, and drugs seemed to be his way of dealing with that.'

Meredith struggles to reconcile this version of Philip with the version she knows, the airline pilot who won't touch alcohol within twelve hours of a flight, the man who told her his worst vice at university was sex with the wrong women.

'You think Phil was… addicted to drugs?'

'Yeah, I do. And I'm beginning to wonder whether he still might be. I mean, you said that he doesn't earn that much. That doesn't sound right. Where's his money going? Maybe, you know, it's going on drugs?'

Meredith thinks about this. Could it be possible that he might be taking drugs when he's away? Could he be successfully keeping that sort of thing from her? It doesn't seem likely, she thinks, but then – she found drugs in her kitchen. Unidentified drugs. And Philip *has* been unpredictable lately. Those monster runs along the tow path at all hours, his moods changing rapidly, his strange about-turn over the house. And if he really is deliberately dosing her with ketamine or whatever in her drinks, maybe that is just an extension of his own addiction? And if he wants her to sell the house, is that to get at money – money for more drugs? It's possible, isn't it? Possible that he might even be deliberately sending her mad so that he can take control of all of her money…

No, no, she thinks. The kind, caring, thoughtful man who held her hand after her miscarriages, who'd taken time off work to grieve with her after her parents' deaths – *that man would never do this.*

'I still can't get my head around...' she says, as the light in the corner flickers, and then turns off. 'Oh.'

Damon leaps up and tries the switch for the main room light. It doesn't work.

'Power's off,' he says.

'Is it to do with the flood, do you think?'

'Dunno. Might be. The electric cable comes overground to here, doesn't it?'

'Yes, I think so. But we have some kind of electrical box out the back – to be honest, I've never really thought about it.'

'I'll go and take a look.'

'I'll come too,' Meredith says, getting up and turning her phone torch on.

'You sure?'

'I'd rather not stay alone here with only the fire and the dog for company,' she says. 'I'd rather be doing something.'

'Fair enough.'

They both put on their coats and shoes, pull up their hoods and open the front door. Poppy dashes around Meredith's feet as they do so. She realises then that she hasn't taken her out yet, so she grabs the dog's lead and attaches it. 'Sorry, Pops, I don't think it's safe to let you run around out there,' she says as she steps out into the rain. The outdoor lights are off too, she notices, so they just have their phone torches to light their way.

As soon as she reaches the bottom of the steps, she realises they're in trouble. The gravel beneath her feet is giving way, like she's walking on wet sand.

'The ground is completely saturated,' she says to Damon, noticing that he's not pausing to examine the ground beneath his feet – he's already heading off around the side of the house. She follows, realising that he's seen this sort of thing before. A reminder of how lucky she is to have him here at the moment. She wouldn't like to be dealing with this by herself. She rushes to catch him up, pulling Poppy, who seems incredibly distracted by every sound and smell, along behind her.

'Come on, silly thing. I know that it's very strange out here at the moment. Lord knows, I agree... The rain just won't stop. But we just need to keep... Urgh...'

The ground was not where she had expected it to be. Instead, she found water, and she has tumbled face first into it, her arms and legs splayed out wide. And in the same instant, a panicked Poppy tugs the lead from her grasp and runs off.

'Poppy! Poppy!' she shouts, her mouth full of water which tastes of earth.

'Merry! Are you OK?' shouts Damon, running towards her.

'I... lost... my... footing,' she says, trying to push herself up, but the ground beneath the surface is so wet, it keeps absorbing her grasp, like quicksand.

'I've got you, I've got you,' he says, grasping her firmly at the waist and tugging her backwards. The effort required is so significant that he loses his balance, and seconds later they are both lying on their backs on the ground, winded.

'Oh God, I'm so sorry,' she says, pulling herself up to standing, noting with relief that all her limbs seem to still be attached and working.

'Don't be. It's treacherous out here. The water has come in at least six metres, maybe more. It's all over the electricity box. Which probably explains the power cut.'

'I've lost Poppy,' she says, reaching for her phone to turn the torch back on to look for her, and then realising with a sinking feeling that it was in her hand when she fell. She checks her pockets, and it's not there. 'Oh God. I've also lost my phone.'

'In the water?'

'Yes, I think so.'

Damon shines his own torch around the area, but there's no sign of it. The water is so muddy, it's hard to see anything. She realises that it could even have been swept away into the main flow of the river.

'It's just a phone. Ignore it. I'll get another one. I care more about Poppy. Can you see her?'

'Let's look for her,' says Damon. The pair begin a slow search around the parts of the garden they are able to reach safely. Meredith stays behind

Damon, who now has the only light source. They scour the trees and the bushes, look in the pump house and beneath piles of garden waste, but there's no sign of her. Meredith begins to panic. Has she drowned? Her lovely, beloved pet?

'Oh God. I've lost her. Oh, God,' she says, her pain apparent in her voice.

'Look, I know it seems bad, but I promise you, dogs often turn up fine when they run off like this. I've lost count of the number of times dogs have fallen into the river, their owners have gone in after them to save them, and the dog has been fine – but the owner has got in trouble and needed rescuing themselves, or sometimes, even drowned. She'll be fine. She'll have found a quiet place to hide. You'll see.'

'Do you think?'

'Yeah, I do. Look, it's wet and cold out here, and you're soaked through.' Meredith realises that her teeth are chattering. Her worry for Poppy has masked her own discomfort. 'Let's get you inside to warm up. Poppy will come back, barking to be let back in. I promise.'

'OK,' she says with great reluctance. 'OK.'

She follows Damon as he finds a safe path back to the front door.

'Here we are,' he says once they are inside. He helps her to take off her coat and her shoes, as if she's a child. She does feel like one, suddenly; she feels disorientated, ignorant, well out of her depth. She also feels unwell. There's a creeping numbness in her limbs and her teeth are chattering. 'Come through to the fireplace.' Meredith sits meekly in one of the armchairs, while Damon removes her soaking-wet socks.

'Are there any candles anywhere?'

'Yes. A few in the kitchen. Under the sink.'

'OK. I'll go and get a few. We're going to need light.'

Meredith nods in acceptance. While Damon is gone, she walks up to the window and stares out into the darkness, hoping to catch sight of Poppy. The muted light of the moon allows only for brief flickers of illumination, however, and all she sees in these are the ripples of water where she knows water should not be. The sight makes her nauseous. She walks back to the fire and stands next to it, trying to absorb its warmth, though even this is now on the wane. She's fumbling around in the dark for new logs when Damon walks back in the room carrying a tray upon which sit two water glasses now functioning as candle holders, and two further glasses filled with liquid. He places them both down on a side table.

'Let me do that,' he says. 'Sit down. You need to rest. You've had a shock.'

'OK.' She retreats to an armchair. Damon brings one of the glasses over and hands it to her.

'And drink that. It'll help.'

Meredith takes a sip and discovers that it's whisky. It tastes like smoke.

'Thanks,' she says, clasping it tightly, watching Damon feed new wood into the fire.

'That'll do us for the next couple of hours,' he says.

They sit in silence for a while, listening to the flames caressing and finally penetrating the seasoned logs, which spark and spit in protest. Meredith's eyes grow heavy. She checks her watch and sees that it's 7 p.m., although it feels much later. She is both frantically worried about Poppy and the flood and achingly tired after all the effort and adrenaline needed to deal with it all. She decides that she will nap for a while. She briefly considers heading to the bedroom, but the lack of heat or light in there makes her change her mind. She will stay here, she thinks, letting her eyes close as she slumps in the chair, the whistling of the wood her lullaby. Here, where it's warm, and light, and safe.

* * *

'There you go, lovely. I'm here. I'm still here.'

Meredith is no longer in the chair. She's now on the floor, lying on a duvet with a pillow beneath her head. She is vaguely aware that she no longer seems to be fully clothed, because her legs don't feel damp any more. What she does feel is warm and dry, which is very welcome. She turns over on her side, to curl up and fall back to sleep.

But there's someone there. Her eyes snap open, startled, and she can make out the shape of a person lying next to her.

'Phil?'

'No, shhh, it's me, Damon.'

'Damon?'

'I didn't want to leave you alone. So I thought we'd both sleep here by the fire.'

Meredith is tired and, because this logic seems reasonably sound, she doesn't reply. She just closes her eyes and waits for sleep to return.

It's not sleep that comes, however. Instead, there's a hand. It's working its way up her leg and around her thigh in light, gentle, swirling gestures. She tries batting it away, as if it's a spider.

'It's OK, lovely. It's OK. I'll be gentle.'

She is wondering what he's about to do – perhaps, she thinks, he's going to remove a plaster, like Philip does when she asks, or perhaps he's going to lift her nearer the fire for warmth – when it becomes very clear what he actually means. His hand is now between her legs, and it's working its way around her knicker elastic, funnelling inside.

'What the?' she says, her outrage now fighting with her addled brain. '*Get off me*.'

'I thought you wanted this,' he says, going all in now, his lips on her lips, his tongue thrashing away, trying to gain access to her mouth. 'That's why I'm here, why you asked me to stay here,' he says, pulling away briefly. 'Because you want me. Not him. Me. You want me. You want this.'

'I... don't...' she says, pushing him away with all the strength she has, which is, in reality, very little. '*I. Don't*.'

Damon is stronger than her, and he keeps her with him, skin to skin, his sour odour filtering into her pores. She begins to thrash around on the floor, but it feels like she's swimming in treacle; she's making no headway.

Why can't I move properly, she thinks, before yelling when one of her hands catches a splinter of wood from a floorboard. The resulting stab of pain is just enough to pull her out of her sluggish state for a few seconds; long enough, she discovers, to reach behind her, grab a glass containing a burning candle, and tip it over Damon's head.

The result is immediate. She can't really see, as the light is so dim, but she can hear his response when the melted wax hits his face.

'Shit! Shiittttt!' he says. 'What did you do that for?'

He lets go of her to try to rip the wax off, and this is all she needs. She rolls away from him, scrabbles upwards, her limbs protesting and refusing to balance properly, but with persistence she manages to make it to the door, then into the hallway, then into her bedroom across the hall.

When she's inside, she slams the door behind her before reaching forward in the dark to locate their wooden bed. Once she's found it, she yanks it towards her with all her might, the wooden legs screeching as they scrape across the oak floor. When it's close to the door, she feels her way around the bed to the headboard and shoves it as far as it will go. She hears it bump against the door and then, with the tiny reserve of energy she has left, she throws herself on top of it and pulls the covers over her. She has only seconds before her adrenaline fades and the drowsiness takes hold of her again, and this time, she doesn't fight it. She is asleep in less than a minute. So deeply asleep, in fact, that Damon's frantic shouts and his fruitless hammering and yanking of the door handle do not wake her.

30
ELLEN

10 February 1944

It is 10.45 p.m. when Ellen puts down the book she has been trying and failing to read and gets herself ready. She has been counting down to this moment all day, mentally preparing herself for the stealthy descent down the hallway, two flights of stairs and through the kitchen to the back door. She knows, because Harry had told her, that Rebecca is on duty on the first floor, so she isn't worried about that. It is the possibility of someone popping out of one of their rooms on this floor to use the toilet, say, or one of the night nurses on the ground floor seeing her that worries her most. And she has to get back upstairs afterwards, of course, running the same gamut each time. She knows that if she's caught, they'll sack her, which is a hundred times worse, for her at least, than being moved. And she doesn't want to give Major Cole the satisfaction, either.

Ellen's heart races as she tiptoes down the corridor, the floorboards creaking nonetheless. As she passes each closed door she holds her breath, aware that the colleagues behind them might wake up and catch her at any moment. She is relieved to arrive at the top of the stairs, where she finds moonlight filtering through the stained-glass window, casting ghoulish shadows on the walls. She descends the stairs to the first floor, noting with relief that it is indeed Rebecca who's sitting behind the desk in the hall. They exchange a look which Ellen feels might not be out of place if she'd seen someone walking to the gallows. It's a melodramatic thought, of course, but not entirely inaccurate. Being forced to leave here, to leave Harry, does feel like a kind of death to her, and this, she knows, will be the final time she will ever see him.

When she reaches the ground floor, however, her heart sinks. Two nurses she knows well are chatting by the nurse's station. She shrinks back against the wood panelling and considers her options. She only has two: one, she waits here until they finish and go back to their wards, or two, go back upstairs. That's no choice at all, she thinks, moving back further to wait. She just has to hope that no one will leave the rooms on the first floor and walk downstairs, because if they do, they'll certainly see her.

It feels like hours, but in reality it's probably about ten minutes, before the two nurses finish discussing their charges and their various grievances against both other colleagues and the army, and head off in separate directions. Ellen breathes a sigh of relief and makes her way down the hallway towards the kitchen. She hopes that Harry will wait for her.

The room is dark, the chef having long since gone to bed. She inches her way past the scrubbed oak table in the centre, her senses alert for any sudden movement inside the room or out. She can see the paved area at the back of the house through the window, with its well and kitchen garden. The rain has eased, and the moon is visible tonight for the first time in at least a fortnight. Its light also allows her to see the river beyond, which is high, fast and furious. She can absolutely understand why Brian isn't prepared to take the boat across at the moment.

She is about to push the door open when she hears a noise. It's almost imperceptible, but definitely there – the sound of a door opening, perhaps, or closing? She stands stock still and holds her breath, waiting to hear if footsteps are coming her way. She waits there like that for at least a minute but hears no further noises. It must have come from one of the floors above, she thinks. Not this one, at least.

She pushes the back door open slowly and closes it at the same pace, before pausing. She's aware that she still has to cross the open area before she reaches the safety of the pump house. She glances at the windows above, checking that all of the curtains are closed – which of course they should be, for the blackout – before darting across to the building opposite. The door is slightly ajar, as she'd hoped it would be. She tugs it open and dashes inside, pulling it closed behind her.

It is less than a second before Harry is embracing her, pulling her so close to him she worries she may struggle to breathe.

'I thought you'd decided not to come,' he says, pulling away for a moment.

'Of course I came,' she says, running her hands up and down his back, hungry to take in as much of him as she can in the short time she has left. 'I just had to wait at the bottom of the blinking stairs. Two of the nurses were having a chinwag.'

'Well, you're here now,' he says, his voice husky.

Ellen melts into him, and for the next twenty minutes, neither of them says a word, because their bodies are communicating for them. Recalling this experience much, much later, Ellen just remembers red. For their tangle of limbs, their frantic need and their acute joy mingling with an unmistakable sensation that they were both drifting towards an abyss was just too much to process, so in the event, she simply recalls the intense colour of the inside of her eyelids as she lay there upon the tiled floor, wanton and unashamed.

'Ellen,' he says afterwards, when he's wrapped her up in his coat and they are sitting next to each other, their limbs entwined. 'Ellen, I want you to come away with me.'

She blinks several times in rapid succession, as if she's testing whether she's awake.

'But… you're married.'

'I know I am, Ellen. I know I am. And I can't divorce my wife. But I think there is a way. If I agree to re-join the RAF, I'll have the independent means to support you, to support us both. My father will allow it. I won't be the first man in my family to have maintained a mistress.'

'Harry, please. Don't call me that. It makes me sound… cheap.'

'I'm sorry, my love, that's not what I meant. You know I love you. I love you more than I have ever loved anyone. I just mean that we wouldn't be married.'

'I see.'

'But we will be able to live together, to be together, forever. We can even tell people we're married. They will never know. And the world is changing anyway, Ellen. This war will end one day, and we will never be able to go back to the way things were before. We just won't. Things will change. Maybe I'll eventually be able to divorce her…'

Ellen is in turmoil. She desperately wants to say yes to Harry; this is the future she has dreamed of, the mistress bit aside. But she knows as well as he does that there are other hurdles to jump over first.

'But they're about to send me away. I'll be gone as soon as the river calms down. And you are still here receiving treatment. You'd have to return to the RAF, and you mustn't do that until you're better.'

'That's the thing. I'm going to leave. I'm going to leave now.'

It's only then that Ellen notices the small rucksack in the far corner of the building.

'You're… packed?'

'Yes, I am. I have everything I need right here. You are all I need. We will leave tonight. I have enough money to put us up in a hotel nearby, and then tomorrow I will find you somewhere more permanent before returning to my unit. They won't question me, they're too desperate for pilots to care.'

'What if the doctors here contact them and ask?'

'I shall say I'm cured. That the ether treatment did the trick. They can assess me all they like; I shall sound as sane as they are. If indeed they *are* sane.'

'But Harry…'

'Yes?'

Ellen pauses. She is trying to formulate what she needs to say next, because her future depends on it.

'Harry, I can't come with you now,' she says, trying to avoid looking directly at him, in case she loses her nerve. 'I can't. If I go AWOL, the army will discipline me and I'll be sent to prison. You know that.'

Harry sinks visibly.

'I hadn't thought of that.'

'And the river is too dangerous tonight, anyway. We can't get across in these conditions, it's not safe. Brian won't risk it, and he knows the river.'

Harry doesn't reply immediately. He seems to be thinking.

'Then, you won't come now. You'll stay here and wait to see where they send you. And then you will simply resign and finish your service honourably. And then you will come to me.'

'I see. Yes, that might work. And would you stay here then, too?'

'Ah, no. That simply won't work,' says Harry. 'Because they are going to move me, too, I'm told. Most likely on the same day they move you. They're going to take me over as soon as the river's safe, I'm told, to somewhere, Cole says, where he can give me ECT.'

'They can't do that...'

'Oh, they can. And they will. They have absolute power over me here. But I won't let them have it, Ellen. That's why I've got to leave, before they take me off here and force me to enter another institution. And anyway, I think they're lying about the boat. They just want to scare us all, to keep us here against our will.'

'But two of the nurses are stuck over the other...' Ellen begins, but Harry doesn't want to hear her. It's like he's possessed.

'Look at me,' he says, taking hold of her face and moving it gently so that their eyes meet. 'Look at me. Yes, that's right. I need to tell you something, Ellen. I promise you, absolutely, that I will leave this island, I will rejoin my unit, I will survive this damn war *and* the war inside my head, and we will always have each other. Do you hear me? I promise. I love you. I will make it happen.'

There's something about his gaze and his voice that quells every doubt that's dancing around her head. She knows that what he's saying has an incredibly slim chance of becoming true, but somehow in this moment that just doesn't matter. She believes him absolutely.

'I love you too, Harry.'

'Good. Now, you need to help me leave.' Harry stands up, grabs his bag and walks towards the door.

'You are really going to go now?' says Ellen, following him.

'Yes. They will certainly move me off the island as soon as they can. If I wait until they take me over in daylight, it'll be much easier for them to stop me.'

'Harry, it's not safe.'

'Well, let's see. I used to row at school. I'm still very strong. It's only about twenty feet to the bank. I'm sure I can do it. I'm in much better physical shape than Brian.'

Ellen is both incredibly worried about this idea and energised by his determination and drive. She takes his hand.

'Look. I'll come with you and we'll see, all right?' she says. 'But we need to be careful, the moon's out tonight, they might see us.'

'Yes, I know. But everyone's either asleep or at work in wards with curtains closed. We'll be fine. Look, let's go now.'

They kiss, and then Harry opens the door to the outside world slowly, checking that no one's in the vicinity. Ellen follows him as he turns left and walks around the side of the house towards the boat landing, shivering, and not just from the cold. The island feels different tonight. The ground is yielding under her feet and the water seems to be much closer than usual, and the river is loud, and getting louder, as they approach the downstream section of the island. This fact is adding to Ellen's unease. Harry, however, seems less concerned. He's bounding on ahead, and she can see he's already reached the boat dock. As she gets closer, however, she can see his expression is now far less optimistic. In fact, he looks afraid.

'It looks like I'm going to have to swim,' he says.

Ellen sees immediately what he means. The boat dock is no longer there. And the boat, which normally sits alongside it, tethered in two places, is listing severely to one side.

'You can't go into that,' she says, looking down at the pitch-black, turgid water, which has transformed in the past few days from benevolent friend to predator.

Harry doesn't reply. He puts one foot forward and steps into the water. Ellen knows that there should be grass below.

'Woah,' he says, almost losing his balance. The water is up to his thigh, and he is in danger of losing his balance.

'Hang on,' shouts Ellen, reaching out as far as she dares, worried that she might also lose her balance, and they'll both fall in. She exhales with relief when he manages to grasp her hand, and she pulls as hard as she can.

Harry grimaces and grunts as he tries to release himself from the mud. It takes much longer than either of them would like, but he does eventually manage to get out. They both stand there in the moonlight for a moment, panting.

'I had visions of you falling in there and disappearing,' she says, pulling him close to her, to reassure herself that he's really there, and not being swept away towards the weir. It's then she realises he's shaking. 'Are you cold?'

'A little,' he says, and she rubs his arms in a vain attempt to warm him up.

'We need to get you inside.'

'No. We need to find a way for me to leave.'

'We can't. Look at the boat, Harry. We can't.'

'I'll try tomorrow,' he says, still shaking. 'But I don't want to go back in yet. I want to spend more time with you.'

'Well, we can't stay out here. Shall we go back to the pump house?'

Harry nods, and they make their way together back to the relative warmth of the outbuilding.

'Come in, let's get you sitting down,' she says, flicking on the light when the door is safely closed. Now that she can see properly, it's clear that he's not just suffering from the effect of the freezing cold water. There's a look in his eye she recognises, too.

'Harry? Are you all right?' she asks. 'Are you feeling... strange?' He doesn't respond. He's staring in her general direction, but not at her. He's with her in body, but not in spirit, she realises. 'Harry, I think we need to get you back to your bed,' she says, taking him by the hand and leading him out of the pump house. He doesn't reply but comes with her without question.

They are passing the well when there's a rumble. It's not the weir, Ellen thinks; it sounds like an engine. She automatically looks up at the sky, wondering if the German bombers have come back for another try, but the sky is clear. Then she realises that it's a boat. She can't see it, because it's probably the other side of the house, but it's getting louder and louder, its engine screaming as it labours against the current. They must be desperate to get wherever they're going if they're out on the river at the moment, she thinks.

Then Harry stops walking. She tries to cajole him, kisses him gently on the cheek to try to help him snap out of whatever he is seeing and experiencing, but it's no use. He's much stronger than her, and he seems rooted to the spot. It's clear that the noise generated by the approaching boat has sparked something in him. She waits beside him as the screeches and grunts of the engine become a cacophony – *gah-dunk, gah-dunk, gah-dunk*. She is wondering when it will pass the island, when there's what sounds like a gunshot – later, she will realise it was the engine backfiring – and Harry suddenly howls. She knows he risks waking up everyone in the house, so she tries to put her hand over his mouth to try to persuade him to quieten. It does the opposite.

'Harry! No! It's me!' she shouts, not caring any more about waking anyone, but it doesn't stop him. The boat engine's relentless labour continues.

Gah-dunk gah-dunk gah-dunk gah-dunk gah-dunk.

He's lashing out at her as if she's his mortal enemy. She tries to grab his wrists to stop him, but he's too fast and much too strong. He lands blow upon blow on her torso and arms, but her cries of pain do not persuade him to cease.

Gah-dunk gah-dunk gah-dunk gah-dunk gah-dunk gah-dunk.

If anything, it gets worse. His flailing, forceful arms are making their way up her body, until they reach her neck. Then she feels his hands close around it and her body floods with fear. *He's going to kill me,* she thinks.

Gah-dunk... gah-dunk... gah-dunk... gah-dunk... gah-dunk... gah-dunk.

He's not Harry now, he's a violent madman, and she has to stop him. Without believing that she has any hope of doing so, she pushes him away. She is far stronger than she thinks; the adrenaline in her body has given her fleeting superpowers. And so it is that she summons the energy for one mighty shove. And this shove is just enough to knock Harry off balance.

Gah-dunk gah-dunk gah-dunk gah-dunk.

As the boat's roar reaches its crescendo, he falls backwards. For a brief moment she thinks he's going to hit his head on the edge, but then she sees they are far closer than that. In what feels like minutes but is really only a few seconds, the backs of his legs strike the well surround; his torso tips backwards, as if he's attempting a macabre limbo dance; his head strikes the far side of the well wall; she surges forwards, suddenly realising the horror that is about to unfold in front of her.

She is too late to do anything about it. For a brief moment, he seems to lie there across the well opening, his expression still blank, his limbs finally still, before he is swallowed – that's the only way she can describe it – *swallowed* down the well shaft. She reaches the well a millisecond too late. She stares into it. She can just make out a flash of brown shoe leather, and then all there is is darkness. She screams down into it, words which might have been 'Harry' and 'Oh' and 'My' and 'God', but they are chewed up by shock and by fear and by grief, and so they are mostly unintelligible. She stands there screaming and screaming until her voice is hoarse, until her brain catches up with what her senses have seen. This is when she falls. She crumples, in fact, onto the ground. But when her knees hit stone, she doesn't even cry out. She doesn't even feel it. Her mind is elsewhere, down in the darkness, down in the water, wrapped around the sodden, broken limbs of the man she loves. The man she will always love.

Although she isn't really listening, her ears can hear the boat beginning to move away.

Gah-dunk... Gah-dunk... Gah-dunk...

And then they hear another sound. It's the back door opening and closing, and then footsteps running across the paving up to the well.

'Miss, *Miss Lieutenant Quinn*,' he says, his voice soft but insistent. 'It's Neil, miss. Neil, Brian's son. Can you stand? I need to get you inside.'

She stirs slightly when he takes her hands, and she is vaguely aware of her body moving through space, upwards, she thinks.

'That's it, miss. I'll take you inside now. It's all right. I promise, it'll be all right.'

31

MEREDITH

10 February 2014

At first light, Meredith gets out of bed and walks to the window. She pulls back the curtain and gasps. May Day House is no longer on an island – it *is* an island.

There is water everywhere. The statue at the centre of the rose garden has lost both its pedestal and its feet; there are ducks swimming on the grass; there are whole branches traversing the path that runs down the side of the house. She even looks down at her own feet to check for flood water, convinced that she can't possibly still be dry. Poppy can't possibly have found anywhere dry out there. *Oh my God*, she thinks. *Poor Poppy.*

Meredith looks for her phone on the bedside table so that she can text Philip, before remembering, with a sinking feeling, that she lost it in the water yesterday. And then everything Damon told her about her husband, not to mention what Damon tried to do to her just last night, comes back to her in one enormous gush. She looks over at the door, checking that it's still shut. Confident that the bed is still blocking it, she collapses onto it and lies on her back, staring at the ceiling, willing the nightmare she now seems to be living to dissipate.

Images come back to her in stop motion, like a flip picture book. In one frame she's sitting in front of the fire; then she's on the floor, trying to sleep; then he's on her, all over her; then she's shouting in protest; then it's his turn to shout, as hot candle wax pours down his face.

How on earth did that happen? How could he have read her so wrong? And honestly, how could she have read *him* so wrong? In an instant last night he transformed himself from a kindly neighbour into a dangerous predator. She can't reconcile this new side of him with the man she thinks she knows, the kind, helpful man who helped fix their water pump, who taught her how to use their boat, who gave up his time to search for it when it went missing. Somehow, this transformation is more unnerving than any of the paranormal experiences she's had in the house.

And then there's what Damon told her about Philip. There's so much to try to process, it's hard to know where to start. Could he really be addicted to drugs? And could he really be so desperate to get at her money that he'd actually consider drugging her to do it? Even last night, Damon's suggestion seemed a stretch, but in the cold light of day, Meredith is more and more convinced that he's wrong. After all, Philip's airline conducts random drug testing on a regular basis. They'd find it in his system, wouldn't they? And would he really risk her health and sanity, something she'd fought so hard to keep after her parents' deaths and their miscarriages, for selfish gain? *No*, she thinks, instinctively. *No.* She might have got Damon wrong, but she is absolutely certain that she knows her husband.

And yet, that story Damon told her about Stuart's death – some of it rings true. It's perfectly possible that Damon and Philip knew each other as boys. And if that's the case, why didn't Philip tell her? Why is it a secret? And if he did buy the drugs that his brother took shortly before his death, perhaps that explains his refusal to talk about the incident in any detail, his almost complete absence from his parents' lives, despite their proximity. *Does he feel so guilty*, she wonders, *that he can't face seeing his parents for any length of time? But lying about being there at all... Why did he do that?*

Meredith's thoughts are interrupted by a knock at the door.

'Merry? Are you awake? I thought I heard you.'

For a brief moment, Meredith thinks it's Philip arriving back from his trip, before realising with a jolt that it can't be. He probably hasn't landed yet, and even when he gets back to the area, he won't be able to get over to the island, will he? *He'll be worried,* she thinks. *And is he wondering why she hasn't been back in touch, since her last message? Did he try to reply to her, and if so, what did he say?*

Oh God, Philip, she thinks. *I need to talk to you so badly. I want to know the truth.*

She tries to remember his flight schedule. Without her phone, she can't check it, but she thinks he's landing at some point this morning. He might even be on the ground now, trying to call her. When he gets here, though, the river will definitely be in his way. How will he get over to her? Their boat is over here and essentially in the middle of the river now, and she doubts that Euan or any other river resident will risk their life to transport him over, if he manages to somehow get to the towpath, which she suspects will be under water now, too. So he'll be stuck over on the other side, won't he? And she'll be stuck here. With Damon.

'Yes,' she replies, seeing no point in pretending that she's no longer in the room she's barricaded herself into.

'Can we talk?' he asks, still speaking through the door.

Meredith wonders whether it's safe to speak to him, before chastising herself for living in the same sort of melodrama he's been spouting. Of course he's safe: he tried to have sex with her, not kill her. She will be fine. Not that she plans to let him close to her again, ever. She has learned her lesson.

'OK,' she says, pulling the bed back against the wall, its legs screaming in protest.

'Can I come in?'

'No. I'll come out,' she says, realising that she's still wearing the clothes she was wearing yesterday. She had flaked out as soon as she'd managed to barricade the door. Meredith walks out into the hall. Damon is standing a few metres away. He has a large plaster on his cheek. She recognises it from a stash she has in the cupboard in the downstairs bathroom.

'Hi,' he says, his voice sheepish. 'I'm so sorry...'

'I'm going to make coffee,' she says, walking past him to the kitchen. She is not intending to forgive him, no matter how much he tries to apologise. He did not back off when it was clear she didn't want to have sex with him. It was very nearly rape, and they both know that.

She enters the kitchen to a scene of desolation. She realises how drunk she must have been yesterday: there are dirty plates and saucepans everywhere, along with several half-empty bottles of wine and an entirely empty bottle of vodka. She takes two cups out of the cupboard and tries to turn on the coffee machine. And then she remembers they have no power. She screams with frustration.

'No coffee, then. Juice.' She opens the door of the fridge quickly, to try to retain as much of the cold inside as possible and snatches a carton of juice from inside the door.

'As I said, I am so sorry,' he says, entering the kitchen and standing on the opposite side, aware, clearly, that she doesn't want him near her.

'You crossed a line,' she says, grabbing a glass from the cupboard, 'that should not be crossed.'

'I'm sorry...'

'And I said no...'

'I'm sorry. I was drunk. I was a bit slow to respond...'

'A *bit* slow? Bloody hell.'

'I thought... I thought... we had a connection.'

'I am married, Damon. I am happily married.'

'To a man who gave his brother drugs and then ran off instead of saving him?'

Meredith spins around.

'What did you say?', She notices his chest is rising and falling rapidly.

'Just that. He ran off when Stuart didn't respond. He literally pegged it, rather than going into the water to see if he could help him.'

'I am not interested in any more of your stories about Phil,' she says, turning round and pouring juice into the glass to give her thinking time.

'That's your prerogative,' he replies. 'I just wanted you to know the truth about the man you're married to.'

She doesn't reply, largely because she doesn't know how to. She no longer sees Damon as trustworthy, for obvious reasons, but she can't deny that he's planted a seed of doubt in her mind about Philip. She feels nauseous all of a sudden, and she doesn't think it's just because of her hangover.

'Have you seen outside?' he says, as she sips from her juice.

'Yes.'

'It hasn't reached the house yet.'

'No.'

'But it might. I think we need to get off the island before that happens.'

'Won't someone come and get us?'

'Who's going to do that?' he says, his eyes alight. 'We aren't a priority. They know the house isn't flooded yet. No, they'll want us to stay put for quite some time. They'll be busy dragging cars out of the water and helping people who are swimming in their lounges.'

The idea of spending several more hours, let alone several more days, alone with Damon, fills her with absolute dread. And getting off the island makes sense. If she does manage to do it, she can find Philip. And maybe even Poppy. Although goodness knows, she surely can't have survived in these flood waters, she thinks. The thought that her beloved dog might have died suddenly overwhelms her. She begins to cry. Damon does not try to comfort her.

'Even if we did want to get off the island, how would we do it? We can't get to the boat,' she says, wiping her eyes.

'Well, I tied up your boat well. It's not out in the main flow. I would need to wade across the front garden to get it, but it's not impossible.'

He does know the river, she thinks. If he reckons he can do it, perhaps he can. And if it means getting off this island and getting away from Damon, then it's worth it for her, despite the risk.

'If you think it's worth a try, then let's do it,' she says.

* * *

It's 8.30 a.m. when Damon dons a pair of waders and heads out across what used to be the front lawn, but is now a subsidiary of the Thames. She watches him lose his balance, stumble and almost fall as he trips over what must be a retaining wall around a flower bed, and realises she doesn't care in the slightest what happens to him.

That's because she's replaying all of the things he's said and done to and for her since they moved onto May Day Island, and something he said quite recently has taken up residency in her brain. It's what he'd said when she'd told him about the ghosts she'd seen. He'd said he'd seen 'all kinds of shit' when doing drugs.

Yes. This is a man who has significant experience with drugs, she thinks. *Enough experience, perhaps, to drug her, to make her see things that aren't there? To plant drugs in a cupboard, to try to frame Philip? And certainly enough experience to drug her last night, by slipping something into that glass of whisky.* Suddenly, she's seeing clearly. Yes, she has questions, but she also knows that Philip has the answers. She needs to get in touch with him, urgently. And if Damon can help her do it, all the better.

'I've got it,' he says, and she sees that he's holding onto one of the boat's ropes, as if it's the golden snitch. She nods but doesn't smile. He's not getting another smile from her ever again. She watches as he pulls the boat towards him, clambers in, releases both ropes and starts the engine. It whirs into life. For a moment she wonders whether he's been playing her, and he's going to head off without her, and she's almost surprised when he sets off very slowly in her direction, trying, she assumes, to choose the deepest parts of the water so that he doesn't risk snagging the engine blades on anything in the garden.

She spends the time it takes for him to reach the house getting herself kitted out for the weather. She finds her thickest coat, hat and gloves, and, in the absence of waders, her wellies.

'You ready?' he says, as he reaches the bottom of the steps.

'Yes,' she says. He holds out his hand, but she doesn't take it. Instead, she shrugs off any residual lack of confidence and, taking hold of one of the grab handles on the side of the vessel, swings herself over and inside, sitting down in one swift movement. *She has come a long way in a short time,* she thinks, determined that Damon will no longer ever see her vulnerability.

'Right, off we go then,' he says, apparently unaffected by the distinctly frosty atmosphere on the boat. In fact, he seems surprisingly upbeat, particularly given their day and night of heavy drinking.

Meredith clings on to the grab handle nearest her as the boat scuds over unknown objects in the garden below – most likely flowerpots, she thinks – and then approaches the main stream of the fast-flowing, engorged river. As soon as it does so, the engine starts to roar and the boat seems to be being carried at disturbing speed towards the trees which are still standing sentry at the island's border.

But instead of responding with understandable fear, Damon whoops like he's riding the rapids at Disneyland. And it's then that Meredith realises she is a passenger on a boat in dangerous flood water piloted by a man who is sky high on drugs.

'You're off your face, aren't you?' she asks, but it's more of a statement.

'Yep,' he replies, revving the engine and ducking as a branch threatens to sweep him off the boat. 'High as a fucking kite.'

'I cannot believe your bloody nerve,' she shouts, her rage about what he did the previous night finally rising to boiling point.

'Tough shit,' he says, finally managing to pull the boat away from the trees. Then he slows down as he looks for a suitable gap, to try to move into the main flow.

Meredith looks across at the opposite bank. She's been harbouring a hope that Philip will be there waiting for her. She's disappointed, however, to find there's no one there at all. But then she realises why: there is no bank. She doesn't know how far the water reaches, but it's certainly obliterated the towpath.

Oh God, she thinks, as Damon heads for a narrow gap at what she feels is an incredibly dangerous angle, the prow of the boat facing into the stream. She's in real trouble.

'So have you decided yet whether you're staying with your absolute arse wipe of a husband?' he shouts over the engine's roar. She does not respond. 'I take it that's a yes. Jesus, you're both even more stupid than I thought.'

Meredith decides to bite.

'I know you drugged me last night,' she shouts.

Now it's his turn not to respond, but that might also be because they are now in the main river, and they have both spotted a large fencing panel which is heading straight for them.

'*Shit, shit, shit,*' she mutters under her breath as it rockets towards them. She knows that the speed it's travelling at means it stands a good chance of turning their own boat over. Damon waits until the very last moment and revs the engine, and then misses it by about a foot.

'Yeah, well, what if I did?' he says, as he fights to keep control of the boat.

'Aren't you sorry?'

'Not at all,' he says. 'I'm not sorry about anything.'

They are making their way with the flow now, and they are almost flying. Trees and bushes whip by. She's surprised he hasn't gone straight for the opposite side of the river, but she assumes that he's searching for a relatively safe place to put down.

But how wrong she turns out to be.

'I hear you like wild swimming,' he shouts, before turning the motor down to a trickle.

'I... what?' she says, confused. Who could have told him that?

'Holly tells me you like wild swimming,' he says, turning the engine off completely. Now all she can hear is the roar of the weir, which is only about five hundred metres further downstream.

'I thought you said you didn't really know her?'

'Yeah, I lied. I screw her most weeks. Actually, she's knows I've been... getting to know you. It's in our mutual interest.'

'It's... what?'

'We need your money, dear Meredith.'

'My... money?' she says, as he takes his hand off the tiller and comes towards her. In an instant, she understands what he's about to do.

'Yeah, well, when I discovered you'd both bought the house, the original plan was to ride on your coat tails. But now, I need you to die,' he says. He's close enough now for her to see that his pupils are enormous. She shrinks as far as she can from him, but in reality, there is nowhere for her to go. If she goes into the water, she knows she'll die. 'Phil isn't giving me enough money. So now I need you to die, so that he gives me everything.'

'And why would he do that?' Meredith rasps, her fear threatening to close her throat.

'Because I will tell everyone that he gave his brother drugs and abandoned him when he jumped into the river, leaving him to die.' She can still smell last night's alcohol on his breath. 'It'll be so sad. You dying when you and I were so bravely taking the flood waters, searching for your dog.'

'But we aren't...' She realises with a start that they are within a hundred metres of the weir.

'Poppy's upstairs in the house, by the way. She came to the door after you barricaded yourself in last night. Someone will find her later.'

And then he lunges at her. She's expecting it, of course. She fights back, knowing that she's fighting for her life. She aims for his eyes but succeeds only in scratching his cheeks. Then she kicks out, landing a heavy blow to his shins, but she cannot keep him at bay for long. He overpowers her easily, his arms pinning her own down so hard, she begins to lose sensation.

'*You. Are. Mad*,' she says, kicking at him uselessly as he starts to lift her up, with his arms wrapped around her torso.

He's about to respond, perhaps with a denial, when he freezes.

'What the...' he says. He's looking at the far bank. She turns her head just a little, and can see that there's someone, a man, she thinks, standing by the water's edge, near a weeping willow. 'No. It can't be...' he says.

What happens next happens very, very quickly.

Meredith seizes her chance. As his attention is directed elsewhere, she shoves her right knee upwards, landing a strike in his crotch. He doubles over in pain. And then she throws herself at him, with every residual bit of energy she has. The strange thing is, he doesn't fight back. He's still staring at the man on the bank, and he continues to do so as his centre of gravity shifts backwards; his shoulders first, then his chest, and then his bottom and legs. In an instant, too short a period of time for Meredith to properly understand what's going on, his calves strike the side of the boat, and then he's falling overboard, backwards, headfirst.

He has barely gone under when Meredith lunges at the engine and tries to get it started again. The weir is now less than fifty metres away. She is frantically pressing the choke in and turning the ignition when she sees a flash of red to her left. As her own engine finally starts, the flash of red becomes a boat, a boat full of people in full rescue gear, and it's heading straight for her. And then someone throws her a rope. It lands in the boat a few feet away, and she scrabbles to get it, catching it just before it rips away.

'*Tie it on*,' someone shouts. 'We're going to tow you. Tie it on.' Meredith takes hold of the rope and tries to tie it to one of the grab handles, but her hands are numb and she seems to have momentarily forgotten how to tie knots. She hears the weir growing louder and louder behind her and cannot bear to look. She knows how close she must be now. So she takes control of the engine once more and forces it as high as it'll go. It groans in protest, but she continues, and soon she's making slow but steady headway towards the bank, the red boat flanking her on her left side. When she feels she's far enough from the weir, she shouts.

'Throw me the rope again.'

And this time, when they throw it, she catches it, and manages to tie it onto the engine shaft.

When the red boat takes over and begins towing her at a snail's pace towards safety, Meredith allows herself to look back at the weir for the first time. There is no sign of Damon. He is not clinging to any of the weir ropes or clambering up any trees.

He has simply vanished.

32

ELLEN

12 February 1944

It has been two nights since Harry's death, although Ellen has been barely aware of time passing. After Neil had part-cajoled, part-carried her back to her room, she'd curled up in a foetal position on her bed and wept.

Ever since then, her mind has been consumed with the monstrous memory of Harry falling down the well, and her only solace, albeit brief, was the hour she spent putting down what happened in her notebook. It had seemed even more stark, written there on the page, but it had also felt cathartic, as if she was sharing the secret with someone else.

The only person she's spoken to at any length since Harry's death has been a very concerned Rebecca, and she hasn't been able to bring herself to tell her the whole truth. And as it turns out, she will never need to, because Neil has sown his own version of the truth throughout the hospital.

Neil, she now knows, followed her out of the house when she went to meet Harry for that one final time, and saw everything that happened near the well. And for reasons she has yet to fully understand – but is beginning to suspect – he has encouraged her to deny her involvement in his death completely. By the time she'd recovered enough to begin to talk about it, he had already done all of the talking for her.

According to Neil, he had been checking on the boat when he'd noticed that Harry was outside May Day House when he knew he shouldn't be. He had challenged him, he said, but Harry had seemed strangely unresponsive. He had run into the flood water without warning and without looking back, so the story went, and now was missing, presumed drowned.

Drowned in a river which, after a week as a growling tiger, has now returned to its usual, benign demeanour of a domestic pet. And that is why she is here. She has to do this now, before she leaves.

Ellen takes a deep breath and knocks.

'Come in.'

Ellen turns the handle, walks inside Captain Huntingford's office and sits down on the chair the senior nurse indicates. 'Now, what can I do for you, Lieutenant Quinn? I thought you already had details of your new posting?'

'Yes, I have, thank you, Captain,' Ellen says, smoothing her skirt down over her knees. 'And I was overjoyed to see that I was due to return to Cairo.'

Captain Huntingford eyes her warily.

'Was?'

Ellen picks her words carefully, because she knows that her senior colleague misses little.

'Yes. I am afraid that I will not be able to continue in the service,' she says, her hands clasped neatly on her lap.

'And why is that, Lieutenant?'

'I have reason to believe I'm pregnant, Captain.'

33

MEREDITH

10 February 2014

'Would you like a cup of tea, dear?'

Meredith has been in the village hall, now functioning as a flood refuge centre, for about an hour. This is the fourth cup of tea she's been offered. She's sitting on an army camp bed and is wearing borrowed clothes which don't fit her and smell like mothballs. She is also wrapped in a blanket; the kind pensioners keep beside an armchair for chilly nights. She's grateful for it. She hadn't realised how cold she actually was until they'd brought her into the warmth.

'No thank you,' she replies, making an effort to smile at the kindly old woman, one of several who are here distributing tea. The other volunteers, including Elinor, the woman who was instrumental in the council refusing their planning permission, and Graham, their unpaid, ancient, un-dismissible gardener, are doing their best. In fact, she hadn't realised until afterwards that the people in the red boat – Surrey Search and Rescue – were also volunteers. Euan, the young man who's been operating as a sort of taxi service for Philip, was among them. She tried to thank him personally but he'd just told her that it was what they were there for, and he'd gone off with the crew on another shout soon afterwards.

'Oh, by the way, I've let the fire service know about your dog, Mrs Holland. They say someone will check the house today, and if they find her they'll bring her back with them. So don't worry about her, OK?'

Meredith nods.

'Thank you.'

'Honestly, don't worry about it. We all have to stick together, we river residents, don't we?'

The similarity between this phrase and Damon's favourite phrase – 'river people stick together' – sends a shiver down her spine.

'Yes. Do you know if they found the... man I was with?'

'I'm sorry dear, I don't. But maybe Neil will know. He saw what happened, you know. Neil? Did you say you'd spoken to the search and rescue people about finding the man Mrs Holland was with?'

The man Meredith knows as Graham walks slowly towards her camp bed.

'Well, I told them about it when I called them,' he says, staring at the floor by Meredith's feet. 'But they haven't given me an update yet.'

'You saw him fall overboard?'

'Yes. I saw him wrestling with the... engine. Struggling, you know. And then losing his balance. He was swept towards the weir. That was the last I saw of him. No news of him yet.'

'Sorry, dear, someone new is coming in,' says the kindly female volunteer. 'I'll just leave you with Neil.'

Meredith and Graham remain silent for a few seconds, each deciding how much they want to say.

'Neil?' she says, finally.

'That's my Christian name, yes. But I go by my surname for work. Always have, since I left school.'

'I see. So, you called the emergency services?'

'Yes.'

'Were you by the bank?'

'When I saw you? No. I was in my boat.' Meredith is puzzled. If it wasn't Graham that she and Damon had seen, then who was it? 'I had wondered if you were going to be all right on the island by yourself, so I was trying to get to you.'

'Goodness. In that flood? Graham, you could have been killed.'

'I've known this river all my life. My father used to be the ferry master for the island. He taught me everything I know.'

'I see. Yes. Are you sure, then, that you weren't on the bank? By the weeping willow?'

Graham looks confused.

'No. I was in my boat.'

'Oh, right.'

'I should go. There's a gentleman over there who needs dry socks...'

'Graham... The account you gave that woman... is that really what you saw?'

The old man looks at Meredith properly. His eyes are milky and tired but incredibly alert.

'Yes. He fell overboard after he lost his balance, when he was trying to get the engine re-started,' he says. 'That's what I've told everyone. That's what'll be on the report.'

Neither of them knows what to say next. And as it happens, they don't have to think of anything, because Holly has just walked through the door. Graham sees that Meredith's attention has shifted and takes his cue.

'I'll be going,' he says, ambling away.

Meredith stares hard at the woman she had thought was her friend. Holly looks awful, she thinks. Her hair is lank, her clothes don't appear to fit, and the skin on her face is raw and red. Her eyes are swollen. She's been crying. A brief flash of sympathy strikes her. After all, Holly has probably just been told that her boyfriend – if that's indeed how she sees him – is missing, presumed drowned. But then she remembers Damon's confession, his unequivocal statement of Holly's involvement in what had occurred, and any sympathy she might have felt fades. But of course, Holly doesn't know that her former friend knows about any of this. Or even, that she is now a former friend. And so she walks towards Meredith like a desert nomad towards an oasis.

'Merry, am I glad to see you.' She walks over to Meredith's camp bed and slumps down next to her, clearly oblivious to the forcefield of anger that's emanating from Meredith. 'Oh God, it's awful, Merry. A friend of mine – a good friend of mine – is missing...' and then she begins to cry large, gulp-filled tears.

'I know,' says Meredith, her voice steely.

Holly looks up.

'You know? About... Damon?'

'I know everything, Holly. Everything.'

There is a brief pause, during which they both sit in silence, listening to the gentle hum of the activity around them: the boiling tea urn, the clinking of washing up in the kitchen, the murmurs of the volunteers in the far corner.

'We kept our relationship on the down low. Damon isn't... the type to settle down, you know? But we care about each other. A lot. We go back a long way.' Of course, thinks Meredith. You all grew up around here together. 'But I'm younger than him. He was in his twenties when we got together. So as I said, I wasn't around when your husband was around...'

'You're still interested in him, though, aren't you? Phil?'

'No. Why would I be?'

'Oh, Holly, don't give me that. I told you, I know everything. I know that you and Damon were in it together.'

'In what together?'

'Jesus,' Meredith mutters under her breath. 'Do I have to say it?'

'Yes, you do. Because I don't have a clue what you're on about.'

'Fine,' says Meredith, clasping her hands together tightly. 'Let's do it your way. You and Damon are together, even though you chose not to tell me that.'

'That's because he didn't want us to tell anyone. He's very private.'

'Yes, he kept quite a few things to his chest.'

Holly shoots her a quizzical look.

'Like what?'

'Like, that he's been extorting money from Phil for years.' Holly looks down at her shoes. 'Yes, you did know about that, didn't you. I thought so. All of that surprise you faked about how little pilots earned these days. You're a good liar, Holly. You were very convincing.'

'I... did know they had some kind of financial arrangement. But I didn't think it was that much. Just enough to keep Damon comfortable, you know? I thought it was... well, he told me that Phil wasn't as nice a guy as he made out, and that he deserved it.'

'Bloody hell.' Meredith snorts with derision.

'But that was why I suggested he might be hiding stuff from you, Merry. Because I knew he was. I thought maybe you might be better off without him.'

'Well, in the end, your delightful Damon decided I'd be better off dead.'

'He... what?'

'Oh, he didn't share that bit with you? Well, I suppose maybe it was a spur of the moment thing. He had a go at seducing me, to try to get me to leave Phil and I suppose to take all of my money with me... But it was an attempted rape, frankly...'

'Oh my God.' Holly's shock is clear.

'Yes. Definitely "*Oh My God*".'

'The absolute bastard,' Holly says.

'So we agree on something,' says Meredith. 'You didn't know that he planned to try to get me to leave Phil for him?'

'Bloody hell, no. I thought... I thought... He wanted to be with me. Why would I want him to be with you instead?'

'Maybe you'd both planned for me to be with him for a bit, until I had an... accident? Like the one Damon tried to stage this morning on the river?'

Holly's eyes are widening.

'Oh Jesus. He... what?'

'Your boyfriend tried to seduce me, then rape me, and when that failed, he tried to kill me. He wanted all of my money to go to Phil, who he was still confident he could control.'

Holly is now weeping again.

'Oh God, I just can't believe this. I knew about the money Phil paid him. I knew that Damon hoped you and Phil would make a go of the island... and that he could get more money from him as a result. And he said... he said he'd share that money with me. The land my house is built on is leased, you see, and I can't afford the new lease, but Damon said we'd get a cut of your profits from the house, and he'd help me buy it. I had no part in... any of these horrible things you're saying. I can't believe that Damon...'

'He was an addict, Holly. You know that, don't you? He would do anything for his fix. He was high when he tried to rape me last night, and he was even more high, if that's possible, this morning when he took me out in the boat.'

This makes Holly cry even more, and the pair sit side by side on the camp bed for a moment, Meredith resisting any urge she might otherwise have had to comfort her former friend.

'You used the past tense,' says Holly, finally. 'Do you think he's dead?'

'I hope so,' says Meredith with a shiver. 'God, I hope so.'

* * *

An hour later, Meredith is lying on the camp bed holding but not actually reading an old magazine someone has donated to the centre. She is tired, and knows that sleep would be restorative, but there is still too much adrenaline in her system for her to be able to relax. And then there's a flicker in the corner of her vision, and Meredith sits bolt upright, flinging the magazine away. Philip has just walked through the door. Meredith struggles to take him in for a moment, worrying that he is a trick of the light or another of her bloody hallucinations.

'Darling, I'm here, I'm so sorry, I'm here,' he says, half-walking, half-running across the room, dodging camp beds and tea urns. He's still in uniform, and Meredith notices that the old ladies doling out biscuits in the corner are eyeing him appreciatively. 'There were all sorts of delays at the airport and then so many roads were closed and you weren't answering your phone and I didn't know where you were and you'd said you were with Damon and oh my God I've been so worried...' He sits down next to her, holds out his arms and she collapses into them, her tears flowing freely.

'I'm sorry. I lost my phone in the water,' she says into his shoulder, in between sobs.

'It's fine. It's only a phone. We'll get you a new one. The main thing is you're OK. Some rescue guy I bumped into told me you'd been in a boat...?'

'Yes.'

'You weren't trying to get over all by yourself, were you?'

'No. Damon was in the boat.'

'Jesus. Is he here?' he says, his eyes sweeping the room, his rage burning in them.

'No. He's gone.'

'He's gone?'

'Yes. I think so,' she says, sitting back and grabbing a tissue from a pack someone left for her on the floor. 'Phil, we need to have a talk. There's a lot I have to tell you. And some things that I think you need to tell me.'

* * *

Several hours later, Philip and Meredith are sitting in the restaurant of a hotel about a mile away from May Day Island. They've managed to book a room for the next couple of days, while they wait for the flood waters to recede enough for them to return home. They've just been to the shops on the high street to stock up on essentials, and Meredith is pleased to now be wearing clothes which are not jumble-sale rejects.

She's pretending to look at the menu while Philip takes a call at the bar. She has a strong suspicion what it's about, and she's using all of her self-restraint to make herself stay in her seat and not run up to him and demand he put the phone on speaker. After what feels like an age, he thanks the person on the other end profusely, and returns to the table. She's incredibly relieved to see that he has a smile on his face.

'They've got Poppy,' he says, sitting down next to her.

'Oh... thank God,' she says, wiping away tears of relief.

'They found her in one of the upstairs rooms, as you said they would. She had some water with her, and some food, too, although she'd finished it all and seemed pretty hungry.'

'Where is she now?'

'She's on her way to the vet for a check-up, they said. We can go and pick her up from there in a couple of hours.'

'Can I get you something to drink?' asks a waiter. Meredith is tempted to ask for alcohol, after what she's been through, but decides to settle for tea.

'Can I have an Earl Grey?' she asks. 'And a glass of water?'

Philip makes his order and the waiter smiles and retreats to the other side of the room.

'So, you said you wanted to talk to me about something,' he says, his face like that of a schoolboy who's been told to report to the headmaster.

'Yes,' she says, sweeping her hair back with her right hand. 'I do. It's about... Damon.'

'They haven't found him yet. I asked.'

'No. I suspect they won't. Not alive, anyway.'

'Did you say he fell over the side of the boat?'

'Something like that.'

'Something like that?'

'Yes. Phil. Why didn't you tell me you knew each other, from before?'

He looks away and stares through the large window to his left.

'Because I didn't want you to think we were friends. He's not... a nice person.'

'When we were on the boat, before Damon... fell over the side... he told me that you had been paying him money. Is that true?'

Phils picks up his fork and starts turning it over and over in his hands.

'Yes,' he says, avoiding her gaze.

'How much? And for how long?'

'It started off small. I couldn't afford much initially. I was a student, obviously. But as I've earned more, he's been demanding more. More, and more, and more...'

'Blackmail?'

Philip nods, but still doesn't look at her.

'This is why you always seemed to earn less than you should?'

'Yep.'

'I see. And what was he blackmailing you for?'

He takes in a deep breath and Meredith watches as he exhales slowly.

'Because... I was involved in Stuart's death.'

'That's what Damon told me. He told me you were there.'

His eyes dart towards hers.

'He told you?'

'Well, I'm not sure he actually told me the truth.' Meredith pauses as the waiter arrives with their drinks and takes their food order. She takes a sip of water as he goes back to the kitchen. Then, she tells Philip the story Damon had told her, about him buying the drugs, about Stuart taking them, and then about him running away from the scene, and not jumping in to try to save his brother.

'He's a liar,' says Philip, taking a sip of the Pepsi he's ordered. 'I bought those drugs because he asked me to. I worked with this guy, Will, and I knew he dealt on the side. Damon was obsessed with drugs. Still is, I think. I'm pretty sure that's where all my money goes. Otherwise, why would he choose to live in a boat?'

'So you bought them and gave them to him?'

'Yeah. We were all meeting up in the park by the river, same as we always did on a Friday. Stuart was there. He was also really shy, really cautious. I was surprised when he took the drugs. But he was in awe of Damon, far more than I was. He was effortlessly cool, I suppose, or at least, as a teenager, I thought so. And then the shy, cautious brother I knew turned almost instantly into someone I didn't recognise. It was as if he'd been possessed, you know? Before I knew it, he was suggesting we all jump from the bridge.'

'I know what happened next. It's OK, you don't need to tell me.'

'That I ran away when he surfaced, face down? Yes, of course Damon told you that bit. I was scared, Merry. Petrified. I did stay for a bit, long enough for Damon to turn him over and say that he couldn't feel a pulse, but yes, after that, I'll admit I did run. I blamed myself for all of it. I'd killed my brother. My shy, sensitive, funny, loving younger brother. And I've been paying for that ever since. Quite literally.'

Meredith puts her hand over his.

'It wasn't your fault,' she says, firmly. 'It was an accident.'

'If I hadn't bought the drugs... if I'd stayed and tried to resuscitate him...'

'You have no idea what would have happened. But the chances are, he was already gone. He fell from a height and had loads of drugs in his system. He could have had a heart attack as soon as he hit the water. It might well have been too late.'

He sits back and looks up at the ceiling.

'Maybe. But what if it wasn't? Damon has held this over me since I was a teenager. I mean, what if he went to the police with it? My parents would never have forgiven me. I'd have gone to jail, maybe. Definitely for drugs, at least. My education would have suffered. And so, I've paid him the money all this time, instead of owning up to what happened...'

'So when I found May Day House for sale and brought you to the viewing, you must have felt really uncomfortable...'

'At the beginning, yes. But I could see how you felt about the place. And then your enthusiasm started to rub off on me, too. I realised I wanted to give this place another chance. I wanted to make my peace with it. And secondly... I saw a way to get out of my situation with Damon. I suggested a deal, and he took it. I promised him a big payout when we got the business at the house up and running, a one and done kind of payment. And he agreed, although honestly, I'm not sure if he'd ever have honoured it.'

'Phil, I'm going to ask you something now, and I want you to promise to answer me truthfully,' she says.

'Yes?'

'Did you, at any point, give me any drugs... that I didn't know about?'

'Oh my God, Merry. Like what?'

'Like... ketamine?'

'Jesus. No. Did Damon say I did that?'

'He did, yes. Well, he strongly suggested, anyway, that you'd been drugging me so that I started seeing things. So you could have me committed, or whatever, and take control of my money.'

He looks acutely distressed. 'That is the most horrific lie I can think of. No, absolutely not. There is no way in hell I'd ever do something like that to you, Merry. Whatever he said to the contrary. I promise. I really do.'

'I believe you. He was good at horrific lies. And horrific acts. Look, there's something I need to tell you. But it's going to make you very angry,' she says, realising that this is not the place nor the time to tell him about the attempted rape, and the fight for her life on the boat. 'Let's eat first, and then we can go for a walk. Then I'll tell you everything.'

34

MEREDITH

12 February 2014

'I don't need you to hold my hand.'

'I just want to.'

Meredith smiles at Philip, acknowledging the mixture of anxiety and relief they're both feeling. She's more than capable of walking down the bank and climbing into their boat, but she's also in need of physical reassurance. The past couple of days in the hotel have been very emotional and very difficult, particularly picking apart Damon's behaviour and coming to terms with the awful things that almost happened to her – *would* have happened to her, she realises, if she had been less lucky.

After talking at length, they have agreed to call the police later today, to report Damon for attempted murder and attempted rape. She'd originally planned to also tell them exactly how Damon had come to tumble out of the boat, but Philip persuaded her that the potential fallout from this – a lack of any eyewitnesses, barring Graham, whose story was very different – would be too stressful for her to deal with. And she knows, of course, that she only knocked Damon over because he was genuinely trying to kill her. No court in the land would convict her for that.

It was an enormous relief when the police called them yesterday and told them that Damon's body had been found in the reeds in Hampton. Part of her had wondered whether he might have somehow managed to survive, and that he still might pose a risk to them.

And then there is Holly. Elinor, the chair of the residents' committee, says that she is still at the flood refuge. Her home was badly damaged by the floods. Part of Meredith wants to offer her support – after all, she's homeless and bereaved – and the other part of her is so furious about her role in Damon's blackmailing plot that she wants to wash her hands of her. She decides to give it time. Holly will have to wait and see if she's ever going to be forgiven. But she might be; Meredith knows that sometimes, holding hatred in your heart is more damaging for the holder than for the person being hated.

As she clambers into the boat with Poppy at her heels, Meredith looks towards May Day House, remembering how excited and joyful she'd felt on that day last autumn when they'd been standing here on the river side watching the removal firm transferring their belongings to their new home. Their *dream* home. How does she feel about it now? After everything she's been through, she could be forgiven, she knows, for wanting to sell it. After all, she almost died in the water. And she has seen strange things there, heaven knows what, of course, because that jury is definitely still out – but despite this, she still can't shake the fact that the island is meant for her. That she belongs there, and she knows Philip feels the same way. They said as much to each other this morning after breakfast, when they'd been packing their few belongings, ready to return to their home. He'd looked at her and said: 'You don't have to, you know.' And she had replied: 'But I want to.'

And so here they are, riding back over the river to the island on a cold but bright February day, the heavy rain and deadly river conditions now a fading memory. Except, of course, that the floods have left their mark on the whole area. As far as the island is concerned, they have been told to expect the worst. Flood waters leave sludge everywhere, the search and rescue guys have said. Inches and inches of it. The pump house was flooded, so she expects they'll have no running water, and she's not certain if the electrics have been restored. The people who rescued Poppy confirmed the water had never made it into the house, however. She's relieved to see that the grand old house is still standing, the paint still flaking off its arched windows, the glass on its orangery still cracked.

'Here we go,' says Philip, who's finished tying up the boat and is now climbing onto the bank with elaborate care, noting the inches-thick mud that's been deposited on them.

'I'll pass you the dog,' she says, and Poppy complies as she is lifted up and handed over to Philip, who decides, wisely, not to put her down on the mud. Instead, he cradles her as he waits for his wife to disembark.

They walk together, slowly and carefully, along the path to the house. She's trying not to look too hard at the damage to the garden, which she knows has undone any progress Graham – Neil – has made in the past five months. She has no idea what you are supposed to do with flood sludge that's been left behind, but she reckons he probably will. He seems to know a lot about this place, and she suspects he's seen flooding like this before.

When they reach the front door, they can see that the water line peaked just below it.

'Ready?' says Philip as he inserts the large key into the front door and turns it. Meredith nods.

When the door is open, Philip puts Poppy down and she runs into the house with enthusiasm, any memory of her imprisonment upstairs obviously not proving troublesome. Then Meredith takes her husband by the hand, and they perform a cursory check of the downstairs, including the orangery, the bathroom, their bedroom and the living room – the latter now indelibly tainted by the memory of that horrible night – and then, finally, the kitchen.

'Did you see that?' she says, suddenly catching a glimpse of someone, or something, through the kitchen window as they walk through the door.

'Yes, I did,' he says, and she is incredibly relieved. If he's seeing it too, it can't be a figment of her imagination.

They both rush across the kitchen to the back door, yank it open, and then grind to a halt a few steps outside the back door, both shocked and spellbound by what they are looking at.

Because on the ground by the well, part-submerged in silt, is a human skeleton. And standing beside it, his cap braced against his chest, is Graham.

EPILOGUE

APRIL 2014

'Do you think you'll be able to support this one, then?' says Meredith, her phone clutched to her ear as she walks around the orangery, noting which buckets need to be emptied today. It's rained a fair amount in the past week, although she's relieved that there are no new flood alerts expected.

'Yes, I think so,' replies Elinor. 'We had a brief discussion last night and we are of the opinion that the slightly reduced footprint, along with your commitment to reduce any noise pollution generated by events and to invest in greener sources of energy, make this a project we can agree to.'

Not to mention the fact that you've actually got to know us during the clean-up and quite like us now, Meredith thinks. The past month has been hard work for everyone in the area, but also a huge community bonding exercise. Teams of residents have been helping everyone affected by the floods, including Meredith and Philip, who were incredibly grateful for their assistance. It allowed them to clear most of the garden, to help the grass to grow back and at least some of their plants to survive.

'That's wonderful news, thank you,' says Meredith.

'Our pleasure,' says Elinor, her tone very much that of a woman who feels she's addressing an equal. 'We must save May Day House for the next generation.'

Miracles never cease, thinks Meredith, walking back through into the hallway and entering the kitchen, where Philip is preparing lunch.

'They're going to back us.'

'Hoo-bloody-ray,' he says, abandoning the hob to embrace his wife. 'Thank God for that.'

Meredith smiles broadly, feeling at least some of the weight she's been carrying around on her shoulders begin to dissipate. It's been happening gradually, in fits and starts, since they returned to the island in February. Their improved financial situation has helped – Philip's full monthly salary, without Damon's 'deduction', is now a thousand pounds more, which will make it much easier to get a new loan – but she knows it's also the difference in the way they are communicating that's made the real difference. They have both acknowledged the part they had to play in the deterioration of their relationship. And this, in turn, has helped her understand and to begin to address the deeply rooted, devastating grief she had been carrying around but refusing to acknowledge. She hadn't realised just how deeply she had been affected by her parents' deaths, coupled with the heart-wrenching loss of each of their future children. It had eaten away at her, she knows now, and yes, it had made her ill. It had even, she believes, made her hallucinate, or at least dream things that felt frighteningly real.

She thinks the tablets prescribed by the psychiatrist she has been seeing – entirely voluntarily – have helped. She hasn't seen any ghosts, or hallucinations, or whatever they were, since the flood. She's been looking for them, checking for faces at windows and shadowy figures in the corners of rooms, but she's found nothing there. The atmosphere in the house seems to have shifted. There is no feeling of menace or pain anywhere within its walls or grounds now, and she seems to have been embraced by its new-found peace.

Even the discovery of a skeleton that had lain in their well for more than seventy years wasn't enough to disturb it, even though, through a combination of Graham's testimony and the notebook she'd found upstairs, she has been able to trace and understand the heart-breaking story behind it. Police opened and closed the investigation into Harry Hennessey's death within a few weeks, happy with a combination of

Graham's witness statement and contemporary army and RAF documents, which had said that Harry had gone missing, in great distress, during the floods of February 1944.

The investigation into Damon's behaviour, meanwhile, was also closed pretty much as soon as it began, because, as they now know, dead people cannot be prosecuted. Part of Meredith is relieved. She has no desire to relive what happened to her in the courts. As a result of this news, they have decided not to tell the police about the blackmail, aware that there is little point in doing so. There will never be any chance of legal redress. Their best revenge, they have decided, is success: hence the new planning application for May Day House, and their renewed determination to see their dream for the island come to life.

Philip is about to return to his cooking when the doorbell rings. They shoot each other a quizzical look. Living on an island with no bridge means that no one drops in unannounced, except Graham, of course, who, despite his age and infirmity, is still turning up with regularity to tend to the garden.

'I'll get it,' says Meredith, patting Poppy as she walks past her on her way to the front door. She opens it and is surprised to find Euan, Philip's occasional ferryman and one of the volunteer rescuers who helped tow her out of the flood, standing on the front steps.

'Hi,' he says.

'I'm sorry, Euan, I think there's been a mistake. Phil doesn't have a flight until tomorrow.'

'I know,' he says. 'I'm not here to give him a lift. I need to talk to you both. If that's OK?'

'Of course,' she says, standing aside. He walks slowly up the stairs and down the corridor, his head slightly bowed. She follows him into the kitchen, where Philip greets him like an old friend.

'Euan, mate, how are you? Did I give you the wrong date for my next trip?'

'Nah. I'm here because... there's something I need to tell you.'

'Oh,' replies Philip, his brow furrowed. He and Meredith look at each other, both wondering what on earth this man is about to say. 'Well, take a seat. I'll turn the hob off.'

Euan nods and takes a seat at the oak table, and Meredith and Philip sit down opposite him.

'This is... difficult,' says Euan, biting his lip. 'But I... was talking to Neil Graham the other day, and he said something which made me feel really shit, so I wanted to come and put some things straight.'

'Like what?' asks Meredith.

'It's probably best if I fill you in a bit, so you understand what's been going on. About a year ago, my gran got really ill. Cancer, same as what got my mum when I was a teenager.'

'I'm sorry to hear that, Euan.'

He acknowledges her condolences, and then continues.

'Yeah, well after my mother died, my gran became a second mother to me. She meant the world, you know,' he says, his hands clasped together on the table. 'And so when she got ill, I wanted to help her, to protect her, to make her better. When she told me that she had this thing that'd hung over her for decades and that I could help put her mind at rest, I promised her I'd try to help.'

'OK...' says Philip, nodding in encouragement. They both desperately want to know where this story is leading.

'Yeah, well, it was a bit of a shock. She told me that... that she'd been in love with a guy, a pilot in the war, who was treated here on May Day.'

'Was her name Ellen? Ellen Quinn?' Meredith now has a name for her mysterious notebook writer, because Graham had told them, after they'd all got over the shock of the appearance of Harry's skeleton, all about Ellen and Harry.

'Yeah. Blimey. How did you know that?' says Euan, clearly shocked. 'Well, she was Ellen Stirling, later, when she married my grandfather. Graham was really sad about that, you know. He had a boyhood crush on her, you see. But she met my grandad at the inn in town where she stayed – my grandad was working at Brooklands, he was an engineer, real clever – and they were married pretty quickly. Which was just as well. Because she was pregnant, it turned out.'

'With your dad?'

'Yeah, with my dad.'

Meredith thinks for a second.

'Oh my God,' she says. 'Then you must be... Harry's grandson? The man they found in our well.'

'I think I am, yes.'

'She loved him so much.'

'How do you know that?'

'It was all in the notebook.'

'You found it?' Euan says, astonished.

'You know about the notebook?' asks Meredith, her eyes widening.

'Yes. It's what I was looking for. When I came to the house.'

'When you came to the house?' says Philip.

'Yeah.'

'When did you come to the house?' Philip asks, clearly angry.

'I... I've been searching for it on and off for more than a year, ever since gran got ill. She told me the book contained evidence linking her to Harry. And she told me about how Harry died, how he attacked her – we reckon he had PTSD, although they didn't call it that then – he was going crazy, triggered by a loud noise, and she thought he was going to kill her, so she pushed him backwards, and he knocked his head and then fell down the well. She said she had been living with the guilt for her whole life, and she wanted to die knowing that the notebook would never reach the wrong hands. So, she asked me to try to find it.'

'That's not quite the story Graham told us,' says Philip. Meredith, meanwhile, is pondering Graham's instinctive revision of what had passed between her and Damon. It wasn't the first time he'd done that then, she thinks.

'Oh, isn't it? You know, I've never spoken to him about it. Gran didn't want me to tell anyone.'

'I see,' says Meredith, more concerned now with the other part of Euan's confession. 'So, you said you'd been searching for it, in the house?'

'Yes. The thing was, Gran was getting a bit confused towards the end, and she couldn't remember where she'd hidden it. And there's such a lot of house and garden to search. I looked quite a lot when the place was empty but didn't find it. And then you moved in, and I... I kept looking.'

'You came to the house after we moved in? And didn't tell us?' says Philip.

'Yeah. I'm so sorry. I really am. I just didn't feel I could let her down. She kept asking...'

'But you didn't find it, because I'd already got it,' says Meredith, the disparate parts of this story joining up now in her head. 'But you kept looking. It's you I saw, up at the window upstairs, wasn't it?'

'Yes.'

'And in the garden?'

'Yeah, that was me.'

Extreme relief floods through Meredith. Here, finally, is evidence that she was not seeing things. That she was not losing her mind. And any anger she has at her young neighbour for trespassing on her property is outweighed by this new reassurance of her sanity.

'But... but... was it you who called out to her in the fog?' asks Philip.

'No, no, that wasn't me. I'd never do that.'

'Maybe that was Damon,' Meredith says, with new confidence. 'Trying to scare me?'

'Maybe,' says Philip, sighing. 'Maybe. He might have graffitied the boat too, I suppose.'

'Oh, nah, that wasn't him. That was... me.'

'You?' Meredith shoots Euan a glare.

'I was hoping it'd make you take fright and leave the house, and my Gran's secret would stay hidden. Because even if you didn't find the notebook, I thought there was also a good chance Harry's body might turn up during the building work. But it was wrong, very wrong. I'm so sorry.'

Meredith is both furious and relieved. At least a real, living person graffitied the boat, and that person hadn't meant to actually harm her.

'Did you steal our boat, too? Just before the flood?'

'No! Of course not. I'd never do that. No, that wasn't me.'

'Maybe Damon took it,' said Phil.

'Yes. Maybe he stole it so I'd ask him to help me find it,' says Meredith.

'That sounds like something the bastard might do.'

Meredith thinks then about the figure she chased up the stairs, and the scene she witnessed on the first floor. That had involved several men, and so it definitely can't have been Euan. But then she realises how distressed she'd been at the time, and remembers her psychiatrist's suggestion of sleep paralysis, and how it might have had a role to play in that particular encounter.

'I'm really, really sorry for scaring you,' says Euan. 'I didn't mean to. I didn't realise you'd even seen me, the first time. But when Graham told me you thought you'd been seeing ghosts, I realised I had to tell you.'

'Why has it taken you so long to tell us this?' Philip asks, clearly less keen to forgive Euan than Meredith.

'I wanted to wait... until she had gone, my gran. I didn't want her last days to be destroyed by police asking difficult questions. I wanted to make sure they could never bother her, when I came to tell you about how Harry died, and about what I'd done. But she's gone now. She died yesterday.' Euan's eyes fill with tears. 'I completely understand if you want to press charges. I would. I broke the law and caused you so much distress. I'm beyond sorry, honestly.'

Meredith and Philip sit in silence for a moment, while Euan dissolves into tears at their kitchen table. And as he cries, her anger dissipates further. What good is it now, anyway, she thinks? The only way forward for all of us, surely, is to let it all go.

'I am happy to give you the notebook,' says Meredith, handing him a tissue. 'It's not mine to keep. But I was wondering... Why didn't Ellen take it with her when she left?'

'Oh, someone else packed her bags. She was taken straight off the island when she told them she was pregnant. They knew she must have got pregnant by someone in the house. They drew their own conclusions. They paid for just one night's accommodation for her at the local pub. Driving her straight into my grandad's arms, as it happened. He was a great man, my grandad. Treated Dad as his own.'

'I see,' says Meredith, her heart suddenly going out to another young woman who must have been mired in grief. 'You know, there were lots of unsent letters in the notebook. Lots to her mother.'

'Yeah, she told me about that. She said she wrote to her mum – she called her Mammy – a lot. But she'd gone by then. She died of cancer before she left Ireland.'

Goodness, Meredith thinks. That explains why the letters were never sent. So much sorrow, so young.

'I'll go and get it for you,' she says, standing up. 'It's in our bedroom.'

'So you won't tell the police about me... trespassing? The graffiti?'

'No,' she says, shooting a look at an astonished Philip. 'Sometimes, I think an apology is all that's needed.'

She desperately wants to draw a line under everything that's happened, and hopes Philip understands that, too. Euan providing a real explanation for things she felt she'd imagined is a huge relief.

Meredith leaves Philip and Euan to make awkward conversation while she goes to retrieve the notebook, which is still sitting on her bedroom table. She picks it up and holds it with both hands and spends a moment thinking about the young woman who wrote it, and the extreme emotion and pain she had poured into it, and, through her words, into Meredith. She feels a bond with Ellen that she cannot quite fathom.

'Here it is,' she says, walking back into the kitchen and handing it to Euan. 'It's yours now. But don't destroy it. Read it. Keep it. We won't tell anyone about her involvement in Harry's death.'

'Yes, we won't,' says Philip, taking his cue from his wife, to her relief. 'It's fine. We won't say anything.'

'You don't know how amazing that is,' says Euan, standing up. 'Look, I should go. I've taken up enough of your time. And caused enough problems. I'll be round tomorrow to take you over to the mainland, Phil. If that's what you want me to do? I understand if you don't...'

'No, it's fine. See you tomorrow,' says Philip, also getting up. Meredith knows he's still angry about Euan's behaviour, but he's hiding it well. Together, they walk down the hallway to the front door, which Meredith opens.

'Thank you so much, both of you, for understanding,' says Euan, holding out his hand, which they both shake, before he turns to leave. 'And on that note – would you be prepared to accept us offering you all of your trips over the river for free, for the next six months? To try to make amends?'

'Thank you, Euan. That would be great,' says Meredith, because anything that will save them money is welcome. And then she realises there's one final question she needs to ask. 'Actually, one more thing,' she says, and Euan stops walking and turns around. 'Was it you, beside the river, when Damon and I were in the boat, near the weir? He saw someone over by the weeping willow. I saw him too, although not very clearly. He was startled by him, I think. Maybe even scared,' she says, leaving out the fact that it was seeing that man that had allowed her to escape.

'On the morning of the floods? Nah, no, I was in the rescue boat, trying to help you. So that definitely wasn't me. Are you sure you saw someone there? That whole area was under water. No one could stand there, really. The flow was too fast. They'd have been swept away.'

'Must have been a trick of the light,' she says, pasting on a smile.

'Yeah, maybe,' he says, waving goodbye as he walks down the path to return to his boat.

Instead of shutting the door, Meredith stands at the top of the steps, frozen to the spot. Philip walks up and puts his arms around her, sensing that she needs support. And as she leans into him, a new realisation dawns.

Whoever was on that bank was not a living, breathing human – of that she is certain. But instead of being frightened by this new revelation, she feels protected, reassured. Loved.

Thank you, Harry, she thinks, *if it was you*. Or if not: *Thank you, Stuart. Thank you both.*

'Shall we go back inside, darling?' Philip asks. 'We can talk all this through over a reheated lunch.'

'Yes, let's,' she replies. 'And then let's get started on the refurbishment. We've had it on pause for too long. Now we're likely to get planning permission, we need to be ready.'

'Yes, much to look forward to, I think,' he replies, slipping his arm around her waist as they step back inside May Day House, closing the door firmly behind them.

'Without doubt,' she says, her hand brushing her stomach. 'Yes, without doubt.'

AUTHOR'S NOTE

In 2007, a year after we were married, my husband Teil and I bought a tiny terraced house on the outskirts of Weybridge. We'd decided to leave London so that we could afford to buy somewhere of our own, and we adored our new location. We'd spend our days off exploring the local area, and one of our favourite walks was to follow the Thames path towards Walton-on-Thames.

It was along here I first spied D'Oyly Carte island, although I had no idea that's what it was called at the time. Just like May Day, it's an island with only one house on it, a beautiful Victorian mansion which back in 2007 looked unloved and abandoned.

Fast-forward fifteen years, and we ended up falling in love with, and buying, a house on another island in the Thames. Unlike Meredith and Philip, we share it with many neighbours, but it's still a very special place in a very special community. We love bringing up our children surrounded by nature, adore taking our little boat up and down the river in the summer, and, like Meredith and Philip, also live with the risk of flooding, albeit in a modern house designed to cope with floods.

And so it was that my interest in D'Oyly Carte and my own experience of island living conspired to create *The House in the Water.* I should point out that the May Day House I created is very different to D'Oyly Carte. It's far more gothic in design, and in a far worse state of disrepair than D'Oyly Carte has ever been in reality. I invented its name, its appearance and its history, keeping only the concept of an isolated house on the river near Weybridge for my novel. I'm also delighted to report that D'Oyly Carte Island no longer looks unloved. Recently, it was bought by new owners who have opened a very popular cafe in its gardens and embarked on an ambitious renovation project. It's well worth a visit if you are nearby.

The eagle-eyed amongst you may have spotted that the flooding Meredith experiences in this novel occurs on the same dates as the real-life, record-breaking Thames flood of 2014. It's not the only real-life event I blended with fiction in this book. I also included the devastating attack on the aircraft factory in Brooklands in September 1940; the bombing of the SS Maid of Kent hospital ship in May 1940; the killing of nine sleeping civilians, six children and four adults, in Westcott, Surrey, in January 1944; and the 'baby' Blitz, otherwise known as Operation Steinbock, which took place between January and May 1944.

Finally – as you might imagine, writing a novel partly set in a World War II psychiatric hospital required a lot of research. I tried to bring as much real detail into the novel as possible, with the usual caveat that this is a work of fiction and not a medical textbook. I'm very grateful to the authors of the following works for helping me understand how things were:

Negotiating Nursing: British Army Sisters and Soldiers in the Second World War*, Jane Brooks, Manchester University Press, 2018.*

PhD Thesis: Treating and Preventing Trauma: British Military Psychiatry during the Second World War*, Nafsika Thalassis, University of Salford.*

'Pitiless psychology': the role of prevention in British military psychiatry in the Second World War*, Ben Shephard, History of Psychiatry, 1999.*

The Hard School: Physical Treatments for War Neurosis in Britain during the Second World War*, Elizabeth Roberts-Pedersen, Social History of Medicine, Vol 29.*

ACKNOWLEDGEMENTS

Firstly, I'd like to thank the wonderful author Kate Thompson for that lunch where I told her about the history of the Thames islands, and she said 'you should write about that.' It was the spark I needed to start my research for what eventually became *The House in the Water*.

And while I'm on the subject of fellow authors, I can't not thank the brilliant community of writers I'm lucky to call my friends. I can't name you all because I'd undoubtedly forget one of you and I'd feel dreadful about it, but suffice to say I appreciate every single one of you. Authors are the best people, I'm certain.

I'd also like to thank my early readers, Catherine Ramsden, Theresa Ricketts and my brilliant husband Teil Scott, for loving this book and giving me such great feedback.

I also need to thank Michaela Grünig, who donated to the brilliant charity Reverse Rett in exchange for the opportunity to choose a name for a character in this novel. She chose Elinor, in tribute to her favourite Jane Austen character, Elinor Dashwood, and Pepperidge because it sounded eccentrically English! Reverse Rett raise funds for game-changing gene therapy for people with Rett syndrome, the condition my sister has. It's an important mission and I was very proud to be able to support them.

I am enormously grateful as ever for the support of my agent Elizabeth Counsell at Northbank Talent and my wonderful editor Rachel Faulkner-Wilcocks, for believing in this book and welcoming me to the Boldwood family.

And last but not least, I'd like to thank you, my readers, for picking up this book and spending your precious time reading it. I appreciate you hugely and always love hearing your thoughts. In fact, I spend far too much time on social media, so please do come and say hello. You can find me at the following handles and on my website, **www.toryscott.com** – where you can also find out about my alter ego Victoria Scott. She writes uplifting book club fiction and looks very much like me.

Instagram: @VictoriaScottAuthor
Facebook: @VictoriaScottJournalist
X: @toryscott
Threads: @victoriascottauthor
TikTok: @VictoriaScottAuthor

ABOUT THE AUTHOR

Victoria Darke has been a journalist for many media outlets including the BBC and The Telegraph. She is the author of three novels as Victoria Scott, and her novel, *The House in the Water* is a Gothic timeslip novel.

Sign up to Victoria Darke's mailing list here for news, competitions and updates on future books.

Visit Victoria's website: www.toryscott.com

Follow Victoria on social media:

- x.com/Toryscott
- facebook.com/VictoriaScottJournalist
- instagram.com/victoriascottauthor
- tiktok.com/@victoriascottauthor

Milton Keynes UK
Ingram Content Group UK Ltd.
UKHW042055230524
442967UK00002BA/11

9 781835 616901